A PROMISE FULFILLED

Further Titles by Connie Monk

★ *available from Severn House*

A PROMISE FULFILLED

Connie Monk

severn House

This first world edition published 2009
in Great Britain and in the USA by
SEVERN HOUSE PUBLISHERS LTD of
9–15 High Street, Sutton, Surrey, England, SM1 1DF.
Trade paperback edition published
in Great Britain and the USA 2009 by
SEVERN HOUSE PUBLISHERS LTD

British

Monk,
A Pro
1. O₁   Var,
1939
(Engl
5. Lo
I. Tit
823.9

WORCESTERSHIRE COUNTY COUNCIL	
658	
Bertrams	25/06/2009
HR	£18.99
KD	

ISBN-13: 978-0-7278-6804-6   (cased)
ISBN-13: 978-1-84751-156-0   (trade paper)

Except where actual historical events and characters are being
described for the storyline of this novel, all situations in this
publication are fictitious and any resemblance to living persons
is purely coincidental.

All Severn House titles are printed on acid-free paper.

Typeset by Palimpsest Book Production Ltd.,
Grangemouth, Stirlingshire, Scotland.
Printed and bound in Great Britain by
MPG Books Ltd., Bodmin, Cornwall.

Prologue

1926

For a brief moment, Jackie stood on the pavement watching the tramcar move away, the familiar rattling sound surely different from anything she had heard before. If she lived a thousand years she was sure there could be nothing to equal the emptiness that gripped her like a physical pain. Wilhelm had gone. Standing in the middle of the street she closed her eyes as if that way she could cut herself off from a future without him.

'Are you all right, missie?' The kindly voice of the newspaper vendor who sat on a box at the corner of West Street brought her back to reality.

'Yes, it was just that the swaying of the tram made me feel a bit sick. But thank you for asking.' There was something old fashioned in Jackie Hunt's manner, the same something that had always set her apart from her classroom contemporaries. It was rooted in the fact that, unlike the others who lived at home with parents, brothers and sisters, she had been brought up by elderly relatives, her great aunt and uncle, Alice and Howard Grant, who kept the newsagents further along Brackleford's High Street. That's why she had got off the tram sooner than Wilhelm, who for the past two years had lived with his parents in Mallard House, a solid Georgian building in the residential district at the far end of the long street.

Putting off going home for as long as possible, Jackie turned up West Street and went into the park. There weren't many people about so late in the afternoon, just one or two children playing cricket – of a sort – on the far side of the grass, and a few dog walkers. She sat on the ground in the shade of a tall elm, leaning back against the trunk and giving herself up to the luxury of remembering. It had all started just two years ago when she'd been walking home after a morning's sketching. What a child she had been – but not now. Childhood was gone; she was a woman, she was Wilhelm's woman, now and forever. With all the fervour of her sixteen years she had no doubt that what had been was emblazoned on her memory to be cherished until they were together again. 'I will come back,' he had said; she could almost hear his voice as she sat there alone. 'We will always be there for each other,' they had vowed.

Wilhelm Furtmueller had mastered the art of fly fishing young. At sixteen he could play a fly on the surface of a lake with the skill of any man. And that's what he was doing when Jackie first saw him. Standing back in the shelter of the trees where she expected to watch unnoticed, she studied him, impressing the image on her mind. If at sixteen he was an experienced fly-fisherman, at fourteen she had her head full of dreams – dreams she shared with no one. Who could he be? There was something about him that set him apart from the local lads. And yet what was so different? He wore pumps and no socks, khaki shorts, a white shirt with the sleeves rolled above his elbows; so might any boy be dressed. What set her curiosity racing was something in his bearing: his straight back and well-set shoulders, the colour of his blond, straight, well-brushed hair. Other boys of his age might be considered fair, but he was more than blond – or less than blond, she corrected her thoughts – his hair was so pale it was almost colourless.

Moving closer, but still not coming from the wood to walk on the lakeside path, she caught her foot on a slender branch that had been brought down in some previous year's gale and lay hidden beneath a carpet of decayed leaves Taken by surprise and thrown off balance by the feeling of a sharp cut on her ankle, she stumbled and reached to steady herself on the nearest tree trunk. The sound broke through the boy's concentration and he turned to see what it was. Just as his image impressed itself on her, so hers did on him. A slender girl with tawny brown hair cut short and worn with a fringe, and – although he was too far away to see them – eyes to match.

'You are not hurt, I hope?' he called to her. Any of the boys she knew would have shouted, 'You all right?' or 'Daft thing! Why don't you use the path?' The stranger pronounced each word carefully and with extreme clarity.

'My own fault if I am,' she answered, coming out from the

trees, 'but no, I'm fine.' With her cover blown she intended to make the most of the encounter. 'Fishermen don't like to be interrupted. I was trying not to disturb you. Are you on holiday?' After all, if you are too shy to ask questions, you never learn anything.

'No. I have come to live in your country for two years. My father is to work at the hospital. Not your hospital here in Brackleford. It's what you call an isolation hospital.'

'Out in the country. I know where it is. That's where my mother was taken when she had consumption.'

'Consumption?' Clearly not in his vocabulary. 'To consume — to eat?'

Jackie chuckled. 'I expect they call it that because the disease eats into you. Is that what you suppose?' She wanted to keep him talking; she wanted to hear again his perfect pronunciation of a language that wasn't his own.

'And is your mother cured?'

'I can't even remember her. She died in the hospital when I was about a year old.'

'That is a most sad thing for you.'

Jackie gave a wan smile, hoping it was appropriate, while uncomfortably aware that she wasn't being honest.

'You aren't English, are you?' She changed the subject. Was she being too curious? Would he think she was rude? Or would he be disappointed that his knowledge of English was letting him down? She wouldn't want to hurt his feelings. 'I know you aren't because you speak each word so well. Most of us gabble away—'

'Gabble away?'

Again she chuckled. She really was enjoying herself enormously. 'Let the words tumble out so fast they fall over each other. But you speak properly.'

'Thank you for saying a thing so kind. I have been learning for one year with a special teacher so that when we arrived in your country I would not be looked upon as different. My parents have enrolled me and I start at the Grammar School after the holiday time is ended.'

It was getting better and better. Brackleford Grammar School, like so many serving country districts, catered for both sexes. Already she felt she had a right to his friendship above the other pupils.

'I go there too. I'm Jackie Hunt. I live at the newspaper shop on the High Street and I'm fourteen.'

With courtesy quite unfamiliar to her, he took her hand in a firm grasp, bowed over it, then told her: 'My name is Wilhelm Furtmueller and I have sixteen years – forgive me, I should say I *am* sixteen years old. My father has taken for us a house also on your High Street. It is called Mallard House. You know it perhaps?'

'Crumbs! That big house! Of course I know it.'

Then, his question relaxing her and showing he was no less curious than she was herself, 'The shop for newspapers – you live there with just your father or have you a what you call . . . stepmother?'

'Yes, I live over the shop,' she answered. 'But no, I've never had a father.' She spoke naturally, not pretending a grief she didn't feel. 'He died before I was born. But Aunt Alice and Uncle Howard were always my mother's special favourites – they were really *her* aunt and uncle – and when they suggested that she should stay there when my father died, that's what she did. From what I'm told, even then she had a nasty cough she couldn't get rid of. Then, like I said, she died in the isolation hospital. So I've always lived with Aunt Alice and Uncle Howard, and except that they are quite old, they seem like my mum and dad. I say, am I butting in on your fishing?'

'Butting?'

'Well, making a nuisance of myself when you want to be quiet. Am I?'

'I came to fish in the lake because it is something I can do on my own. Now I have you to talk to, Jackie. I have no need to – ah, here is something I learnt from my teacher – no need to tickle the trout.'

'You must have had a jolly good teacher to have learnt to speak so well in just a year. I have been learning French ever since I started at the grammar school and haven't got much further than "*Ou est la plume de ma tante?*". And as for Latin, I know about "*amo amas amat*", but not much more and that does limit conversation.' She giggled. 'What did you say your name was? "Vil" something?'

'Wilhelm. That is the German way of saying what you call

William.' He pronounced the 'W' with great care. 'If I pack up my rod perhaps we could walk back together to the town.' Then, with a smile that belied his formal manner, 'We are almost neighbours. Perhaps I will come with you to your uncle's newspaper shop and purchase from him a daily newspaper. I would like to meet him if, to you, he is as your father.'

Friendship developed naturally between Jackie and Wilhelm. Each day of the remainder of the holiday they were together, he a boy in a strange country, she a girl who, perhaps because of her circumstances, had always been a loner. They went for all-day hikes, played tennis on the court in the park; perhaps most important was that they talked, sharing their views, listening to each other with respect ahead of their years. Neither of them had ever had a friend like it. The following spring, Dr Furtmueller, Wilhelm's father, bought a tandem. They rode for miles, Wilhelm on the front, Jackie on the back. Life had never been so good.

So the months went by, each one better than the last, while like a dark cloud coming closer loomed the time when he would be gone. Sometimes she would make herself look beyond, resolved to make a success of her future, for although she was undoubtedly in love, it was impossible not to feel a thrill of excitement at the idea of stepping out into the world. She had persuaded her uncle and aunt that when she was sixteen she should start at art school, and during that summer of 1926 they had even found what they considered suitable lodgings for her in Maidenhead. Anticipation of her forthcoming adventure helped her face the parting she dreaded.

Her final day with Wilhelm came during one of England's brief but intense heatwaves. The tandem had already been returned to the bicycle shop where Dr Furtmueller had purchased it, so they walked the two miles to the river where Wilhelm rented a punt. She sat at the far end, taking the rudder, while he handled the pole with an expertise that made her gaze on him with open adoration. It wasn't the first time they'd taken a punt out there, and the man who took the money and watched them start off had no fears for their safety. The first time had been different; he'd been glad then to see them come back just as dusk fell, for many a man came unstuck once he got into deep water with a pole. But he had no need to worry about that lad. He wouldn't mind being young again himself and having a pretty lassie like that on the river for the day.

In her basket she had packed a pile of sandwiches, four apples, two bananas, a big bottle of lemonade and a bag of toffees. In his he had glasses, knives, forks, enamel plates, two meat pies and biscuits. When he'd called for her at the shop he had transferred her things to his rucksack so that he carried everything, while Howard looked on approvingly and Jackie swelled with pride.

While Wilhelm stood at the back of the punt, working the pole through his hands until it reached the river bed then propelling them forward as he raised it ready for the next stroke, she gazed at him, trying to impress the image on her memory so that these last precious hours would stay with her until they met again. For they would meet again. It was no good praying for something and not trusting; one day he would come back.

'Wake up from your dreams,' he called. 'Are you sleeping? See those blackberry bushes on the edge of the field there? Shall we stop and collect some? Steer us that way.' She was in charge of the rudder so now she did as he said and they brought the boat to the bank near a tree where they could tie up. 'We have finished the lemonade so we will put them in one of the glasses.' He leapt on to dry land and caught the rope she threw, then, the punt secured, held out his hand to help her to the bank. Even carrying the empty glasses, she was perfectly able to leap just as he had, and if she had been with any of the local boys that's what she would have done. But this was Wilhelm: he had the gallantry of every hero who had ever caught her imagination, and trustingly putting her hand in his she was no longer a daydreaming girl in an outgrown cotton frock; she felt herself to be cherished and beautiful.

As if he too wanted to overplay his role, he raised her hand to his lips. Surely he must know how her heart was racing!

'You hold the glass,' he told her. 'Leave me to reach for the berries. Anyway, I don't want you to scratch yourself. You have the prettiest hands I have ever seen,' he added. And he certainly seemed loathe to let go of her as they walked towards the bushes.

The prettiest hands he'd ever seen . . . His words echoed and re-echoed, embossed on her memory. 'Silly,' she mumbled, hearing herself as ungracious. Why couldn't she simply have thanked him for the compliment? Why? Because she was just a gauche child, she answered her silent question. But in her heart she was neither gauche nor a child. In her heart she was full of the strangest sort of emotion: she wanted to shout with pure joy; she wanted to cry until she had no tears left, because this time tomorrow he would be gone; she wanted—

'Pass the glass,' his voice broke into her self-analysis. For ten minutes or so the blackberry picking went on, while the sun blazed down on them. 'I have filled both the glasses, so the rest we will leave for the birds. And once I get away from the scratches of these branches I am going to divest myself of my shirt. You will not be offended?'

'Of course not. You are lucky; it is all right for you to take off your shirt.'

'There is no one about, no one for miles, I expect. Take off your dress, Jackie, let the air and the sun get to you.'

She knew it would be wrong to do that. When they'd first met she could have stripped to the waist and looked no different from a boy. Even now, at sixteen, she was less developed than anyone else who'd been in her form at school, and when they changed for gym she'd been ashamed of her small breasts.

'Come on, Jackie. Don't be shy. We are what you call "mates", are we not?'

She nodded and started to unbutton her frock. He watched her pull it over her head and felt a great surge of excitement. Dressed, she looked as straight as a young lad, but the sight of the two firm mounds of her breasts was an insight into a new world. By the time she stood before him wearing nothing but sandals and knickers he had himself in check and didn't let his gaze fall lower than her face.

'Doesn't that feel better?'

She nodded, but she was uneasy; it was like trespassing on private and forbidden territory.

'Let's eat some blackberries,' she suggested, saying the first thing that came into her head.

'I have a better idea. Just look at that water, see how it shimmers in the sunshine. You swim, do you not? Jackie, this is our last day, our last few hours. Let us make them perfect. Together we will swim.' And without waiting for her reply he pulled off his khaki shorts and, naked, started towards the punt. 'We will lower ourselves into the water from the end of the punt. The bank of the river is too muddy.'

Yes, yes, that's what they would do. Naked and free they would swim. So off came her sandals and then her knickers and, discretion forgotten, she climbed down into the punt just as he lowered himself into the water.

'You are like a water baby,' he told her. 'This is so superb, is it not? There are no weeds, clear water, and if you swim over here you can put your feet on the ground of the river – that is not what it is called?'

'River bed,' she told him, swimming to join him. So they stood, side by side. 'I thought it would feel muddy, but it's firm and gravely. It's not like anything real, you and me, standing here with water up to our shoulders, nothing on.'

'Jackie, I am going to miss you so much when I am back in my own country.'

She nodded, moving close to him, his naked body touching hers, cold and unfamiliar and yet as if they had always been together. He was going to miss her – surely that was what she had longed to hear him say. She moved even closer.

'You say nothing. Are you not going to miss me? It is something I don't want to contemplate.'

'I'm going to miss you so much that I can't bear to even think about it. Us being together is the most important thing that has ever happened to me.'

'Just a few hours, that's all we have left.'

Her mouth was trembling; she held her chin firmly in an attempt to stop it. She mustn't cry, even though her future was an empty void. She shivered and felt his wet arm around her. She felt his hand cupping her small breast too, and covered it with hers, proud that he knew she was no longer just a child. She felt him move his face against her wet hair.

'We will swim back to the punt and then go and lie in the field to dry in the sunshine.'

They didn't talk as they swam back across the river. He helped her to clamber on to the punt, then followed her. Hand in hand ('the prettiest hands I have ever seen' came the echo again) they walked to where they'd left their blackberries, and then lay spreadeagled on their backs, glorying in the warmth on their wet bodies. In minutes they were dry but they made no attempt to dress. The afternoon had been a new experience for both of them, not only in the adventure of swimming nude, but also in an overwhelming and nameless emotion.

'I'll never forget, Jackie. As long as I live I'll remember how it's been for us to be together. And we will be together again.'

'Will we?'

'I swear we will. And Jackie,' then softly and almost timidly, as if he were experimenting with the word, '*darling* Jackie, let us both make a solemn promise, lying here under God's clear blue sky. Let us promise that we will be together again and that we will never fail each other.'

'I promise it with all my heart. We were just children in the beginning, but we've been growing up, both of us moving together.'

He rolled on to his side and raised himself on his elbow as he looked at her, then almost reverently he moved his hand over her body. She watched him, saw how he closed his eyes as if that way the sensation of touching her was being stored in his memory. 'We've done all the childish things,' she said softly, 'but we're not children now . . .' Her mouth felt dry, she had a strange tingly feeling and hardly realized what she was doing as she pressed his hand to her warm groin. 'I want us to share everything.' The words came straight from her heart; she heard herself say them and heard him make a strange, strangled sound as he changed his position and moved over her, taking most of his weight on his elbows.

'Let me just lie touching you, nothing between us. I dreamed of this, and when I've gone I want to remember.' He too spoke in a whisper, cutting the rest of the world off from these precious shared moments.

'I want us to . . .' She knew what she wanted but not how to tell him. 'I want to be yours.'

She wrapped her legs around him, and even though all either of them knew was what nature was telling them, she reached to guide him into her. They were driven by something outside their understanding, both of them as ignorant as most of their contemporaries in an age of innocence. For her the next minutes were a combination of heaven and hell. And for him heaven was short-lived as his climax came. His dreams were so often of Jackie, dreams that pulled him out of sleep, ashamed of and yet excited by his loss of control. There on the sun-parched field his control was no greater, but his dreams had never held the wonder of this. As he rolled off her they lay close, neither of them speaking, for they knew no words to encompass the journey they had taken, a journey from carefree childhood to what they believed to be adulthood.

'Did I hurt you, darling Jackie?'

Yes, he had hurt her, she had felt as though she was being torn apart. But now that it was over she gloried in the pain.

'You were wonderful,' she told him.

'I read that the first time it always hurts a woman.' This was Wilhelm the man speaking.

Jackie's mouth softened into a smile as she snuggled closer to him. 'I'm glad it hurt. I knew it was making me yours.'

'We don't need to start back for ages,' he whispered into her still damp hair. 'Next time it will be wonderful for you, like it was for me.'

Secretly she was puzzled – puzzled but excited. He'd said 'next time'. It wasn't over yet. She turned on her side and caressed him just as earlier he had caressed her. How soon would 'next time' be? The warmth of the sun helped his recovery, that and youth. The cows meandered across the field to gather by the sloping and muddy area where they went down to the water. Nothing hurried them as in twos and threes they dabbled and drank, then started their plodding progress back to the shade on the far side of the field.

'Nature,' Wilhelm said, watching them. 'Here we are in their field yet they did not even look at us.'

The word 'nature' raised Jackie's hopes. Surely that's what they were doing, following what nature demanded.

'"Next time", that's what you said,' she murmured, and knew his thoughts were turning in the same direction as hers. 'When will that be? If not today, when? Not for years.'

'We can't wait years. Why do we whisper, my *liebling*? The cows, they are not listening. The world is just ours.'

And for the next half hour, so it was. This time they both knew where they were going, so certain were they that there was no rush as they explored each other's bodies. They'd believed they knew everything there was to know about each other, but what many a couple learn from the guidance of textbooks, they discovered for themselves. And yet there was innocence in all they did.

Lying gazing at the sky and, in the certainty of what was to follow, feeling her body alive with joy at his touch, she murmured, 'In the marriage service they say something about the comfort of each other. Is this what they mean?'

'I believe it is,' he whispered, 'so long as two people love each other.'

'I do love you, Wilhelm. I never want anyone else to touch me except you.'

'And I love you, my *liebling*. One day we will be together again.' He moved above her and she knew that 'next time' was now.

Later they dressed and repacked their picnic things. The black-berries no longer looked appetizing, except to the insects that had taken up residence inside the glasses, so they tipped them on to the ground and rammed the dirty glasses back into his ruck-sack. Then, before they climbed back into the boat, they stood for a moment, both of them knowing that for them this was the real moment of farewell.

As his mouth gently covered hers, she realized that this was the first time they had kissed. She wanted to cling to him, and yet the kiss was gentle, solemn.

'We've made our promise,' she whispered. 'You will come back.'

'Until then we shall have letters. We shall always be there for each other. You will tell me everything about art school and I will tell you all that I do. Because of you, these have been the most wonderful two years of my life.'

'And, Wilhelm, this afternoon. I'm glad – oh, that's a silly nothing sort of word – I *rejoice* that we did it.'

He nodded, holding her gaze. 'The first time for both of us. Whatever happens to us, nothing can take that away from us.'

She wished he hadn't said that. Hadn't they promised what would happen to them? He would come back for her; they belonged just to each other.

They didn't talk on the way back in the boat. To talk would have been to break the spell that held them.

They caught the tram on the outskirts of town, even though it would have been no more than ten minutes' brisk walk to the newspaper shop. As it rattled and clanked along its track they sat quietly side by side. When she stood up to get off, in the almost full vehicle they felt every eye was on them.

'Remember.' He said just the one word.

She knew her smile was forced, but to be cheerful was important. 'Don't imagine I shall forget. Have a good journey – and write soon.' She might have been talking to a casual acquaintance; there was nothing to suggest that her young heart thought itself broken.

'Enjoy art school.'

'You bet.'

The conductor was getting impatient. 'Come along now, missie, these folk have all got homes to go to.'

'Sorry,' she mumbled, her fledgling adulthood dropping from her as she felt her face flush with embarrassment. 'Bye Wilhelm.' Then she stood alone on the pavement as the tram clattered on its way.

One

'I'll take twenty Gold Flake, Jackie, and while I'm here I'll give you my weekly paper money. I shan't be in on Saturday. Guess where I'm off to? I'll tell you. Naomi has finished her training; she gets her certificate saying she is a qualified nurse. Our little Naomi! Her Dad and I are going to the hospital to see her get it.'

'That's splendid, Mrs Griffith.' Jackie made sure her face wore the expected smile of delight. It was nearly eleven in the morning. Wherever had he gone? Whatever could he be doing? The last she had seen of her poor, confused Uncle Howard had been at half past five that morning. By herself she had made up the boys' delivery rounds then looked after the shop. In his depressed, confused state was he kneeling in the churchyard by the mound of earth where Aunt Alice had been buried? 'When you see Naomi, give her my congratulations.' Somehow she hung on to her smile.

'That I will. Oh dear, Jackie, you must be going through a difficult time with poor old Mr Giles. Freddie, my husband, you know, he said he met him the other day and the poor old soul didn't seem to know where he was going or what he was up to. "Can't find my Alice," he said. Poor old lad. Of course his mind has been going for some time, we've all seen it. Even though she'd been so ill, at least she had been *herself*, he knew where she was. But now – oh dear, oh dear – and this is no life for a young girl like you, stuck in the shop day after day, looking after him. It's not like an illness he might soon be better from; minds don't mend. But what age is he? My guess would be not more than about seventy-five. The sad thing is, Jackie, he might go on for years. Once a person's mind goes, it seems to me that as long as they are fed and watered they just drift on. Isn't there someone else in the family could take him on? It's not fair a girl of your age being saddled.'

Jackie shook her head, fighting for control so that she could trust her voice. 'Even if there were, I couldn't think of it. I promised Auntie Alice. He's no trouble, he tries to carry on just like he always has.'

'Dear oh dear. A broken leg, loss of sight, loss of hearing . . . none of them are as sad as a person who's lost his marbles. Anyway, I must run, I'm having my hair permed. Must look my best for Saturday.'

Alone in the shop, Jackie perched on the stool behind the counter. 'Might go on for years . . .' Mrs Griffith's words echoed. She would soon be twenty-one and what had she to show for her years? Just before she had been due to start at art school, Alice had been taken into hospital. After an operation she had come home, a tumour removed. But release from hospital hadn't meant return to health. All hope of art school was gone; Jackie had been needed at home. As her former classmates had been learning professions and trades, some even getting married, *she* had been tied to the newspaper shop in the High Street, while her aunt had grown more and more frail as the disease tightened its grip. Jackie had always loved the elderly couple – elderly in her eyes, even when she'd been a child – but over the four years since the onset of Alice's long illness, it had become more and more difficult to recall the happy atmosphere of days gone by. Probably seeing his beloved Alice suffer had triggered Howard's confused state, just as her death had taken the final toll.

That day Jackie watched for him to come home, half frightened of what each hour would bring. 'He's had no breakfast, he's been gone for hours.' She voiced her thoughts aloud in the empty shop. 'He must have gone straight out after – after . . .' She pulled her mind away from where it was taking her. She couldn't bear to think of her last encounter with Howard. By afternoon she had no choice but to put the *CLOSED* sign on the shop door and go to the police station.

It was two days later, an unseasonal afternoon in late September, a foggy day that had hardly managed to get light at all, when Constable Withers brought her the news. A fisherman had noticed a photograph in the reeds by the lake and, retrieving it, had recognized Alice Giles as she had been twenty or more years before. A local man, he had known Alice and Howard from as far back as he could remember and, like the rest of the small town, he had heard that the poor old boy had gone missing. So he'd taken the photograph to the police station. A few hours later Howard's body had been lifted from amongst the weeds.

That night, alone in the rooms above the shop, Jackie tried to concentrate on her future. But she couldn't. Instead she walked from room to room through the only home she had known. She picked up ornaments and put them down again; she gazed at faded photographs; she opened the wardrobe in Alice and Howard's room and looked at their clothes hanging side by side, shoes neatly in trees, Alice's hats in boxes on the high shelf, Howard's 'best suit' with mothballs in its pockets and his Sunday bowler hat in a wrapping of tissue paper. Tears blinded her. It was as if that wardrobe encapsulated what life used to be. And yet she had longed to be free, to get away. Had they sensed that she'd felt herself to be a prisoner; had they known her smouldering resentment and felt hurt and rejected? When her aunt had been dying she had begged her to care for Howard: 'His poor mind is so muddled, poor darling. Promise me, Jackie, promise you'll stay with him.' So she had promised.

Duty, resentment, longing, despair . . . on that evening, alone above the closed shop, to those were added guilt, shame and hopelessness that, now it was too late, above all else she wanted to be able to tell them how much she loved them.

There could have been delays and complications, but in the event things happened fast. It had been only weeks since her aunt had died and it had been Jackie who had registered the death, so she knew exactly what she had to do. Then she went to see the solicitor.

Howard had died towards the end of September; by the first week of October she had agreed with Stephen Picher, who with his wife ran the general store at the other end of the High Street, that she would hand the business over to him at the end of the month. It was arranged that he would pay the valuation price for the stock and for the household furniture. All the finances were handled by the solicitor. Jackie simply had to be out by the time Stephen Picher moved in. He and his wife Nellie would live over the paper shop where the accommodation was bigger, and each day Nellie would cycle the length of the High Street to the grocery premises which would be her responsibility. By mid-October he had signed the new lease.

Jackie's future was an unknown. She would inherit all her great uncle and aunt had possessed, but not until her twenty-first birthday the following March. She had a little money in her Post Office savings account, but she must find a room and a job. On one point her mind was made up: she would get a job away from Brackleford. But doing what? Serving in a newspaper shop in Reading? No. This was her new beginning; she craved adventure. Each day she scanned the vacancy columns in the evening papers, but the work was always for people with experience. She pictured herself packing her bag and going to London, then reason reminded her that without work she might lose what little she had.

Then, on the third Wednesday in October, she opened the paper and the words seemed to jump out at her: *Wanted to live and work at a fruit farm in Gloucestershire, lady prepared to live as family, be a companion-help indoors and be keen to assist as necessary outdoors. Only someone prepared to work hard and treat the situation as a way of life should apply.* There was no name, simply a box number.

She wasted no time. As soon as the *CLOSED* sign was on the shop door at six o'clock she wrote her letter. If she'd meant it to be brief and businesslike, that certainly wasn't the way it developed. Her pen raced, the writing on the first page neat, but by page three the words tumbling out into something of a scrawl. She frowned, annoyed with herself. It was too late to do anything about it; the last collection went at seven and she had to get to the Post Office to be certain it would go that evening. Some people might have used the long, straight-from-the-heart letter she'd written as a base on which to produce something more efficient, the handwriting neat from beginning to end, the whole thing less rambling. But not Jackie. She literally ran to the Post Office, not allowing herself to imagine the host of other, probably more suitable, applicants. In her mind's eye she could see a farm kitchen, on the walls shining dish covers, on the dresser willow pattern crockery, and in the room the cheery family – and soon she would fit in as if she were one of them.

Only later as she lay in bed was there no way of escaping the seriousness of her situation. The vision of a warm farm kitchen faded and in its place she saw herself walking the streets of Reading looking for lodgings and work.

It was exactly six o'clock the following afternoon; the whole day had been quiet and Jackie would be glad to lock up. First, though, she went outside to look up and down the street to make sure no one was rushing to get to her before it was too late. She put the remaining evening papers on the doorstep with her usual notice asking that the money be put through the letter box, then seeing the street as empty as the shop had been all the afternoon she came in and pulled down the blind. It was just at that moment that a car drew up. She had better wait, the driver was getting out. He didn't look as though he belonged in Brackleford where, except for two or three who caught the London train each morning attired in dark suits and bowler hats, everyone looked what she would call 'ordinary'. By Brackleford standards there was nothing ordinary about the man who approached the shop. She guessed him to be in his mid-thirties, quite a good-looking man with well-cut hair, clean shaven, and wearing a smart dark grey suit, his narrow striped grey and white tie matching the handkerchief in his breast pocket. She held the door open for him to come in.

'I tried to get here before you closed. I want to speak to Miss Hunt, Miss J. Hunt,' he said as he stepped inside.

'That's me. Jackie Hunt.'

'I had your letter this morning, Miss Hunt.'

His appearance was so different from what she had expected that her next words were out before she could stop them.

'You mean you're a farmer — a fruit farmer?' Her disappointment must have been apparent from her tone.

'Indeed, no. If you remember, your letter went to the newspaper box number in London. My parents run a fruit farm in Gloucestershire. The employment of someone to live in was my idea, but I don't live there. Is there somewhere we can talk?'

'I'm sorry.' She was embarrassed. She ought to have thought to invite him to the living quarters; his having to make the request himself got them off to a bad start. 'Yes, of course there is. I'll just lock the shop. Now, if you'll come down the passage – and mind the step at the end. It's a bit dark along here.'

The room behind the shop was sparsely furnished with only the items being taken over by the new tenants. She had a large box on the floor of her bedroom in which she had put ornaments, pictures, games, trinkets, all the treasures of their lives as the three of them had lived in the humble but scrupulously clean rooms soon to belong to the Pichers.

'Would you care to sit down?' She indicated the fireside chair that had been her aunt's.

'Thank you, we can talk better sitting.' His stiff manner was infectious; Jackie was usually relaxed and natural, but she had the impression that if she were less formal than he, it would be a mark against her. So, as straight as a ramrod, she sat in the opposite chair as he continued, 'I think at this stage I should tell you something about Crocker's End, my parents' establishment. It is in a somewhat isolated situation, about a mile from the village and seven miles from the nearest town. You may not care for such a quiet region?'

'I expect I would. I've only ever lived in Brackleford, so I don't know. But whether you give me the job or not, I am going to move away when I pass the shop over to the new people at the end of the month.'

He looked at her with a puzzled expression. 'You wouldn't care to see it in new hands, perhaps? But surely you must be certain your move is to your liking?'

'I hope it will be. But the thing that will be to my liking, as you put it, is that it is new, different, an adventure.'

'At Crocker's End your main responsibility would be to keep my mother company, give her life more interest.'

'But you can't employ a person – even one with lots of knowledge about things – to give interest as if it can be handed out; we have to look for our own interests.' Whatever sort of a woman could his mother be, that she was prepared to pay someone to keep her amused?

'Unfortunately Mother can't look for anything. She has lost her sight. There is someone from the village who comes in each morning so the housework is dealt with, and Mother's vision deteriorated gradually so she has been able to adjust and tries to be independent. But her life is restricted and she is alone for most of her days.'

'I'm sorry, that's awful for her. And if your father looks after the fruit, he can't have much spare time to be with her?' A picture was beginning to form in Jackie's mind: a hard-working, rosy-faced countryman, his hands work-roughened, and a portly woman typical of farmers' wives in storybooks. She believed she detected a tightening of her visitor's mouth at her words.

'There is a manager looking after the fruit, with casual labour brought in as the seasons require. My father has become immersed in local affairs, council work and so forth. You may find the environment of the place not at all what you are looking for.'

'The advertisement said to live as family. So the family is just your parents?'

'I fear so.' And this time she could almost imagine the hint of a smile. 'As I say, it may not be at all what you are looking for.'

'I told you in my letter, I don't know anything about proper jobs. I've always just been here looking after things, with Auntie not being able to do much, and then helping in the shop. So anything I do will be new to me. But I promise you, Mr Bennett, if you give me a chance I will try and be all your mother wants.'

'Whether or not you are given the job will be up to her, not me, so I suggest that I pick you up at, say, ten o'clock Saturday morning and drive you to Crocker's End to meet her.'

'Saturday? I'm really sorry, but I can't possibly come on Saturday. It's not like an ordinary weekday. On Saturdays people come in to pay for their papers; some of them walk right from the other side of town especially. I can't have them arrive and find I've gone off and put *CLOSED* on the door.' How could she expect him to understand? You only had to look at the smart way he dressed to know that he did something important, that he could take a day off whenever he wanted. And why was he looking at her like that?

'It is customary to make oneself available for interview when one applies for a post.' Still he didn't take his gaze off her as he waited for her answer. She supposed he expected her to say she'd put the interview before her regular customers. But she couldn't do that; it would be a sort of betrayal of her uncle and aunt, as if what they'd done here didn't matter.

'Yes, I know. And I'm truly sorry. But if you knew how trade works in a place like this you would understand. They are regular customers, you can almost set the clock by the times some of them come each week.'

He stood up to leave and her heart dropped to the soles of her boots, believing this would be the end as far as he was concerned. Then he smiled. It was a smile that started in his brown eyes, the brightest eyes she had ever seen, before his mouth got the message.

'Well done,' he told her. 'I was testing you. Anyone who would neglect an established duty would be of no use to Crocker's End. How about Sunday? Sunday morning at around ten o'clock?'

She nodded, relief flooding through her.

'Yes, Sunday would be lovely. Gloucestershire . . .' From the way she said it, it might have been on the moon. 'And do you mean you are taking me in your car?'

This time he laughed, although she had the uncomfortable feeling he was laughing *at* her. 'I'm certainly not suggesting we walk. We shall see how you and my mother take to each other. If all goes well and she offers you the post, assuming you accept . . .'

'But of course I shall if she thinks I'll do. And, Mr Bennett, thank you for understanding about Saturday.'

'If you're not prepared to fail your customers here, then I believe I can entrust you with my mother's well-being.' Kind enough words, but she wished his manner wasn't so stilted.

As she saw him out it occurred to her that neither of them had mentioned wages.

Sunday dawned cold and bright. At precisely ten o'clock the car drew up outside the shop. Jackie had already put the remaining newspapers on the doorstep in three neat piles: *News of the World, People* and *Sunday Times,* about a dozen papers in all, for there was never much over-the-counter trade on Sundays and the delivery boys had already done their rounds and returned the bags. Underneath the *CLOSED* sign she had stuck a notice, written in bold capital letters: *Please put money through letter box. If you don't have the right change you can pay me next time you're passing.*

With a purposeful slam she shut the shop door and turned the key in the lock.

'I'm all ready, Mr Bennett.' She believed she'd managed to let no hint of excitement creep into her voice, but it was impossible to hide her smile as he opened the door for her and she settled into the passenger seat. She supposed he was dressed for the country, for Thursday's immaculate dark suit had been replaced by a sports jacket and flannels, and his tie by an open-necked shirt and cravat. 'I'm especially glad it's sunny and bright, we'll be able to see *everything*. If I'm honest I'm really excited. I've never been to Gloucestershire before, but I hear it's very beautiful and has lots of stone houses, Cotswold stone houses.'

'Beautiful mellow stone. Something of an artists' paradise, I believe.'

'That's funny. Perhaps Fate is telling me something. Ages ago, when I was leaving school, I wanted more than anything to be an artist. I was never top-of-the-class clever at most things, but I loved to draw and paint. I was all booked in to go to art school – we'd even found lodgings for me in Maidenhead. But then Auntie was taken into hospital and it got put off. Well, I told you about why I never got a job or anything when I wrote, didn't I. Don't you think that it seems like Fate that the first time I go anywhere it's to what you call an artists' paradise? Perhaps it's a sign that your mother is going to think that I might do.'

He glanced at her as he drove. What a funny child she still was. Plenty of girls were married and even had babies by the time they were her age, and yet lots of girls, for all their show of sophistication, hadn't her wisdom. Never top-of-the-class clever, but wise beyond her years.

'You're not used to long car rides? Some people don't enjoy them.'

She chuckled. 'I'm not going to be one of those. This will be my first one and I mean to love every second of it.' She was conscious that he turned to look at her and she could see how those bright eyes were shining with laughter.

'I'm glad to hear it,' he said, 'because, assuming my mother offers you the post, and assuming you don't see how isolated the place is and take fright, it will be necessary for you to learn to drive.'

'*Me!* Drive a car? It's usually men who drive, although I have seen a few women, I suppose.' There must be a motor car no one used; perhaps his mother drove before she lost her sight. Following her own thoughts she almost missed what he was saying.

'Whoever Mother engages, I intend to buy a small car and arrange driving instruction. To my mind, one of the most import-ant services you – or whoever is appointed – can offer will be to take her out sometimes, to town perhaps, to the hairdresser, even to church. At one time she used to drive herself.'

'Mr Bennett doesn't drive?' But what about all that local work he did, surely he didn't get around on a bicycle?

'Indeed he does. But he has outside engagements, his life is very full.' Again he looked at her, seeming to consider before he added, 'To my mind, the whole point of having someone with my mother is to put colour and meaning into her days. Imagine what it must be like to be alone for hours of each day, alone and in a dark fog.'

Jackie nodded. 'You can't really imagine, can you? It must make her angry and bitter.'

'So I have often thought. But not Mother. You will see for yourself. It's as if she has some sort of inner . . . joy? Contentment? You will form your own opinion, Miss Hunt, as she will of you.'

They drove in silence for some time, but Jackie was so enrapt with all she saw that she hardly noticed. Then her mind went to the woman who waited at Crocker's End.

'Fancy living with so much beauty all around you and not be able to see it,' she said softly, more to herself than to her companion.

'A warning to you,' he answered. 'Never let her suspect you pity her. You will understand why I say that as you come to know her – *if* you come to know her.' Another reminder that in a few hours' time she might well be on her way home to a future of job seeking.

They covered the rest of the journey in silence.

'Here we are,' he said at last. 'This field is the start of Crocker's End. Down there is the house. The drive is quite a slope.' Then through the opening where the five-barred gate was hanging on a single hinge and to the house.

Her ears alert for the sound of the car, Verity Bennett came out of the back door to meet them. Jackie's first impression was one of surprise. This sprightly, slightly built, white-haired lady wasn't a bit as she had expected Richard Bennett's mother to look.

'Miss Hunt, this is my mother. Mother, Miss Hunt.'

'Come away in, my dear. Miss Hunt did he call you?'

'Jackie Hunt, Mrs Bennett. To be honest, I'm not used to being Miss Hunt, I'm usually just Jackie.'

'Then Jackie it shall be.' With a manner so different from her son's, there was friendliness and warmth in the voice. It wasn't that Richard had been unfriendly, but he was so stiff and formal that Jackie felt uncomfortable with him. How different his mother was; even those few words put her at her ease. 'Now, Richard,' Mrs Bennett was saying, 'just you scoot off somewhere for ten minutes, leave Jackie and me to get to know each other without having to mind our Ps and Qs. We can't talk with you standing there weighing up every word we say.' Jackie was surprised that he should have been dismissed so positively, and yet the words were spoken with affection, even as if the two of them shared some joke.

'I'll give you a quarter of an hour. Come on, Montague,' he said to the yellow Labrador who had come to meet them and was flailing his tail in anticipation. 'We'll take a walk.'

Verity watched him go, or rather she turned her head in the direction of the retreating footsteps and watched them in her imagination.

'Is the dog yours?' Jackie asked.

'Yes. Richard gave him to me for company. Montague. I ask you! What a name for a dog. But that's Richard for you. Our dear old Lab died, he was called Chum, and Richard knew how I missed him. So he arrived one weekend with this wee puppy, for that's all he was then, and said his name was Montague.'

'I bet he was Monty in no time,' Jackie suggested.

'In no time at all. Almost before Richard's car had got out of the gate. But not to Richard – dear me, no. To Richard he is Montague. And the animal seems to know.'

Jackie smiled a smile that was lost on Verity. Clearly, Richard didn't go in for abbreviations.

'Come and sit down, Jackie. A quarter of an hour isn't long to get to know each other, but somehow I think we shall manage.'

And this, Jackie thought, is the start of my interview. But it didn't turn out to be a bit as she had expected. She found herself talking easily and naturally, and listening too. The pride in Verity's voice when she talked about her husband, Ernest, didn't escape her. It seemed that he wouldn't be home for their bread and cheese lunch as he was playing golf with three more members of the Parish Council, of which he was chairman.

The fifteen minutes melted. 'I see your son coming back,' said Jackie.

'Now, I don't want to press you into taking a place here because you don't like to refuse. But for my part, I think you and I could rub along very easily. Money's a nuisance, I hate bringing things down to pounds, shillings and pence, but it has to be done. I had thought twenty-two and sixpence a week and your keep. But I'm out of touch with things these days. If that's not right, you tell me. Always supposing you think you could be happy here. In the season it's a busy place to be. It's not an orderly, routine sort of job I'm offering.'

'Do you know what? If you were able to see me clearly you wouldn't even have to ask, you'd know what I was thinking because I can't stop smiling.'

Verity laughed delightedly. 'Thee and me, we'll get along fine.'

So the day went on. Bread, cheese and chutney for lunch, then Jackie scraped new potatoes while Verity insisted on shelling the peas. 'Peas are something I can still do. After all the summers I've done them I could shell peas blindfold just as long as you look them over and make sure I haven't let any maggoty ones slip through.' Richard played his part too, improving on the butcher's scoring of a joint of pork, making sure the cuts were narrowly placed and perfectly in line, then rubbing oil and salt into it so that the crackling crackled.

Earlier he had told Jackie that his mother seemed to have an inner glow of contentment. Certainly it was true that afternoon; it was a contentment that turned a normal daily chore into fun. With the joint in the oven, Richard suggested leaving Jackie in charge while he took his mother and Montague out in the car so that the dog could have a good run. 'Leave the meat to the Lord to cook. We'll put the vegetables on when we get home.'

'Richard, we can't go off and leave the poor girl behind like that.' Verity might have been talking to a child who had forgotten his manners.

'Of course you can,' Jackie cut in quickly. 'I think I'd like it if you did, really. It would make me feel I belonged. And while you're gone I'll see to the apple sauce.'

As they drove off, her wave was intended for Verity, but of course it was lost on her. Her only acknowledgement was a flail of Monty's tail Once they'd gone she wandered around in the yard, she strode out between the raspberry canes, she breathed deeply of air filled with the unfamiliar scents of the countryside. This was to be her new home. Mrs Bennett said they would rub along fine, and so they would. Already she had come a little way towards understanding her, and she could see why Richard had warned her never to show pity. You can't pity someone who still retains that love of life.

Hearing the shrill ring of the telephone, she rushed indoors and picked up the receiver. Should she have, or was she over-stepping her position?

'Hello?' she said.

'Oh damn, sorry, I must have the wrong number.'

'This is Crocker's End,' she offered.

'That's not Verity. Oh, you must be the home help Richard was bringing. This is his father speaking.'

'Yes, I'm Jackie Hunt. And Mrs Bennett has told me I can stay – well, not actually stay today because I can't come till the end of the month. She said you were playing golf. Did you win?' For some reason she expected him to be as easy-going as his wife.

'I had the best round of the four!' he answered, not disguising that he was pleased with himself. 'Lunch at the clubhouse was extremely good, too. Better than the bread and cheese I'd been told to expect at home. Is my wife there?'

'No. That's why I answered the phone. Your son has taken her out in the car.'

'Well, just give her a message for me, will you? Tell her that I shan't be home until late, don't know what time. Tell her not to wait up.'

'She'll be sorry. There's a leg of pork in the oven.'

He laughed. 'Trying to tempt me with food, are you? Don't worry, I shan't go short. Something has cropped up, Parish Council work. A few things I want to go over with one of the other members. At present we're still at the golf club, but I've been invited to stay for a meal with my colleague after we've dealt with the business at hand. Now don't forget – she's not to wait up. I'll see to locking up when I get in.'

Jackie was surprised, even offended, although she supposed she had no right to be, that he had asked no questions about *her* – who she was or what sort of a person was to be his wife's daily companion. 'Too full of himself' was her silent opinion, although she had to admit he had sounded jollier than his son.

When she delivered his message, Verity's immediate questions were: 'How did he sound? Did he say how the golf went?' And when she was told that his was the best round, she beamed with pleasure. 'He was always good at ball games. You've either got an eye for the ball or you haven't, that's what he says. I'd love to have been able to see his face when he was telling you,' she laughed; a laugh filled more with love than with mirth. 'Bless him.'

At that moment Jackie happened to glance in Richard's direction and noticed his tight-lipped expression. He appeared to dote on his mother, but surely he couldn't be jealous of his own father?

'I was so looking forward to your meeting Ernest.' The pride in Verity's voice spoke as clearly as any words that she expected that anyone meeting Ernest would love him. This time Jackie purposely didn't look towards Richard.

'May I come in?' a voice called from the front hall. 'I saw your car, Richard. How's life?' And the owner of the voice appeared in the room: a man, probably in his late sixties, and, looking at him, Jackie immediately recognized the sort of figure she associated with a countryman.

'Michael,' Verity greeted him. 'What a lovely surprise. I didn't hear your motor.'

Stooping to where she sat, the man she called Michael planted a kiss on her cheek. 'That's because I didn't bring it,' he answered. 'I came on my bike – thought the exercise would do me good. And you, Richard? How do you go on for exercise up there in that grey old city, then sitting behind the wheel of a motor car?'

'There's plenty of walking space in London. Nice to see you, Michael.'

'I say, though,' Michael stood a little straighter, as if the sight of company demanded it, 'here I come barging in. Forgive me, Verity my dear, I hadn't realized you had a visitor.'

'You must get to know each other, you and Jackie. She is coming to live here and keep me company. Richard's idea, bless him.'

'This is Miss Hunt,' Richard introduced her. 'Mr Southwell, our nearest neighbour and an old friend.'

'Not that being the nearest neighbour puts me within hailing distance, but my fields run alongside Crocker's End. Nice to meet you, Miss Hunt. One of your better ideas, eh, Richard, old son.'

'I'm sure it will prove itself to be so.'

Loss of sight seemed to have given extra clarity to Verity's other senses. How else could she have known that Jackie felt put down by Richard's reply?

'Prove to be so, indeed. Hark at him!' Verity laughed, holding her hand in Jackie's direction and moving it in an obvious invitation for it to be held. 'We've found our proof already, haven't we, Jackie? Slotted together immediately. Like a handmade decanter and its stopper. Isn't that so, Jackie?'

'I thought so, Mrs Bennett,' Jackie said. 'With some people it's so easy to be your natural self.'

Richard turned away and she felt she had scored a point. Yet why should she feel the need to? He had never been less than polite to her.

At about six o'clock they ate the best meal Jackie had had for years, for food had become a necessity rather than a pleasure. Richard sharpened the carving knife with the expertise of a professional, then carved the joint, cutting the meat on the first plate into bite-size pieces before passing it to Jackie, with: 'Mother's. Will you see to her vegetables.' Verity turned a loving smile in his direction. It was clear to Jackie just where that inner contentment was rooted: Verity had a husband she idolized and the best son in the world.

Much later, lying in bed, Verity listened as the sound of the car faded into silence. What dears they were, staying so long with her and seeing her safely tucked up. Now she would relive every moment of their visit. If Ernest had said she was to go to bed, that must mean he would be very late home. Poor darling, he worked so hard for the council. Only three days ago he had been at a meeting until after eleven. When they were young, before he'd ever dreamed of standing for the council, she'd had no idea how much time councillors gave voluntarily. If only she could look after him better. This business with her sight was as hard on him as it was on her, yet he never complained that he was neglected. Hark, was that his car? She would be awake when he came up to bed . . . she'd call out to him so that he would come into her room – well, it had always been *their* room, but lately he was so often out late, and when he came in he always slept in the 'small spare'.

'I'm not asleep, darling. I want to hear all about your game.'

'You would have been proud . . .' and he started a hole-by-hole description of his success. He sounded excited, not a bit ready for bed. 'How tired are you?' he asked finally as he climbed in beside her.

'Not a bit. I've had such a lovely day.' If hers was a voice of contentment, his was of pent-up tension.

'I'm glad you're awake. I didn't fancy the thought of that lonely single bed tonight. I need some loving care.' He took her hand and drew it to the evidence of that need.

'Um,' almost a purr, as she wriggled close to him. She knew that tonight he was going to make love to her, something that happened so rarely recently. She had been aware of his mood as soon as he'd come into the bedroom. An evening at home and he would have gone to their shared bed and straight to sleep; a very late meeting and usually he would have gone quietly past her door to the single bed in the little spare room. But sometimes, as on his return tonight, she would recognize his mood of excitement, hear the way he drummed his fingers on the brass rail at the foot of the bedstead while he was telling her about his game. Darling Ernest, he had so enjoyed the day, he was keyed up, he wouldn't be able to sleep until he was satisfied, and she smiled as she pressed close against him, grateful that he would turn to her to find that satisfaction.

Putting her arm around him she could feel the tension in him and knew that sleep was a million miles out of his reach. Always she had given herself to him willingly, eagerly, even though her

own satisfaction had only come from knowing he had found what he wanted. And so it was that night, as wordlessly and without preamble he climbed above her and she guided him. He was a noisy lover, but she had known no other so she wasn't aware that not every man grunted or even shouted as his pleasure heightened. She gloried in the sound, holding him closer until the final cry that brought him to a trembling weight on her. Then, rolling away from her, he was asleep within seconds. Still she lay awake, sending up a silent prayer of gratitude that she had brought him the peace that had eluded him. Lying by his gently snoring body, she once again gave herself over to reliving her own day, this time adding its final few minutes – for it had been no more.

At about the same time, Richard and Jackie came to the outskirts of Brackleford.

'I trust you found it a satisfactory day. Certainly I did,' he told her. 'I have been increasingly worried about my mother, but knowing you will be there with her, Miss Hunt, is a great weight lifted from my mind.'

'You can't go on calling me Miss Hunt,' she answered, 'not if your parents call me Jackie.'

He turned to peer at her by the glow of the town's newly fitted lights. The old gas lamps had been taken away and electric brought to town, lights that were supposed to be akin to daylight but in fact cast a greenish hue over everything and everybody.

'You are right,' he agreed. 'You are to live as family with my parents. Does that make brother and sister of us?' She felt uncomfortable. He was really more difficult when he tried to talk lightly than when he retained his starchy mode.

'Silly! Of course not. But it would be better if you could call me Jackie, the same as they will.'

'Impossible!' His answer knocked her off balance. Had she been too familiar? Then he went on, 'Jackie you will never be. You have a very beautiful name and I shall use it. I shall call you Jacqueline.' His pronunciation of the J intrigued her; it was almost as if the word began with a soft G.

She found herself laughing. 'Like the Lab is Montague, not Monty,' she chuckled.

'Precisely. And perhaps you will be good enough to call me

Richard. For myself I don't care whether I am Richard or Mr Bennett, as you have been saying, but I know Mother will be pleased to hear we are on Christian name terms.'

He drew up outside the shop and came round to open the passenger door.

'I shall collect you in ten days' time, the first of the month, at ten o'clock.'

'It's an ordinary working day. Can you come during the week?'

'Ten o'clock on the first,' he replied. 'Goodnight, Jacqueline.'

'Goodnight – and thank you for taking me and, well, goodnight, Richard.'

He waited until she had unlocked the door and gone inside, then he left her.

In the silence they each heard the church clock at the other end of the street chime and strike midnight. In less than five and a half hours she would be taking the newspapers in from the doorstep, but the thought did nothing to detract from her eager anticipation for all that lay ahead.

Driving her home Richard had again spoken of her need to learn to drive. He said he had selected the car and arranged for it to be delivered as soon as whoever was engaged arrived at Crocker's End. After that, Sidney Holmes, the owner of the garage from which he'd bought it, had agreed to come each day to take her out for an hour's drive until he was confident she was safe to be on the road unsupervised. His tone implied that it was part of the job, so she made sure she didn't let him see her excitement at the prospect.

Listening to Richard driving away, she leant on the closed door, wanting to remember the whole day in detail, but in fact simply letting the changes to her life wash over her. In ten days' time Mr Bennett – Richard, she corrected herself silently – was fetching her and driving her away from Brackleford forever. The gate of her cage was open, she was free to fly, and strangely the certainty of her freedom brought her closer to Alice and Howard. Her old irritations were wiped clean; even her revulsion at some of Howard's recent behaviour had lost its power. Now, in the dark she walked around the shop, touching things so familiar that she needed no light: the spines of the library books, the piles of cigarettes – Gold Flake, Players, Ardath, paper

packets each containing five small cheroots, she knew exactly which was which – the till, the rack where weekly or monthly magazines were put out for over-the-counter sales. Only a month before, all these things had filled her with resentment. Now their hold had slackened, and all she was left with was the memory of being part of the team with her aunt and uncle, of games of cards in the little sitting room on winter evenings before Alice became so ill, of a childhood when although she had been brought up more strictly than most of her peers, yet the home had been filled with love. In the dark she smiled as memories crowded her mind.

It was raining when Richard put all her worldly goods on the back seat of the car: two large suitcases that had always been kept well polished even though they weren't real leather and had seldom been used, two carrier bags, the box full of mementoes of her years, and the straw basket she used to take shopping. Then he swung the starting handle to crank the engine.

'All set?' he said as he got in beside her.

'Yes. I wonder if I'll ever see all this again.' She turned around as he drove off.

'Look forward, not back. And yes, of course you will see it again, you're not leaving the country. There is nothing dramatic about relocating to another county. You'll be only a car drive away, and on any day off you can come and see your friends.'

But the truth was, she had no friends to leave behind.

'It seems to me more like entering another world,' she said, not wanting this vast step she was taking to be so belittled.

They were both of them right: it was only an easy car journey away, and yet it carried her into a life different from anything she had known.

As good as his word, Richard ensured the car was delivered the day after her arrival, and the very next day she had her first lesson in a vehicle that was to be her own, or more accurately hers to drive but Richard's as far as the expense of running it was concerned. She loved her lessons and soon grew confident on the quiet country roads.

She certainly wasn't idle, and as for set hours of freedom, there were no such things. 'Living as one of a hard-working family' was an accurate description, not that Ernest Bennett's contribution to the running of Crocker's End was worth considering. He spent far more time out than at home and took no interest in the management of the fruit farm. He seldom talked to Algy Cross, let alone put in an hour working there. Algy had been employed at Crocker's End all his adult life, just as his father and grandfather had before him. In those days there had been other men working there as well, but Ernest had decided that it was better to invest in a petrol-driven cultivator than to pay a man fifty-two weeks of the year to use a fork and shovel. So Algy was now the only man employed. The Romany travellers knew there was work to be had there for the winter pruning, and again in the summer for fruit picking. In Verity's youth all the family had worked the land under her father's watchful eye, but she would hear no criticism of Ernest and never ceased to champion him for the hours he gave to helping the local community. So why was it Jackie held back from joining in the chorus of admiration? Perhaps it had to do with Richard's expression as they'd listened to Verity regaling his wonders.

On a normal day Verity would go to her room for a rest in the afternoon, and it was then that Jackie suggested to Ernest that she might find something helpful to do outside.

'I think Cross is putting fertilizer round the bushes,' he told her. 'If I had the time I'd be out there with him. Yes, a good idea if you offer your services. One thing about this place, there's never a slack moment. And of course we miss the extra pair of hands now that Verity doesn't work. It worries me that I have so little time to give to the place. And just look at it, look at the state of this yard!'

Jackie resented the way he spoke about his wife. Or, more accurately, because there was something about him she didn't trust she clutched at what she heard as a criticism of Verity.

'You can't say she doesn't work,' she said, regardless of whether or not it was her place to speak to him like that. If she were to live as one of the family, then she would speak as one of the family. 'Just shut your eyes for a moment and try and do even the most everyday thing and it takes twice as long. She works jolly hard. And she never grumbles about all the hours you are

away do-gooding in the community.'Then realizing she had probably overstepped the mark, 'I'm sorry if that was rude. I spoke
first and thought after.'

He laughed, not in the least offended. Sometimes it was hard
to maintain her anger at what she considered his neglect; he had
such natural charm. 'And quite right, too. I like people who speak
their minds. I do the same myself. Do-gooding, as you call it, has
to be done by someone, Jackie, and it snowballs. Verity certainly
has a champion in you.'

'As you have in her.'

He didn't answer; probably his mind had moved on to something else. He was something of a mystery to Jackie, and it seemed
to her unfair that men wear so much better than women. He
looked years younger than Verity, and yet he was Richard's father
so he couldn't be. There he stood surveying his reflection in the
small mirror hanging from a nail in the wall of the lobby where
they left their Wellingtons and outside work clothes, straightening
his tie, smoothing his hair, something about him telling her that
he was pleased with what he saw. And, she told herself, how could
he not be? He was good looking in the fashion of Douglas
Fairbanks, with his neatly clipped moustache, his dark hair greying
at the temples, and his slim, upright build. Yes, he had every right
to be satisfied with what he saw.

'Before I go out to Mr Cross, I'll tidy up the yard and give it
a scrub.'

'That shouldn't be your job. Jane Carter is here each morning,
but there never seems anything to show for what she does with
her time. The trouble is she has no one to supervise her. But I
can't do everything. I must go, I have to drive to town. You'll
manage here without me?'

This time Jackie bit back her words. Yes, they'd be perfectly
all right without him, and for any evidence of what he did at
Crocker's End he could stay out as long as he liked. But all she
said was, 'Yes, of course, Mr Bennett.'

'I've a PCC meeting this evening, so if I get held up in town
I shall go straight there. I'll put my papers in the car in case I
don't have time to come back here.'

The yard hadn't been so spruce for years as it was by the time
Jackie was satisfied with it. She was about to go and offer to help

Algy Cross when the phone rang. It was the Secretary of the Parochial Church Council to say the meeting had had to be cancelled as the Vicar had been called away. She made a note and left it on the desk in what Ernest grandly called his study, then put the incident out of her mind as she went in search of Algy and the fertilizer.

The sun was shining and there was something invigorating about working out of doors; she felt herself to be at one with nature. She'd been at Crocker's End little more than a fortnight, and despite having always lived in town, she felt as if she had been tossed in the air and come down right side up. Of all the jobs she might have applied for, she knew that Fate had guided her in bringing her to Crocker's End.

Ernest was forgotten, and there was nothing unusual about there being no sign of him as she helped Verity prepare a meal later on. That was how she termed it, but in fact the situation was reversed and she cooked the meal while Verity scrubbed the potatoes and chattered.

'Hark, there's the hall clock striking seven. Poor Ernest. He had to go to town for something, and he must have been delayed. The PCC meeting was to start at seven; he must have gone straight there. He misses so many meals, it's not good for him.'

Uninvited into Jackie's mind came the image of Richard's expression on the day he brought her to meet his mother. Something stopped her telling Verity about the phone call. But it wasn't to protect Ernest that she was silent. What was he doing? She held on to the thought that when he came home he'd tell them what had kept him so long. But the evening progressed, she and Verity listened to a play on the wireless, and still Ernest didn't come. At ten o'clock she helped Verity to bed then went to her own room.

It was nearly midnight when Ernest's car turned into the driveway. Verity listened; she could always tell from his tread what his mood was. Trying to make no sound he crept up the carpeted stairs. With all her might she tried to will him to come into their bedroom. Even if she pretended to be asleep, she wanted to feel he was close beside her. If she called to him she knew he would come, but the message of his footsteps was that his mind was elsewhere and he wanted to be by himself. She lay there silently as he crept past her door on his way to the 'small spare'.

Two

'Hark! That's Richard's car,' Verity said, speaking with certainty. Living in a world of dark mist, how could she be so sure? 'I'd know the sound anywhere.' Her voice held that lilt of happiness – contentment? excitement? Jackie could never be sure – that had become familiar.

'Did he say he was coming again this weekend? I thought you said he didn't come each week,' Jackie reminded her, trying to prepare her for disappointment. Richard had come the previous weekend and the one before that.

'It's different now,' Verity chuckled.

Yes, Jackie thought, I suppose it's different now because *I'm* here and he's making sure I'm doing all he pays me for. Because I'm pretty certain it *is* he who pays my wages, just like he pays for my driving lessons. Verity and I get on so well on our own, what does he want to keep butting in for? If he didn't trust me, why did he bring me here? But she said nothing, and even if she had, Verity wouldn't have been listening; already she was outside in the dark yard, waiting for the bear-like hug that would make her happiness complete.

Attired in his city garb, which looked so out of place in the sprawling kitchen of the old house, Richard came in, his arm still around Verity's shoulders.

'Hello, Jacqueline. How's life in the country?'

'I love the country,' she answered, hearing her answer as brusque, then as an afterthought, 'Hello, Richard.' The fact that she'd 'put the cart before the horse', as she could almost hear her Aunt Alice telling her, seemed to get the weekend off to a bad start. Keeping her back to them, she continued preparing the vegetables for the evening meal.

'And the driving?' he asked, seemingly unaware that he'd been cold-shouldered.

'Mr Holmes says I'm ready to be on my own. But he won't give his permission because he says it has to be up to you. I've been out every day for nearly a month and I can do three-point turns and go backwards round corners – oh, and start on the steepest part of Silham Hill without slipping backwards too. I did that yesterday with Mr Southwell.'

'That's good. You don't want to get used to being with just the one person. That was kind of him, Mother. Did you go along too?'

'No. Michael said I could next time, but he wanted to make sure Jackie was really safe – and he says she is. They went right into town, didn't you, Jackie?' She wanted Jackie to speak for herself. With that extra perception she had acquired, Verity was sure that if she listened to the two of them she would be able to pick up the vibes and perhaps confirm what she hoped. She understood Richard so well, and that polite, unbending manner of his didn't fool her. She hated to blame darling Ernest for anything, but in her heart she did hold him responsible for Richard's refusal – or was it inability? – to show emotion. Ernest hadn't meant to harm the boy when, even while he was still at junior school, he had made teasing remarks because secretly he was disappointed that his son should be what he called a 'blue stocking'. Everyone was different, and just because Richard hadn't got into the First Eleven or the school rugby team didn't mean he grew up to be less of a man. But Ernest had been disappointed, there was no doubt of that. As her thoughts wandered, she missed the beginning of what Jackie was saying.

'. . . kind of him to say I could drive him in. The roads were quite busy, and a policeman was directing the traffic at the cross-roads. Then I had to park by the kerb between two other cars.' She tried to say it casually, but the truth was she had had a hundred butterflies in her stomach. Michael was the perfect passenger; he'd given the occasional 'Jolly good' or 'Well done', and with every mile her confidence had grown. When she finally parked in the barn where he had left his bicycle, he'd said, 'Nothing wrong with *your* driving, my dear.' But to repeat that to Richard would sound as though she were blowing her own trumpet.

'Good.' Richard's expression conveyed neither pleasure nor congratulation; it simply accepted the information. 'So, Mother, you'll soon have the freedom of the road. Tomorrow Jacqueline will drive both of us, how would that be?'

Jackie told herself he had every right to want a progress report considering he was paying for her lessons. But why did he always have to sound so – so – 'buttoned up'? And why couldn't he have spoken to *her* about tomorrow and said, 'How about if tomorrow you take Mother and me out for a drive,' instead of acting as if she wasn't a proper thinking person and arranging the outing with his mother? If Jackie had been a cat her fur would be standing on end down her back; she was no more important than Monty – sorry, she corrected herself in silent sarcasm, glaring at Richard: Montague.

'I have promised to work with Mr Cross tomorrow,' she said, making sure her tone was as aloof as his. 'He is always so busy. Keeping the weeds from taking over is a full-time job. I don't want to let him down.'

'And neither shall you,' Richard told her. 'I'll help him with whatever it is you intend to be doing. Four hands for three hours will be as productive as two hands for six. And where's Father? He can't expect to leave everything for Cross to do.'

'He's always busy, Richard, love, you know he is.' Verity defended her increasingly absent husband. 'Meetings, visits to the Urban District Council, calling on people who write to him with their problems, I've never known a man like it. These days he never seems to have an hour to be undisturbed at home.' She had an unfamiliarly troubled look on her face as she talked, but now she shrugged off her gloom and her usual cheerful expression was back in place. 'So you two do as you say, Richard, both of you help Cross in the morning, then Jackie can take us for a spin after lunch and show us how well she has got on.' Then that chuckle, 'I knew when I got up this morning that the day was going to bring something good. But you being home three weekends in a row, dear, and so near to the Christmas break – that's the icing on the cake.'

All Richard said was, 'I'll go and change out of this suit.'

Jackie was busy scraping the carrots so she hadn't been aware of his expression as he'd watched her. Yet despite Verity's almost total lack of sight, there was little that escaped her where Richard was concerned. She heard him going up the stairs and, even though reason told her she should keep her thoughts to herself, she found herself voicing them aloud.

'Thirty-three, that's how old Richard is. I know from some of the things he tells me that he mixes with plenty of women – just friends, I mean. But I'd swear hand on heart he has never had a sweetheart. Sometimes it's worried me, Jackie. All fine and good when a man's young, but you know what I've always thought to be one of the saddest things? A man getting on in years, all by himself, propping up the bar somewhere just for the sake of a bit of human company.'

'He's lived away from home for a long time, Mrs Bennett. He probably has a very full life. You oughtn't to worry about him.'

Verity gave a mischievous chuckle. 'Not now, I don't. Home three weekends in a row. It's not home that's the attraction, and it's not me either, nor yet Monty here. When he telephoned to say he'd be bringing you on that first Sunday, I could tell there was more to it than he was telling me.'

The carrots were forgotten as Jackie turned to face her. 'I don't understand?'

Verity was enjoying herself; there was evidence of that in her beaming smile and the twinkle in her sightless eyes as she held out her hand towards Jackie.

'What was it he said? Oh, I shouldn't be telling you. But, Jackie, you and I are on the same wavelength. If I love him – and the Lord knows how dear he is to me – then it seems to me that you could love him, too. I was telling you how he described you . . . I don't remember the words, but it was that you were as innocent as a child but with wisdom far beyond your years. Something in the way he said it – I knew it was important.'

'Mrs Bennett, you're dreaming dreams because you want to think he has a special girlfriend. He has been very kind to me. I dare say he pays my wages, and he certainly pays for me to learn to drive the car he has bought, but it's all for *you* he does it.'

'Oh yes, I know that. But sometimes, just sometimes, Fate plays into our hands. Perhaps I shouldn't have said anything.'

'It doesn't matter your saying it to *me*, just as long as you believe me when I tell you that you're dreaming dreams. He and I are poles apart. I shouldn't think for a minute we'd even laugh at the same jokes.'

'Love takes no account of things like that.'

'Perhaps it doesn't, I wouldn't know.' In that instant her mind was back more than four years. Oh but she did know. She and Wilhelm had always laughed at the same jokes, been serious about the things that mattered, and had such discussions about the things that make life important. 'You say love takes no account of what two people have in common, but surely it *should*. Please, *please*, put those thoughts out of your head. Honestly, it's embarrassing for both of us – not that he knows what you are brewing up, but he'd feel as awkward about it as I do if he ever found out. Truly, I'm not the sort of girl who could ever interest him – and neither could he interest me. He's – he's . . .' How could she say to his adoring mother that he was starchy and dull? 'He's set in his comfortable ways, he's probably forgotten what it is to dream.'

Neither of them had heard Ernest come in through the front door, so they hadn't been aware that he had heard their conversation from the hall.

'Forgotten?' His laughing voice surprised them. 'More likely he never knew. He's about as much fun as a foggy November teatime, and has always been the same. You're fantasizing, Verity, my dear. Leave the poor girl alone. Our son "Einstein" has a mind like a calculating machine, he always has had. How I was ever responsible for creating a chap so lacking in the joy of living I shall never know.'

Jackie found herself about to jump to Richard's defence, but Verity spoke first, the previous conversation, fantasy or not, pushed out of her mind by the pleasure of Ernest's arrival.

'I didn't hear you come, Ernie, darling. Richard's home, did you see his car? Didn't I say what a good feeling I had about the day?' His criticism of their son left her unmoved; she'd clearly heard it all before. 'What a pity you have to go off to that Council meeting.'

'I just called on the Clerk, Mrs Schofield, and asked her to type a note for each of the members changing the time to eight o'clock. She's letting her lads walk round the village together and deliver them.'

'That means another really late night for you. Oh, Ernie, you ought to put yourself first sometimes. The village managed without you before you got yourself so involved. You never have a few hours to relax and enjoy yourself. You'll end up damaging your health.' She couldn't see his expression as he watched her talking.

'My health's as good as any man's,' he said, and then, tapping her bottom and speaking in a tone that implied more than its words, 'and well you know it. Ah! Einstein approaches.'

What was there about the men of this house that made Jackie uncomfortable? Richard was so stiff-necked she could well believe his father's opinion wasn't far from the truth. Father and son were so different, the only thing they had in common was that they were both difficult. Why was it she didn't trust Ernest? She couldn't put her finger on any one thing, yet she was sure that home was no more than a convenient place for him to be fed and watered. It was obvious that Verity adored him, so where was the logic in her uneasy feeling that all wasn't as it should be? Perhaps the fault was in herself; she had known no man except her uncle. But even as she thought it, the image of Wilhelm sprang to mind for the second time. The memory of him was as vivid as it had been four years ago, and, if she faced the truth, the hurt was just as deep as when his letters had become less frequent until they finally stopped. Just thinking about it brought alive how it had hurt to realize that he couldn't have cared as she had. The echo of the words they had spoken on their last afternoon had never grown dim: their sacred promise that they would never forget each other, that they would always be there for each other. Did he ever think of her? She pulled herself up short as Richard came into the room.

'Good evening, Father. Are you well?'

Jackie heard the mockery in Ernest's tone as he replied, 'I'm blessed with more vigour than some desk-bound Johnnies half my age.'

'I understand from Mother that you are busier than ever.'

Ernest's sarcasm and Richard's 'buttoned-up' reply appeared to be lost on Verity, who looked from one to the other, seeing neither as more than a dark shape and loving both of them unquestioningly.

'Come along now, boys,' she chuckled. 'Here we are, warm and comfortable, all of us together, what more can we want? We'll have the meal ready in no time, Ernie, so you can eat up quickly before you have to go out.'

'You must count me out. I only came back to collect my papers for this evening. I altered the time of the meeting because there is someone I want to discuss something with beforehand. Don't wait up for me, Verity, you know how these things drag on.'

And that was the second time Jackie was aware of Richard's tight-lipped expression as he heard his father's words.

When Jackie and Verity were alone their meals were relaxed, filled with easy chatter. Add Ernest to the equation and the atmosphere changed, but wasn't as bad as when Richard was home. His presence took away Jackie's self-confidence. She felt like a child on her best behaviour, and annoyed with herself that it should be so. Yet, seeing Verity's patent joy in having him there made her feel ashamed. What did *her* feelings matter? She was only an employee, here now and perhaps somewhere else right out of their lives in a year or two. So for Verity's sake she made sure she appeared to be agreeable.

Afterwards, while she washed the dishes, Richard took Monty for a walk and Verity listened to the wireless. Later, while Jackie amused herself with a pack of cards and a game of patience, at his mother's suggestion Richard played the piano: Beethoven's *Moonlight Sonata*, a Chopin Étude, a ballad Jackie had never heard but Verity must have known well for as soon as he played the opening bars she started to sing. Leaning back in her favourite chair, her eyes closed, her sweet voice soft, she sang every word. Jackie might have been surprised if she could have seen Richard's tender expression as he played the accompaniment. There was something about the atmosphere that put her in mind of evenings in the room behind the shop, evenings when she and Alice and Howard had played rummy or sometimes shove ha'penny: home entertainment that cast a spell.

The following morning, as soon as he had finished breakfast, Richard went out to find Algy Cross. It was almost an hour later by the time Jackie had cleared away the evidence of the meal, prepared a cottage pie ready to be cooked for lunch, and seen Jane Carter, the daily help, set off upstairs with her routine remark: 'Off I go then to make a start on m'bedrooms.'

Ernest shut himself in his study saying he had things to attend to and phone calls to make.

'It's one of those magic mornings, Mrs Bennett,' Jackie told Verity as she piled the mashed potato on the pie. 'The sky suddenly thinks it's spring instead of nearly Christmas.'

'It's not so cold either,' Verity agreed. 'It won't last; it can't at this season of the year. But to waste it would be a crying shame. Be a dear, Jackie, and run upstairs to my bedroom and bring my fur coat down. It's in the wardrobe. And you'll see my mother's old fur muff on the hat shelf. I've always kept it even though I doubt if anyone uses them these days. Then we'll take a chair outside and I can sit somewhere near to where Richard is working.'

'It's not "sitting outside" warm.'

'I'll be all wrapped up. And it will be second best to being able to make myself useful and get my hands dirty with you others. Yes, get a deckchair out of the shed for me and put it where I can smell the fields.' There was never any hint of self-pity in Verity, but her remark did make Jackie wonder whether 'smelling the fields' wasn't a flight of fancy. However, she did as Verity asked and saw her comfortably settled with Monty lying across her feet near to where Richard was busy hoeing round the loganberry bushes. Then she went to find Algy Cross, who was working in the next and more steeply sloping field they called Dilly Hill.

'Where do you want me, Mr Cross?'

'Be a help to me, missie, if you would take a hoe to some of these little devils of weeds. They get in there between the rasp-berry canes like as if they had a right to be there. I've done from the top down this far. So if you start at the bottom we'll see how we go. That would be a help. But I tell you, Miss, and it's no secret, I've said the same thing to the boss often enough, and not just this last season that's gone – with bushes and canes as knack-ered as these, how can they expect to make a good return? But does he listen? Does he, heck! Too busy out there making a big name for himself with the Council and the like. You know what? If he doesn't heed my words and put some new stock in, I don't reckon they'll sell enough fruit from all this land to make a half-decent living come next year.'

'You mean the bushes should be replaced?'

'Bushes, ah, and raspberry canes, too. They're like people: none of them go on forever. And you think of the day's work you can get out of a strong young chap compared with what can be done by some old buffer – one like *me* if I tell the truth. Most of these bushes have been in the ground long past their time. Still, missie, nowt we can do but our best, 'cos it's a sure thing the gaffer won't do anything to improve matters. Maybe that son of his might see the state the place has got into.'

'Would he recognize a bush that has served its time any more than I would?'

'Likely not. Truth to tell, this morning is the first time I've ever known him come out and offer to give a hand. His father used to complain about him, oh, years back it was, when the boy was leaving school and going on to Oxford. I can hear him now. "Bloody beats me," those were the boss's words, "that a son of mine can want to spend his life mucking about with sums when he could be out in God's fresh air." That's what he said. In those days he used to work out here and seem keen to do it. And the missus too, poor soul. Sad thing it is to lose her vision like she has. When my dad – aye, and grandad, too – were working here and I was just a bit of a nipper, I used to come along with them sometimes. The missus, she was just a lass, pretty as a picture she was, ah, and keen as mustard to help. Brought up to it, you see, this place being her father's and her grandfather's before that. Now then, we can't stand here gossiping all the morning. You get your hoe and start from the bottom. Take the old barrow that's leaning against the outside wall by the water butt and I'll see to emptying it by and by. Nothing like working as a team. Ah, those were the days, nowt but a memory now, though.' He started along between the rows of canes, but after no more than half a dozen steps, stopped and sniffed deeply, took off his cap and ran his fingers through his thinning hair, then put it on again. 'Just take a sniff of that air, won't you? Better than all the riches, blowed if it isn't.'

Jackie collected her hoe and barrow and set to work. It was probably her imagination, but she liked to think she could feel the warmth of the sun. How could Richard leave this place and go to work in noisy, dusty London? In fact Jackie had never been there herself, but in her imagination it fell into that bracket, as did any other large town

So the morning passed, Richard talking to Verity as he worked.

Jackie broke off just long enough to put the cottage pie into the Aga, then she was back again, scratching at the soil with her hoe and adding to the pile of weeds in her barrow. Just before one o'clock Richard folded the deckchair and guided his mother to the house before going back to make sure he was satisfied with what he'd done and to put away his tools.

With a feeling of excitement, Verity took the old bell she had used when there had been more workers than just Algy Cross, and then, standing outside the back door, she shook it with all her might. This was great! This was like the old days. Even as a child she had loved to be the one to ring the bell when it was time to knock off for the lunch break. In her mind's eye she could see it all, then and now. And the image wasn't so far from the truth, for like well-trained children they pushed their wheelbarrows and hoes back to the shed.

'Grub time for me and knock-off for you two. When I've eaten whatever my Flo has parcelled up for me, I'll just do a couple more rows before I get off home,' Algy Cross said as he stood his wheelbarrow against the side wall of the Dutch barn.

'Why don't you call it a day?' Richard answered. 'If anyone has earned a half day it's you.'

'Well, I look at it this way. I've been here too many years to look on it as a job o' work, that and no more. I'm going to do all I can to keep the wheels turning, as you might say. No use any of us thinking the gov'nor will take the interest he used to before – before . . . Oh well, it's none of my business how he spends his time. But one thing I will say: last year wasn't good and the next crop will be as bad or worse. I've told your father till I'm blue in the face, what this place needs is some new stock.'

Richard looked worried. 'I'll have a word with my father. Some of them must be replaced for next season.'

'Humph! None so deaf as those who won't hear. Time was when this place produced the best fruit in the area. That was when your mother's people tended it. I dare say I'm speaking out of turn, but to my mind it's not fair to her to let it go to the dogs like it is. If she had eyes to see it, it would break her heart.'

Jackie didn't let herself look at Richard; she didn't want to see the tight-lipped expression she was sure such familiarity would foster.

'You're right,' his tone surprised her, 'it's not fair to her – and not fair to the farm either. I can remember when it was – was . . . Dammit Cross, the canes were hanging with fruit! The pickers used to fill their baskets in no time – or so it seemed to me as a child.'

''T'ain't just hindsight, Mr Richard. This place has gone to ruin, don't make a scrap of difference how much work anyone puts in, *old* is *old*, and like I was saying to Miss Jackie here, they're worse than old, they're knackered. Fair breaks my heart. There are times when I reckon perhaps it's a blessing your mother can't see how things are.'

Jackie told herself there would be no difference driving with Richard sitting beside her instead of Sidney Holmes from the garage in the village. But telling herself was one thing, believing it quite another. She felt tense, sure she would crash her gears every time she double declutched to change down.

'Comfortable, Mum? Perhaps Jackie can put her seat forward a notch.'

'Don't fuss, Richard,' his mother laughed. 'I'm fitted in with room to spare.' And even if it hadn't been true she had no intention of asking Jackie to move her seat; it was important that the first time she drove Richard she should feel at ease.

'If you're sure. Montague! Here boy!' The dog had been sitting watching, hope written all over him as his tail beat a steady tattoo on the ground. Now he leapt in and clambered on to the seat by Verity's side, immediately laying down with his head and the front half of his large body on her lap. Had she not been there he would have been on his hind legs watching out of the rear window, but Monty knew without being told that his job was to take care of Verity.

'Pretend we're not here and you are out on your own,' Richard said as he settled into the passenger seat by Jackie's side. It ought to have put her at her ease, but why did he always have to speak in that authoritative voice? She had enjoyed driving with Michael Southwell, but this was quite different; she hadn't felt so nervous since her first outing with Sidney Holmes.

Off they went, the car moving forward smoothly while Jackie sent up a silent 'Thank you'. They skirted the village and took the road towards town some seven miles away. It was a reassuringly uneventful drive, the roads more or less empty until they reached the outskirts of town.

'I've been sitting here thinking,' Verity said. 'Do you know what I'd like? I wish one of you would pop into Hadley's' – a name that meant nothing to Jackie, but that Richard knew as the ladies' hairdresser – 'and see if anyone can do something to my awful hair. It's been nigh impossible to get here for ages so I've been taking the scissors to it myself. I'd like them to smarten me up for Christmas.'

That's how it happened that Richard, Jackie and the dog found themselves with an hour and a half to kill. Under Richard's guidance – it being only her second attempt – she had reversed to park alongside the kerb a little way up the street from Hadley's, where they left Verity, and it was as she started to pull away that an elderly man came out of the tobacconist's and made for the bicycle he had left propped against the kerb just in front of her. Like all accidents it happened in a second. He reached to take hold of the handlebars, caught the cuff of his jacket, lost his grip, and the bike fell to the ground right in front of the slow-moving car. Had Jackie been more experienced she might have braked in time. As it was they heard the sound of metal against metal.

'What the devil do you think you're doing?' the elderly man shouted, fright giving his voice extra volume. Then, as Richard got out of the car, closing the door quietly but firmly behind him, 'How old is that child? She's never eighteen! I shall report this to the police.'

By contrast Richard's reply was calm. 'The driver, who incidentally is twenty years old, had no way of avoiding your machine. She was already starting to pull away with her arm clearly out of the window to indicate what she was doing. Unfortunately, you didn't look. I suggest we take your bicycle down the road to the cycle shop and see if they can put it right.'

'I'm dreadfully sorry.' Jackie couldn't just sit there and let Richard take over. The poor old man sounded cross, but that was probably because he'd had a fright. So she'd got out of the car and joined them where a small crowd was already gathering. She understood about fright. If only she could stop shaking, but even her breath felt as if it was catching in her chest. She *must* look calm; she mustn't let Richard see how near to tears she was.

'You have nothing to apologize for, Jacqueline, you couldn't avoid the bicycle,' Richard said in a matter-of-fact voice that did nothing to calm her. Then, again to the bicycle owner, 'Had you looked you would have seen the car was pulling out. You should be grateful the bike fell or you might have been getting on it when it was hit. However, I'm sure we all three of us regret the occurrence. It's an unnecessary inconvenience. Wait in the car, Jacqueline, and this gentleman and I will go to the cycle shop.'

'It won't push,' the owner of the sorry-looking machine said. 'I tell you, that bike's my lifeline.'

While the owner tottered along by his side, Richard carried the cycle. Less than five minutes later he returned to find Jackie in the back of the car with Monty.

'Why are you there?'

'You drive home. Mrs Bennett can sit with you.' Please don't let him argue. I feel awful, as wobbly as jelly.

'Out you get.' Richard held the door open as if she hadn't spoken. 'And you, Montague. Mother will be more than an hour yet. We'll walk in the park.'

She felt like a chastened child. If he'd shouted at her she would have fought her corner, but instead he must be making allowances for her, thinking she wasn't fit to be on the road, probably wishing he hadn't wasted his money on having her taught. At the back of her mind, not admitted even to herself until that point, had been the hope that she would surprise him with her skill, that he would say 'Well done!' Instead, look at what a mess she'd made. They walked in silence, Monty staying by Richard's side even though he had no lead. The scene misted before Jackie's eyes and she dug in her coat pocket to find her handkerchief, then made a pretence of blowing her nose so that she could wipe away the tear that had escaped. Once inside the park Richard picked up a stick and hurled it for Monty to retrieve.

'Suppose you think you've wasted your money,' Jackie mumbled, and felt her breath catch in her throat.

'Let's sit by the pond here. You won't be too cold? That is not what I'm thinking. Jacqueline, my dear Jacqueline, you mustn't let yourself be upset by that little incident.'

'Not "your dear Jacqueline".' She sounded childish and knew it, but she was on a slippery slope and couldn't stop herself. "Spect you wish you'd employed someone else, not some silly kid just looking for dreams.' What was the matter with her? She couldn't believe what she was doing and yet it was as if she was stood outside herself and had no control.

'Do you really want the truth?'

She nodded, feeling the hot tears on her face and not even trying to hide them, too miserable to care that she was behaving so badly. In her mind's eye she saw Howard and remembered how he used to cry after he lost his beloved Alice, letting his tears fall unchecked. She wished things were like they used to be. All the years when she'd longed to be free crowded back on to her: Aunt Alice, Uncle Howard, the cosy little sitting room, the warmth and the love. When Alice had died she had made herself stay cheerful for Howard's sake, but now, sitting hunched on the park bench, she sobbed.

Richard drew her into his arms. He'd seen how her hands shook, but holding her close he was aware of how her slight body trembled. Moved with tenderness, he felt inadequate. Gently he moved his hand on her back, a silent message that she wasn't alone. Surely the incident ought not to have upset her to this extent.

She leant against him, hardly aware of who it was who held her.

'It's happened to us all, Jacqueline. I doubt if there's a driver on the road who hasn't hit something – I scratched the car on the garage door the first time I tried to put it away. Today, if I had been driving instead of you, the same thing would have happened.' Short, quietly spoken sentences and probably an exaggeration of the truth, but under the circumstances it was allowable. Whatever he might have said, his words hadn't penetrated her misery.

'Not just that. It's everything.' She was beyond being comforted.

He eased her away from him so that he could turn her tear-blotched face towards his. 'I thought you were happy at Crocker's End?' It was a question not a statement.

She sniffed, gulped in an effort for control, and then spoke in a rush. 'That's just it. You don't understand. It's like a dream come true – and I haven't any right to it. I used to long to be free, never thought about *them* – Auntie and Uncle – just dreamt of getting away. I was selfish and I'm so ashamed.'

'Rubbish. You've nothing to be ashamed about. You always stayed with them, that proves you weren't selfish.'

'Not in what I did, but in my – in my *soul*.'

Not releasing his firm hold on her, he said, 'Can't you tell me about it?'

At any other time she would have been surprised that he could speak like this, as if he really cared. But now she gave it no thought beyond her need to talk.

'I expect it was different when I was little. They were so kind, so – so – sort of full of goodness. They didn't spoil me, but I always knew I was loved; I was important to them just like they were to me. At school other girls went to each other's houses, played together. I never did. We didn't have a garden and I never asked if I could bring anyone home, partly because living over the shop it wasn't like other people's houses, and partly because I was never lonely. Then when I left school, all the others went off to jobs or to train to really *be* something, nurses, typists, that sort of thing. I was booked into an art school but Aunt Alice was taken ill and I was needed at home. We said "next year", but by then we knew she wasn't getting stronger.' She snorted and sniffed her way through her tale, almost as if she were reliving the years aloud. 'Then just before she died she asked me to promise always to look after Uncle Howard. I didn't want to, but I couldn't not promise. It was like hearing the prison door being locked. Those weeks were so awful. His mind had been going for ages, but after she died he was so lost. I did try, I *did*. But he was so miserable, he cried; every time he remembered she'd gone, he cried. Then that morning . . .' Richard could feel the sudden tension in her body. He tightened his hold on her. 'I was in my bedroom, bending to get clothes out of the bottom drawer to start dressing to go down and sort the papers. I had my back to the door and didn't hear him come in. He thought I was Aunt Alice, you see.' As she recalled it, she couldn't stop shaking. 'He was old, sort of thin and frail, but suddenly I felt him leaning on me from behind, his bare skin against mine. It was revolting. His arms were round me, his hands sort of kneading my – my . . . It was disgusting.

He thought I was her, he must have thought they were young. I just hurled him as hard as I could and he stumbled back and landed on the edge of my bed.'

Once started she couldn't stop, the words poured out even though she was crying so much it was hard for him to understand all of them. 'He sat there; all he had on was his unbuttoned shirt. His face was crumpled up as he cried, he looked shrunken and – and – defeated. "My Alice, thought it was my Alice. Can't find her . . ." He kept saying things like that. I'd put my nightie back on, but he didn't seem conscious of me being there. I tried to tell him to forget it, but I don't think he even heard me. He went back to his own room and I dressed and went to sort the papers for the boys. I expected him to come to help but he didn't. I never saw him again, not after I pushed him off me that morning. Two days later they found his body in the lake.'

'So he found his Alice. Just try and tell yourself that.' Richard hoped his words penetrated her misery.

'It was because of me, because I threw him off me and sort of looked at him with disgust for what he had become, that he couldn't stand even another day. And I'd promised Auntie I'd take care of him. Sometimes it all comes back to me and I know I have no right to feel so – so – *joyous* living at Crocker's End, getting on so well with Mrs Bennett, working outside – all of it. There was such warmth, such *love* in that little room behind the shop, and all the time all I wanted was to get away. It's there in my – in my *soul* – festering.'

Richard was silent for a second or two, then he spoke slowly, choosing his words carefully.

'Listen, Jacqueline. When you have a wound that festers, it is lanced to let out the poison. And that is exactly what you have done this afternoon. And after it's been lanced it has balm to help it heal and a dressing to keep the wound clean. So that's what we have to do now. You have told me about your frustration, your resentment and this feeling of guilt, now tell me the important thing: your aunt and uncle gave you great affection – and what about you? How deeply did you care for them?'

'I loved them. Truly I loved them both and I always will. If I hadn't loved them I wouldn't feel like I do about it all. Even now, although I blame myself that he couldn't face living after that morning, the *real* Uncle Howard, the one who was like a father for me, he is as clear as anything in my mind and I'll always love him. I doubt if any child had a more caring home than I did: the home was built on love, theirs for me, mine for them, theirs for each other. Yet I couldn't be content, I wanted more.'

'Of course you did. Just as when they'd been your age they must have wanted something other than the homes they'd been brought up in. Just as I did. A lot of girls would have put their own ambitions, their own dreams, before their responsibilities. But you didn't. Think what their lives would have been if you'd put your own wishes first, but instead you were with them right till the end. So that, Jacqueline, is the balm, and the dressing for this lanced wound of yours.'

She eased herself away from him.

'You make it sound so easy,' she said. This was *Richard* she was talking to: stiff-necked and starchy Richard. Whatever could have come over her? Or him? Even making a fool of herself crying like that was nothing compared to the things she had told him. 'I don't expect you believe in an afterlife, do you?' She hoped he would say he didn't; that would help her slot him back where, in her opinion, he fitted.

'Indeed I do – absolutely. But don't ask me what I expect. I am simply confident that when a person dies leaving behind someone who has been loved in life, then that love cannot be snuffed out. Is each of us not a body and a soul? A body dies – probably tired, old, worn out, sick, ready to go – but nothing ages or destroys a soul; surely it lives on as long as that person is remembered.' As he paused, she didn't say anything. Perhaps he hadn't said enough. 'Suppose that between two people there is a relationship, shared by just themselves, observed by others. One of that couple dies, be it a husband, wife, parent, grandparent, sibling, lover – the bond that had bound them on earth was between two souls, something that will last as long as either of them draws breath.'

She had been watching him as he talked, seeing him as she never had before.

'You make it sound so easy,' she said again.

'I have never been tested and tried. But I pray that when I am, my certainty won't waver.'

'Don't know about praying,' she said, not meeting his gaze. 'That's not the sort of heaven we used to get told about in Reverend Wood's sermons.'

Something hinting at a smile touched the corner of Richard's mouth. 'Ah,' he said sagely, 'and I dare say your esteemed Reverend Wood might look on my humble faith as that of an agnostic. But I assure you it is sincere.'

For a full moment they sat in silence. He could almost feel her gathering together some semblance of normality as she blew her nose one last time and put away her handkerchief, smoothed her rumpled hair and sat a little straighter.

'You have been very kind,' she told him with a dignity so reminiscent of the childlike creature he'd found in the shop in Brackleford. 'Please don't tell anyone about how badly I behaved – not even your mother.'

'I give you my word. This afternoon has been our own and that's the way it will remain. And Jacqueline . . .' It seemed it was *his* turn to be uncertain of how to phrase what he desperately wanted to say. 'This afternoon has meant more to me than you know. I am thankful, grateful, that it was to me you talked.'

'I feel sort of empty, hollow.'

This time there was no doubting his smile. 'I think perhaps that's because you have shed that festering wound. If you are happy at Crocker's End, clutch at it, Jacqueline. I believe that is what your aunt and uncle would want.'

He could tell she was weighing up his words. Then she turned a watery smile on him, despite her sore and swollen eyelids, and nodded. 'Yes they would. I know you're right. We'd better start back to collect Mrs Bennett. If you want to drive home, Monty and I will be fine in the back. But if you say I ought to, then I will.'

'You know my answer.'

Back in town, he went to collect his mother while Jackie and Monty got into the car. If Verity was surprised that he should have fetched her from the hairdresser's instead of Jackie, she didn't say so. In fact it probably didn't cross her mind. Her out-of-control mop of hair had been razor-cut into a short bob, giving its natural wave a chance. Shampooed and coaxed into shape, it took years off her, although nothing could detract from the lines on her once pretty face.

The homeward journey was uneventful. It was as the car turned into the gateway of Crocker's End that Richard said, 'You did splendidly, Jacqueline. There's no doubt you are competent. I would trust you to take my mother anywhere.' His tone was just as she'd come to expect from him, neither friendly nor unfriendly, simply distant. Later she might remember how he'd talked to her in the park, allowing her to see the man behind the barrier that held him aloof. Now, she thought, he's speaking to me as though we were strangers. No, not true, came another thought, more likely as if I'm an employee, and so I am. Without answering him, she slowed the car to a neat halt about three inches from the back wall of the old barn where it was kept, her antagonism all too ready to surface. But Richard appeared not to notice as he got out, opened the back door and held out his hand to guide his mother.

Hearing them come through the front door, Ernest came out of the study where he'd been watching for their return. .

'Good, I'm glad you're back. I've been waiting for you.'

'A refreshing change, Father,' Richard said. 'It's usually Mother who is left to do the waiting.'

Aware of something uncomfortable in the atmosphere, Jackie went to the kitchen and pulled the kettle forward on the Aga to bring the water to the boil. Why were Richard and his father always looking to score points off each other? .

'Never mind all that. Now, here we are, all of us home,' Verity said with a laugh. 'Ernie, look at me and tell me what you think.'

'They've certainly cropped you. You've had a proper short back and sides.'

'Is it too short? It feels about right to me – like I used to have it.'

'Different colour in those days, eh? Yes, she's cut it very well. I don't know if it's a good idea – I'd got used to you as you were.'

'But this was how I always had it. I remember how pleased you were when I first had it all cut off. You always liked short hair.'

'Yes, I do. But – God, though, isn't it frightening what the years do to us?'

Only Richard sensed his mother's hurt, and even he wondered if perhaps he hadn't imagined it for almost instantly she laughed.

'I'm sorry, my darling,' she told Ernest in a voice that implied she was joining in the fun with him. 'I can have my hair done, but you'll just have to put up with the ravages time has wrought on my face. It's not fair, you know, Jackie,' for even though Jackie had come back quietly into the room, Verity hadn't missed her entrance, 'men are allowed to mature like fine wine, we women just grow old.'

'Not you, Mrs Bennett,' Jackie answered, hoping her tone disguised her anger that Ernest could dash Verity's pleasure. 'If you live to be a hundred you will never be old.'

Ernest looked impatient. 'Perhaps growing old has something to do with what I want to talk about. Just listen and say nothing, Verity. I said I was watching for you. I can't go ahead with what I mean to do without your approval. Utter nonsense, of course; as your husband it's for *me* to make our decisions, just as I always have. When have you ever not seen that what I decide is for the best, eh?' While he talked, Richard watched him speculatively, wary of what it was his father might be planning to do. He guided his mother to her chair and when she sat down kept his hand firmly on her shoulder. 'Even while you could still see, that condition in your father's will was an unnecessary nonsense, but now – why, you must realize it has to be me who holds the reins.'

Verity didn't answer, but Richard was aware of the way she raised her head as if it gave her extra alertness. His grip on her shoulder tightened in a silent message, and from that message she drew her strength. They both knew Ernest could do nothing regarding Crocker's End without her approval.

Three

'As I say, it's a ridiculous formality – an insult to my honesty and intelligence. And I know, Verity my dear, you will see the wisdom of what I have decided. If you were able to see the place instead of always imagining it in the days it was teaming with activity, you would realize that the offer I have received must be the way forward.'

Richard moved his position so that as he stood directly behind Verity he held a hand firmly on each shoulder. Seeing the movement, Jackie became even more aware of the atmosphere in the room and turned to leave. Whatever they were discussing was for family alone.

'Tea.' Richard mouthed the word soundlessly, turning his head in her direction.

She was glad to escape, but now the water in the kettle was bubbling. Ought she to hurry back with the tray or give them longer? She believed Richard's silent request meant that he wanted the conversation to be interrupted and thought tea and cake might ease the tension. So she prepared the tray and carried it back, hovering just outside the drawing room door and hoping for a sign that the moment was right.

'Why don't you tell her, Richard? You've got eyes, for God's sake, you can see the state it's in. For two years it hasn't even brought in enough to keep the place going. Am I to be expected to turn down an offer like this just so that Cross has a wage? I tell you, he's the only one who makes anything out of it.'

'And the only one who puts any effort into it, too.' Richard's voice was cold and expressionless, yet Jackie was sure that his sentiments were far from cold. Even twenty-four hours ago, would she have been so sure? She put the tray down on the occasional table and started to pour the tea as he went on, 'Have you listened when you've been told the stock needs replacing? No. And you know that's the truth.'

'I'll take no sermons from you. What the hell do you know

about growing fruit, sitting there in your comfortable office playing about with your sums? I tell you there is no longer a living to be made here. I've negotiated a top price from Hulbert and Blakeley and I've talked to the planning people and been given their word that they won't put any objections in the way. In today's economic climate it's little short of a miracle.'

Verity sat very straight in her chair, her head raised as she listened. 'Is that you, Jackie, with some tea? Now let's say no more about all this nonsense. If the bushes need replacing, Ernie darling, surely we have money enough to see to it?'

'Damn the bushes! Listen to me, my dear. Richard says the place needs restocking, and yes it does. But I'm not getting any younger; even if I did nothing to try and help people in the community, if I were prepared to slave seven days a week out there, how long do you think I could do it for? Your grandfather had your father to help him as he got older; your father had me. But I have no one, only a son who can see no right in what I do and who isn't prepared to raise a finger to help.'

'We should be proud of how well Richard has done. Jackie enjoys helping Cross, don't you, Jackie? And if we need more help replanting, feeding some good fertilizer into the soil – oh, I may have lost my sight, but not my memory. I know how to look after the place, even though I'm so useless these days. But we'll say no more about it. And Ernie, darling, if you're terribly disappointed after all the trouble you've gone to, I truly am sorry. But Crocker's End is in my trust and I couldn't possibly part with it just because we've hit a bad patch. Let's all pull together and make sure next year is a profitable one. Think how happy we always were here, Ernie.'

'Yes, I'll look back and think *that*. And you, Verity my dear, look forward and picture the years ahead of us. I tell you, I'm beginning to feel my age. The thought of grafting as I used to when I was young and fit terrifies me.'

Verity frowned, trying to imagine Ernest any different from the man he always had been. 'We'll engage a strong young man to work under Cross. How would that be?'

Ernest didn't answer, and perhaps it was as well she couldn't see his expression.

★   ★   ★

At Hideaway Cottage, Ben and Chesney Schofield were making paper chains, clearly neither of them with any enthusiasm for the job. Ben was five years old, and his memories of the way the house was bedecked when they'd lived in America had nothing in common with strips of sticky paper and a tub of glue.

'Stupid things,' he growled. 'Just a mess, Mom, that's what they are.'

'Sure they are, honey, but keep at it and when the chain grows long you'll see how good they can look. When I was little I used to make them every year.'

'Mom, look, I got sticky all down my jumper,' Chesney observed. 'I 'spect it'll stick to me. Will it, Mom?'

'Maybe.' It seemed she didn't care one way or the other. And that was probably what was behind Ben's discontent. If Pa were here they would be out in the car choosing a tree tall enough to touch the ceiling like they had last year.

'Silly chain. Hate them,' he croaked, and as if to show just how much he hated not just the boring decorations but the whole of life, he screwed his afternoon's work into a heap and threw it on the floor.

'Hey, hey, hey, what's all this?' Ernest's voice surprised them all. Ben's face crumpled and he started to cry.

'Come on, lad, big chaps like you don't have to cry. They have to decide what's to be done if there's something gone wrong.' Then to Hilda, his words accompanied by a kiss on her cheek, 'Hello, my darling. Having a frustrating time?'

As neither Ben nor his three-year-old brother understood 'frustrating', his question passed, and Hilda was so thankful to see him that her reply was simply a laughing nod of her head.

'Ah, paper chains . . .' From Ernest's expression it was clear his opinion was much the same as Ben's. 'Verity would never have them, she always wanted to fill the house with greenery.'

'Hate paper chains,' Ben said, sniffing and swinging his feet so that he kicked the table leg.

'Um, not what you've been used to, I dare say. I believe in America the shops are filled with the sound of sleigh bells – so much more exciting than gluing tacky bits of paper together. How would it be if you get your coats on and we go to see if we can find some holly and perhaps a sprig or two of mistletoe?'

'What's that? The mistle— whatever it was you said?'

Ernest warmed to the subject, explaining the traditions of rural England. Both children were fond of him and, as is so often the way, he who had had little time or patience with his own son was ready to make of himself a father figure to someone else's. It was the last Saturday before Christmas, so he drove them to town where they pushed their way into the crowded weekly market, Chesney riding high on his shoulders. Then the homeward trip armed with holly, mistletoe and two Christmas trees, which had to be tied on to the roof of the car

It would be the first time since Verity had been unable to organize Christmas that there would be a tree at Crocker's End, and for Jackie the first time ever. By the time Ernest surprised everyone by dragging it into the house, the table was laid ready for their evening meal.

'What do I hear?' A rare thing for Verity not to be able to imagine what was going on around her. 'Ernie, that's you, isn't it?'

'Yep,' he answered in what he believed to be an American accent, 'it sure is me, ma'am.'

Verity chuckled, a sound of pure delight. Her darling Ernie, home in time to sit at the table with them and in such a jolly mood, too. She sniffed deeply. For it wasn't only her sense of hearing that was enhanced, but of smell, too.

'Can it be? I believe I can smell a spruce tree.'

'Clever girl she is,' he laughed, stooping to kiss her forehead. 'Do you know where I've been all this time? No, of course you don't. I had some typing I wanted Mrs Schofield to do for the Committee, so I dropped it in at her house. And there were those two boys of hers, plastered in glue and having a miserable time trying to make paper chains. A far cry from the Christmases they'd known before she broke up with her husband and brought them home to England. And they miss their father, too. There's no doubt, boys need a man about the house.' If he could feel Richard's cold stare, he gave no indication. 'So I bundled them all in the car and took them into town to the market. A few bunches of holly and a tree, that's all it took to make them happy. I suppose she hasn't money to fritter on decorations; it must be a real struggle. Then we went to Woolworths and picked up a few bits of tinsel and baubles. It'll be a poor show compared with the things we've got up in the loft. I suppose I got carried away with their excitement, so I bought a tree for us too. Young Jackie will be in charge of decking it out, eh, Jackie? And before you go back to town, Richard, you can make yourself useful and get up into the loft to bring the decorations down.'

So often Jackie looked on him with mistrust, but this was one of the moments when she fell for his charm. Perhaps she'd misjudged him; perhaps when he was out so often he really was doing work he deemed necessary. Certainly on that evening, with time to relax, he seemed quite different. Usually he had no time to spare for Verity, but on that evening he was so pleased with himself to have given her pleasure, he couldn't have been nicer to her. In fact, if it weren't so implausible, Jackie would have thought he was flirting with her. Yet Richard still didn't unbend; Jackie felt he was watching his father, putting two and two together and not able to make four (as her Aunt Alice used to say if there was some problem they couldn't solve).

'What about some music, Richard? That would be lovely, wouldn't it, Ernie darling?'

'Um, very nice. I'll have a stab at the crossword if you'll just pass me the paper, Jackie.'

So often Richard played the piano when his father was out and there were just the three of them in the room, and always Jackie loved the atmosphere, the almost tangible feeling of contentment. So why with Ernest sitting across the fireplace from Verity was everything different? When the familiar opening chords introduced that favourite ballad and Verity sang it from beginning to end, just as she always did, Ernest clapped his hands and told her, 'Very nice, my dear. A pity you had to give up singing in the choir, you always had a good voice.' So was it *his* fault the atmosphere seemed changed?

Next day Richard got a ladder and climbed into the loft, carefully walking on the rafters.

'May I come and help?' Jackie's voice surprised him as she too clambered up. 'I've never been in a loft before. It's huge.'

'It ought to be floored in – even a few planks laid across the rafters. Mind you don't step off them. Hold the roof beam to balance.'

As he spoke he lifted an empty trunk and used it to straddle two rafters. 'Then sit on this while we see what we have.'

Apart from the open trap door where the ladder was propped, the only light was from his torch. She told herself she was being childish and stupid to have such a feeling of excitement; what could possibly be exciting about being in a dark loft with stiff-necked Richard? In answer to her silent question came the memory of that afternoon the previous weekend when she had been given a glimpse of a man so different, so sensitive; someone who'd called her 'My very dear Jacqueline'. But of course that was stupid. She wasn't his very dear Jacqueline (and why couldn't he call her Jackie, the same as everyone else?), and neither did she want to be. He was dull, starchy.

'Move along a couple of inches,' his voice cut into her thoughts, 'and I'll sit this end. God knows what there is in this box. Mother used to love doing the tree.' Then, instead of opening the box which he had balanced across the rafters in front of them, 'Jackie, you've no idea how thankful I am to have you here with her. When she was on her own – because most of the time she was – each time I left her I dreaded it, seeing her standing at the door and knowing she'd turn back into her dark, lonely world.'

'She's a very special lady,' Jackie said, speaking quietly and yet aware that for both of them what she said was important. 'I've not been here even two months and yet I – I – It sounds stupid, but it's true – I really love her.'

'Does that sound stupid? To me it doesn't. Not just because I too love her, but because . . .' And here he hesitated in a most un-Richardlike way. 'Because I know love can come in many ways: sometimes it grows over years, probably out of respect; sometimes it hits you like . . .' He didn't finish his sentence. She waited, believing that there in the almost dark loft he was going to confide something in his own life, some hurt that lay behind the aloof, unemotional front. She turned to face him, trying to give him some sign that she was his friend and was ready to listen and understand. And, without warning, there in her head was the echo of Wilhelm's promise to love her always, to come back for her. Even though it was too dark to see her expression, surely Richard could feel her sympathy. The seconds ticked by. 'Remember the day I came to the shop?'

'Yes, of course I do.'

'So do I, every second of it. I knew from that evening that nothing would ever be the same for me again. You put some sort of spell on me with your honesty, your refusal to shut the door of the shop on a Saturday, your wisdom – and your loveliness.'

Jackie had never known what it was to be shy, but in that moment she was lost for words.

'Say something. Tell me I'm stupid too, but believe me, my dear, dear Jacqueline, I never knew I could feel like this. I want to cherish you . . .'

'Now you are being stupid.' She tried to make a joke of it. 'I'm not the sort to be cherished. I'm tough as old boots.'

'I love you.'

'How can you say that when you hardly know me at all? Two months ago you didn't know I existed. You're – you're – well, you're a clever person – I know because your mother has told me about how well you've always done. Me? I was never anything special.'

'Cleverness has little to do with wisdom, and of that you have plenty. In fact what you call cleverness stems from the fact that I was never any good at sporty things, never had any wish to be. So I worked hard and passed exams. Darling Jacqueline, if you don't feel the same for me as I do for you, I can understand that. I shouldn't have spoken about it so soon. As you say, two months ago we neither of us knew the other existed. But I shan't change.'

'If you've never fallen in love before, that's because you haven't met the right woman. But Richard, that woman isn't me. Because you're a nice man, a kind man, and you found me all alone, you felt chivalrous towards me. I expect that's what happened.'

'Perhaps. But feeling protective, or chivalrous as you put it, doesn't alter the fact that I love you as a woman, not as some fledgling unable to take care of herself. I've never taken account of my age until now. I wish I were younger.'

'Oh no, I can't imagine you being younger. You're extremely serious, not like a young person.'

It was too dark for her to see the way he smiled. What a precious, quaint creature she was. He wanted to draw her into his arms, to feel her leaning against him as she had in the park only a week ago. He wanted that and so much more.

'Yes, of course I do.'

'So do I, every second of it. I knew from that evening that nothing would ever be the same for me again. You put some sort of spell on me with your honesty, your refusal to shut the door of the shop on a Saturday, your wisdom – and your loveliness.'

Jackie had never known what it was to be shy, but in that moment she was lost for words.

'Say something. Tell me I'm stupid too, but believe me, my dear, dear Jacqueline, I never knew I could feel like this. I want to cherish you . . .'

'Now you are being stupid.' She tried to make a joke of it. 'I'm not the sort to be cherished. I'm tough as old boots.'

'I love you.'

'How can you say that when you hardly know me at all? Two months ago you didn't know I existed. You're – you're – well, you're a clever person – I know because your mother has told me about how well you've always done. Me? I was never anything special.'

'Cleverness has little to do with wisdom, and of that you have plenty. In fact what you call cleverness stems from the fact that I was never any good at sporty things, never had any wish to be. So I worked hard and passed exams. Darling Jacqueline, if you don't feel the same for me as I do for you, I can understand that. I shouldn't have spoken about it so soon. As you say, two months ago we neither of us knew the other existed. But I shan't change.'

'If you've never fallen in love before, that's because you haven't met the right woman. But Richard, that woman isn't me. Because you're a nice man, a kind man, and you found me all alone, you felt chivalrous towards me. I expect that's what happened.'

'Perhaps. But feeling protective, or chivalrous as you put it, doesn't alter the fact that I love you as a woman, not as some fledgling unable to take care of herself. I've never taken account of my age until now. I wish I were younger.'

'Oh no, I can't imagine you being younger. You're extremely serious, not like a young person.'

It was too dark for her to see the way he smiled. What a precious, quaint creature she was. He wanted to draw her into his arms, to feel her leaning against him as she had in the park only a week ago. He wanted that and so much more.

'What's that? The mistle— whatever it was you said?'

Ernest warmed to the subject, explaining the traditions of rural England. Both children were fond of him and, as is so often the way, he who had had little time or patience with his own son was ready to make of himself a father figure to someone else's. It was the last Saturday before Christmas, so he drove them to town where they pushed their way into the crowded weekly market, Chesney riding high on his shoulders. Then the homeward trip armed with holly, mistletoe and two Christmas trees, which had to be tied on to the roof of the car

It would be the first time since Verity had been unable to organize Christmas that there would be a tree at Crocker's End, and for Jackie the first time ever. By the time Ernest surprised everyone by dragging it into the house, the table was laid ready for their evening meal.

'What do I hear?' A rare thing for Verity not to be able to imagine what was going on around her. 'Ernie, that's you, isn't it?'

'Yep,' he answered in what he believed to be an American accent, 'it sure is me, ma'am.'

Verity chuckled, a sound of pure delight. Her darling Ernie, home in time to sit at the table with them and in such a jolly mood, too. She sniffed deeply. For it wasn't only her sense of hearing that was enhanced, but of smell, too.

'Can it be? I believe I can smell a spruce tree.'

'Clever girl she is,' he laughed, stooping to kiss her forehead. 'Do you know where I've been all this time? No, of course you don't. I had some typing I wanted Mrs Schofield to do for the Committee, so I dropped it in at her house. And there were those two boys of hers, plastered in glue and having a miserable time trying to make paper chains. A far cry from the Christmases they'd known before she broke up with her husband and brought them home to England. And they miss their father, too. There's no doubt, boys need a man about the house.' If he could feel Richard's cold stare, he gave no indication. 'So I bundled them all in the car and took them into town to the market. A few bunches of holly and a tree, that's all it took to make them happy. I suppose she hasn't money to fritter on decorations; it must be a real struggle. Then we went to Woolworths and picked up a few bits of tinsel and baubles. It'll be a poor show compared with the things we've got up in the loft. I suppose I got carried away with their excitement, so I bought a tree for us too. Young Jackie will be in charge of decking it out, eh, Jackie? And before you go back to town, Richard, you can make yourself useful and get up into the loft to bring the decorations down.'

So often Jackie looked on him with mistrust, but this was one of the moments when she fell for his charm. Perhaps she'd misjudged him; perhaps when he was out so often he really was doing work he deemed necessary. Certainly on that evening, with time to relax, he seemed quite different. Usually he had no time to spare for Verity, but on that evening he was so pleased with himself to have given her pleasure, he couldn't have been nicer to her. In fact, if it weren't so implausible, Jackie would have thought he was flirting with her. Yet Richard still didn't unbend; Jackie felt he was watching his father, putting two and two together and not able to make four (as her Aunt Alice used to say if there was some problem they couldn't solve).

'What about some music, Richard? That would be lovely, wouldn't it, Ernie darling?'

'Um, very nice. I'll have a stab at the crossword if you'll just pass me the paper, Jackie.'

So often Richard played the piano when his father was out and there were just the three of them in the room, and always Jackie loved the atmosphere, the almost tangible feeling of contentment. So why with Ernest sitting across the fireplace from Verity was everything different? When the familiar opening chords introduced that favourite ballad and Verity sang it from beginning to end, just as she always did, Ernest clapped his hands and told her, 'Very nice, my dear. A pity you had to give up singing in the choir, you always had a good voice.' So was it *his* fault the atmosphere seemed changed?

Next day Richard got a ladder and climbed into the loft, carefully walking on the rafters.

'May I come and help?' Jackie's voice surprised him as she too clambered up. 'I've never been in a loft before. It's huge.'

'It ought to be floored in – even a few planks laid across the rafters. Mind you don't step off them. Hold the roof beam to balance.'

As he spoke he lifted an empty trunk and used it to straddle two rafters. 'Then sit on this while we see what we have.'

Apart from the open trap door where the ladder was propped, the only light was from his torch. She told herself she was being childish and stupid to have such a feeling of excitement; what could possibly be exciting about being in a dark loft with stiff-necked Richard? In answer to her silent question came the memory of that afternoon the previous weekend when she had been given a glimpse of a man so different, so sensitive; someone who'd called her 'My very dear Jacqueline'. But of course that was stupid. She wasn't his very dear Jacqueline (and why couldn't he call her Jackie, the same as everyone else?), and neither did she want to be. He was dull, starchy.

'Move along a couple of inches,' his voice cut into her thoughts, 'and I'll sit this end. God knows what there is in this box. Mother used to love doing the tree.' Then, instead of opening the box which he had balanced across the rafters in front of them, 'Jackie, you've no idea how thankful I am to have you here with her. When she was on her own – because most of the time she was – each time I left her I dreaded it, seeing her standing at the door and knowing she'd turn back into her dark, lonely world.'

'She's a very special lady,' Jackie said, speaking quietly and yet aware that for both of them what she said was important. 'I've not been here even two months and yet I – I – It sounds stupid, but it's true – I really love her.'

'Does that sound stupid? To me it doesn't. Not just because I too love her, but because . . .' And here he hesitated in a most un-Richardlike way. 'Because I know love can come in many ways: sometimes it grows over years, probably out of respect; sometimes it hits you like . . .' He didn't finish his sentence. She waited, believing that there in the almost dark loft he was going to confide something in his own life, some hurt that lay behind the aloof, unemotional front. She turned to face him, trying to give him some sign that she was his friend and was ready to listen and understand. And, without warning, there in her head was the echo of Wilhelm's promise to love her always, to come back for her. Even though it was too dark to see her expression, surely Richard could feel her sympathy. The seconds ticked by. 'Remember the day I came to the shop?'

'Let's forget it, Richard, forget we've talked about it. One day you will meet someone who can talk to you about the things that fill your life, about your work and all that sort of thing. You think you love me because I expect you haven't had much experience of people of my age. I truly am – well, I don't like to say it, but I suppose it's true: I'm really quite ignorant.'

'Forgive me, Jacqueline, I shouldn't have let myself speak to you about how I feel. You've had adjustments enough to make in your life recently without me badgering you. But – but . . .' With his hand under her chin he raised her face to his. They were only inches apart. She didn't love him, how could she when she knew he was aloof and boring, and yet in that moment, when those inches between them melted, her lips parted as his mouth found hers and she had no power to pull back. To be held close, to feel the warmth of another human being and to be told she was loved, brought home to her how utterly alone she really was. But this was madness. She drew away from him.

'No, Richard. Don't. Please don't.' And yet, had it been Richard any more than she who had been driven by something stronger than reason? Again she was back in that water meadow, lying naked under a hot sun and whispering, 'I want us to share everything.'

'I'm sorry, I shouldn't have let any of this happen.'

'Let's just forget it. Come on, is that the box of decorations?'

'You go down first and I'll pass it to you. Can we forget? I can't, and neither do I want to. I was just a fool to rush you. If, as you say, we hardly know each other, then don't you think we might enjoy rectifying that?'

She gave a chuckle. 'There, you see what I mean? You make it sound like a sort of business agreement. Truly, Richard, you will find someone more like yourself.'

'Someone who has lost the glorious innocence of youth, the honesty and trust I first recognized in you?'

'Even if I were the perfect creature you seem to think, no one falls in love for the sake of a good character reference.'

This time it was his turn to laugh, giving her a quick hug and then standing up, careful not to let his foot slip from the rafter.

'Go carefully,' he warned her, 'then when you get down the

ladder I'll pass the box down. We'll get the tree decorated before
I go back, if you like.'

Moving gingerly to the ladder took all her concentration. It
drew a line under the incident and she made herself put it right
at the back of her mind; or, more accurately, she told herself that's
where it was, but it was ready to spring out and catch her unawares
when she was alone.

Richard was late setting out for London. The tree was decorated,
the heady smell of pine already filling the house. At the newspaper
shop they had never had a tall tree; it was just one more thing that
made this Christmas different from any Jackie had known.

The hours had been strange since the interlude in the loft.
Working together, she and Richard had purposefully tried to blot
it out of their minds. Had he succeeded? She knew she hadn't.
But their good intentions had been made easier by their joint
effort in setting up the tree. Verity knew exactly where they would
find the wooden tub which, by tradition, had been brought in
each year. They half filled it and brought it indoors to stand in the
corner of the drawing room. Then the fun really started as the tree
was 'planted' so that Jackie could hold it straight while Richard
brought in buckets of soil to be piled around it until they were
satisfied it was stable.

As excited as a child, Verity wanted to know whether it reached
the ceiling, just as she wanted a description of where every bauble
was placed. Then came the final touch: the box of fairy lights
had to be tested before they could be draped over and around
the tree. Of course, they didn't work.

'It's always the same,' Verity said with a chuckle. 'Each year they
would be put away working as good as gold, but come the next
Christmas and there's not a flicker. Can you do something to
them, Richard?'

'I hope so. I'll take each bulb out and test it on my meter.'

'He'll get them right, Jackie. You see if he doesn't. It's all part
of the routine, isn't it, Richard, love.'

'Seems so, Mother. But when I come home on Christmas Eve
I shall bring some new lights with me just in case these die on
us over the festival. Turn the switch off, Jacqueline, and I'll get
the meter.'

'Isn't this fun,' Verity said as she heard him going upstairs to his room. 'You know what? This is going to be the best Christmas we've had for years. Fate has such a way of knowing what's best for us. Two months ago I couldn't have dreamt it would be so – so magic.'

How strange, Jackie thought; two months – isn't that just the time span Richard and I spoke about earlier? Could he have meant the things he said or was it just that we were sort of cut off from everyone but each other up there in the loft? I won't think about it. Mrs Bennett has such an uncanny way of knowing what's going on, if I even think about it she'll get the vibes . . . It's what she wants – perhaps she has put the thought into his head.

'Here comes Richard with his meter.' She guided the conversation away from where it had been heading. 'Now we have to hope he finds the duff bulb. I hope there are some spares.'

'Never doubt it. Richard will have seen to it that there were spares when he put them away the last time we used them.'

And she was proved right. Two duff bulbs were removed and replaced with new ones, then the tree was given its final touch of glory just as they heard Ernest ushering people into the front hall.

'Now, how's that for timing! And what do you think of it, boys, eh?' It was apparent from his hearty tone that he was delighted to bring the children into his home.

'Oh boy! You've got proper lights like Pa put on ours back home,' the elder of the brothers gazed wide-eyed at the lighted spectacle.

'I've brought you some visitors,' Ernest announced, sounding as pleased with himself as the conjuror pulling a rabbit from his hat. 'Verity, my dear, you've heard me speak of Mrs Schofield and her two boys.'

'How nice to meet you, my dear. You're the American lady Ernest has spoken of from the Parish Council. You've come at just the right moment. Five minutes earlier and Richard was still diagnosing the fault with the lights. They tell me it's a fine tree.'

'It surely is, Mrs Bennett. The boys and I helped choose it. Maybe Ern— Mr Bennett told you. He was kind; he took us into town. The boys were being a real pain, wanting all the razzmatazz they used to have. I tell them, Christmas is different in England – more old fashioned than back in the States.'

'You've had Christmases here before?' Verity asked with genuine interest, delighted that Ernest had brought unexpected visitors.

'I grew up here. I guess I'm as English as the rest of you. I travelled to America with my boss,' then, smiling as she remembered, 'but he travelled back home without me. I just fell for it there. It seemed to me to have all that was good about England, with the difference that it seemed smarter, brighter, the folk more ambitious. I was out there for more than ten years.'

'Do sit down, Mrs Schofield.'

'How did you know Mom was standing up?' Ben's curiosity got the better of his good manners.

'Don't be rude, Ben,' his mother cut in.

'That's not rude,' Verity said. 'It's an honest question and deserves an honest answer. You see, Ben – isn't that what your mother called you? Nice name. You see, you get clever at that sort of thing as you get used to not seeing. I could tell from her voice that she was standing. Jackie, be a dear and see about some tea for everyone. You said you brought some chocolate biscuits back from the village, didn't you? I've never known a boy who can't eat a few chocolate biscuits.'

Jackie was glad to escape to the kitchen and surprised when, while she was still waiting for the kettle to boil, Richard joined her. He looked particularly tight-lipped and critical, in fact his appearance exactly fitted the slot where until very recently she had managed to keep him.

'I take it he hasn't brought her here before?' he asked.

'No, I've never seen her. Oughtn't you to be in there being hospitable?'

Ignoring the suggestion, he frowned. 'Jacqueline, I am here so seldom, I can't know what goes on. How has he been towards her this last week?'

'To Mrs Schofield?'

'Don't be purposely obtuse. Mother, of course. Since her refusal to do as he wanted and sell Crocker's End, have you heard him refer to it again? And this Schofield woman? Is she the reason he is seldom home? You're not stupid, surely you know as well as I do that there can't be meetings and commitments all the hours he is out of the house. She's the sort he might well be attracted to – different from most of the women around these parts. Didn't you see the way he watches her? If she makes a fuss of him, no doubt he's fool enough to fall for it and be flattered. He could end up being the laughing stock of the district. And what about Mother? Does she honestly believe he spends his life on good works?'

He perched on the edge of the kitchen table, and without thinking what she was doing Jackie hoisted herself to sit at his side.

'Mrs Bennett would never suspect him of doing anything that wasn't upright and kind, she loves him far too much for that. I don't really understand them. But then I've only been here a few weeks, I've no idea how things used to be before her sight went.'

'She almost worships him, she always has.'

'You wouldn't be jealous of him by any chance?' Jackie always spoke her mind, and she had wondered about that from the first time she had seen the two men together.

'Am I jealous because of Mother? Indeed, no. Mother and I are very close; we understand each other perfectly. For anyone to love her husband as completely as she does, to my mind is wonderful as long as it's a two-way thing. But is it? I don't pretend to know how his mind works. I don't care how he amuses himself, just as long as he's good to Mother and she doesn't get hurt. Keep your eyes open, won't you?'

The lid of the kettle started to bob and rattle as the water boiled, and she slid off the table and made the tea

'I'd not really thought about it,' she mused, 'but in fact over this last week he has been *more* attentive to her rather than less. Did you notice how he kissed her when he came in? That's not habit. He has such power, you know; a few gentle words from him and her day is made. I expect with Christmas nearly here he is less busy outside. He was at home on two evenings this week and seemed content to listen to the wireless with her.'

'Humph.' Richard wasn't convinced.

'Perhaps he'll listen to what Mr Cross says and replace some of the fruits. Then things will be better. Do you mind carrying the tray while I bring the biscuits and some plates?'

And so the incident was closed. Jackie was quite pleased with herself that she and Richard had done the tree together, then talked in the kitchen, and never once had either of them referred to the nonsense he had spoken in the loft. He must be as glad as she was that they were trying to pretend it hadn't happened. He was really a very good man, she admitted: dependable, methodical, kind too behind that austere manner. Since last weekend when she had made that scene in the park, and he had listened and been patient, she had felt much more relaxed with him. She wished he hadn't said those things about being in love with her; it made her uncomfortably aware of how young and inexperienced she was. Just imagine the sort of woman he ought to fall in love with, surely the woman who one of these days he would meet and it would happen. She would he intelligent, probably a mathematician like he was himself, or at any rate she would be something professional. And the more Jackie thought about it the more her estimation of herself shrank.

Pushing the loft incident out of her mind during the day was one thing. But by night it was quite another. If the last afternoon she and Wilhelm had spent together had been different and she had still been an innocent virgin, would she have felt as she did, not only on that night but so often? Like lifting the lid from Pandora's box, there could be no way back. In the first months after he'd gone back to Germany, she had tried to rekindle the wonder of that hour of discovery. Nothing she did could ever make it as perfect as the joyous closeness of Wilhelm's naked body against hers, but in the sanctuary of her own room, the covers pulled over her head, she had reached out to him. Then, with the passing of time, as she'd made herself face the truth that he must have put her out of his mind, she had willed herself not to think of him. That's when she'd realized that the craving she couldn't escape went far beyond what had happened between the two of them; he was part of it simply because it had been he who had shared her first sensual joy.

On that December night everything was forgotten except the quest that drove her as, with the bedcovers making a tent over her, every nerve in her was alive as she arched her body in the final seconds. Then, as always, came the moment of truth. She was alone. The aching desire that had driven her only minutes ago was gone, but there was no satisfaction, no contentment; she felt degraded. She threw off the covers and climbed out of bed, going to the open window to lean out, breathing deeply of the cold air. Was it normal to behave like she did? Was every woman without a partner to love and share her life with driven by some nameless yearning she had no power to deny? And, as always happened, as if to punish herself, she was filled with utter desolation.

With a shiver she closed the window and moved back into her room where by the cold light of the moon she gazed at her naked reflection in the pier-glass. To other eyes she would be seen as slender, her small breasts firm and pert, but to her own eyes she appeared thin and her chest flat. Hopelessness swamped her. She loved being at Crocker's End, living as if she were family, but supposing Richard talked to her again as he had that morning? How could she stay? But he wouldn't. Soon he would tire of her just as Wilhelm had; he would see her as inexperienced, with no scintillating conversation, no claim to a profession or even trade that would earn his respect. There were millions of women like her, women who knew nothing beyond their homes and family. But she had no home and she had no family. And even if she were as beautiful as a Hollywood film star with breasts to make men's eyes stand out like organ stops, she would never meet anyone isolated here. Again came the memory of what only minutes ago she had done under her solitary tent of bedcovers. Would it always be like that for her, that fall from the heights to the depths, no warm human body sharing the miracle that came from being with a person you loved and who loved you? Without that, what was it but lust? Silently she spat the word, hating herself.

She had been disgusted with Uncle Howard, who had come near to raping her, believing she was his beloved Alice. But she had sunk lower than ever he had. For him, love and sexual need had been one and the same thing; for her there had been no thought of love.

She pulled her nightgown over her head and climbed back into bed, but her mind was still racing. Richard had tried to make her believe he loved her; he was alone just as she was. Would he be driven by a desire he couldn't escape? Would sleep elude him just as it had her? Richard, calm, unemotional Richard . . . yet, running her tongue around her lips, she relived the moment when his mouth had covered hers and she had been crushed close to him. If his day was ending driven by the same need as hers, where would his mind be when he brought himself to those final seconds? Would he be thinking of her? Her eyes were wide open, her lips parted as her imagination ran riot. But such thoughts were ridiculous, she told herself. There could be no moment of his life when he wasn't in control.

That night, just as he had for nearly a week, Ernest shared Verity's bed. Lying side by side, he took her hand and carried it to his lips.

'Thank you dear, you made the Schofields so welcome. It's their first Christmas away from all they've known. And, I say, didn't I get the timing just right, arriving when Einstein had just got the lights to work. I wish you could have seen those children's faces.'

'Poor little souls. I was thinking about them while you were getting ready for bed and I wondered if you wouldn't think it a good idea if you went to town and found something to put on the tree for them. They can't get many presents. She'll do their stockings, of course, but it's such an unfair world. Adults have no right to put themselves before their children.'

If she could have seen the sudden tightening of his lips, her own feeling of peace and contentment might have taken a jolt.

'There are limits to what a woman should have to put up with.' Then, moving her hand to his chest, 'Rub me just there.'

'Why's that? Have you got indigestion?'

'I expect that's all it is. Until tonight I've felt better this week, being able to spend time more quietly.'

She turned on her side and wriggled closer. 'You ought to see Dr Hamilton, let him listen to your heart. Ernie, darling, you don't think there's anything wrong, do you?' He could hear from her tone that she was frightened. In the dark, a smile played around the corners of his mouth.

'No, no, no. If the pain would just loosen its grip, I'd soon show you how fit I am, eh?' His voice hadn't its usual strength, something he knew wouldn't be lost on Verity.

'Never mind that, darling. Here, take one of my pillows, you'll feel better if you don't lie so flat. How long have you been getting these pains?'

'Not long. Since the weather's turned colder, I suppose. Thanks for the pillow, dear. Now try and get to sleep. Don't you worry; there can't be anything seriously wrong with me. Why, I've never had a day's illness.' He took the hand that was still working on his chest, kissed it and moved it towards her, then turned his back as if he was settling for sleep and expecting her to do the same.

Five minutes or so later she whispered, 'Are you asleep?'

Was this his moment, he wondered. 'No, I can't sleep. I keep thinking.'

She turned towards him and put her arm around him. 'You're worried about something. Please, Ernie darling, *please* tell me the truth. Whatever worries you is for me too.'

'I can't. You've set your heart on keeping this place. How can I expect you to understand how frightened I am. I'm a fraud, Verity. I try and make myself sound like a fit, strong man, but I'm so bloody frightened. I know I ought to be out there working with Cross, managing the place as it should be managed. But I dread it. Do you know what I believe? I believe that an hour digging out the old bushes, planting new, pruning, even pushing a wheelbarrow on that sloping ground, and before winter's done with us you'd be burying me.'

'No! Don't even think of it, Ernie. We'll find a way. Of course you mustn't even attempt to work outside. Is that why you haven't been helping Cross all this time? And you never told me.'

'You have troubles enough of your own. I've been glad of the committee work I do, it's not a physical strain like working on the land. And I suppose I've been hiding behind it rather than admit to – to this bloody fear I have.'

'You do too much. This week you've been home more, resting. And that's what you must do, Ernie. Forget working outside. We'll get it all sorted out. And let someone else take on some of the committee work you do.'

'Bless you, darling.'

The next day Verity took the law into her own hands and asked Jackie to dial Dr Hamilton's number. Ernest had said he meant to have a quiet morning and would be in the study, and that's where he was when the doctor arrived.

'He always seems so well,' Jackie said to Verity while they waited for the examination to be over and the two men to reappear.

'He wouldn't admit to being less than well,'Verity said. 'At any rate, not by the light of day. If you feel poorly in bed at night, somehow you are more vulnerable. I was really frightened and – oh Jackie, I'm so helpless. He wouldn't want me to be talking about it, but you and me tell each other most things.'

'There's one blessing, Mrs Bennett. There won't be meetings this week with Christmas. And Richard is coming home on Christmas Eve.'

'Yes.' The thought of Richard coming obviously helped. 'We shall have to take on someone else to work outside with Cross. Then poor Ernie won't feel so bad about not being able to do it.'

It seemed to Jackie most unlikely that he would have any compunction about leaving everything to Cross, just as he had previously. She felt uneasy – she even wondered if Ernest was play-acting to serve his own purpose – then was ashamed to be harbouring such uncharitable thoughts.

'Well, Mrs Bennett,' Dr Hamilton's booming voice reached them before he appeared in the doorway of the drawing room, 'your husband tells me he gave you a fright last night. I've given him a thorough going over and I don't think there's any need for anxiety as long as he remembers he isn't the boy he used to be. Time to slow down, that's my advice.'

'If it isn't one committee it's another,' Verity answered.

'They exercise his mind, keep the grey cells going without exertion. No bad thing for a man when physical work sets the alarm bells ringing. Lovely tree you've got. He was telling me he brought it home on Saturday and got it erected yesterday.'

'That's right. Richard and Jackie set it up and decorated it. This is Jackie, she's living with us now.'

The doctor glanced briefly in Jackie's direction and acknowledged her with a brief nod of his head.

'Richard is still in London? A shame, a great shame. If he were here his father could hand over the running of the fruit farm and take life more slowly. But, there you are, the young are all the same, they put their own wishes first. I dare say we did too.'

'Richard is splendid,' Verity championed, thrown temporarily off course by the criticism.

'Dr Hamilton,' Jackie knew she was speaking out of turn but surely *someone* had to ask the question, 'is there anything we should take into account about looking after Mr Bennett? If it's his heart, does that mean he has to watch his diet?'

'Oh no, no. His heart is sound. For a man of his age he is in extremely good shape. Cut down on dairy products by all means and see if that helps his digestion. His heart is strong, his pulse is good, his blood pressure is good. No, indigestion can be painful, and it's no use telling a sufferer that there's nothing wrong. Now then, I must get on my way, I've a lot of calls to make.' He moved towards the door then stopped, seeming uncertain for a second before he made up his mind to speak. 'And there's another thing that can bring about the symptoms of illness, something that should never be disregarded: fear. And in your husband's case, Mrs Bennett, I could see his agitation as soon as we talked of the work waiting to be done outside. Think about it. Don't let him imagine you see him as an invalid, but don't discount what, to my mind, is the root of his trouble.'

For the rest of that day Ernest stayed at home. He sat close to the fire, playing at doing the crossword in the newspaper, every few minutes sighing deeply.

'You mustn't worry, Ernie darling,' Verity told him. 'I'll see to it that everything is all right.'

Jackie was watching closely, so she didn't miss the sudden movement of his head at Verity's words, as if he were waiting for her to enlarge on how she meant to 'see to it'.

'The grocery order came this morning, I need to go and pay for it,' Jackie told them. 'I'll take the money from the tin, shall I, Mrs Bennett? Do either of you want anything brought in?'

'Get me a box of fifty Players, Jackie,' Ernest answered, with a sorry-for-himself sigh. 'I really don't feel like turning out in the cold. I was telling Hamilton this morning, the cold air seems to affect these pains in my chest. He says he couldn't hear anything wrong, but why should there be when I'd spent the morning on my behind in the warm?'

Before Jackie went to the general store, she walked to the corner and into the telephone kiosk. She had taken a note of Richard's number from the telephone book, so with a small pile of shillings ready, she dialled the exchange and read it out to the operator.

After a minute or so came the cool, expressionless voice down the line. 'Bennett speaking.' She wished she hadn't called him; she felt small, her confidence gone.

'I don't know if I should have phoned you at work . . .'

'Jacqueline! Of course you can phone me. What's happened?' This was the Richard she had begun to feel familiar with. Immediately, her fear melted and she told him all she knew; all she knew and all she suspected.

'I don't know what I expect you to be able to do. But I'm afraid he'll get her to agree to what he wants simply because she is worried about him. It sounds hateful, I know, but I'm *sure* he's playing up to her on purpose.'

'You did right to phone. Jacqueline, go home and try not to give him an opportunity to persuade her. She can't live anywhere but Crocker's End; it means the world to her.'

'I know.'

'I'll fix things this end and I'll be home this evening. I'll take leave. But don't tell them I'm coming – not even Mother.'

Jackie returned home with a box of fifty Players, the grocery bill paid and a much lighter heart.

'. . . won't give our minds to it until after Christmas. At this season of the year everyone has more to think about.' She only heard the end of Verity's sentence as she walked into the room where the two of them were together on the sofa in front of the fire. 'And how did you get on, Jackie, dear? Did you remember Ernie's cigarettes?' Then with the chuckle that was a signal of her contentment, 'He's run right out of them, and he needs calming down with today's crossword.' Ernest managed to chortle at her poor attempt at a joke as he undid the box, put two cigarettes in his mouth, lit them and passed one to her. 'Thank you, darling. Now give me another clue before my brain goes to sleep again.'

Jackie wished she could have spoken to Richard again and set his mind at rest that whatever schemes were afoot, nothing was to be done until after Christmas. It was a shame he had to waste precious leave days coming home when it wasn't necessary. But there was no way she could telephone him from the house, so instead she went to the kitchen and tried to think of something above the ordinary to cook for the evening meal.

His unexpected arrival was the icing on the cake of Verity's delight. Ernest looked less impressed.

'The season of office parties,' he said while his son was upstairs changing out of his city clothes, 'and one thing is certain: our Einstein's boot-faced absence won't so much as be noticed.'

'Hark,' Verity sat straighter as she listened, 'footsteps. That's Michael's step. My word, but who wants office parties when you can be with family and dear friends?'

Before Richard joined the family he went into the kitchen where Jackie was preparing vegetables to eat with the Somerset pork casserole that was giving out such appetizing smells from the Aga. He wanted to make sure there had been no further developments, and when she told him what she had heard said about doing nothing until after Christmas, he nodded his approval.

'I shall tell them that, this being an easy time to take leave, I decided to start Christmas early. How's that?'

'Plausible.'

'It − it almost hurts to see Mother's pleasure in having him with her. There's the door bell, I'll get it.' But he was too late. As was Michael's recognized and approved custom, he rang the bell then came straight in. At Crocker's End the front door was only ever locked last thing at night.

'I saw Cross at Sid Holmes' garage. He stopped for petrol for his motorcycle while I was picking up a welding job Sid had done for me. He tells me you're under the weather, Ernest. That's not like you.'

'He does too much,' Verity said, 'but he won't listen to me.'

'I've been feeling rough ever since the weather turned so damned cold. Get these chest pains. Quite frightening. How you work out of doors, I don't know. Sitting here now in the warm, resting, I feel fine.'

'Cross said Hamilton's car was here. What had he got to say?'

Richard had come into the room and was watching his father closely.

'If you ask me he doesn't know his arse from his elbow.

Says it's indigestion. I ask you! I know when the pains come:
if I exert myself, and especially in this cold weather. Frightening,
quite frightening. Then if I hide myself away in the study and
sit quietly by the fire, gradually I feel better. You tell me that's
indigestion? The only way to ease indigestion would be to
burp. Do I ever burp? No. No, I've been crawling away quietly
so that Verity wouldn't suspect how rotten I sometimes feel.'

'Oh Ernie, darling, you ought to have told me. But never a
word until last night.'

'Well I had to tell you then, old thing. Suppose I'd suddenly
turned my toes up.'

'Not very likely, Father,' Richard said in a voice of encour-
agement. 'Did Dr Hamilton not listen to your heart?' He lit a
cigarette and threw the match into the fire.

'I tell you, the man's no better than a quack,' Ernest snapped.

'He's always been very good to me,' Verity defended.

'Yours was an easy case. You told him your vision was going
and he sent you to the specialist. A cure wasn't even on offer.'

'Well, darling, your cure is to take life quietly. No more outside
work for you, that I promise you.'

Richard said nothing, but his glance met Ernest's and each of
them knew what was in the other's mind.

'Stay to supper with us, Michael,' Verity suggested. And in the
usual way Michael would have accepted, but on that evening
there was something in the atmosphere that made him want to
escape. After thirty-five years of marriage Verity was as much in
love with the man who'd snatched her from his grasp as she had
been on her wedding day.

During supper it was Verity who brought up the subject of
the Schofields.

'I've been thinking about those dear little boys you brought
in yesterday, Ernie. What a sad Christmas it will be for them –
for them and their mother, too. Nothing is worse than a broken
home. She sounded a nice enough woman; she must have good
memories as well as sad ones. I was thinking, if Jackie and Richard
went into town tomorrow they might buy something to put on
the tree for the children.'

'Bless you, my dear, but I've already got it in hand. I bought
presents for them and left their mother to wrap them. However,

they will have very little to open, so perhaps we could put some little thing on the tree. They'd like to come in and collect a gift, I'm sure.'

'We'll ask them to lunch on Boxing Day, how would that be? They can run wild out of doors here, every boy needs to do that,' she said.

Ernest raised his eyebrows. 'I seem to remember my son didn't.' His voice was heavy with sarcasm as his eyes mocked Richard.

'Parents and their offspring aren't automatically suited to each other,' Richard replied, and Jackie felt a laugh trying to escape. Point scored by Richard.

Next day she and Richard went to town with a list of things to do. She half dreaded the outing, driving alone with him. But no reference was made either to her scene of some ten days ago or to his unexpected outburst in the loft. Both of them seemed glad to move on.

'Your father has gone off to see how the decorating is getting on in church,' Verity greeted them on their return. 'He promised me faithfully he wouldn't be persuaded into helping. But you know what he is; he feels that being on the PCC he must show an interest. What did you buy the boys?' Although she couldn't see the toys, she wanted to hear a good description of the wind-up car for Ben and the wind-up pecking bird for Chesney. 'Put them on his desk in the study, dear. He'll want to wrap them up himself.'

Jackie did as she said and was just turning to leave the room when she noticed a ring box on the mantelpiece. What made her open it she would never know, but seeing the sapphire set in the gold ring, she felt excited – excited and relieved. She could hear Richard coming down the stairs so she went to the open doorway and silently signalled to him. Together they examined the ring.

'Thank God,' he whispered. 'Over Crocker's End and his so-called illness we may not be misjudging him, but just think of the joy she will feel when he puts this on her finger. Put it back just where you found it.'

On Christmas morning they expected to see the ring on Verity's finger. But there was no sign of it, and neither was it mentioned.

Hilda Schofield was delighted to accept the invitation to Crocker's End for lunch on Boxing Day. Christmas Day itself had been one of the gloomiest she had ever experienced: the boys, particularly Ben who had a longer memory, had been disagreeable and burst into tears for the slightest reason. By Boxing Day morning there was an air of relief in the house; mother and sons felt a sense of release. At precisely midday her car turned into the driveway of Crocker's End and Ernest went out to greet them.

'Jackie will take you upstairs and show you where to put your coats, my dears,' Verity said, 'and tell you where everything is.' By 'everything' Jackie knew she meant the bathroom.

Banging their small feet, the boys went ahead of them then waited at the top to be shown which way they had to go. It was as Hilda took her comb from her bag and tidied her hair at Verity's dressing table that Jackie noticed her hand with its beautifully manicured nails – and on one long, slim finger, the ring.

Four

For a fleeting moment Jackie wished she hadn't called Richard to see the ring. Would he be able to stand by and see his mother deceived? Or would he accuse his father and destroy Verity's pleasure in the Boxing Day party? Perhaps he won't notice it, she hoped, knowing there was little chance of that. On Christmas morning they had both looked at his mother's hand, expecting to see the deep blue sapphire, and even when she had shown them a pair of navy blue leather gloves Ernest had given her, they had clung on to the hope that the ring had been bought in advance of their February wedding anniversary.

I must behave naturally, Jackie told herself. If I let it show that I've noticed, Richard will know something is wrong.

'I'll go on down, the vegetables are calling me,' she said, making sure the smile she gave Hilda was warmer than she deserved. 'That's the bathroom, if any of you want it before lunch.'

The children were on their best behaviour, and whether it was because they wanted to please their mother and Ernest, or whether it was the sight of the presents on the tree, they were a credit to the way they were being brought up. The remains of yesterday's goose was in the cool larder, and today's prepared feast was a huge joint of roast beef with Yorkshire pudding that would have been a credit to a chef and had been one of the first things Aunt Alice had taught Jackie to cook.

'Are you ready to carve, Father?' Richard asked as he carried the serving dish to the dumb waiter.

Ernest started to stand up, but Verity was quick to answer for him.

'You do it, Richard, dear. And be sure to give him just lean meat.' Then, looking towards where she knew Hilda had been seated, 'He's told you of the scare he gave us. I've never known him to have a day's illness in all our years – nearly thirty-six years.'

'You didn't tell me, Mr Bennett. I'm sorry you've been poorly.'

'Nothing to fuss about.' He was clearly irritated that Verity should discuss his health with an outsider. 'I wonder you even mentioned it, Verity. No, Mrs Schofield, as Verity says, illness and I are not acquainted. Think nothing of it.'

'Well there is no Council meeting for a few days, so you have time to get right back on form.'

Jackie noticed Ben watching them as they spoke, looking puzzled. Then her mind took a giant leap in a different direction – a different direction leading to the same result: Hilda Schofield wore no rings!

Although Richard had to return to London that evening, he didn't set out on his drive until late. Before he went he followed Jackie to the kitchen where she was busying herself getting the tray ready for bedtime drinks.

'Jacqueline, I'm leaving in a minute.' He took a cup out of her hand and put it down, then held both her hands in his. 'Having you here takes a great weight off my mind. I hate to go. Because of you, I shall treasure memories of this Christmas—'

Avoiding his eyes she cut in, the words tumbling out in an attempt to steer him away from where he seemed to be heading. 'It's been really good. I'd dreaded what it would be like. Our Christmases were always quiet, but they never varied, year after year. It was church at eight o'clock, boiled eggs for breakfast, turkey for Christmas dinner and home-made pudding. Last year Auntie barely ate a thing – but they never broke the pattern. In the evening Uncle banged out some carols on the piano and we all sang. I dreaded what it would be like this year. But it's gone well.'

'I'm glad. I'll be back to see the New Year in.' He tilted her face towards him. 'For me too this has been like no other Christmas. Shall we be together this time next year? If prayers are answered, we shall.' He was speaking quietly, willing her to meet his gaze. 'We said we'd forget. That's what you want, isn't it? What have you done to me that I have no pride, that I can beg you to think of what I said? Then perhaps one day you'll begin to see me differently.'

'Don't, Richard. Somewhere out there is the right partner

for you.' Then, making an effort to get them back on course again, 'But I'll tell you one thing: when you picked me up to bring me here and meet your mother, you saw me just as some sort of day dreaming, old-fashioned kid, and I saw you – it sounds rude to tell you this, but it was true at the time – as stiff-necked and dull. Now we've come to know each other much better and I believe we're friends.'

'Indeed we are friends.' She liked to think his half-smile was simply an expression of that friendship, yet how was it she didn't draw back when he bent and held his lips on her forehead? 'There should never be love without friendship, too,' he whispered. 'I can't change my feelings, Jacqueline. But if all you can give me is friendship, then I will take it and be grateful. Until New Year's Eve . . .'

She raised her head, looking directly at him. Was it an invitation? Was it no more than an innocent movement? She could feel the warmth of his breath, her lips parted as, hardly realizing what she did and having no power to stop herself, she clung to him. His mouth covered hers; he held her so close that when she felt her heart pounding she believed it was his.

'You believe you could never love me as I do you,' he whispered, his lips so close to hers that she could feel his mouth moving with each word, 'but one day you will. I swear I'll make you love me.'

When she pulled away he didn't try and hold her back. He was talking rubbish: she didn't love him and she never could. She ought not to have let the last minute happen, it had left her breathless and with a funny, hollow feeling. And what about him? A mocking smile tried to tug at the corner of her mouth as she looked at him. If she had been thrown off balance, so too had he. She'd thought of him as starchy and buttoned-up, but from the way a nerve in his cheek was twitching, emotion had burst the buttons!

'You've got a long journey. It's a horrid night.' She made a supreme effort to get them both back to familiar ground. 'Drive carefully.'

'Indeed I will,' sounded much more like the Richard of old.

Jackie had always loved New Year's Day, the feeling of promise it brought, a wiping away of old mistakes and a chance to start

again. Not that she belonged to the brigade who made resolutions – resolutions that usually didn't last even to the end of
January. The previous evening, Verity had insisted the meal should
be held back until Richard had had time to get to Crocker's
End, but Ernest had cut himself a plate of cold meat and eaten
it with bread and cheese rather than wait for a hot meal with
the others.

'I don't see why being on the PCC means you have to go
to church for a midnight service,' Verity had said. 'Do all the
members go?'

'I expect so. You forget, my dear, this time last year I hadn't
been elected to the committee. At any rate, those with any sense
of responsibility will be there.'

'Let's hope God takes note that you're there,' Verity chuckled.
'Wrap up well. I just let Monty out for a run and, my word, but
it's a bitter night.'

'Keep the fire made up, it'll be well after midnight when I get
home. But you won't lack company, you two girls. Einstein will
be here and so, I imagine, will Michael. He won't want to be
home with just a housekeeper to see the start of 1931. Can you
believe it? 1931. Frightening where the years go.' Since Christmas
he had made no reference to chest pains and on that evening
was in a particularly good mood. Sitting on the arm of Verity's
chair he reached and took her hand in his. 'What has this next
one got in store for us, eh? New Year, a fresh page for us to write
the story of our lives on.'

'We've had our share of good years,' Verity said, locking her
fingers through his. 'We must get something sorted out. We said
we wouldn't think about it until after Christmas, but once we're
into January it's time to start looking to the future.'

She couldn't see his expression, but her reward came in the kiss
she felt on the top of her head

With a pinafore tied around her slim waist to make sure she
didn't get a mark on the new dress she liked to think gave her
a touch of sophistication, Jackie was in the kitchen preparing
what she hoped would be a festive supper. She liked it when
Michael Southwell came for a meal; his presence always ensured
an extra cheery atmosphere.

There was no doubt that the warmest room in the house was the kitchen where the Aga burnt night and day, and for that reason it was where the family usually ate in winter. Since Jackie had been at Crocker's End, the dining room had only come into its own over Christmas, and on that New Year's Eve she had lit the fire at teatime ready for the evening. But going in to lay the table she gave an involuntary shiver. What if she suggested they let the fire die down and stayed in the kitchen as usual? The door of the drawing room was closed, and as she reached for the handle, she stopped in her tracks. Ought she to go in? Richard had as good as asked her to be his mother's support. Unashamedly she put her ear against the wooden door, as if that way she would hear more clearly.

'. . . until after tomorrow. Then there's the weekend,' Ernest was saying, his tone strong and eager. 'Monday morning I'll go and see him. You'll like him, dear, he's a good, honest man, he'll not try and wriggle out of the offer he made.'

Jackie's mouth felt dry. She wished Richard would arrive. But she must just be grateful for the weekend. No matter how he'd managed to get his own way, nothing could be done until the following Monday. Then came Verity's reply.

'The builder man you talked about? No, Ernie darling, I've already told you, Crocker's End is in my trust. One day it will belong to Richard. I shall never sell it.'

'But damn it, Verity, you just said—'

'I certainly didn't say I could be pushed into a plan that we'd regret for the rest of our days.' There was no anger in her voice; she simply had to be sure he understood that Crocker's End was where they should be. 'Can you see us living in some modern bungalow?' She laughed as if the very idea was funny. 'No, of course we couldn't. Listen, Ernie, I've got it all thought out. We'll write a card to be put up on the newsagent's notice board, and while Jackie's taking that we'll get her to pop into the newspaper office too and put an advert in next Friday's paper. Poor Cross can't battle out there all by himself, except for when Jackie can find the time to give him a hand. We must take on a strong lad, someone Cross can train, someone fit and keen. One thing is certain, you mustn't do it, whether it's winter or summer, we mustn't risk your health. See how much better you've been, resting here in the warm.'

'It's my place to be out there. As long as it's in our possession I'm the man at the helm. Or I should be. What sort of a man do you think I am, that I could lounge about while other people do my work?'

'Darling Ernie, you have more than enough to do with the village things. I wondered if you did too much there too, but Dr Hamilton said it was good for you. He said it kept your brain active.'

'God, you make me feel a hundred! Get rid of this place and I'd be as fit as I ever was.'

'Darling, you don't have to work with the fruit, you mustn't. And neither must you worry about any of it. We'll find a good man. You needn't even interview him if that would make you feel you ought to be showing him the job. Richard can do it—'

'Einstein? What the devil does he know about anything here? It would kill him to do a man's work for a day.'

If he was trying to pick a quarrel he was unlucky, probably because Verity had heard it all before.

'Silly,' she laughed. 'Who's suggesting we ask him to work on the land? He must be able to size a man up and know a good worker when he sees one. What's the time, darling? He'll be on his way by now, won't he?'

'Another year nearly gone, Verity. Where will 1931 take us, eh? Young Jackie has settled well.'

At that Jackie moved stealthily away from the door, then approached it again, making sure she trod firmly before walking in on them.

'I was just going to lay the table in the dining room, Mrs Bennett, but even though the fire is roaring up the chimney it's horribly cold in there compared with the kitchen. Wouldn't we be better to eat out there?'

'Not very festive,' was Ernest's view, but he added, 'still, it won't make any difference to me. I'll have some cold beef before I go out.' Then with a twinkle in his eye as he addressed himself to Jackie, 'Someone in this house has to go and put in a word with "Him Upstairs" so good fortune will befall us in this bright New Year.'

'What rubbish the man talks,' Verity chuckled. 'You know as well as I do, Ernie my darling, you want to get there early so that you can greet each person and hand out the books. You were never one to hide your light under a bushel.' There was no criticism in her words, only understanding and devotion. To her, he was perfect just as he always had been.

'True,' he agreed with a laugh. With Richard well on his way home, he decided this was no time to pursue the future of Crocker's End.

'Where shall I lay the table, Mrs Bennett?' Jackie turned the conversation back to where she had lost it.

'In the kitchen, dear. On a night like this Richard must be frozen in the car – and we don't term Michael a visitor. Let's be warm and comfy. We'll make our own festivity.'

Ernest looked at his sightless wife with his eyebrows raised, his chuckle holding more mockery than mirth.

'That'll be the day! With Einstein leading the fun and poor old Michael the prize jester, you'll be as hard pushed to find a festive atmosphere as I shall with the Reverend Sobersides Stoughton's sermon.'

If he could have looked into the kitchen an hour or so later he might have been surprised. There was a buzz of conversation; everyone was relaxed and pleased to be where they were. Verity was having a lovely time, her mind at last at rest about Crocker's End. Ernest hadn't argued about taking on a second worker, so when Jackie went to the village to pay the paper bill she could take a notice for the board. Jackie was aware of the euphoric atmosphere and didn't look for its reason. Richard and Michael were talking to each other and Jackie listened with interest. When she'd lived in the newspaper shop she had been so much more aware of what was happening in the world than she was now. Certainly she read the *Daily Telegraph* when she had the chance, but usually Ernest carried it off almost as soon as it came through the door, whereas standing behind the counter of the shop a day never went by when she didn't read the news and the editorials. Perhaps one of the things that set her apart from most of her contemporaries was that whereas they read the film weeklies and glossy magazines, she was fascinated by world affairs. Listening to Richard and Michael, she remembered how just before she left the shop she read that Haile Selassie was about to be crowned King of Kings in Addis Ababa. How long ago it seemed that such things had made up her life.

'It seems,' Richard was saying, 'that the Rastafarians believe he is a living god.'

'Ah, I read something of the sort in an editorial a week or so ago,' Michael agreed, while Jackie listened and absorbed. 'And who was it who prophesied that the crowning of a black king foretold the day of deliverance was nigh?'

'Surely it was Marcus Garvey,' Jackie said. 'I read about it in an editorial. He wrote: "Look to Africa where a black king shall be crowned, for the day of deliverance is near." ' She had spoken automatically, remembering how the article had impressed itself on her, giving her a feeling of excitement that she was living in an age of change. Now, though, she was aware from the way Michael and Richard were looking at her that they were surprised by her words. Embarrassed, she rushed on to say, 'In the paper shop I used to read a lot. And that was just something that stuck in my mind.'

'Well done, you.' Michael beamed his admiration. 'That's what comes of having a young mind. At my age I forget the names of people I've known for years, let alone someone I've never even heard of before.'

The subject was changed, but she knew she had gained respect, whether or not she deserved it. The meal over and the hands of the clock telling them there were only twenty more minutes left of 1930, she got up to clear the dishes. Just for a moment she imagined the thousands of parties, the dancing, the balloons – but then that's the way her thoughts had turned on New Year's Eve for as long as she could remember.

'Are we clearing up?' Michael asked, passing plates to be put on her tray. 'Or do you stack it for the morning?'

She shook her head. 'We can't start a brand new year with last year's dirty dishes waiting,' she answered. How often she'd heard her Aunt Alice say those words. A smile played at the corners of her mouth as she remembered. She felt Richard watching her and wondered whether he suspected the expression was part of her past. He stood up and took the tray from her, while Michael brought the heavy kettle from the top of the Aga and poured the water.

'You wash, Richard, and I'll dry while Jackie sorts the bits out and puts things away. We have eighteen minutes.'

'Not quite,' Richard answered, 'we have to leave time to uncork the champagne.'

Verity laughed. 'Champagne? When did we last have champagne? Your twenty-first? No, our thirtieth wedding anniversary.'

'Then it's time we did. I brought it from London.'

Verity was satisfied. Why else would he have thought to bring champagne if it wasn't because he and Jackie were moving in the right direction? The old year was ending with everything going her way.

The advertisement appeared in the local paper the following Friday. Ernest gave the impression of knowing when he was beaten and said no more about the builder's offer. Instead he interviewed three applicants, made his choice and hired a young Irishman called Eddy O'Neil.

With Christmas over, the committee meetings that kept him out late started up again. And was there ever a village with so many troubles? Almost daily he would drive off in answer to someone's call for official help. But for all that, Jackie was able to reassure Richard that the idea of selling Crocker's End appeared to be forgotten.

'We're starting pruning today, Mr Bennett,' Jackie told him early in February. 'Did you tell Algy where the new bushes are to go? We don't want to waste time pruning any that are going on the bonfire, do we.'

'I decided we'd give the old ones another chance. Now that Cross has a full-time helper the place will be better looked after. He seems to think I'm made of money, but unfortunately he's wrong. This year he has O'Neil working all day and you as often as you can get out there. I'm afraid if Cross thinks I can pay for extra workers and restock a place that doesn't even earn its keep, then he'd better think again.' Then, as she opened her mouth to air Algy's argument that the bushes were knackered, he looked at her with the smile that never failed to win folk round. 'I'd be out there like a shot seeing to things myself if only I were fit. That fool Hamilton can say what he likes, *I'm* the only one who knows how I feel. Time was, young Jackie, when I used to work out there from dawn till dusk – ask Verity, she'll tell you. Getting old is no fun. An old car you can send to the garage, get a new engine put in; that's what I could do with – a new engine. Then I'd be there with you others, I wouldn't be frightened of hard manual work.'

'Well, with three of us, we shall manage. But Cross says the bushes are knackered.' Then with a chuckle, 'As knackered as he is, that's what he said.'

'In that case we needn't worry too much about them. As knackered as *me*, then I might get my cheque book out. But Cross still works with the same vigour as he always has and never has to take so much as a half day off.'

She knew it was useless to argue.

In the way that Fate and coincidence often go hand in hand, it was as she turned away from him to go up to help Verity with her morning bath that the phone rang.

'Crocker's End. Bennett speaking . . . Good God . . . I can't believe it . . . do they give you any indication how serious it is? . . . yes, yes, naturally . . . are you all right for transport? Leave it with me, I'll be with you in five minutes.' Then, putting the receiver back, he took the stairs two at a time and went straight into the bathroom where Verity was just feeling her way into the bath with Jackie close by, her hands only inches from the thin, naked body, ready to hold her if she took a step wrong. 'Did you hear that?' Ernest sounded breathless, something that wasn't lost on Verity.

'You've been rushing about. You *mustn't* do it, Ernie. Did we hear what?'

'No of course you didn't hear. Cross has been taken to hospital, that was his wife on the phone. Apparently he collapsed when he got up this morning. She thought it was a faint, but she couldn't bring him round. Hamilton came. It was a stroke, a severe stroke by the sound of it.'

Jackie had helped Verity with her bath for more than two months; Ernie had been her husband for nearly thirty-six years. Individually Verity was perfectly comfortable with either of them, and if the combination of the two might have made most women ill at ease, perhaps it was her lack of sight that protected her from any such sentiment. Lying back in the warm water she gazed towards some point on the ceiling, believing she was lined up to face Ernest.

'What can we do for them? Is he very bad? She must be so frightened.'

'I'm going straight there to take her to the hospital. Jackie, you and young O'Neil will have to do what you can. You know, Verity, I'd just been saying to Jackie how I used to work out there myself when I was younger and fitter. I can't do it, though. There's no point in pretending. If Cross had thrown the towel in sooner, probably this wouldn't have happened.'

'How will they manage if he can't work?' As she thought of Algy, in only seconds Verity's imagination saw him from the boy who used to love to come and help his father, to young adult, through middle age to the present day, and in all those years nothing had taken away his enthusiasm for what he did.

'If only we could afford it, we ought to give him a few bob a week pension. But if he doesn't come back we shall have to look for someone with experience to replace him. We've already taken on young O'Neil – and Jackie here. This place didn't make enough to pay the bills last year, God help us this year.'

Embarrassed, Jackie said, 'If it helps you needn't give me any wages just so long as I can live here. I shall have some money coming to me as soon as I'm twenty-one.'

'I haven't come to that.' Ernest's curt answer did nothing to lessen her discomfort. 'We won't discuss it now. Mrs Cross will be waiting for me. Expect me back when you see me; you know what hospitals are. They may not let her see him for hours.' And he was gone.

'It's frightening how suddenly a life can change,' Verity said as she heard him going downstairs. 'Ernie says Cross should have given up sooner, but he's not old. I can't imagine Crocker's End without him. No, he's not more than two years older than Ernie. You've worked out there with him, Jackie. Tell me, did he seem to find it too much? Or would he not say because he needs his wages every week.'

'I've not known him long so I don't know whether he's changed. But I *do* know that he loves Crocker's End as if it were his own.'

Verity nodded, her gentle smile full of affection as she said,

'That's what I thought. Yes, I must see he gets his wages. Sickness isn't a time to have extra worries. And when he's better he might like to come back sometimes – just to potter.'

'I meant what I said, Mrs Bennett. I've hardly spent anything since I've been here – except for my new dress for Christmas. And once I get what uncle has left me I really won't need wages. Just so long as I can stay here – go on being part of it all.'

'Bless you, Jackie. But you guessed from the beginning who pays your wages. Richard insisted that I should have someone for company. It was his idea and one of the best ones he's ever had. You're like the daughter we never had.'

'It's very kind of Richard to pay me, but I wish you'd tell him I'd rather he didn't.'

Verity stood up in the bath and held her hands in Jackie's direction, ready to be guided out. To her it seemed so straight-forward: she was sure Richard loved Jackie – Jacqueline, she corrected herself – she was sure Jackie was happy at Crocker's End and wanted to be part of it. Two such dear people – what was wrong with them that they couldn't see how right it would be for them to be together? In her mind's eye she had a vivid picture of Jackie, known only to herself and probably completely unlike the reality. When she'd asked Ernest what she looked like he had said she was 'a pretty enough child'. But Jackie was not a child, of that Verity was certain; no matter what she looked like, she had the heart of a woman and more understanding than most.

The next quarter of an hour was given over to getting Verity dressed, her hair done and even a little make-up on her face.

'This is a pretty coral lipstick,' Jackie told her, 'it exactly matches your jumper. Yes, you'll do. You look very pretty.'

For so long, unable to do more than dress with difficulty, looking pretty had been something she hadn't dare hope for.

'You're good for me, Jackie. You know what I think? My face has seen better days but you do your best for it; the one thing about me that must have improved with the lazy life I have nowadays is my hands. When we go into town, I want you to help me get some nail varnish. You could paint them for me, couldn't you?'

'What fun. Yes, we'll do that when we go in to the hairdresser's on Friday. Get you all prettied up ready for when Richard gets home.'

They giggled like a couple of conspirators, then, leaving her in her chair next to the up-to-the-minute press-button wireless – Richard's present to her for her last birthday – Jackie put on Wellington boots, an old coat Verity hadn't used since her own gardening days and old leather gloves from the same stable, and went off to find Eddy O'Neil, who had already started work cutting back the old bushes.

No more was said about taking on a replacement for Algy Cross. Instead, Ernest gave Eddy an extra seven and sixpence a week and the responsibility of organizing the work, which he had to do himself with Jackie's help. Whether or not Verity told Richard of Jackie's offer to work without a wage, she didn't know. No one mentioned it to her and her twenty-two and sixpence was in its envelope on the kitchen table each Friday morning.

Ernest apparently considered that having passed responsibility to Eddy, he was free to continue with his life of good works, the only difference being the occasional days when he might take Monty for a walk and do more than his share of sighing and oh dearing when he got home.

It was as he got up from the breakfast table, picked up the not-yet-unfolded *Daily Telegraph* and made for his study that he gave a deep and sorry-for-himself sigh that made Jackie glance at him.

'You've a lot to do out there, Jackie. God knows, I wish I could help.' He was grasping the back of his chair, his chest heaving as he breathed. 'But it's no use, I seem to have no strength at all this morning and the cold air would about finish me off. When you get Verity dressed, tell her I'm having a quiet morning. I've warmed the room with the gas fire, I dare say I'll have a doze, that's about all I seem fit for. I feel quite – what is it Cross would say? – quite knackered.'

He seemed to be steadying himself, standing a little straighter. Despite her frequent suspicions about him, Jackie felt responsible.

'Why don't you sit here a minute and I'll get you a sip of brandy.'

'Bless you, my dear. But no. I know just what it is: while you were cooking my breakfast I went outside and scraped the ice off the windscreen. I shouldn't have done it. It's the cold – and the exertion. I'll just sit quietly. Verity will be frightened if she thinks I'm ill again. When you tell her I shall be having a doze, make her see that it's nothing to get alarmed about. Tell her it was my own fault, I shouldn't have exerted myself in the cold air. Oh dear . . . talking too much . . . just have to sit a moment.'

'If you're all right by yourself, I'll go and run Mrs Bennett's water.' But as she pulled the door closed behind her Jackie looked back with a worried frown.

A few minutes later, leaving Verity in the bath, she ran back down to fetch a clean blouse from the airing cupboard, and that's how it was that she heard the ting of the telephone as he lifted the receiver in his study. Did that sound like a man who, only minutes before, hadn't been able to muster the strength to cross the hall from the kitchen? What made her do it she didn't ask, she simply followed her instinct and walked round the outside of the house until she could glance through the study window. Ernest was sitting at his desk with his back to the window, the telephone to his ear, his frailties forgotten. She heard him laugh as he talked; this was no duty call to do with parish work. She knew immediately who was on the other end of the line. It was surprising how rapid his recovery could be, given the right incentive.

'A different world now the sun's up . . .' His voice surprised Verity as she listened to the mid-morning story on the wireless. Immediately she switched the set off and turned in his direction with a smile.

'Jackie was worried about you. But she said you wanted to be left to have a quiet sleep. Are you feeling better, darling?'

'Yes, I must have slept for more than an hour. But it did the trick. It was my own fault, didn't Jackie tell you? I took liberties and went out to scrape the ice off the windscreen. It really knocked me for six. Never learn, do I, eh? But I'm fine now and it's degrees warmer now the sun has come through. I'd promised to run someone to the garage to collect a car that's been in dock. Didn't think I'd be able to do it, but thank God I feel better. I wish you could see me, I look as if I'm dressed for a polar expedition.'

'Can't you let Jackie go? I shall be worried until you get home again.'

'No, the poor soul would think I couldn't be bothered, sending the home-help instead. I'll be fine. It takes my mind off myself to be doing things.'

She heard his car climb the slope to the lane, then turn left towards the village.

So the weeks went by. They were used to hard winters there in middle England, and until that year Ernest had accepted them as easily as the next man. But he rang Verity's alarm bells when she woke during a night just before Easter. Something was wrong with him!

'Ernie? What is it, darling? You ought to let Dr Hamilton have another look at you,' Verity whispered, aware of his heavy breathing as he sat in bed by her side. 'Is it that nasty pain again? Perhaps it's an ulcer. He could give you something better than you can buy at the chemist for indigestion.'

'Not bloody indigestion. It's nearly three in the morning, nine hours since we had a meal. I came to bed randy as a man half my age – would I have felt like that with indigestion? I ought to have more sense.' Then, with a mirthless laugh, 'Can't you just imagine the report in the local rag: Councillor's Wife Finds Him Dead at her Side After Sexual Orgy.'

'Don't, Ernie! Let me call Jackie to bring you a brandy.'

'No, no, its getting easier. Just let me rest quietly.'

'If it's making love that's too much for you, it's high time we stopped doing it. Poor darling.'

'And what sort of a husband does that make me?'

'The only husband I want. As long as we have a cuddle, that's all I need.' Perhaps it was wicked of her, she thought, but she would much rather they just cuddled up and perhaps talked quietly for a while before going to sleep. In fact thinking back to what he called a 'sexual orgy' – it made it sound so nasty – she had felt on edge, thinking Jackie must hear him and be worried that something was wrong. Tonight he'd grunted louder and louder with each thrust. He was quiet now, though, and breathing nice and evenly as if he might be asleep already. Poor darling, if he has to give up making love he'll feel it's a slight on his manhood. Then, fervently, mouthing the words silently, 'Please, don't let him be ill. Please, I *beg* you, make him feel well, give him his strength back – not for my sake, not for Crocker's End – no, that's not honest, it is partly for *my* sake, because I can't bear to think he is suffering. *Please.* Hurt me if you like, but not Ernie. *Please.* And if Jackie did hear the noises he made tonight, there's nothing you can't do, so wipe it from her mind. She's young and inexperienced; she must think of us as ancient.' The thought faded and Verity slept.

At her side, Ernest purposely made his breathing border on snoring, while his mind went on an excursion of its own and his handsome face relaxed into a smile. Verity was a good old stick; without realizing it she was coming round to seeing things his way. It was much wiser not to mention selling the place, just to let her get used to the idea that it was a liability and that the worry of it was more than he could stand. Softly, softly, that was the approach. By now he had expected the sale to be going through and they would have found a small place, or even a flat. Once this was sold and the money in a joint account . . . His face took on a look of contentment.

But the softly, softly approach was taking time. The pruned bushes grew tall again, sprouted leaves, then the fruit started to form. But as Algy Cross had predicted, the crop would be no better than last year, in fact it showed signs of being worse. As the weather grew warmer, Verity often had her chair near where the work was going on, and at weekends Richard helped too. But Ernest, the man at the helm as he called himself, did no more than arrange for the casual workers to come in when it was time to pick the ripe fruit, so that Eddy could take the daily delivery of punnets to the fruiterer in town and then the rest, boxed, to the railway station to be taken to the wholesaler.

It was the second Monday in August, an oppressively warm morning. From where her deckchair had been put in the shade, Verity listened to the laughing banter that was so often the background to Jackie and Eddy's working day. Monty lay in his usual position by her feet, occasionally raising his head to rub it against her leg to remind her that he was there and would appreciate his ears being fondled. She probably didn't even realize that she was smiling as she sat there. With her acute hearing she believed she heard the telephone, but certain that it would be for Ernest don't let him be ill. Please, I *beg* you, make him feel well, give him his strength back – not for my sake, not for Crocker's End – no, that's not honest, it is partly for *my* sake, because I can't bear to think he is suffering. *Please.* Hurt me if you like, but not Ernie. *Please.* And if Jackie did hear the noises he made tonight, there's nothing you can't do, so wipe it from her mind. She's young and inexperienced; she must think of us as ancient.' The thought faded and Verity slept.

At her side, Ernest purposely made his breathing border on snoring, while his mind went on an excursion of its own and his handsome face relaxed into a smile. Verity was a good old stick; without realizing it she was coming round to seeing things his way. It was much wiser not to mention selling the place, just to let her get used to the idea that it was a liability and that the worry of it was more than he could stand. Softly, softly, that was the approach. By now he had expected the sale to be going through and they would have found a small place, or even a flat. Once this was sold and the money in a joint account . . . His face took on a look of contentment.

But the softly, softly approach was taking time. The pruned bushes grew tall again, sprouted leaves, then the fruit started to form. But as Algy Cross had predicted, the crop would be no better than last year, in fact it showed signs of being worse. As the weather grew warmer, Verity often had her chair near where the work was going on, and at weekends Richard helped too. But Ernest, the man at the helm as he called himself, did no more than arrange for the casual workers to come in when it was time to pick the ripe fruit, so that Eddy could take the daily delivery of punnets to the fruiterer in town and then the rest, boxed, to the railway station to be taken to the wholesaler.

It was the second Monday in August, an oppressively warm morning. From where her deckchair had been put in the shade, Verity listened to the laughing banter that was so often the background to Jackie and Eddy's working day. Monty lay in his usual position by her feet, occasionally raising his head to rub it against her leg to remind her that he was there and would appreciate his ears being fondled. She probably didn't even realize that she was smiling as she sat there. With her acute hearing she believed she heard the telephone, but certain that it would be for Ernest

on Friday. Get you all prettied up ready for when Richard gets home.'

They giggled like a couple of conspirators, then, leaving her in her chair next to the up-to-the-minute press-button wireless – Richard's present to her for her last birthday – Jackie put on Wellington boots, an old coat Verity hadn't used since her own gardening days and old leather gloves from the same stable, and went off to find Eddy O'Neil, who had already started work cutting back the old bushes.

No more was said about taking on a replacement for Algy Cross. Instead, Ernest gave Eddy an extra seven and sixpence a week and the responsibility of organizing the work, which he had to do himself with Jackie's help. Whether or not Verity told Richard of Jackie's offer to work without a wage, she didn't know. No one mentioned it to her and her twenty-two and sixpence was in its envelope on the kitchen table each Friday morning.

Ernest apparently considered that having passed responsibility to Eddy, he was free to continue with his life of good works, the only difference being the occasional days when he might take Monty for a walk and do more than his share of sighing and oh dearing when he got home.

It was as he got up from the breakfast table, picked up the not-yet-unfolded *Daily Telegraph* and made for his study that he gave a deep and sorry-for-himself sigh that made Jackie glance at him.

'You've a lot to do out there, Jackie. God knows, I wish I could help.' He was grasping the back of his chair, his chest heaving as he breathed. 'But it's no use, I seem to have no strength at all this morning and the cold air would about finish me off. When you get Verity dressed, tell her I'm having a quiet morning. I've warmed the room with the gas fire, I dare say I'll have a doze, that's about all I seem fit for. I feel quite – what is it Cross would say? – quite knackered.'

He seemed to be steadying himself, standing a little straighter. Despite her frequent suspicions about him, Jackie felt responsible.

'Why don't you sit here a minute and I'll get you a sip of brandy.'

'Bless you, my dear. But no. I know just what it is: while you were cooking my breakfast I went outside and scraped the ice off the windscreen. I shouldn't have done it. It's the cold – and the exertion. I'll just sit quietly. Verity will be frightened if she thinks I'm ill again. When you tell her I shall be having a doze, make her see that it's nothing to get alarmed about. Tell her it was my own fault, I shouldn't have exerted myself in the cold air. Oh dear . . . talking too much . . . just have to sit a moment.'

'If you're all right by yourself, I'll go and run Mrs Bennett's water.' But as she pulled the door closed behind her Jackie looked back with a worried frown.

A few minutes later, leaving Verity in the bath, she ran back down to fetch a clean blouse from the airing cupboard, and that's how it was that she heard the ting of the telephone as he lifted the receiver in his study. Did that sound like a man who, only minutes before, hadn't been able to muster the strength to cross the hall from the kitchen? What made her do it she didn't ask, she simply followed her instinct and walked round the outside of the house until she could glance through the study window. Ernest was sitting at his desk with his back to the window, the telephone to his ear, his frailties forgotten. She heard him laugh as he talked; this was no duty call to do with parish work. She knew immediately who was on the other end of the line. It was surprising how rapid his recovery could be, given the right incentive.

'A different world now the sun's up . . .' His voice surprised Verity as she listened to the mid-morning story on the wireless. Immediately she switched the set off and turned in his direction with a smile.

'Jackie was worried about you. But she said you wanted to be left to have a quiet sleep. Are you feeling better, darling?'

'Yes, I must have slept for more than an hour. But it did the trick. It was my own fault, didn't Jackie tell you? I took liberties and went out to scrape the ice off the windscreen. It really knocked me for six. Never learn, do I, eh? But I'm fine now and it's degrees warmer now the sun has come through. I'd prom-ised to run someone to the garage to collect a car that's been in dock. Didn't think I'd be able to do it, but thank God I feel better. I wish you could see me, I look as if I'm dressed for a polar expedition.'

'Can't you let Jackie go? I shall be worried until you get home again.'

'No, the poor soul would think I couldn't be bothered, sending the home-help instead. I'll be fine. It takes my mind off myself to be doing things.'

She heard his car climb the slope to the lane, then turn left towards the village.

So the weeks went by. They were used to hard winters there in middle England, and until that year Ernest had accepted them as easily as the next man. But he rang Verity's alarm bells when she woke during a night just before Easter. Something was wrong with him!

'Ernie? What is it, darling? You ought to let Dr Hamilton have another look at you,' Verity whispered, aware of his heavy breathing as he sat in bed by her side. 'Is it that nasty pain again? Perhaps it's an ulcer. He could give you something better than you can buy at the chemist for indigestion.'

'Not bloody indigestion. It's nearly three in the morning, nine hours since we had a meal. I came to bed randy as a man half my age – would I have felt like that with indigestion? I ought to have more sense.' Then, with a mirthless laugh, 'Can't you just imagine the report in the local rag: Councillor's Wife Finds Him Dead at her Side After Sexual Orgy.'

'Don't, Ernie! Let me call Jackie to bring you a brandy.'

'No, no, its getting easier. Just let me rest quietly.'

'If it's making love that's too much for you, it's high time we stopped doing it. Poor darling.'

'And what sort of a husband does that make me?'

'The only husband I want. As long as we have a cuddle, that's all I need.' Perhaps it was wicked of her, she thought, but she would much rather they just cuddled up and perhaps talked quietly for a while before going to sleep. In fact thinking back to what he called a 'sexual orgy' – it made it sound so nasty – she had felt on edge, thinking Jackie must hear him and be worried that something was wrong. Tonight he'd grunted louder and louder with each thrust. He was quiet now, though, and breathing nice and evenly as if he might be asleep already. Poor darling, if he has to give up making love he'll feel it's a slight o his manhood. Then, fervently, mouthing the words silently, 'Pleas it didn't really interest her. At least, it didn't interest her until a minute or two later when he came in search of her.

'Did you hear the phone? It was Aunt May. When did we last have contact with her except for Christmas cards?'

'Yes, I remember her. But Ernie, she must be in her nineties. You say she phoned herself?'

'She's ninety-three, she just told me. And she's moving to what she calls a rest home for retired gentlewomen.' He chortled as he repeated what she'd told him. 'She manages very well looking after her home, she says, but she finds the shopping more of a problem. She's sure things are heavier now than they used to be.'

'We haven't seen her since Richard was at prep school. Nice lady.'

'Yes, quite a character. Don't make her sort any more. An independent old girl, she must have hated asking – no, not asking, she did no more than hint that she was struggling to organize things on her own. She intends to sell the house and everything in it, except for anything I would like.'

'Is there no one to help her?'

'No, it seems not. I suppose if I stopped to think about it I would know I'm the only Bennett. Anyway, I did the only thing I could: I told her I would come up to help her and see her settled into this residential home.'

'You can't drive all that way on your own. Please, Ernie darling, please—'

'My dear, I know my limitations. I shall get the train to Hull and go on by taxi. Jackie will be here with you.'

'Don't worry about me. It's you I worry about.' Verity bit her lip. 'I'm so useless,' she surprised him by saying, 'it's a wife's place to be there. You ought to ask Dr Hamilton if he thinks you're fit to go off like that on your own. I wonder if Richard could change the dates of his leave. He's coming home at the end of next week.'

'Don't even think of it. I like to muddle along in my own sweet way, I couldn't cope with Einstein breathing down my neck.' Ernest stood straighter, breathing deeply of the pure country air. Tomorrow he'd be on the train. Aunt May was going into the home at the end of the week; he would give her his full attention until then, make himself responsible for seeing the estate agents, and once she'd moved out, arrange for the furniture to be taken to the sale rooms. But far more important than that, by the end of the week heaven would have dropped into his lap.

'I'll drive into town to the station, find out where I change and get my ticket. Aunt May insists I travel first class at her expense and I didn't argue. The old dear has never been short of a bob. It'll be a long, tiring journey so I'll appreciate the extra comfort.'

Once again she heard his car climb the hill to the lane then turn left. Just through the village he would take the right hand turn; she liked to imagine how far he'd got. What she didn't know was that as she imagined his car drawing up in Station Square, it still hadn't got beyond Hilda Schofield's cottage where his news had aroused excitement equal to his own.

Next morning Jackie drove him to the station and, under instructions from Verity, waited to see him into an empty first-class compartment, then lifted his leather suitcase on to the rack for him.

'I can't say when I'll be back,' he told her. 'At Aunt May's age who can say how well she'll settle. I can't just abandon her. But I know you and O'Neil will do your best to keep the wheels turning. Goodbye, my dear, take good care of Verity.'

Jackie waited to wave as the train puffed its way out of the station, but Ernest's mind had already moved on. Leaning back in his comfortable seat, the compartment to himself, he let his imagination carry him beyond the end of the week.

Here he was, approaching sixty but never had he felt like this. He and Verity had rubbed along very well – she was a good sort and it was rotten to think how her life had changed – but never had he known such intensity of feeling as he had for Hilda. Poor old Verity, a truly good woman – although she had a bloody stubborn streak in her when it came to Crocker's End – but for all that she was a *good* woman. It was a strange thing how the years took everyone differently. In the beginning she'd been so pretty, so girlish, he hadn't given it a thought that she was more than six years older than he. But lately – oh well, he ought not to criticize her, it wasn't to be wondered at if losing her sight had aged her. He didn't need to be told that she never got any natural pleasure out of sex. Was she a prude or simply one of those women who see it as part of her wifely duty? But how different Hilda was. Each time was a glorious adventure; just thinking about it as the train puffed on its rhythmical way made him 'stand up and take notice'.

Good old Aunt May, he thought, his mouth softening into a smile as he relived the previous day's unexpected telephone conversation. From out of the blue had come his salvation. Folding his arms he leant back contentedly. He was fond of Verity, he mused, she was part of the familiar structure of his life and he had no wish to hurt her. Even before she lost her sight she had never interfered with the financial side of things, but the wretched place was keeping them poor and for her sake as well as his it was time it went. And after what May had told him yesterday, he could almost smell the sweet scent of independence. And thank God when he could make a 'recovery' and live a normal life; he had had more than enough of playing on Verity's love and sympathy in an effort to tip the scales his way. Heigh-ho, but life was pretty good. In fact, just at the moment, life was full of promise.

The hot weather held all through that week, and from morn till night Jackie and Eddy picked fruit. It wasn't an easy job, for the bushes were even older this year than last. Two women came from the village to help, and at half past twelve and again at five o'clock each day Jackie went to the wooden building next to the barn where they brought their baskets of fruit to be weighed. Her next job was to divide the crop into punnets to be boxed ready for Eddy to take in the van to the railway station on his way home at the end of the day.

On the Friday of that week the heatwave had built to breaking point, there was a difference in the atmosphere and a storm threatened. So the pickers stayed later, everyone working against time. Eddy took the van to get petrol, so that even if the garage was closed by the time they called it a day, he could still get today's crop to the station in time for the evening train. That was at six o'clock. Verity left her deckchair and went indoors, followed closely by the faithful Monty.

'We're packing it in now, Jackie,' one of the pickers said half an hour or so later, as she passed her last basket for weighing, 'our ol' men'll be giving us the sack if we don't get some food on the table.' So the working day came to an end, they cycled off up the slope to the lane, Jackie made up the last of the boxes for the wholesaler and covered them ready for Eddy to take to the station before he went back to his lodgings. It occurred to her that he was a long time getting back from the garage, but perhaps he'd stopped to get something to eat if he meant to work into the long summer evening. The first heavy raindrops were falling and the wind had blown up from nothing; a long rumble of thunder announced the arrival of the storm.

'I stopped off to slake my thirst.' Eddy's voice surprised her. 'Everyone gone home? Just you and me, eh?'

'Let's try and get these loaded into the van before the rain gets too bad. The tray of punnets is for Mitchell's, so you can drop it off as you come through the village on your way in the morning.'

'Ah . . .' But had he even listened to what she said? Why was he standing so close? 'All right in here, out of the wet.'

'You take that tray, I'll take this, and we'll get them in the van before the storm really breaks.' And with that Jackie moved towards the open doorway, the tray of punnets in front of her keeping him at his distance. There was something about the way he was looking at her that made her uneasy. She got her fruit into the van just as the heavens opened, and by the time she was back her sodden thin cotton frock clung to her.

'Can't go out to the van in that, we'll have to hive up in here for a bit,' he said. She was relieved that he sounded normal, so perhaps she'd imagined there had been something odd in his manner just now.

'Gosh, I'm soaked in just that minute,' she said with a laugh, unprepared for his sudden unexpected movement as he pushed her into the corner and, holding her by the shoulders, pressed her against the side of the wooden building, his eyes devouring her.

'Ah, I can see you are.' He ran his tongue around his lips. 'Might as well be in the starkers the way that wet dress clings.' He moved nearer, pressing his body against hers.

'Stop it, Eddy. Don't fool about.' But she knew he wasn't fooling. They had worked together for months, but suddenly he was a stranger. His face near hers, his tongue that had been moving on his own mouth reached to explore hers. That's when she managed to free her arm and started to hit him.

Rather than pull him back from where he was heading, as she beat him his excitement mounted, she could tell it from his breathing. When he moved one arm and started fumbling with his trouser buttons, she tried to escape, She wriggled, she beat his chest, with clenched fists she hit his shoulders, but she was no match for him. That any man's passion could be heightened by being beaten was something she didn't know and wouldn't have understood. Working out of doors through a week when the temperature had soared, she wore nothing except her cotton dress and knickers. Her firm young breasts needed no bra, but now with her frock wet and clinging to her body, Eddy was beside himself. He forced her to the ground, passion adding to his strength as he sat astride her and tore the material from the undone buttons at the neck of her dress almost to the hem. His mouth open, he was like a madman as he pulled at her knickers, forcing them down, his weight crushing her. All she could do was thump his shoulders as she felt his greedy hands on her naked breasts, his hot, beer-laden breath adding to the horror of what was happening.

'Open your legs,' he hissed.

'Get off! *Get off me!*'

'Damn you, open your legs, can't you? Quick, quick, damn you, open your knees.' He tried to force them apart. If Jackie could punch, so could he, and he brought his fist down on the side of her head. For a second she lost control and in that second he forced her knees wide apart.

'Quick!' If he had become a stranger to her, for him she might have been anyone, any woman. 'It's going to come. Quick!' Fumbling, he tried to guide himself into her as she rolled and squirmed, crying and still hitting him. He knew only one thing: he had to force himself into her before it was all over. She knew only one thing too, and with her knees forced apart she pushed her hands to her groin, baring his way. Neither of them were aware of anything beyond the moment.

Then, bringing his fist down on her again, he gave the first convulsive shudder. A healthy young man, his passions flaming, but his goal was lost as she felt the sudden wet warmth on her hands, on her stomach, even on her breast and, as he jerked convulsively, on her neck. That's when the scene was suddenly changed, his weight gone and her eyes shot open.

Five

The roads were awash. Only those who had no choice were driving, and what few cars there were on the road were moving slowly with their headlights doing little to improve visibility as the rain lashed down. Richard's journey had taken nearly half as long again as normal, but at last he turned into the drive of Crocker's End. For once Verity didn't hear his engine, which wasn't surprising as the guttering couldn't cope and sent a waterfall splashing on to the yard.

He was startled to see the van parked by the weighing-in shed, for by this time of evening he would have expected Eddy O'Neil to have gone. Probably Jacqueline was still there too, sheltering. He'd drive on round there rather than park at the end of the drive as he usually did, then he could give her a lift to the house. Even in that short distance she would get soaked.

He drew up just behind the van then ran to the open door of the shed. Not a man of violent emotion, or more accurately not a man to show emotion, but one look at the scene inside and he was filled with rage such as he'd never known. Neither Jacqueline nor Eddy were aware of him; indeed Eddy was beyond being aware of anything in those seconds. And it was that that made it possible for Richard to cross the stone floor and lift the convulsing form of the younger man off his prey. With a superhuman effort and not questioning his own unfamiliar strength, he carried Eddy outside and dropped him to his knees with no thought for the weather.

Eddy's passion spent and with it the wild emotion that had driven him, he was a weak and sorry sight, hunched on the ground, gasping for breath.

'Young swine,' Richard heard himself say, 'filthy young swine. Get up on your feet and clear off out of here. And don't show your face again.'

With reason returning, Eddy thought of his landlady waiting with her hand out on this Friday evening. 'Not been paid,' he

whined. Then, with the start of recovery, cunning making him
bold, 'Takes two. She begged for it.'

'You heard me. Get out. Your wages and stamped insurance
card will be brought to your lodgings in the morning – I'll do
it myself. Now clear off. And leave the van where it is.'

Without waiting, Richard turned back into the shed, shut the
door and switched on the light. Jackie was still lying on the hard
ground, holding her torn dress together and keeping her legs
tightly closed as if she feared the nightmare might return. If Eddy's
strength was returning, hers seemed to have left her; her whole
body shook.

Richard knelt at her side. 'He won't come back. We must get
you home.' He was taking off his jacket as he spoke. Then he
stood up, laid it on the bench behind her and, stooping down,
raised her to her feet, while still she held together the rip down
the front of her frock.

'. . . never feel clean again,' she croaked. '. . . in an awful mess.'
She looked at her hands, then with a shudder wiped them hard
against the material.

'Yes you will, Jacqueline. Now take your dress off and put my
jacket on.'

'Can't. He's made me – made me . . .' she hesitated, not knowing
how to explain. 'It's your good London suit, it'll be messed up.'

It was as much as he could do not to take her in his arms,
but all he said was, 'It's as well I have a fortnight's leave. My suit
can go to the cleaners. You'll find a clean handkerchief in the
breast pocket; clean up as best you can with that. Then we'll
throw your dress away.' And with that he turned his back and
wandered to the small window to gaze out at the desolate scene.
The thunder was further away now, but the rain showed no sign
of easing.

'I've got your jacket on. What shall I do with your hanky?'
Her voice surprised him; he hadn't heard her come towards him.

Turning, he looked down at her, her hands lost in the too-
long sleeves, the jacket buttoned up and just long enough to
cover the fact she was wearing nothing else. It was a moment
that caught them unprepared. He held his hands towards her and
in that same instant, as a shuddering sigh escaped her, she leant
against him as if for support.

'I could kill him,' he breathed, 'doing this to you. Darling Jacqueline,' he moved his cheek against the side of her head, 'you are the most precious thing on this earth to me. Nothing can ever change the way I feel.' Then, fearing that after what she'd just been through he was handling things badly, yet unable to stop himself, he rushed on, 'You say you don't love me—'

'I'm fond of you. When you're here I know everything will be all right. Perhaps romance is just dreams, really.'

'No, romance is life. Marry me, my dearest, precious Jacqueline. Let me teach you what real love is, love that is the most necessary ingredient in life.'

'I don't know. Richard, I don't know if it would be right for you, or for me either. I can't seem to think straight.'

'Of course you can't, not after what's happened. I was a fool even to ask it of you.' He tilted her face up and she didn't look away from him. 'Just at this moment I expect marriage is the last thing you want to think about. Come on, hop in the car and when we get indoors I'll tell mother you've gone straight up to have a long bathe because you got soaked through.'

Settling beside him for the short drive to the house she was aware that her emotions had done a complete turnaround; not only was the horror of what had happened starting to recede in her mind, but she also felt safe – 'cherished' would have been how Richard would have described it. Yet when she turned her head to glance at him she knew a momentary disappointment: his expression told her nothing; he looked as cold and unemotional as the first day she'd met him.

'I was just talking to Mother about O'Neil.' Richard's remark took her by surprise as, bathed, with her hair washed and wearing a clean cotton frock, she joined the others in the kitchen where Richard was scraping potatoes.

'You were?'

'A bolt from the blue, his walking out like that. But Mother says he has talked to her of his uncle's market garden in Surrey, so I imagine this might have been in his mind for some time.'

'Did he say that was where he was going?' Jackie joined in the charade.

'He said nothing about his future. And I certainly didn't enquire.

In my book one doesn't put personal convenience before responsibility. At least you have *me* to give a hand for the next two weeks, but we must see his post is filled by the time I leave. I've looked in the larder and I imagine it's cold pork and salad for supper. Can you go and cut some mint for the potatoes, Jacqueline? The rain seems to have stopped.'

He sounded so normal that it was easy to reply in the same vein as she took the kitchen scissors and went towards the herb patch on the far side of the yard. But once outside, seeing the rows of bushes on the sloping land, the weighing-in shed and the van, memories rushed back. Standing still she closed her eyes, listening to the steady dripping of water from the roof, and seeming to hear Eddy's demented 'Quick, quick, open your legs, damn you, quick!' She remembered her sick fear as she fought with every ounce of her might, and all to no avail; she lived again the hopelessness of finding that the more she thumped him, the more excited he became; she remembered the sharp pain of his clenched fist on her head, the horror of feeling him finally forcing her knees wide apart and his barely human shout as he believed his goal would be reached. Every sickening second was clear in her mind. All of it was revolting, carnal, unloving.

She made herself walk on to the mint patch and cut two large sprigs. She wouldn't give memories a chance; she would hurry back to the warm and loving atmosphere of the kitchen. Yet still she stood there, with no more chance of escaping the horror that replayed in her mind than there is of fighting to be free from the hold of a nightmare. As clearly as the moment it had happened she recalled how, as he pressed against her and tried to guide himself, she had forced her hands between his body and her own to bar his way. She shuddered. Her hand had been on his bare, angry flesh in her attempt to shield herself when, with the first convulsive shudder, his control had been lost. Now she looked at those same hands as if they had a life of their own. Her steaming bath might have cleansed them and her soiled body, but there was no forgetting. Did a murderer feel like this? Once he had had blood on his hands, even with a lifetime of bathing, could he ever be free of the stain?

How was it neither of them had heard Richard come into the shed? And where had he found the strength to carry Eddy out as if he had been a rag doll? Dear Richard. Why couldn't she fall in love with him? He was so safe, so unchanging. Life was romance, he'd said. But that was nonsense. With no warning, that other memory filled her mind and chased everything else away: a young blond god, the laughter they'd shared, the love they'd shared . . . Oh yes, that was romance, that was *love*, love that had consumed her. But it was years ago, she ought to learn to forget. Had Fate sent her to Crocker's End purposely? Was Richard her destiny? Why couldn't she suddenly see him afresh, not as buttoned-up and aloof, kind and steady, but as someone who would sweep her off her feet? He really did love her, of that she was certain, for he wasn't a man to give way to sudden unthought-out emotion. He was good looking, distinguished, always immaculate enough to stand out, whether in a small provincial town like Brackleford, here in the country, or even in London. He was well up the ladder of a first-rate career as senior statistician in a department of government, and yet for her sake he was even prepared to spend his annual holiday helping with the fruit picking. Then there was Crocker's End . . . if she agreed to marry Richard there would be no thought that one of these days she would be leaving to find a job somewhere else. Reason told her that as his wife she would find contentment. But she wanted more than content-ment, she wanted excitement, she wanted to feel love that filled her soul and aroused passion and desire.

Since she had come of age she had received the legacy from her uncle so her outlook was very different from when she had left the paper shop. Now if she were to decide to move on she would need to find work, but there would be no pressure on her as there had been when she answered the advertisement that brought her here.

Standing with her back to the house, the sprigs of mint clutched in her hand, her gaze moved up the sloping field of fruit bushes and beyond to where Michael Southwell's herd of Herefords grazed aimlessly. After the rain the air was filled with the smell of country. For ten months this had been her home, for ten short months she had lived here as an employee, yet she loved the place as if it were woven inextricably into her spirit.

The distant lowing of one of Michael's herd woke her from

her daydream and she hurried back to the house, embarrassed that she had taken so long to cut two pieces of mint.

Richard looked up from setting slices of cold pork on a serving dish in a straight, neat row, each slice overlapping the previous one to exactly the same degree. She wished he'd thrown each one to land in higgledy-piggledy disorder, but that wasn't his way and nothing would ever change him.

'All right?' he mouthed silently, to be answered by a nod.

'Does it look as if the rain has cleared away, dear?' Verity asked.

'Yes. It's lovely out there, the world smells fresh and clean. Sorry I was so long, I was just daydreaming. I'll rinse the mint and pop it in the saucepan.' She knew Richard was watching her; his glance made her feel that he could read where her daydreaming thoughts had carried her.

'In the morning I shall take an advert to the local paper,' Richard said as the three of them sat round the table eating supper.

'Is there any great panic?' Verity wondered. 'If you tell the Romany workers that we need more help with the picking, I'm sure they'll know of someone. Then when Ernest gets home he can be the one to engage someone permanently. He might be hurt if he thought we wouldn't wait those few days until he is home again. I do feel badly about him being up there on his own, and there must be so much to organize. His Aunt May was going into the retirement home today. What a sad night for her, leaving all her things to be disposed of and her home put on the market.'

'Indeed it must be,' Richard answered. 'But, as I recall, she was a very sensible, practical sort of person, and she must acknowledge she will be better looked after where she is going than struggling alone.'

'I believe she isn't completely alone, except for nights. She's had the same daily help for years,' Verity told him.

The shrill bell of the telephone interrupted their conversation and Richard got up to answer it, returning a minute later to fetch his mother.

'Verity?' Ernest's voice came down the line. 'The plans have been thrown out of the window up here. The old girl fell when she was walking in the garden this morning. Got her hat and coat on all ready to shift off to the home, then she said she wanted one last look. There are a couple of steps down to the brick path and she must have known them well enough to walk there blindfolded. But she apparently caught her foot. She went down a hell of a crash. I saw it happen. Mrs Cummins, the daily help, came out to give me a hand but we couldn't get her up, she's quite a weight – I thought the last thing we wanted was for me to keel over – so I called the doctor. When he finally came he said it was a hospital job. I've been stuck there most of the day. She's broken her hip, poor old thing. But worse than that, she cracked her head on the brick path. What a day I've had. God, how I hate hospitals! I've only been back at the house half an hour, just long enough to have a bath and get the stench of hospital off me. Now I must go out and find somewhere to get a meal.'

'How long do you think they'll keep her? Poor old dear. I expect she wasn't quite herself, going to say her goodbye to her plants.'

'God knows. I've no meetings through this month, so I shall go on organizing the sale of the house whether she's in hospital or not. Once they release her, the people in the home can collect her. She won't be coming back here. I thought I'd just tell you what's happened. Problem enough having to come up here at a moment's notice, without this added inconvenience.'

'I'm glad you're there for her, darling. Imagine what it would be like if she had just no one.'

'That's true. She was certainly glad to have me to discuss her affairs with before all this happened. No messages of any importance for me?'

'No. Oh, O'Neil has gone. Found greener pastures somewhere else, I imagine. I suggested we wait until you come home before we engage a replacement. Richard is here for a fortnight.'

Ernest's guffaw was his only answer.

At a time when a woman of May Bennett's age with a broken hip would have faced spending her remaining years in bed, Fate dealt with her more kindly than it might. When she'd lost her footing and been thrown down those two steps, the full brunt of her fall had been taken by her head as she'd hit the brick path.

That same night, just as Ernest was climbing the stairs to bed, the call came from the hospital: Miss Bennett's condition had worsened, her pulse was weak and it was unlikely she would last the night. She hadn't regained consciousness, but if he wanted to be with her at the end they suggested he should return to the hospital. To return there was the last thing Ernest wanted, but he owed it to his aunt that when she departed this life someone should be with her, and with no family except himself there was no question who that someone had to be. So with a sigh, he telephoned the taxi company. It was more than a quarter of an hour before his transport arrived, another quarter of an hour's journey into town to the hospital, then a long walk through the corridors with gloss-painted walls and the occasional highly polished bench until he reached the department he'd left only a few hours before.

May had died only minutes before he arrived and was still in the same bed as he'd left her earlier, the curtains pulled around her. They said he could see her for a minute or so before the stretcher bearers moved her.

Poor old girl, he thought, looking down at the elderly relative he'd only started to know during the last few days. Well, I suppose you've had a longer life than most and I shouldn't think you've ever been hard-up for a bob. I say, though, this is going to put a different complexion on things. I expect when you arranged your will you imagined I'd be glad to put the money into Crocker's End. You as good as said so when we talked about it. Well, if that's what you wanted, then I'm sorry, Aunt May, old dear. All these years Verity has looked on me as the keeper of the purse strings, I've never been able to escape the feeling that when it comes down to it I'm nothing of the sort. Well, she proved it, didn't she, when I told her what a liability the place was, not even paying for itself let alone giving us an income. And if that's what she wants, so be it. When I sell the house and everything goes through probate, my days of never having money that is really my own will be over. And tomorrow, when Hilda and the boys come for their holiday, they won't have to find rooms in a hotel. No, they can stay in the house – *my* house.

Glancing round at the closed curtains to make sure he was alone, alone with the old lady who looked remarkably peaceful, he bent over and kissed her forehead. I wish I'd got here in time, but I suppose you wouldn't have known the difference. Anyway, goodbye old dear, and bless you – I really mean that – bless you for what you've done for me. Verity is never mean, you know, but to have a bank account in my own name after all these years, you don't know how much that means to me. I don't know how I ought to say goodbye to someone who's already dead, but, well, I hope you've woken up in a better place than the rest of us struggle around in. That's it then, I'd better get back home or the night will be gone before I get to bed.

Next morning he telephoned Crocker's End and was told by Jane Carter that the others were all 'out there with the picking. Do you want Mrs Bennett to ring you back when they bring her in? Another beautiful morning it is after yesterday's storm, and I can see her out there near where Jackie's picking, with that great dog Monty on her feet. I'll get her to ring you, shall I?'

'No. I shall be out most of the day, I have a lot to see to. Tell her my aunt died during the night. I have to register her death, go to the solicitor, and go to the estate agent, a hundred and one things. Just give her the message and say I'll phone either this evening or tomorrow.'

Replacing the receiver, he looked round the room, not even conscious that he was smiling. He held his arms up and stretched as hard as he could – neck, back, arms, even his legs so that there was no sag at his knees – then finally, as he reached towards the ceiling, he spread his fingers. God, but it was good to be alive.

Richard drove to Eddy O'Neil's lodgings taking an envelope containing his wages, his stamped insurance card and a brief note:

O'Neil,
Enclosed find wages for week ninth to fifteenth August and one week in lieu of notice.
    R. Bennett

Jackie and the two Romany women, Rita and Flo, were busy, but three people couldn't hope to cover an acreage such as Crocker's End.

'Is anyone working on the hill yet?' Verity asked when she heard Jackie moving near her.

'Yes, both the women are there, but we need more help, Mrs Bennett. They're working their way down the hill, but while they're moving on down there's fruit higher up still getting ripe.'

'It's no use waiting for Ernest to get back to arrange things. He'll have so much to attend to now that Aunt May's gone. He may be away for ages. Have a word with the two who are working, Jackie, and ask them if they know anyone else who could help. The trouble is, this is a busy time all round; with the hot weather the corn is ripening off, I expect, and the farmers will be after extra help.' It was as if, in her mind's eye, she could see it all. 'See what you can do, dear. School holiday time – perhaps there are some youngsters who'd like to earn the money. Oh, but I remember how I always loved gathering in the fruit, such fun we always had with a whole gang of people. That's the way to do it, such happy times they were.'

'And still are, Mrs Bennett. No one could fail to be happy doing this job. Mr Cross said it was a poor yield last year and he had no hope that this would be any better, but I've never picked fruit before so I don't know how big a crop we should get. I'll talk to Rita and Flo, they'll probably know people who'll be glad of the chance to earn. I suppose now that Mr Bennett's aunt has died he'll wait for the funeral and then come straight home. If he gives them details at the Labour Exchange of the sort of person he's looking for, by this time next week someone might apply.'

'It sounds cruel to say, but it will be easier for him now his aunt has gone. He would have been loathe to come home until he was sure she was settled in the home. What a blessing he was there when she fell; at least she wouldn't have felt frightened and alone. Dear Ernie, he likes to hide his soft side, but there's not a kinder man living.'

'And here's another kind man. Mr Southwell's car is coming down the slope. He's parking in front of the house, but he's seen where you are,' Jackie said as she waved her hand in greeting to Michael. 'I'm going to pop indoors to put something in the oven and then I must get on or there won't be enough picked to be worth Richard driving into town at midday ready for the afternoon shoppers.' She knew the routine exactly: from Monday until Friday the trays of punnets would be trained to London at the end of the day ready to be sold in the early morning market at Covent Garden; but on Saturdays, either during the morning or at any rate by lunch time, the fresh fruit would be delivered to the local shops in town. As she turned to go indoors another thought struck her. 'Not much of a holiday for Richard now that Eddy's gone,' she said.

Verity chuckled. 'He'll enjoy it more than he would dabbling his toes on a beach somewhere. And it's a rare treat to have him home for so long.'

'Where does he usually go for his holidays?'

'He usually goes walking, sometimes on the Continent, sometimes in the Lake District. Always on his own.'

'If I worked all the year in a noisy, crowded city I think that's the sort of thing I'd want to do. Just imagine the freedom and the silence.' Then, as Michael approached, 'I must go and put the food in the oven. See you later.' By 'see you', what she meant was that she would collect Verity and see her back to the house at the end of the morning.

But it didn't work out that way. Ten minutes later, as she was picking raspberries on Dilly Hill, Jackie was surprised to recognize Verity's voice only feet away. Standing up straight she turned in the direction of the sound in time to see the back view of Michael with his arm linked through Verity's to guide her as they did a circuit of the field. She could see from the way he was pointing to things as they walked that he was giving her a detailed picture of the place she loved so well. She recalled how Michael had talked to her when he had taken her out driving, telling her of how dear Verity was to him, and how until Ernest had come on the scene he had hoped she would have agreed to be his wife. 'Long years ago,' he had said. 'There have been many times when I have envied those who can accept when they're beaten and move to pastures new. I tried. Indeed there was no other way except to accept defeat. But you can't alter your nature and I could never change the way I felt.'

Wasn't that almost word for word what Richard had told her about himself? If Verity had accepted the unchanging devotion Michael had offered, would her life have been happier? It was easy to say 'yes', but was it true? In his own fashion Ernest loved her, and surely there had been more joy in being swept off her feet by a glorious passion than settling for faithful devotion.

Squatting on her haunches she checked the next bush, finding a few well-hidden fruits to be added to her basket while her thoughts went their own way. Somewhere, some day, she would know the sort of love that demanded everything she was, the sort of love she had felt for Wilhelm. But that was years ago, she had been little more than a child. Did that sort of thing happen to adults, to people with experience of living?

'I'm back . . .' Richard's voice pulled her from her reverie and not for the first time gave her the uncomfortable feeling that in her face he would be able to read where her mind had been. 'I would have been sooner but I met Cross and his wife. He tells me that he has a nephew he thinks would be interested in working here. Apparently the farm where he was has been sold and he isn't happy with the new set-up. So I told him to wait until Father is home and get in touch. Where do you want me to start?'

'Thank you, Richard,' she answered. 'You'll find a basket in the shed and then perhaps you could make a start, say, halfway down this hill.' Hearing herself giving instructions, she covered her embarrassment with a chuckle as she said, 'Hark at me giving the orders. I'm only the new girl here.'

'It doesn't feel that way to me.'

She sensed he was leading her to dangerous ground, so with a quick smile she attacked the next bush, defying a single fruit to escape her eye.

During the fortnight of his leave they worked together, chattering in a manner as relaxed as any brother and sister. Either one or other of them brought Verity to sit nearby so that she felt included in all that was going on, Richard even taking her with him in the van when he went to put the fruit on the late evening train. Only once during that time did Ernest phone, and that was to say that the funeral was over but he had a lot of loose ends to tie up.

It was only as Richard was leaving to return to London, his mother not attempting to come further than the back door where

she would hear his car move off, that he passed his briefcase to
Jackie saying, 'Perhaps you'd give me a hand carrying that,
Jacqueline, would you please?' Clearly it wasn't necessary; he had
two good hands and only one other case. 'I won't run away with
her, Mother, she'll be back in a minute . . .' Perhaps said just to
make sure he meant his mother to stay where she was. Then, as
they came towards where he'd parked, 'It's been a wonderful fortnight, Jacqueline. A leave I shall remember. We are a good team,
you know.' As he reached the car and laid his things on the back
seat, he turned back to her, taking both her hands in his.

'Jacqueline, precious Jacqueline . . .' His voice trailed into silence.

'It's been good. We're friends, Richard, proper friends, not just
two people who know each other.'

'I know. I honestly have tried to make myself feel that that is
all I want. Until you came here I had just one goal – my work.
Nothing is the same any more. You don't want to hear me say
it again. But – but just tell me you'll think about what I've asked.
Asked? Begged. You are my friend, is that a start?'

'I don't know, Richard. I don't want to hurt you – not now,
not ever. But friendship is not the same as being in love.'

'But being in love without friendship is like a house without
foundations.'

She put her hands on his shoulders and reached to kiss him
lightly on the cheek. 'We have deep foundations,' she spoke lightly,
trying to stop the conversation getting out of hand.

And with that he had to be satisfied.

The conversation came back to her much later when she was
laying in bed, and with it all the uncertainty. Suppose she agreed
to marriage with Richard and turned her back on the shapeless
dream of an all-consuming love that would fill her life – wouldn't
that be the sensible thing to do? Their friendship was as stable
as a rock, a foundation to build on for a good life together. Lying
in the dark she let her imagination carry her where it would:
back to what she repeatedly told herself had been a childish dream
of love with Wilhelm; forward to an extension of that friendship
with Richard.

What would he be doing now, she wondered. It was nearly
three hours since he'd left; he would be back at his lodgings in
London, probably in bed like she was herself. If he were, then

where would his thoughts be? Perhaps imagining her, perhaps wanting her. Supposing she were married to him: he'd be here by her side, the hands that caressed her breasts and awoke such a strange empty ache in her would be his. Forget Richard, forget everything except this . . . Minutes passed as the deep need in her drove her; she knew nothing else as desire reached toward fulfilment, then finally brought her from the heights to the depths. She tried to imagine he was here with her, that she could feel the weight of his naked body on hers, that for him passion had carried him just as it had her. In the darkness she seemed to see him clearly – not the man she had worked with, laughed with and who was her friend, but the other Richard, aloof, unemotional, unnaturally precise. Turning her pillow cool-side upward, she rolled on to her side and closed her eyes as if that way the incident was over and thoughts of him gone.

With Richard gone, the next day it fell to Jackie to take the van to the station.

'It'll only be for a day or two. Once Ernest gets home I'm sure he'll do the station run, it's not the sort of hard work we know he mustn't try and do.' That was Verity's optimistic expectation, but Jackie hadn't the same faith. There would be meetings, someone who needed his wisdom; if not one good excuse then he'd find another.

'Yes, of course he'll do it when he can. But we'll work it out. The only thing is, it means supper will be a bit late.' Jackie was pleased with her confident reply. They had telephoned twice to the number in the book against May Bennett's name, but neither time had there been a reply, and it hadn't escaped her attention that Verity had waited expectantly for letters that hadn't come.

On that Monday evening, the fruit weighed into punnets and stacked into containers, the containers covered, sealed and named, she packed them into the van and headed for town. Although she had never been the one to check them in at the railway station, she enjoyed doing it; it rounded off her day's work. Driving home she hummed cheerfully, feeling at one with where life had brought her. Before she'd gone back into the field after lunch she had made a macaroni cheese, so all she had to do when she arrived home was put it in the oven. From her own point of view it suited her very well that Ernest was delayed; it wasn't the sort of snack she could have served up to *him*. By the following week his round of meetings would have begun, but during August it was no use there being any sudden local emergency, for the August council break was sacrosanct.

With the van locked, she crossed the yard to the back door. 'I'm—' The word 'home' died before it was born. From the drawing room came the sound of voices. Ernest had come back. She crossed the hall and had her hand on the doorknob when she seemed to freeze in her tracks; his words were unnaturally clear, spoken as if to ensure there could be no argument, no misunderstanding.

'I'm not a hard man. But, Verity, I have a right to a life. To say I'm sorry would be a lie. How can I be sorry when I have never in my life known such – such complete joy. Yes, I do feel sorry for what it must do to you. But it's not in my power to change.'

'I didn't know . . .' It was hard to hear Verity. Her voice was small, as if she had lost her grasp.

Jackie gripped the doorknob. Should she go in? If she were to interrupt them perhaps it would stop him saying things that later he would regret. But she was an outsider, she had no right to interfere. If only Richard were still here!

'How long have you known all this?' Surely it wasn't only Jackie who realized the effort Verity was making to stay calm and speak without emotion.

'Almost since I first met her. I've never known a woman like her. When I take her into a dining room I can feel every head turning. Verity, I never wanted to hurt you.' Then, his tone changing and sounding aggressive, 'And I'll tell you something. If you'd not been so damned pig-headed when I wanted to get rid of this place, if you'd let it go and we'd had some money so that I wasn't always made to feel beholden to you for every penny, then I would have tried to make the best of the situation.'

'I don't ask for your charity or your sympathy.' Cold dignity was her shield. Hearing her, Jackie felt a physical ache, as if she were bearing the pain Verity wouldn't allow to show. It was an ache rooted in anger, in pity and in love for the woman who surely had borne more than her share of trouble and never let it scar her spirit. Now, wounded by the deepest cut of all, it seemed that from somewhere she had found a new dignity. 'I am grateful

you don't feel you are tied to me out of sympathy. But, Ernest . . .'
Saying his name almost destroyed her, but after a second she went
on, 'Ernest, if you stayed here for the sake of a home and your
keep, which is what you are as good as telling me, and if your
aunt has left you the money from the sale of her house, which
I'm sure she has, why is that so different from what the outcome
of your scheme to sell Crocker's End would have given you? You
say that with independent means you would have let things go
on as they were.'

'I shan't sell the house. Hilda and the boys have been there
since the day after the old lady fell. It has been a – a . . . Oh
damn it, Verity, what am I doing, trying to make you understand?
I never knew it was possible to feel as I do for Hilda. You're the
last person I should say that to. I suppose all through our years
together we have both believed that a relationship like ours was
all there could be.'

'Indeed.' It might almost have been Richard answering, and as
she continued to speak, her manner didn't change. She gave no
hint of what she was feeling. 'But then how much do either of
us know of what the other believes?'

'That's just it. Not only over these last years when we'd got
into a rut and took the way things were for granted. But even
when we were younger, our lives were no more than a placid
sort of routine. There should be more than that. Did either of us
ever know the meaning of real love?'

Listening, hating herself for eavesdropping and yet doing it out
of care for Verity, Jackie felt Ernest was saying the same words that
had so often come into her own mind when she had contemplated
marriage to Richard. A placid routine, no passion that consumed
them – didn't that exactly describe what their lives would be? Ernest
said there should be more; she *knew* there should be more. And yet
she condemned him with every fibre of her being. How could he
bear to hurt Verity? For surely even he, his thoughts going no further
than himself and that hateful woman with her American accent and
her oh-so-smart clothes and beautifully made-up face, must know
the wound he was inflicting on Verity.

'If you have been given this wonderful second chance, I suggest
you get back to her.' Still Verity managed to maintain the same
cool manner, as if she were untouched by what he was doing.

'I suppose you intend to move in with her until the council appoint a new chairman? Your name will fall from the dizzy heights you've worked for in the village. That seems a great pity.'

'Doesn't that just show how blind you have been . . . Oh, I'm sorry, that was a tactless thing to say to you. But fancy you believing I spent every evening looking after the village affairs. You've lived a sheltered life, my dear.'

'I took it for granted you were telling the truth. I have been blind, indeed, with a blindness of the soul. I dare say when you crept past our room on the way to the small spare, she had entertained you to your liking first?'

'You make it sound sordid. But if you mean she had lain there while I pounded her till I was satisfied, then you're wrong. Verity, if we had had a loving, joyous relationship, do you think I would have needed to look outside marriage? We are as we are. Can't you just accept and see there is no future in the lie we are living?'

'Indeed, I believe no one's life should be based on a lie.'

'I've only come back for one night, just to collect my things and collect the car. She's sorting the boys into a school up north. I shall leave here in the morning.'

Until that point their conversation had moved fast, their answers spontaneous. But this time there was a silence, perhaps no more than two or three seconds, but it felt like eternity. Then Verity spoke and Jackie could imagine her sitting very straight in her chair, her head held high.

'I prefer you collect what you intend to take and leave tonight. No doubt you have your key to your paramour's house in the village, you can always sleep there.'

'But you can't kick me out like a badly behaved lodger. Damn it, Verity, this is my home. I'll sleep in the—'

'I prefer that you leave. And, in case it escapes your memory, this is my house.'

'Of course I have a key to her house, but – Christ, Verity, I would never have believed you could be so petty minded.'

'Indeed . . .'

'For heaven's sake stop *indeed*'ing. You sound like bloody Einstein, he who can do no wrong.'

'Very likely I do. Now –' with a wave of her hand indicating where she knew the door to be – 'I'd like you to leave.'

Jackie moved silently back across the hall to the kitchen, and so it was that she didn't hear his final request, nor yet Verity's reply to it. Ought she to telephone to Richard? No, it wasn't her place to interfere. All she could do was be there for Verity. Perhaps she was wrong in thinking that that cool voice was armour against showing her broken heart; perhaps he was right and their relationship had been no more than placid routine; perhaps her way of calling him 'Ernie darling' had been so much habit that neither of them had even been conscious of it.

Taking the macaroni cheese from the larder, she put it in the oven. Very likely Verity would say she wasn't hungry, but whether she wanted it or not, food would help. Upstairs, doors were slammed; Ernest must be packing. Then footsteps as he came down, crossed the hall, and with a final slam of the front door, left the house. Jackie watched his car disappearing up the slope to the lane. Verity listened to the sound of the engine; she knew when the car turned left towards the village, and gradually the sound faded into silence.

Uncertain what to do next, Jackie waited, hoping that Verity would come to join her in the kitchen as she often did while she was preparing their supper. There was something unnerving about the complete silence. She had to do *something*, there was no one to help except *her*. Perhaps the best thing would be to go into the drawing room as normal, saying she'd checked the fruit in at the station and the supper was in the oven. It was probably a vain hope that Verity might take her cue from that, but anything, *anything* would be better than this silence.

'I'm back!' she announced as she opened the drawing room door.

But at the sight before her she forgot everything but her need to help. Usually in her blindness Verity heard every sound, but she was unaware of Jackie's presence as she sat where Ernest had left her, her hands gripping the arms of the chair and her body rocking backwards and forwards, as if by movement she would escape her agony. Sitting in front of her, Monty had one paw on her lap, but she didn't seem aware of him.

Crossing the room to her, Jackie fell to her knees by the side of the chair. Poor Monty gave two thumps of his tail on the ground, as if to acknowledge that he knew that, like him, she was there to help his beloved mistress.

'Can't you tell me?' She covered Verity's hand with hers and the action had an immediate effect. It reminded her of a time she had seen a child fall over, and when her mother had picked her up she couldn't get her breath; it was only when her mother had given her a sudden shake that she had gasped and started to cry. And so it was with Verity that the touch of Jackie's hand on hers broke her silence and released her pent-up misery. Still her body rocked, but now she made a dreadful unearthly sound, part wail, part scream. Jackie moved to sit on the arm of the chair and drew her into her arms.

'Gone – not coming back – never knew what love was – never been happy . . .' Then the tearless, unearthly sounds she'd been making turned to crying, and as Jackie held her she sobbed. 'Nothing left,' she wept, 'not even memories. All the time I thought we were happy, he had nothing, *nothing*, just routine, boring routine. I thought he was happy, I thought – I thought . . . She's young – he said he's proud to be seen with her – not with me – I was just part of the background – I thought he loved me like I did him – nothing left – Jackie, how long have I got to live like this? I've tried not to mind about my eyes – but I thought he loved me – just want to die. Nothing left . . .'

'There's Crocker's End. There's Richard.' And when the tail knocked on the carpet, 'There's Monty.'

Verity seemed to have wept all her tears, but her breath was still catching in her throat. And when she said those words again, 'I just want to die,' there was no hysteria in her voice, only the truth that looking ahead she believed there was nothing. Jackie looked at the small, shaking figure, and with a rush of love and tenderness knew exactly what she would do.

Six

Holding the shaking figure close to her, Jackie spoke clearly, each word so distinct that it defied being drowned in Verity's misery.

'We weren't going to tell you until Richard is here at the weekend. But I can't listen to you talking about having nothing to live for.' She turned Verity's tear-blotched face towards her. 'Richard and I are going to be married.' There! She'd said it; after weeks of indecision she had committed her future. She felt surprisingly elated, as if a weight had been lifted. 'It may not seem like anything wonderful to you at the moment, I can't expect it to. But Mrs Bennett – no, you won't be that any more, you'll be Mother – except that what I really want is a Mum. We'll be a proper family. Perhaps I'm being selfish to expect you to be excited, but – but we'll all belong with each other.'

Verity turned in her chair, buried her head against Jackie's small breast and clung to her. Still she was crying, but now her tears were quieter, the hysterical frenzy of grief over. Did Jackie imagine it or was there relief in the sound?

'I've prayed for this, Jackie, dear, dear Jackie. You don't know how hard I've prayed. I knew from the day he first spoke about you that for him you were special. But you said he was – I forget what you called him, but what you meant was that he was dull. Now you know him better and God has answered my prayers and you have learnt to love him.' The news had broken through her wall of misery. 'Why didn't he tell me before he went yesterday?'

'I didn't give him my answer until he was leaving – you remember he wanted me to go to the car with him.'

'Richard to be married and his father gone. When he was born I believed I had everything any woman could want. But they are so different; they never met at any level. I used to wish they would play games together, or Ernie would teach him as a child to love working out of doors.'

'If he had, Richard might be a very different man today. And you wouldn't want to change him.'

'You're a wise child,' Verity said, making an effort to regain control. 'You'll be the daughter I always hoped for.'

Jackie dropped a kiss on the top of Verity's head, with its beautifully cut white hair which these days was cared for at the hairdresser's each Friday afternoon.

'On your feet my Mum-to-be, there's a macaroni cheese in the oven and we don't want it cremated.'

At the thought of food Verity's stomach seemed to turn a somersault, but some of her natural determination was returning and she wasn't going to fail Jackie.

The two original fruit pickers had brought another two with them, so once Jackie had given them their baskets and told them where to work she made the excuse to Verity that they needed one or two things from the village shop. If Verity had hoped to go with her for the ride she was disappointed. No sooner did Jackie call to tell her where she was going, than she hurried away to get the car from the barn. She felt mean, for she knew how precious even a short outing must be, but it was vital that she went by herself.

Flour and coffee had been her excuse, even though neither were really needed. Once they were bought she left the car where it was and walked on up the village street to the red telephone box, put a small pile of shillings on the ledge by the instrument and asked the operator for Richard's number.

'Bennett here,' he answered. Ordinarily she would have heard his voice as reassuring, but there was nothing ordinary about this call. And instead of being reassured, without any prompting on her part, her mind took her back to the day she had promised her dying Aunt Alice that she wouldn't leave poor confused Uncle Howard and the door of her cage had closed on her.

'Richard, it's me.' She made a supreme effort. 'I had to come out to phone you.'

'What's happened? Is something wrong? Is my father home?'

And so she told him. 'I shouldn't have heard it, but – well, there was something different in the way he was talking to her so I listened from outside the door. He was telling your mother that he was leaving her. It was horrid. He said he'd never known what real love was until he knew that woman – the clerk to the council woman. She's living with him at his aunt's house. Well, I gather it's his house now. But Richard, your mother doesn't know I was eavesdropping. Richard – can you hear me? Are you listening?'

'How could he do it to her? She's better without him.'

'It was so awful. She didn't cry, she sounded so sort of dignified. It would have broken your heart to hear the way she asked him to leave. But after he'd gone, it was awful. She was – was almost demented, I've never heard anyone cry like it, sort of moaning and screaming. Said she wanted to die.'

'How is she this morning?'

'I haven't got that far yet—'

'Christ! She hasn't—' Only then did she understand where his imagination was taking him.

'No. But last night I couldn't seem to get through to her. Perhaps a shake or a smack might have pulled her out of her awful crying. So I could only think of one thing that would help her accept the future: I told her that we were going to be married. I said we had agreed to tell her when you came home at—'

'Jacqueline, just stop talking for a moment. That's better. Are you telling me that you are accepting me?'

'Yes, Richard. Unless you've changed your mind. It was the only thing I could think of. She said it was what she had been praying for.'

'I dare say.' He spoke in what she called his buttoned-up voice. 'And you? I hardly think it's what you have been praying for.'

She imagined his face, aloof, expressionless. She felt as small and gauche as she had on the day she had met him. She stood to her full five foot four and looked at her reflection in the smeary glass set in the wall behind the telephone. 'You know it wasn't. But I promised you I'd think about it, and once I'd heard myself tell your mother, I know it sounds silly, but I felt as if a weight had been lifted.'

'And now, Jacqueline, by the light of another day?'

'You can't ask me how I feel if you don't say whether you think I did right. That's not fair, Richard.'

'Right for whom? For Mother? For yourself? For me?'

'I suppose for all of us. I thought it was what you wanted.'

Again, her confidence had left her. 'But I don't want you to pretend, Richard.'

'I don't change, Jacqueline. Perhaps like my mother it's what I have prayed for. But I'm sorry your decision was made on the spur of the moment in an effort to help Mother, rather than because you discovered it's what you want.'

'Of course I wanted to help her, and so would you have if you'd been home. She was tearing herself to pieces. I didn't think a human being could cry like it, she was *frenzied*. I would have done *anything* to help her. And, being quite truthful, it was almost as if I stood outside myself hearing myself say it. But Richard – and this is the God's honest truth, too – as soon as I'd told her, I had a sort of feeling of – I don't know, a sort of thankfulness.'

'And that's the feeling I have at this moment. I know you don't love me as I love you, but you are giving me the opportunity to change that. I shouldn't be sitting here in an office, miles away from you. Jacqueline, I will *make* you care.'

'It's going to be all right, Richard. We'll turn Crocker's End into the sort of happy home your mother remembers. You haven't said anything about your father and Mrs Schofield. I think I'd better tell your mother that I rang you up to tell you what he's done. She won't think it funny, she will expect that I'd want to talk to you.'

'Tell her I'll phone her this evening. How is she this morning?'

Jackie thought a moment before she answered. 'She's pretending she's all right and I went along with her charade. But she looks as though she's had no sleep and her eyelids are horribly red and swollen.'

'I could kill him,' Richard said, his quiet voice filled with suppressed passion. 'How can he do it to her?'

'The pips have gone again and that's my last shilling. Richard – I've got such a *safe* sort of feel—' The line went dead leaving the sentence unfinished.

Replacing the receiver, Richard leant forward, his elbows on the desk and his head in his hands. Safe . . . that was what she'd said. Was he wrong to let her marry feeling no more than that? And yet his soul was filled with thankfulness. Help me to make her discover a full and meaningful love, he begged. She's such a child;

and me, how could I expect her to fall in love with the dull, sober creature that I am? Have I the right to take advantage of her affection for my mother? Because that's why she's doing this. Just a child – and yet there's a woman there waiting to be woken. She's hungry for love, I don't need words to tell me that.

Pushing his work to one side he gave himself up to imagining the years ahead, Crocker's End ringing with the laughter of children, his and Jacqueline's children; his mother, his dear mother, finding her way again. In those moments he saw more clearly than ever before how Verity's ever-ready smile had hidden her inner misery. How was he so sure? Jacqueline hadn't hinted at it. Yet had she had her sight, had she still been able to work outside as she used to, her grief would never have been as wild and hysterical as it had when his father dealt the final blow.

Reaching for the phone again, he asked for Michael's number.

'What time is it now?' Verity asked.

'Ten past seven. Supper's nearly ready. Richard will probably phone while we're eating.'

They both made sure they didn't let the note of cheerfulness – albeit forced cheerfulness – slip. Jackie truly did feel relieved that she had made her decision, and yet surely she ought not to force that hint of suppressed excitement; surely it ought to come from an inner happiness. But of course I'm happy – if I weren't I wouldn't be so sure that what I have done is *right*.

'If you'd like to sit up, soon-to-be-Mum, I'll take the bones out of the fish for you. Then it's new potatoes and runner beans.'

'Lovely, dear. Yes, I expect the phone will ring in a minute.'

Words, just words, in Verity's battle to pass the time until she was safe in bed and the mask could slip. In bed . . . his side of it empty . . . but then so it had been so often when she had heard him come home and creep along the passage to the small spare room. He hadn't wanted her then . . . perhaps for years he hadn't really wanted her . . . She mustn't think about it . . . but she couldn't think about anything else . . .

'There you are, no bones in it and I've cut the potatoes. They call themselves new but they are getting big now.' Jackie's voice cut into her thoughts and saved them slipping so far downhill that she couldn't hold them back.

'I thought that when I scrubbed them,' Verity said, playing her part in the charade.

So they ate their supper, but no call came from Richard. While Jackie cleared up, Verity went on into the drawing room, Monty padding along behind her. Knowing every step of the way she went straight to her usual chair. She ought to have stayed in the kitchen with Jackie; in here the echo of Ernest's voice was waiting for her, that and the memory of her battle to hold on to control until he was gone. Gone . . . gone because he'd found real happiness, the sort of happiness he hadn't known possible . . . No, she mustn't think. She sat very straight in her chair, her hands on the arms as if she was about to get up. She ought to have stayed with Jackie . . . when she was alone there was nothing to protect her. As she got to her feet to retrace her steps to the kitchen there was a ring at the doorbell, followed immediately by Michael's 'All right if I come straight in?'

'I'm in here, Michael.' And this time she didn't have to force her voice; his unexpected visit had caught her off guard and her relief was genuine.

Jackie heard him arrive, and even though she had finished the dishes she didn't hurry to join them. The hall clock struck eight and still Richard's call didn't come, but now that Michael was there, he would answer the phone and give Verity time to reach it. So Jackie went outside, taking deep breaths of the fragrant summer air. She loved the stillness and silence of this time of evening. Yes, she had done right, she *must* have done right. Her very soul belonged here at Crocker's End. 'We are each of us a body and a soul,' Richard had said. She wasn't marrying Crocker's End, she was marrying Richard. Soon they would belong to each other. Would she ever find the same wonder with him that she had when she'd fallen in love with Wilhelm? Body and soul. She wasn't in love with Richard, and yet the thought of them making love excited her. But what about her soul? Making love with Wilhelm had fulfilled every romantic dream. As her thoughts drifted she walked to the weighing-in shed to lock it for the night, then stood gazing towards Michael's fields and the outline of the hill silhouetted in the fading light. Way above, the pale waning moon rode high in the darkening cloudless sky.

Lost in thought, letting her imagination carry her forward in

time, in those few minutes the future passed before her: she lay
in Richard's arms, she raised a family, she looked ahead through
the years – in fact so engrossed was she that she didn't hear the
car come down the drive. The first she knew was his voice, quietly
speaking her name as if he didn't want to disturb the peace of
the scene.

'Jacqueline.' His hand reached out to her. This was no moment
for normal friendly chatter – 'I didn't hear the car' or 'What a
surprise': trite, empty remarks. Instead, aware of the silence that
held them, she took his hand in hers. A moment later he was
holding her close against him. Why wasn't her heart racing with
excitement? Instead, she nestled her face against his neck, savouring
the delicate aroma of – of what? Shaving soap? Brilliantine?

'Mr Southwell is here,' she whispered.

'I phoned him. He said he'd come this evening.' He held one
hand under her chin, tipping her head back then bending to
cover her mouth with his. 'I had to come,' he spoke with his lips
almost on hers, 'not just for Mother, but for you, for us. My
blessed, precious Jacqueline—'

She silenced him by pressing her parted lips to his mouth.
Hardly aware of what she did and following instinct, she drew
his hand to her small, firm breast, and when she felt the movement of his thumb caressing her nipple she felt rather than heard
the barely audible moan that escaped her. Her body was crying
out for him to touch her, to love her, but what of her soul? The
question sprang uninvited into her mind. Why, why couldn't she
fall in love with him? She was fond of him, she believed she even
loved him, but where was the wild excitement, the longing to
be with him every second of the day and night? She wouldn't
think about it, not now. Instead she pressed her hips closer, moving
against him, glorying in knowing that he was as hungry for love
as she was herself.

'No, Jacqueline.' Her answer was to move the tip of her tongue
around the inside of his lips. 'No. We must go indoors.' She was
an innocent child, he told himself, she had no idea what she
was doing to him. But fast on that thought came another: in her
innocence her young, healthy body was led by instinct; surely she
must care for him or her instinct would have been different?
'We must go indoors.'

time, in those few minutes the future passed before her: she lay in Richard's arms, she raised a family, she looked ahead through the years – in fact so engrossed was she that she didn't hear the car come down the drive. The first she knew was his voice, quietly speaking her name as if he didn't want to disturb the peace of the scene.

'Jacqueline.' His hand reached out to her. This was no moment for normal friendly chatter – 'I didn't hear the car' or 'What a surprise': trite, empty remarks. Instead, aware of the silence that held them, she took his hand in hers. A moment later he was holding her close against him. Why wasn't her heart racing with excitement? Instead, she nestled her face against his neck, savouring the delicate aroma of – of what? Shaving soap? Brilliantine?

'Mr Southwell is here,' she whispered.

'I phoned him. He said he'd come this evening.' He held one hand under her chin, tipping her head back then bending to cover her mouth with his. 'I had to come,' he spoke with his lips almost on hers, 'not just for Mother, but for you, for us. My blessed, precious Jacqueline—'

She silenced him by pressing her parted lips to his mouth. Hardly aware of what she did and following instinct, she drew his hand to her small, firm breast, and when she felt the movement of his thumb caressing her nipple she felt rather than heard the barely audible moan that escaped her. Her body was crying out for him to touch her, to love her, but what of her soul? The question sprang uninvited into her mind. Why, why couldn't she fall in love with him? She was fond of him, she believed she even loved him, but where was the wild excitement, the longing to be with him every second of the day and night? She wouldn't think about it, not now. Instead she pressed her hips closer, moving against him, glorying in knowing that he was as hungry for love as she was herself.

'No, Jacqueline.' Her answer was to move the tip of her tongue around the inside of his lips. 'No. We must go indoors.' She was an innocent child, he told himself, she had no idea what she was doing to him. But fast on that thought came another: in her innocence her young, healthy body was led by instinct; surely she must care for him or her instinct would have been different? We must go indoors.'

Again, her confidence had left her. 'But I don't want you to pretend, Richard.'

'I don't change, Jacqueline. Perhaps like my mother it's what I have prayed for. But I'm sorry your decision was made on the spur of the moment in an effort to help Mother, rather than because you discovered it's what you want.'

'Of course I wanted to help her, and so would you have if you'd been home. She was tearing herself to pieces. I didn't think a human being could cry like it, she was *frenzied*. I would have done *anything* to help her. And, being quite truthful, it was almost as if I stood outside myself hearing myself say it. But Richard – and this is the God's honest truth, too – as soon as I'd told her, I had a sort of feeling of – I don't know, a sort of thankfulness.'

'And that's the feeling I have at this moment. I know you don't love me as I love you, but you are giving me the opportunity to change that. I shouldn't be sitting here in an office, miles away from you. Jacqueline, I will *make* you care.'

'It's going to be all right, Richard. We'll turn Crocker's End into the sort of happy home your mother remembers. You haven't said anything about your father and Mrs Schofield. I think I'd better tell your mother that I rang you up to tell you what he's done. She won't think it funny, she will expect that I'd want to talk to you.'

'Tell her I'll phone her this evening. How is she this morning?'

Jackie thought a moment before she answered. 'She's pretending she's all right and I went along with her charade. But she looks as though she's had no sleep and her eyelids are horribly red and swollen.'

'I could kill him,' Richard said, his quiet voice filled with suppressed passion. 'How can he do it to her?'

'The pips have gone again and that's my last shilling. Richard – I've got such a *safe* sort of feel—' The line went dead leaving the sentence unfinished.

Replacing the receiver, Richard leant forward, his elbows on the desk and his head in his hands. Safe . . . that was what she'd said. Was he wrong to let her marry feeling no more than that? And yet his soul was filled with thankfulness. Help me to make her discover a full and meaningful love, he begged. She's such a child;

and me, how could I expect her to fall in love with the dull, sober creature that I am? Have I the right to take advantage of her affection for my mother? Because that's why she's doing this. Just a child – and yet there's a woman there waiting to be woken. She's hungry for love, I don't need words to tell me that.

Pushing his work to one side he gave himself up to imagining the years ahead, Crocker's End ringing with the laughter of children, his and Jacqueline's children; his mother, his dear mother, finding her way again. In those moments he saw more clearly than ever before how Verity's ever-ready smile had hidden her inner misery. How was he so sure? Jacqueline hadn't hinted at it. Yet had she had her sight, had she still been able to work outside as she used to, her grief would never have been as wild and hysterical as it had when his father dealt the final blow.

Reaching for the phone again, he asked for Michael's number.

'What time is it now?' Verity asked.

'Ten past seven. Supper's nearly ready. Richard will probably phone while we're eating.'

They both made sure they didn't let the note of cheerfulness – albeit forced cheerfulness – slip. Jackie truly did feel relieved that she had made her decision, and yet surely she ought not to force that hint of suppressed excitement; surely it ought to come from an inner happiness. But of course I'm happy – if I weren't I wouldn't be so sure that what I have done is *right*.

'If you'd like to sit up, soon-to-be-Mum, I'll take the bones out of the fish for you. Then it's new potatoes and runner beans.'

'Lovely, dear. Yes, I expect the phone will ring in a minute.'

Words, just words, in Verity's battle to pass the time until she was safe in bed and the mask could slip. In bed . . . his side of it empty . . . but then so it had been so often when she had heard him come home and creep along the passage to the small spare room. He hadn't wanted her then . . . perhaps for years he hadn't really wanted her . . . She mustn't think about it . . . but she couldn't think about anything else . . .

'There you are, no bones in it and I've cut the potatoes. They call themselves new but they are getting big now.' Jackie's voice cut into her thoughts and saved them slipping so far downhill that she couldn't hold them back.

'I thought that when I scrubbed them,' Verity said, playing her part in the charade.

So they ate their supper, but no call came from Richard. While Jackie cleared up, Verity went on into the drawing room, Monty padding along behind her. Knowing every step of the way she went straight to her usual chair. She ought to have stayed in the kitchen with Jackie; in here the echo of Ernest's voice was waiting for her, that and the memory of her battle to hold on to control until he was gone. Gone . . . gone because he'd found real happiness, the sort of happiness he hadn't known possible . . . No, she mustn't think. She sat very straight in her chair, her hands on the arms as if she was about to get up. She ought to have stayed with Jackie . . . when she was alone there was nothing to protect her. As she got to her feet to retrace her steps to the kitchen there was a ring at the doorbell, followed immediately by Michael's 'All right if I come straight in?'

'I'm in here, Michael.' And this time she didn't have to force her voice; his unexpected visit had caught her off guard and her relief was genuine.

Jackie heard him arrive, and even though she had finished the dishes she didn't hurry to join them. The hall clock struck eight and still Richard's call didn't come, but now that Michael was there, he would answer the phone and give Verity time to reach it. So Jackie went outside, taking deep breaths of the fragrant summer air. She loved the stillness and silence of this time evening. Yes, she had done right, she *must* have done right. very soul belonged here at Crocker's End. 'We are each of body and a soul,' Richard had said. She wasn't marrying Cro End, she was marrying Richard. Soon they would belong to other. Would she ever find the same wonder with him th had when she'd fallen in love with Wilhelm? Body and so wasn't in love with Richard, and yet the thought of them love excited her. But what about her soul? Making l Wilhelm had fulfilled every romantic dream. As her drifted she walked to the weighing-in shed to lock night, then stood gazing towards Michael's fields and of the hill silhouetted in the fading light. Way abo waning moon rode high in the darkening cloudless

Lost in thought, letting her imagination carry b

She felt rebuffed and made a supreme effort to firmly ground herself, as he obviously was, as they started walking towards the yard and the back door.

'You're not driving back to London tonight?' she said, as she might have asked any casual acquaintance.

'Indeed, no. I shall be on the road by seven in the morning.' Then, stopping and turning her to face him, 'How soon can a wedding be arranged? Do you have hundreds of distant relatives who will be offended if they don't come?'

She shook her head. 'Auntie Alice and Uncle Howard were the only family I've ever had.'

'Friends?'

Again she shook her head. 'Once I left school and everyone else trained for things or started work, I just lost touch with them all. You can get married without each one of the couple having to have someone, can't you?'

'Certainly you can. So there is nothing for us to wait for. Do you want to wear a white gown and look like a fairy princess?'

She chuckled, once again feeling comfortable with him.

'I'd look a bit silly with no one to see me all dressed up.'

'Then I suggest we see the vicar on Saturday and arrange for the banns to be called. Is there any point in waiting?'

'I think it would be good for your mother if we did it quickly. Silly to say that it would take her mind off what's happened; nothing could do that, I know. But at least she could pretend to be thinking about other things, and perhaps the hurt would start to fade without her realizing it.'

Jackie didn't go into the drawing room with Richard, and after a minute Michael came to join her in the kitchen.

'My congratulations, my dear. Or rather, my best wishes; the congratulations are due to Richard. And what wonderful timing. I could swing for that devil of a husband of hers.' He shook his head, seeming lost in thought as he mumbled, 'My poor Verity.'

'You know what I think? I think he's better gone. She's a thousand times too good for him.'

'And always has been. The one good thing he did was sire Richard. So when's the great day? Any thoughts on it yet, or is it too soon?'

'Richard talked about seeing the vicar on Saturday to arrange for the banns.' Then, seeing the look of surprise he wasn't quick enough to hide, she laughed and said, 'What's the point of waiting? Don't you think a wedding in the family might be the best medicine we can give his mother? Mr Bennett wants her to divorce him, you know. It's so hard for her. Divorce is like wiping all those years away, like cleaning the blackboard.'

'You can't make a new start until you're free of the old,' was Michael's opinion. 'I'm phoning Harvey Grant in the morning, from Taylor and Grant, the solicitors in town, to get an appointment for her. Then I've told her I'll drive her in.'

Jackie nodded, secretly relieved. 'You must be her oldest friend; you've known each other for ages, haven't you?'

'I was thirty-two when I took the farm. Fell for her like a ton of bricks. I wish you could have seen her; never seen a girl like it. Bowled me right over, she did. Ah, and still does. We were great pals, Verity and me. If I'd had anything about me I'd have thrown my hat in the ring and asked her to marry me. But I just about scraped together enough to pay the mortgage on the farm. Crocker's End was very different in those days – well looked after, the house had a feeling of comfort and prosperity. How could I even dream of taking her away from all that to live as I did? Have you any idea of the way people who worked the land had to live and work in those days?'

'I've never been to a farm.'

'Well, take my word for it, my dear, life was hard. No hot water, no indoor lavatory, boiling buckets of water on the kitchen range to fill a zinc bath in the kitchen; all that and barely enough coming in to live on. Things got better – the War made the country realize they needed their farmers. But that was too late. She'd been married to Ernest for years by the time I had a home fit to bring a wife to.'

'Did you never marry?'

'Yes. Millie was a farmer's daughter. She was a good soul. We rubbed along pretty well, and it's thanks to her that I have a pretty comfortable place now. Worked like a Trojan, she did. Then suddenly she got taken ill in the influenza epidemic after the War. Like thousands more, she died.'

'How awful for you. But you never look as though you don't live comfortably.'

He laughed at her childlike honesty. 'I get looked after very well by an excellent housekeeper, Mrs Trout. She came to give me a hand looking after Millie when she was ill and she never left. But how did we get on to all this?'

'I said that you must be Mrs Bennett's oldest friend.'

'Oldest indeed. I've known her since I was thirty-two and I'll be seventy at the end of the year. And I'll tell you something else, young lady, seeing that you are starry-eyed and in love: I lost my heart to her the first time I set eyes on her and I've loved her ever since. Both of us married – happily married, I suppose in my case; like I said, Millie was a good woman, worked as hard as any man, a real partner on the farm . . . But none of that made a scrap of difference to how I felt for Verity – and still do.'

'Yet you stood by and saw her marry Mr Bennett. Didn't she know how you felt?'

'It has to be a two-way thing. She was fond of me, she always has been and still is, and had Ernest not come on to the scene we should have got married – sort of drifted into it as far as she was concerned. But once Bennett appeared on the scene it was as if she'd suddenly come to life. No, that's not fair, it makes her sound as if she'd been dull – and that she never was. But he cast a spell on her. I knew my case was hopeless.' There was silence for a moment then, his mind still on Verity. 'I wonder how Richard is getting on with her. He's always been so good to her. I sometimes felt his dislike of his father – and there's no other word for it – was because he was aware Ernest was womanizing, not just with this American dame, but before she came on the scene. Frightened of letting himself grow old, that's his trouble. He always looked for compliments, and handsome young stag that he was there were always plenty of women ready to encourage his vanity. Ah, I hear Richard coming.'

A few minutes later Richard went out to his car and came back with a bottle of champagne he had brought with him from London. So the four of them drank a toast to the engaged couple. Verity forced herself to smile despite her inner misery. None of them were fooled, but it was a small step forward.

The day finally over, Jackie lay in bed, the memories of it

playing out in her over-wakeful mind. Next Sunday the banns
would be called in the parish church; she and Richard and his
mother would be there to hear them. She *must* be doing the
right thing, she reassured herself for the umpteenth time. You
can't live on dreams. Richard was real, he was very dear to her
and would never change; this would be her home, this was where
she belonged, his mother would be her mother. So how was it
that when she turned on her side and made herself settle, determined to stop chasing shadows and to sleep, a hot tear rolled on
to her pillow?

They were married on the first Saturday in October. The bride
wore a knee-length white 'sailor dress', and on her head a straw
hat with its wide brim evenly turned up all the way round and
a navy blue and white band; on her feet navy blue court shoes.
Since she'd been at Crocker's End she had spent little money,
and most of her twenty-two and sixpences were in her under-
wear drawer in a trinket box she'd had since she was a child.
Even when she had inherited from her uncle, rushing out to buy
clothes had never been high on her agenda. It was a new experience to go to town knowing she need not look at the price tag
before she chose her outfit.

For such a quiet wedding, clothes were of no great importance, but Verity insisted she too needed something different. None
of them knew the effort it took for her to involve herself, but
there was no effort too great for the day Richard was to take
for his wife the girl she had come to love. She alone knew her
underlying and constant grief. Through the time her sight had
been gradually fading, she had trained that ever-ready smile never
to fail, and even Jackie, who was with her more than anyone,
didn't fully realize the hurt it hid. The two of them spent a whole
afternoon in Cheltenham, where Jackie described anything she
thought would suit her almost-Mum. A pale violet dress and coat
of the same material led them on to the hat department, where
the assistant joined them and poor sightless Verity sat before the
mirror while one headpiece after another was put on her. At last
the decision was made and satisfied – or in Verity's case, making
a show of her delight in her purchases – they went home.

Richard had no such problem; he dressed as he did for work

in what Jackie thought of as his London clothes. As for Michael, who have been delighted and flattered to be asked to walk Jackie up the aisle and give her away, he surprised them all by appearing on the morning of the wedding in a charcoal grey suit bought for the occasion. 'I wasn't going to escort this pretty young lady up the aisle in my old tweeds!

And anyway –' with a knowing wink at Jackie whose mind immediately took a leap back to his confession of his ever-faithful love for Verity – 'who knows when I might find myself needing to smarten up for some other occasion?'

They had envisaged only their own party and the vicar would be in the church, but they had overlooked the way word is passed around in a country district. That Ernest had run off with that 'red lips' from America was soon public knowledge, for after the summer break the Parish Council had met to find the meeting was to be taken by the Vice-Chairman, who read Ernest's letter of resignation for both himself and Mrs Schofield. Not much else was discussed on that evening. 'Can't say I'm surprised, haven't we all seen the way he's been looking at her' . . . 'Makes you sick, a chap married as long as he has been' . . . 'Fancies himself a bit of a Jack m'Lad' . . . 'Never thought he'd leave home for her, and that poor wife of his, too . . .' And speaking freely amongst the all-male committee now there was no lady clerk to curb their choice of words, 'If you'd have asked me, I'd have said he was getting his oats right enough as things were. That car of his was outside her place some nights till gone eleven o'clock. Some nights, did I say? More often than not. I always looked out for it when I took Boots for his last walk of a night' . . . 'Well, if you want my opinion, we're better off without the pair of them. Got no patience with a man who cheats on his wife just when she must have needed him most.' So the committee members carried the news home to their wives, and the wives spread it to friends. By the time Verity visited her solicitor, following Ernest's instructions and taking with her the details of where he and Hilda Schofield were living, there wasn't a person in the village who didn't know she'd been deserted. Then, from Jane Carter, the daily help, came the next piece of gossip – and for some this was even more interesting than the break up of the Bennetts' marriage: with no engagement, or so it seemed, their son was marrying the young girl who had come as a general help. There could be only one reason for that sort of rushed ceremony. What girl of her age didn't dream of floating up the aisle in wreath and veil? Wicked, it was, to take advantage of an innocent young girl like he must have done.

So public interest was high. Instead of just the four of them and Mrs Trout, Michael's housekeeper, the village women turned out in full force, and when Richard said in a clear, firm voice, 'I, Richard James, take Jacqueline to be my lawfully wedded wife, to love and to cherish . . .' there were some who secretly wondered if perhaps they'd misjudged him. Only time would tell.

The five went back to Crocker's End for a lunch that had been prepared in advance and only had to be reheated. In the drawing room Richard uncorked the first bottle of champagne and filled five glasses.

'I ask you to raise your glasses and drink to the bride and groom,' Michael bid them. 'May they have many happy years together. You're a lucky chap, young Richard.'

'Indeed I am. I know I speak for both of us when I thank you Michael for your help and support, now as always. Jacqueline and I will go away with easy minds knowing you and Mrs Trout will be staying in the house with Mother. And one more word of thanks, and that's to you, Mother, the best mother in the world, and especially on this occasion for knowing as soon as you met Jacqueline that she was right for you, for Crocker's End – and for me.'

In her mind's eye Verity saw him as she listened, holding the image that for her would never change with the passing of time. How often through recent years she had wished he could meet the right girl and fall in love. And always when she had pictured his wedding it had been a happy affair: a bride in white, music, laughter – and most of all, she had taken it for granted that Ernest would be with her. 'The best mother in the world . . .' Richard's words echoed, but not a word of his father. And why should there be when Ernest had turned his back on both of them? Smile, look as though your body doesn't ache with misery . . . Smile and hold your chin high. This is Richard's day, Richard's and Jackie's. It's the day you have prayed for.

It was late afternoon by the time the bridal couple drove off, turning right out of the gate and heading towards the South-West.

They would only be away for four days as Richard didn't have limitless leave and he wanted to keep some back to help on the land in the New Year when new bushes must be planted. Michael had promised that while they were away he would divide his time between the farm and Crocker's End. His small acreage of arable land had already been harvested, thanks to a good summer, and he had two reliable herdsmen.

'Do you remember when you brought me to meet your mother? My first long car ride.' Jackie broke the silence.

'Indeed I do. But I prefer to look to the future.' Without looking at her he held out his hand in her direction. She knew he wanted her to take it in hers, a silent assurance to him that she was ready for that future. Only for a second she hesitated, then she did as he wanted, locking her fingers through his.

She took a quick glance in his direction. How stilted he sounded. Over the months she had come to know him, he had relaxed and lost the formal manner she had met with in the beginning and which had seemed to hold her at a distance. And yet to hear him now was to take her back to that first drive. Yes, he remembered it just as she did, hadn't he just said so? 'Indeed I do.' Was it because he was as uncertain as she was herself? He loved her, she was sure he did, so she ought to be excited; she ought to be prepared to help him. He probably expected her to be innocent and ignorant, frightened of the unknown. That other voice echoed in her memory: 'Whatever happens in the future, we will never forget our first time.' The first time and, looking back through the distance of five years, she realized how innocent they had been. Both of them had been consumed by the passion that drove them, passion that left room for nothing else; both of them with nothing to guide them but nature. Nothing could ever be like that again. What was she doing marrying a man she admired, respected, but didn't love with a longing that couldn't be denied. If only she loved him as she knew she was capable of loving. But there could be no repeating that first miracle, the wild joy, the abandonment. She'd been just a child, silently she reminded herself; it was senseless to believe that either she or Wilhelm had brought adult emotions to the earth-shaking experience that had been the culmination of a friendship that they'd believed had matured to the richness of adulthood.

Now she was a woman, with a woman's needs and yearnings.
And with the thought came the image of her lonely bed, the
need she couldn't deny, didn't try to deny – and the shame and
degradation that followed. And what now? Her mind raced on:
sometimes I'm sure he's felt the same, but look at him now, his
expression tells me nothing . . . Please don't let him be starchy
and remote. Or am I some sort of oversexed trollop? I'm not in
love with Richard, but I am his wife. I want him to touch me,
I want us to make love, I want us both to be driven with that
same relentless passion as before, and I want the final moment to
leave me exalted just as it did that first time. Of course tonight
we will make love, it's the first night of our honeymoon. But
what if he's buttoned-up, precise? What if he doesn't know about
that sort of untamed longing, what if he just climbs on top of
me and . . . and . . . I don't know the words.

'You're very quiet.' His voice took her by surprise, giving her
a feeling of guilt, as if he had been able to follow where her
thoughts had taken her. 'You're not feeling car sick, are you? Do
you need to stop and get some air?'

'No. I'm fine. I was just thinking about things.'

'Thoughts you can share?'

'Nothing interesting. Anyway, you aren't exactly chatty.'

'No. I too was thinking, about our future. It's a strange start
to married life, me in lodgings in London, you left behind in the
country. But it's difficult to expect Mother to get used to someone
else in the house when she's going through such a bad patch
with the divorce ahead of her.'

'Whatever would I want with living in London? I've never
even considered it. What is there about Crocker's End that casts
such a spell? I've felt it from the day you took me there and it
digs deeper into my – into my *soul* with every day.'

'Then it's as well you only have four days' honeymoon to
keep you away from it.' If only he wouldn't speak in that expressionless voice.

'I know,' she answered. 'When we get home, Richard, I'm going
to get on with digging out the bushes we are replacing. And then
there are the year's figures to be finalized now that the season is
over. It's not going to be good. I checked back in the ledgers for
the last few years and the income has gone steadily down. I believe

this year will be even worse than last – just like Mr Cross forecast. Over the next few weeks we'll have to engage more staff. My feeling is that what we want would be two or three strong young lads, plenty of energy and willing to learn.'

He looked at her thoughtfully. Strong young lads, willing to learn? And who was there except her to teach them? They must engage an experienced manager, one who not only understood the care of the stock but had some idea of marketing. For years his father had taken no interest, and for all her enthusiasm how much could Jacqueline possibly have learnt?

'When we get home on Wednesday we'll go over the figures together.'

Jackie settled more comfortably into her seat, she even reached her hand and laid it on Richard's knee. It had been good to talk to each other about Crocker's End. Some of her doubts melted.

'I've made you cry. Did it hurt you? I should have been more gentle.'

Jackie rubbed the palms of her hands across her cheeks, shaking her head. 'Not that sort of crying,' she sniffed. 'I expect it's because it's been too much living all packed into one day.' She tried to laugh as she said it. 'We're going to be all right, you and me, aren't we?'

'Too much living? For me, the day brought all I have dreamt of. Jacqueline, my wife, lying here by my side.'

In the car she had let her imagination carry her forward; she had known she wanted Richard to make love to her. But even in her mind she hadn't been completely honest and admitted that what she wanted was to feel the warm weight of his body moving against her – against her and inside her. And as she reached the goal she'd been striving for, so too would his control be lost in a convulsive shudder and she would grip him tightly and press him closer, closer into her as they shared the miracle of true union. She knew it could happen like that; it had happened before as she and Wilhelm had lain on the sun-scorched earth.

And so it had been, so why the tears? The answer made her ashamed, for honesty made her face the truth: it had been wonderful, all she had yearned for, but not because it was Richard. He was her husband, and more than gladly – even thankfully – she would be his willing partner. No doubt, being a man of orderly routine, it would be a Friday night occurrence when he arrived from London, and probably again during the weekend. And she would be ready and willing – but not because she was in love with him so much as because it was what her body craved.

Soon she would lay the ghost of Wilhelm. That had happened years ago, she told herself as she had a thousand times; it simply lived in her memory because it had been a journey of discovery.

She drew Richard's hand to her small breast, moving his fingers over her hardened nipple.

'No more tears,' he whispered, reaching his other hand to pull the cord and turn off the light over the bed. 'Our first night together, Jacqueline, my precious love.' In the dark he could speak from his heart.

'I want us to do it again,' she whispered. With Wilhelm she had loved the sunshine, but with Richard she felt freer in the dark, her mind carrying her where it would. 'If you can't, then just hold me,' and she wrapped her leg across him, her hands caressing him. So it had been on that sunny day by the river.

Their short honeymoon over, they returned to Crocker's End and the beginning of the routine of their new lives. It was a routine not so very different from the old one, except that they took over the large spare room – as opposed to the small spare where Ernest had so often ended his days.

Even to Richard, Jackie didn't talk of the charade she knew Verity was playing. That smile they had all come to take for granted never failed, and only she knew the heartbreak it hid. She had been home from her honeymoon less than a week when she woke in the middle of the night believing she had heard something and yet not knowing what. Lying still she listened. Yes, there it was again. She got out of bed and, as silently as she could, opened her bedroom door. There was no mistaking what it was she had heard: from Verity's room came the sound of stifled sobbing. Jackie tiptoed across the passage and was about to go in when she stopped herself. What Verity fought for was an illusion of happiness; to intrude on her would be more cruel than to leave her believing she hadn't been heard. So Jackie went back to her own room as quietly as she had come. Wide awake, her mind was racing. Something had to be done; she had to think of some way to lift her new Mum out of her despair. After that, each night she listened. It didn't happen every night, but often enough for her to worry increasingly and know that they must do *something* to give the future new shape, new colour. Of course the answer would be if she were pregnant. She had assumed it was easy for anyone to conceive – she had thought even on their honeymoon it must surely have happened. But in October her period was regular to the day, just as four weeks later so it was again.

Outside, she spent two or three hours each day digging out the old bushes, and as she worked, the thought of Verity haunted her. The digging was a tough job, but slightly built though she was, Jackie had stamina. In the first instance she expected that they would be replaced by the same varieties of fruit: raspberries, loganberries, blackcurrants. But with Verity's restricted lifestyle and so many memories of happier times at Crocker's End, surely it must be *here* that they involved her in a new beginning, something to carry her thoughts forwards, not backwards. Even if the new stock produced healthier fruit, next year would be nothing but a repeat of all the seasons that had gone before. Jackie's mind was working overtime, and that's when the idea came to her.

She read avidly, learning everything she could, and a plan started to form, one about which she said nothing. If she discussed it with Richard he would consider that he being a man and she only a mere woman it would be up to him to carry the scheme forward. So she strode the borders of the plots, counting her strides, which she had initially measured to be a yard for each step she took, then writing down the approximate measurements. Next came nursery catalogues and, finally, calculations. And why hadn't she seen from her first thoughts that this was the way she wanted to use the money she had inherited when she came of age the previous March. It represented a lifetime's hard work and savings for her great uncle and aunt, and she knew it would soon be swallowed up here – in fact it might not even be sufficient in the outset. But she wanted to invest in Crocker's End; she had a lightness of heart imagining it.

'Michael is taking me for a drive this afternoon,' Verity said to her as they ate their lunch on the last Wednesday of November.

'We'll take Monty with us and stop somewhere for him to have a run.'

'That's nice, Mum. It's such a gorgeous day. The end of November but it still smells like autumn – bonfires, decaying leaves, and even the air has a different feeling.' Then, with a laugh, 'And I don't mean because it's getting colder. It's something to do with the hazy air, I expect.'

Verity nodded. She knew exactly what it was Jackie was trying to describe. 'He's calling for me at two o'clock and he said to tell you not to worry if we are some time. I think he has in mind to stop at a tea room he knows. What about if I suggest he comes back here for supper? Will it stretch to an extra?'

'I'm going into town, so I'll bring something back. There's a sale at Toms and Blake – you know, the department store in King's Street? I thought I'd see if they have anything exciting, perhaps something to wear at Christmas.'

In truth, what she was looking for had nothing to do with Christmas. She intended to buy a suit, a tailored skirt and jacket, then to wear with it a pair of high-heeled court shoes. She envisaged something in charcoal grey or navy blue, a suit that would give her the appearance of a proficient businesswoman. But she didn't share her secret with Verity, for to give even the slightest hint of her need for such attire could all too easily lead to telling more than she intended. So, at the department store on King's Street, she took the lift to Ladies Clothing on the second floor, where she explained to the assistant what she wanted. The selection was wide – she could have purchased what she had envisaged in grey, navy, or even forest green – but while the assistant was regaling her with the excellent workmanship, she caught sight of something quite different. That's how it was that her plans took off in another direction. What would a businesswoman dressed for the city know about growing fruit? No, the speckled tweed in forest green, dark brown and a hint of russet shouted 'country'. It fitted her perfectly, and to wear with it she bought a russet jumper. Then in the hat department she found the ideal thing: a jaunty Robin Hood hat with a pheasant's feather. With brown leather court shoes her image would give just the impression she intended. As she passed up her money, she felt the ghost of her great aunt and uncle close by and had a moment's guilt as she realized how long it would have taken them to earn what she had just spent. Clutching her purchases she hurried out of the shop to the car parked outside, still thinking about the elderly couple. Her expression softened into a smile as she imagined them. She had told no one of her plan, but it needed no words for *them* to understand the way her mind was turning. With her right arm stretched out of the window to indicate that she was pulling out from the kerb, that hint of a smile deepened. Spending money on fancy clothes was something they had never done, but they would realize that there was purpose behind today's purchases; they would know and approve. Long, long ago when they had been young and had taken the lease on the newspaper shop, they must have felt this same excitement.

Seven

Michael had always paid frequent casual visits to Crocker's End, but since the summer day when Ernest had dropped his bombshell the visits had changed. Still he often arrived unannounced with his customary ring of the bell, as he opened the door and called 'All right if I come in?', but these days he stayed longer and often took Verity out with him.

It was a Friday morning, the end of the week when Jackie had bought her new outfit and brought it home without a word to be hidden in her wardrobe. 'All right if I come in? Not too early for you ladies?' Michael called as he came through the hall.

'Never too early,' Verity answered, her voice as bright as her smile.

'It's just a thought, Verity, and tell me if the idea doesn't appeal to you, but I have to go to a village near Reading to a farm where they want old Horace to go and have his evil way with some of the herd.'

'That's a long way to take an animal. Has no one nearer to them got a bull?' Verity asked.

'There are bulls and bulls. This is a prize herd and old Horace has a pedigree that cost me more than I could afford at the time I bought him. But he's been worth the outlay many times over. Anyway, I wondered if you'd take pity on my lonely state and keep me company. We could stop off somewhere and get lunch – and maybe find a little tea shop too so that we can meander around a bit.' Then, seeing her hesitation, 'You'll be fine, my dear, trust me.'

The change in his tone, the gentle way he said those last words, almost got through her defences.

She nodded. 'I've always trusted you, Michael.'

'I'll go and find Jackie, shall I, so that she can give you a hand getting ready?'

Jackie had been digging for a good half hour, grubbing up loganberry bushes. Always willing when Verity needed her, on that morning she answered the call with alacrity, not even stopping to clean her shovel before she propped it against the side of the barn. They would be out all day! It was as if Fate was playing into her hands. Leaving her muddy Wellingtons in the porch, she hurried upstairs to find Verity.

'He's so good to me, Jackie. I'm sure he'd have a better day without me – chatting to the farmer without thinking of me waiting in the car.'

'If that's what he'd wanted, he wouldn't have suggested your going with him. He wants your company. He is very fond of you.'

Verity sat on the dressing table stool while Jackie brushed and combed her hair for her, then raised her face while a little vanishing cream, powder and lipstick were applied. She didn't speak while that was going on, but when she sensed Jackie stepping back to inspect the result, she said, 'When we were young we used to be such friends. We always have been, of course, but I could feel that he and Ernest never liked each other.'

'And you still are *special* friends, Mum.'

Verity looked in Jackie's direction with that over-bright smile. 'Will I do? Do I look respectable?'

'More than respectable, you look pretty as a picture. Mr Southwell will escort you into your lunchtime restaurant with pride. Hold your arms out, here comes your coat.'

'That's what Ernie said – he escorts his wretched woman with pride, knowing he's the envy of the room. That's what he said.'

Jackie wished she'd steered the conversation in a different direction. She had to think quickly how to repair the damage, for she feared Verity was near to losing the tight grip on cheerfulness she fought so hard to maintain.

'Pride is a two-way thing, Mum. And if Mr Southwell is proud of you, so you can be of him. He's a dear, isn't he – one of those people you take to the moment you meet. You're going to have a splendid day. I'll expect you when you get home, and I'll make sure there's plenty to eat, just in case he stays.'

Verity nodded. 'I can't remember when I last had a whole day out. Now then, if you're sure I'll do him justice, here we go.'

One look at Michael and it was clear she did him justice. Holding her elbow he guided her to the waiting car. Jackie watched them drive out of the drive and then hurried to the telephone.

'Crownley 273, please.' Then a wait while she heard rings, clicks, and finally, 'You're through now, it's ringing for you.'

'Findlay's Cordials, good morning,' came the voice of the telephonist.

'This is Mrs Bennett speaking from Crocker's End Fruit Farm. Will you enquire of Mr Findlay whether he can spare me a few moments of his time either later this morning or this afternoon, please.' Another ringing tone, more clicks and voices she couldn't hear clearly enough to understand, then the telephonist was back with her.

'Are you there, Mrs Bennett? Mr Findlay says he will be here all day today, so he will see you whenever you find most convenient.'

A smile – nearer the truth to say a beam of delight – spread across Jackie's face. 'Then I'll be with you at, say, eleven o'clock.' That would give her time to scrub up and don her new outfit. The drive wouldn't take more than half an hour at the most. Luck was on her side today. Please make things go well, make him be nice and easy to talk to, make him be prepared to back me.

Perhaps it was the tweed suit and new court shoes or, more likely, it was the Robin Hood hat with its pheasant's feather, but from wherever it came, her confidence had a boost. Driving up the sloping driveway she seemed to hear Algy Cross's voice as she looked back at the fields of 'knackered' bushes. She would bring new life to Crocker's End. Today was a challenge, one she looked forward to; if life didn't present a challenge, what hope could there be of success? If Mr Findlay didn't want to listen to her – she pulled her thoughts up before they burst her bubble of optimism.

At three minutes to eleven she parked her car in the forecourt of the cordial producing plant and, with a firm step – she knew it was firm, she made sure of it – went up the steps to the main entrance of the building.

'I have an appointment to see Mr Findlay, will you tell him I'm here. Mrs Bennett from Crocker's End.' How strange it sounded. She realized that today was the first time she had introduced herself with her new name, a name that belonged to her mother-in-law.

'I'll take you up to his office. This way . . .' The middle-aged woman behind the desk seemed to look on her as someone important, a far cry from the truth. Jackie decided her new outfit was already paying dividends. She was ushered into a large room, sparsely furnished and with no floor covering on the bare boards. It wasn't at all the setting she had envisaged for head of the Findlay's Cordial empire.

'Mrs Bennett? Mrs Bennett from Crocker's End?' It was apparent from his tone that she wasn't the sort of person Charles Findlay had expected. And if he was surprised at the sight of her, she certainly had expected him to be very different from the wizened man who stood up to greet her. In his youth he had been slightly built, but the years had left their mark. Never had she seen a face so deeply lined. With his tatty black jacket unbuttoned she could see his braces, which hoisted his trouser top inches above his skinny waist, and even when he held out his hand to take hers, his greening-with-age bowler hat remained firmly on his head. 'You know I must be getting old and silly, or how could I have thought I was to expect a visit from the Mrs Bennett I remember. Well, when first I met her she wasn't Bennett at all.'

'That's my mother-in-law, Verity Bennett. It was good of you to see me, Mr Findlay. I hope you'll be interested in what I intend to do at Crocker's End.'

'Well, we shall have to see, shan't we?' That seemed to Jackie an indication that although he looked something of a scarecrow, he wasn't going to be putty in her hands. 'Back in the days when I first had dealing with Crocker's End it was run by Verity Bennett's family and no one grew finer fruit. That was when I was just a youngster – much the age that you'd be now, I dare say – and I hadn't gone into cordials. Preserves, that's how I got my foot in the door, so to speak. It was a start, but I did a lot of reading and did my sums, you might say, and I made the change. In a small way to start with. But like they say, from a little acorn a great oak tree grows. Now then, my dear, you didn't come here to listen to how I climbed up the ladder. So what is it you want with me?'

Jackie's planned speech was forgotten. 'If you knew Crocker's

End in its heyday, Mr Findlay, you'd be sad to see it now. My
mother-in-law has lost her sight, and as Algy Cross, who looked
after it with no help but seasonal casual labour—'

'Algy Cross, you say. Don't recall the name Algy, but there were
two or three from the same Cross family working there, as I
recall. You're telling me that that pretty girl I remember has lost
her sight? What a dreadful thing. And that fop she tied herself
up with, you say he leaves Algy Cross to look after the place?'

'Not now. Mr Cross had a stroke, he had to give up some
months ago. And Mr Bennett has gone off with another woman.'

'God bless my soul! Whatever next!'

'My personal feeling is that the place is better without him, but
it's so hard on her. My husband is a government statistician –'
she was pleased with the way she dropped that into the conversation before the astute old man asked questions – 'but I have
been in charge of things since Mr Cross was taken ill and I know
he was speaking the truth when he told me the place has been
going steadily downhill over recent years. The idea was that we
should replace stock in the New Year, and I've already started
clearing some of the ground. But – and this is why I wanted to
talk to you – I want to concentrate just on blackcurrants. I know
you must take fruit from various sources, one grower couldn't
possibly meet your need, and I hoped you might be prepared
to give me a contract to take what we can supply from
Crocker's End.'

She knew he was more canny than at first he appeared, and
while she'd been talking he had been weighing her up.

'You say the place is run down and you have been looking
after it. I don't want to judge what I haven't seen, but what makes
you think you have the ability to turn the place around?'

'Put like that, it does sound a tall order. But–' for a second
she hesitated, wondering whether she was wise to trust her instinct
and tell him the truth – 'well, there are two reasons for making
me so sure I'll not let the place down. The first is that it's a challenge, a challenge I *relish* because I truly love the place; I knew
it from the day I went there, and every day it gets more and
more important. That's one reason. The second isn't so easy to
explain; it has to do with my mother-in-law. I hate to talk about
her like this when she makes such a huge effort not to let anyone

see how unhappy she is, and she'd feel humiliated if she knew what I was saying. But when her husband left her it sort of destroyed all her pleasure in the future. Richard and I got married and she was pleased, I know she was, but deep down she is . . . without hope. She loves Crocker's End and, even though she can't see, it's the background to her life. If we replant the older stock with the same fruit as before, then the only difference is that Mr Bennett has run off with a younger woman. What I want to do is get her interested and involved in a new project, one that is still Crocker's End but without all the old connections that hurt her to think about. Does that sound crazy? When I said just now I'd started digging out the old bushes, I know that if you are prepared to back what I want to do, we will have to hire machinery to clear the land and then see the soil is fed and fertilized.'

'Jigger me, it seems a rum way of starting a business. Or perhaps it doesn't. If you were a chap with some experience behind you, then I'd have more hope for what you intend.'

'I'm as good as any chap. If I'd talked to my husband I wouldn't be here today – not because he wouldn't approve the scheme, but because, like you, he would think the person at the helm should always be a man. Well, I told you, he is a government statistician in London. Look, if you can spare the time, I mean – I've brought these to show you.' And from her bag she produced a sheaf of papers. On the first sheet her measurements of the fields had been drawn out; on the second, her calculations of how many blackcurrant bushes would be needed to stock the whole area, her estimate of the cost per bush and the final figure; on the next the amount of fertilizer an acre and then the final quantity and cost; and finally, on the fourth sheet she had written the cost of hiring machinery to dig out the old bushes, to plough the land and to spread the fertilizer. All of it was written clearly and neatly. Charles Findlay was surprised and, despite his deep-rooted belief that businesses should be run by men, there was something about this 'pretty little filly' that impressed him.

'There's no doubt you've done your homework. Now, Mrs Bennett, this is the proposition I'm prepared to make . . .'

★   ★   ★

With hope and confidence riding high, Jackie walked out of the building and down the steps to her car. She made a detour to go to town; there were a few things she needed for the weekend meals. Catching a glimpse of her reflection in a shop window, she wouldn't have been human if she hadn't been pleased with what she saw: 'All dressed up and nowhere to go' – an expression she'd heard often enough but never been more aware of than at that moment. In a second her decision was made: she would go to the Green Dolphin Restaurant, a place she had only admired from the outside, and have her lunch. No one was waiting to be fed at home and her successful morning ought to be celebrated – to say nothing of her smart appearance.

Yet by the time she turned down the drive of Crocker's End at about four o'clock, her initial confidence had deserted her and even hope was having a struggle to survive. What right had she to take it upon herself to map out the future of what had once been a thriving fruit farm? If Richard and his mother considered she had interfered in what didn't concern her, wouldn't that be just what she deserved? She would put the car away then go and change into her old clothes. She had time for an hour's digging before Verity and Michael would be back, even if they didn't stay out for tea, and it was usually well after seven by the time Richard got home on Friday evenings.

Halfway down the slope she realized there was a car following her. She felt as guilty as someone caught with her fingers in the till, even though, unless Michael remarked on her appearance, Verity wouldn't know she was dressed in anything special. Then she realized the car was Richard's. Now there was nowhere to escape; the truth would have to be told.

She drew up just in front of where he always parked, got out of the car, and with her fingers tightly crossed for luck walked towards him.

'I wasn't expecting you for hours yet. Is everything all right?'

'It was a morning of disturbances and interruptions so I decided to call it a day and bring some work home instead. You are looking extremely elegant?' It was a question, so what he really meant was, 'Why are you all dressed up on a Friday afternoon?'

'It has to be told, Richard, so can we get in your car together so that we can talk? It's no use putting it off. I'll make a clean breast of it. Don't interrupt me, just listen. And when you've taken it in, I promise I'll do whatever you say is right.'

She felt rather than saw his fear, and only then realized what he must have thought he was going to hear. Without a word he opened the passenger door for her, and, clutching her bag, she climbed in.

'You didn't tell me if you liked my rig-out,' she said in an attempt to put them into a more relaxed mood.

'And you didn't tell me why you are wearing it.'

'Listen, Richard, and don't knock me down before you've heard all I have to say. This morning Mr Southwell collected Mum and took her to a farm in Berkshire and then on to lunch. So I knew that had to be my opportunity. I phoned Findlay Cordials and asked for an appointment with Mr Findlay.' And so the whole story was told. She took her drawings and calculations from her handbag and passed them to him – and then she waited as he gave the neatly written sheets his full attention.

After a few moments he folded them and passed them back. 'For someone who once told me she had never been top-of-the-class clever, you have done an amazing job, Jacqueline.'

'But what do you think about the idea? It's not me who would have to sign the contract with Mr Findlay, it's *you* on behalf of your mother. So if you don't think a completely new start is a good idea, then we'll forget the whole thing and not even mention it to her. I expect you think I have an awful cheek—'

'Indeed I don't. On the contrary, I feel touched – humbled – that you care enough to have done all this then rigged yourself out and taken the plan to Mr Findlay. And, by the way, you look enchanting.'

'You don't have to go over the top,' she chuckled, basking in his admiration. 'So if you think it's a good scheme, the next thing is to persuade your mother to think so too. I want you to be the one to tell her about it. You will do that, won't you? At the moment I don't think she'd notice if we said we were going to drill for oil instead of growing fruit. She'd just give us that bright smile. Oh, Richard, we *have* to do something to set her moving forward. Just replacing the plants like Mr Cross had been telling your father was needed would do nothing to shake her out of herself. This way it's new to all of us, it would be a challenge.

I know you have your own work, and I know she wouldn't be able to actually see any changes if we made them, but at weekends when you're home we could all three talk about it, and I want to make her see with her mind's eye every step of the way. Oh, and one more thing, always supposing you both agree to sign the contract with Findlay's, what money I have won't go very far with the expenses, but I want to invest what Uncle Howard left me. I can't just fritter the money he worked so hard to be able to save; I want to invest it in Crocker's End.'

'Is that what they would want?'

'I believe it is. But we'll have to see the bank about a loan, I expect, shan't we?'

'No doubt we shall. But with the contract from Findlay's we ought to be able to get the money. Another outing for the suit?'

'No. Crocker's End belongs to Mum, but you'd have to go with her. You have her authority to sign things, don't you?' Then, looking at him with a teasing twinkle, 'I'll tart myself up and come as well if you think my new attire would add tone to the interview.'

'You'd add tone to anything, Jacqueline. Have you the slightest idea how proud I am of you, of what you've done? Take that very fine hat off; I can't kiss a lady with a hat on.'

By the time supper was over there was a buzz of conversation in the kitchen, where they all sat around the table, and an unfamiliar atmosphere of hope. Michael had stayed to the meal, and he was throwing his weight behind Richard and Jackie, probably sensing where the basis for change lay. Looking at Jackie's 'homework', which Richard passed across the table, he too felt the need to be involved and was quick to offer to take on the work of clearing and preparing the land.

It was difficult to tell whether Verity's apparent interest was real or as much a façade as the smile she presented to the world.

'We'll be staking everything on it being a success,' Jackie said. 'The quantity and quality has to be good. That will be written into the contract. But, assuming the crop is good, it will be a secure income – and no rushing off to the station in town every day.'

'We're responsible for picking, of course,' Verity said, her words causing the other three to glance at each other, silently noting the 'we' as a huge leap forward, 'but does that mean that the currants have to be taken to the cordial plant in the van? That's a much longer daily trip than the station.'

'No, Mum. He said that first of all they will come to see the crop, size up what it looks like, then we get the pickers in. We shall need more people, but not every day; it'll be all hands on deck on picking days, then the lorry will come from Findlay's to collect the filled baskets. I imagine once a week or something like that. But when they come to look before picking starts, they will give us details.'

'I seem to remember years ago, when the firm first started, we used to supply Charles Findlay with a variety of fruit – gooseberries, strawberries, raspberries, logans – but in those days he was making jams. I remember him clearly, a skinny young man with a big smile and always in a black suit and a bowler hat. It used to strike me as so out of place here in the country, when we were all in short sleeves and the men with no jackets, and no collars on their shirts, sleeves rolled up. You remember how it used to be, Michael?'

'And still is on the farm.'

'Mr Findlay's the same man, the same suit and bowler hat, I shouldn't wonder,' Jackie laughed. 'I liked him. But I got the feeling he's no pushover; he's a real businessman.'

Later, when Michael had gone home, Verity went up to bed. She could manage very well in her familiar room, but it had become a habit that Jackie always went to see that she was safely in bed and had everything to hand that she might need.

On that night, as Jackie went into the bedroom, she found Verity in her nightdress, standing by the window where she had opened the curtains as if she could see out.

'It will be the same and yet different,' she said when she heard Jackie come into the room. 'I've never wished for my sight so much. How I would love to be out there with you, doing something useful.' She felt Jackie's arm around her shoulder.

'You'll be the foreman, Mum. Mum . . .' She hesitated. 'You didn't think it was pushy of me to go to Findlay's? I know it ought to have been Richard, but, well, we women are more capable than people give us credit for, and I wanted to be the one to do it. You don't mind? I bet you would have felt the same.'

Verity thought about it. 'Yes, looking back I can see that was
what I would have wanted. And of course during the War, when
so many of the village lads had gone off to the Army, women
had the chance to show what they could do.' She felt her way
to the bed and climbed in. 'Jackie, it has been a really special day.
I know there will be others not like it, days when I feel hopeless and – and rejected. But today I almost forgot all that. We
had lunch in such a nice place, somewhere Michael had been
before. He is so easy to be with, he doesn't fuss me, and yet he
always seems to anticipate.'

'He's very fond of you.' It was the second time that Jackie had
said it that day.

'Yes, it was one of those days I know will stay with me. And
then to come home and find that you and Richard had been
planning a way to pull Crocker's End up again, you don't know
how much that means to me. Not just whether we make our
fortunes. No, it's something more important than that. You *thought*
about it, *cared* about what happens out there.'

'Crocker's End does that to you, Mum.'

Verity pulled the covers around her shoulders, then, just as
Jackie was feeling satisfied that with a future to look forward to
she would be able to let go of the hurt Ernest had done her, she
said, 'What a silly man Ernie is, letting his head be turned by
that woman. We could all have been so happy and he would have
enjoyed the new venture.'

Jackie kissed her goodnight but said nothing. If Ernest had
been there, nothing would have been done – not so much as a
few replacement bushes planted. Surely reason must have told
Verity much the same thing, or is love blind?

Lying in the dark bedroom, Jackie felt satisfied and content.
Perhaps it had been the unexpected turn of events that had given
Richard's Friday night homecoming bedtime ritual such fervour,
or perhaps it was because the previous weekend it hadn't been
possible for her. She smiled as in her mind she relived the last
half hour; tonight had made up for the long wait. Thinking about
him she longed to believe she was in love with him, but she was
too honest to pretend. He was unfailingly kind, unfailingly fair,
yes, and unfailingly efficient. If he helped her clear up after a

meal, just a simple thing like putting knives and forks away, she always knew if he had done it. She threw the cutlery in the right sections of the drawer; Richard stacked them neatly. If he read the newspaper he always folded it precisely, the corners exact. Each night he put his wallet on the bedside table, his loose change in a neat pile on the dressing table, then hung his jacket in his wardrobe and put his trousers in the press. Lastly, pyjamas on – even though he would soon be wriggling out of them – he brushed his hair with the pair of silver-backed brushes before fixing them together, bristles into bristles. Yes, he was methodical in everything he did, even in making love. Jackie had never heard the word 'orgasm'; she thought of it as the 'miracle', and he never failed to give it to her. But there had been a difference about this last half hour: routine had been broken, pyjamas left folded and untouched . . .

'Are you asleep?' she whispered.

'No. I'm not even tired. You must be, you've had quite a day.'

'Shall we talk if you're not tired? Shall we make plans?'

Richard laughed softly, hearing her childlike excitement. But Jacqueline was no child, she was a passionate, sensual woman. How many women were as honest and natural? Just as hers had, his mind went back over the recent scene. With the bedroom door closed, the world had been their own. If she'd consciously been a temptress he would have drawn back, but sex with Jacqueline was as natural as it was joyous. She was neither bashful not blatant, she was young, healthy, hungry to satisfy and glory in the need of her body, and his too. From the day he'd first met her he had loved her and wanted to cherish her. He remembered the day, much later, when she had first guided his hand to her small, firm breast and he had felt her hardened nipple through her cotton dress; he remembered the rush of desire he had felt for her, but even then he had had no idea of the strength of her sexuality. She was wonderful – and she was his. When they made love he could make himself believe that she loved him as completely as he loved her.

'We'll go over the figures again tomorrow,' she was saying. 'I don't know anything about what money there is in the bank, but you can work out how much we need to borrow – and when we go to see the manager we'll transfer mine into the account.'

'We'll talk tomorrow,' he whispered, drawing her close. 'Jacqueline, my Jacqueline.'

With no prompting, her body responded to his tone. She snuggled her face against his neck, then wriggled to lie on top of him before drawing up her knees so that she sat astride him. Nature had always been her guide, and unquestioningly she followed.

'Closer, deeper, deeper,' came muffled whispers in the dark. Was it his voice or hers? Or was it both?

Soon it was over and this time she didn't suggest talking; she knew Richard was immediately drifting into sleep. For a long time she lay awake, her body at peace. But what of her soul? Everyone is a body and a soul, wasn't that what he had said way back, in what seemed like a lifetime ago even though it was hardly more than a year? He satisfied every hungry yearning in her body, but what of her soul? He was the best person she had ever known, he was good looking, he had a successful career, so why couldn't she give him her soul as willingly, eagerly, as she gave him her body. I want to love him – I do love him, of course I do – but I love him like I do Mum. If he suddenly walked into a room where I was, I would be pleased to see him, but my heart wouldn't race. Or does that only happen in silly books? In real life is the sort of safe, solid love I feel for him all there is? No, there should be more, there must be more. Please make it happen for me, make me know that wonderful churned-up excited sort of feeling – I know it exists, I used to feel it when I was with Wilhelm. But we were so young, perhaps I felt it because my hormones were just waking up and crying out. So why aren't they now? Why aren't they when I'm with Richard, dear Richard?

Despite herself, her eyes were closing; she was only just enough awake to know the comfortable, contented feeling of snuggling close to the warmth of his sleeping body.

There was no time to spare. By Christmas of that year the contract had been signed, the bank manager had arranged the loan, the order had been sent to three different nurseries for blackcurrant bushes, and Michael had brought his tractor and digger and grubbed up all the existing stock. The bushes were left in separate piles at the top of the slope just inside the boundary of

Crocker's End. Having started his farm on a shoestring and learned the hard way, Michael hated anything to be wasted, so he suggested they should put a notice in the local paper saying there were fruit bushes for sale at a nominal price, either in bulk or in twos and threes. But Richard favoured putting a board bearing the name of the fruit on each pile, and another outside in the lane saying: 'Fruit bushes for sale. Serve yourselves inside gate and put whatever you consider in the bucket. Thank you.'

'There are sure to be some who consider nothing the best price to pay, but, by and large, I'm sure folk will put what they can afford,' he said, speaking to none of them in particular.

'We aren't looking to make a lot of money out of them.' Verity had been listening and saying nothing up to that point. 'I wasn't deaf to what Cross had been saying for a long time, and I don't want us to take money for something that won't give the pleasure people hope for. So I want you to alter the wording of the notice. Say something like this: "If you can use any of these bushes, please help yourself. There is no charge, but, if you care to, you may put something in the bucket for the Society for the Blind." I'd like that. It would be my "thank you" for being so much more fortunate than a lot of poor souls. And it's all due to you, all three of you.' Then, with a slight shrug of her shoulders, an uncharacteristic movement which, quite wrongly, she believed would disguise her embarrassment, 'Well now, that's my little speech said and done with.'

The first consignment of bushes arrived on a Friday afternoon towards the end of January, too late to go to town to the Labour Exchange. So, with Michael making a third, Jackie and Richard started the long job of planting. Busy though they were, they made sure that Verity was involved, even though she could do no more than sit with Monty by her feet and imagine the scene before her. As so often happens during the winter months, the changeable weather had turned mild, but even so it wasn't the season for a deckchair, so Richard and Michael carried her easy chair almost to the top of Dilly Hill where they were to be working.

'Here comes your fur coat, Mum . . .' Jackie made sure she was well wrapped up. 'Hold out your arms. And your mother's muff and a hat. It's your pretty violet velour, your best hat.'

'For sitting about in?'

'Yes, that's it, for sitting about in. This is a day worthy of
your best hat. It's the first day of – of something splendid, with
the beginning of planting. Like laying the foundation stone on
some important building. We ought to have a fanfare of trum-
pets when the first bush is trodden in. Hold tight to my arm
and off we go.'

Richard saw them coming as they started up Dilly Hill, his
mind on what Jackie had told him that morning. It was much
too early to be sure, he reminded himself, but it was impossible
to stop his imagination rushing ahead through the months. Three
days late, she'd said. He could almost hear the pride in her voice
as she told him. But surely three days was too soon to even start
to hope? He watched her bringing his mother up the hill, saw
the easy companionship between them and felt a great rush of
love.

Jackie guided Verity to her chair and saw that she was comfortable with a rug over her knees and the faithful Monty close by
before she went back down the hill to collect her shovel from
the shed. This would surely be the best year she had ever lived:
she was seeing the beginning of her plan take shape, and even
though some people might say she was hardly late at all, she felt
certain it was the beginning of a baby. Seldom was she even a
day late, but this time, despite the long hours of quite heavy
outside work she had been doing, already three days had gone.
If we have a child, perhaps like him, perhaps like me, or a bit of
both of us, that must be the most natural way to make a marriage
complete. Perhaps then the horrid empty sort of feeling I sometimes get will be gone. Please make it be like that. Make me have
our baby and make that give us the sort of union we surely ought
to have. He's such a dear. He deserves a wife who thrills at the
sight of him. That's how he feels about me, I'm sure it is, which
is silly because I'm nothing special. Come on now, Jacqueline
Bennett, take your shovel and go and show the chaps you can
work as hard as they can.

First thing on the Monday morning she went to the Labour
Exchange and was able to get all the help they wanted, for it was
a time of unemployment and even something so temporary
was welcome. The national economy was in a bad way and men

were being stood down from jobs they had expected to be in for life. And even for Jackie there was a problem. She had always been remarkably healthy – even as a child she had had nothing worse than a mild dose of measles. Add to that the fact that she had never known anyone who had been pregnant, and so she was unprepared for the bouts of nausea that assailed her almost as she stepped out of bed each morning. She felt humiliated by her dash to the lavatory and the uncontrollable retching that left her weak and shaken.

'Poor Jackie,' Verity said when, later than usual, Jackie went to help her dress. 'I hate to hear you being so poorly.'

'I hate it too. I do try to be quiet. Does it go on for nine months, Mum? I'm not ill. Once it's over and I'm washed and dressed, it might never have happened.'

'It's only in the beginning, and then not everyone gets sick. You're sure you feel better? I can manage if you'll just put my water in the basin.'

'Honestly, I feel quite normal, as if it hadn't even happened. Today I'm going to start on the lower field and get a couple of the men to work there. We're getting on really well; by the end of another week the planting will be done.'

'I thought Jackie looked a bit off colour when I saw her just now. She works as hard as any of those chaps,' Michael said the following week as he drove Verity to her hairdressing appointment, having assured her that he had things to do in town while she was being prettied. 'She's such a slip of a girl, do you think she is doing too much?'

'A slip of a girl she may be, but you just try stopping her.' Then, deciding to take him into her confidence, 'It's early days yet, but the truth is, Michael, she's expecting, and she's so sick in the mornings, poor child. Such bad luck. Some women get it and some – like me – waltz though it with no problem. I'm so useless, I can't do anything to help her. Well, to be honest, no one can. She always says don't tell Richard, but he must see for himself at the weekends.'

'A baby, a grandchild for you, Verity. You say it's early days, but that outside work she does, shovelling the earth, bending around with the planting, it's enough to make her lose the baby.'

'Don't let her know I've told you about it, Michael.'

'I wouldn't dream of it, my dear. I was just thinking what I might do. It's my quietest time of the year and, as I've said before, Cload and Higgs are reliable. They do all the milking. You tell her that you know how I liked to feel I was involved when I was preparing the land, and say you believe I'm disappointed not to be asked if I can give a hand with the planting. That way she needn't know you've told me anything.'

'Oh Michael, what would I do without you?'

He didn't answer immediately, and then he said, 'And what would I do without you, Verity? You know how I feel about you, the same now as forty years ago. You've had a husband, I've had a wife – bless her, she was a real helpmeet – but nothing has, or ever could dim that first love.'

'All long years ago,' she answered softly, as if she were looking back and seeing them as they had been. 'I believe we would have drifted into marriage, we were so fond of each other. Then Ernie appeared and knocked everything else out of my head. It was as well you hadn't asked me to marry you because, if you had, I would have said yes, and then what a mess it would have been. But we've had a wonderful friendship all these years.'

'And so we always will have, till the end of our days.' Another mile and they would be on the edge of town. Perhaps he was a fool, he told himself; perhaps he was risking damaging the friendship that was precious to both of them. But, as if Fate was setting the scene, they were approaching a viewpoint where the road widened. So he drew the car to a halt and turned to take her hand in his.

'Are we there?' she asked, holding her head up and listening. 'The town sounds very quiet this morning.'

'No, we're on Colman's Ridge. Remember when we used to ride our bikes out here?'

'They were good, carefree days, weren't they?'

'Verity, can't we share the time we have left? Perhaps we've come full circle, taking us round to where we were all those years ago. When you get your freedom, marry me – I beg you, marry me. Don't say anything. Just listen.'

'No, Michael, I mustn't listen. Yes, we might well have married nearly forty years ago. Hardship wouldn't have mattered. We were young, we might have had a family, everything would have been different. But that would have been if I hadn't fallen so completely for Ernest. Now here we are, neither of us young any more, I've lost my looks—'

'You'll always be beautiful,' he interrupted.

'Don't, Michael. I know I have lost my looks, so let's be honest. It's frightening what the years do to us.' And as she said it she remembered Ernest using those same words when he had seen her with her hair cut as it used to be. 'When Ernie rejected me, at least he was honest. And I'm lucky, I have Richard and Jackie – and by the end of the summer there will be a grandchild.'

'Perhaps I'm being selfish, because I'm on my own and have never stopped wanting to be with you. I forget that you have a family.'

She turned to face him, imagining him as he'd been when she'd last had vision enough to know. 'Selfish? You? You are dearer to me than I know how to tell you. But marriage is for the young. Then you grow and change gradually, hardly aware of what time is doing to you. You accept each other without consciously seeing each other.'

'Darling Verity, are you saying you can only give me friendship? Perhaps at my age that ought to be all I want from you. It isn't. I want us to have a union that is complete. No, we're not young, we're falling apart at the seams a bit, I dare say, but that isn't important, except that it reminds us that time isn't on our side. But if you can give me nothing but friendship, then marry me and I'll settle for just that. It may not be all I dream of, but to have you as friend and wife would be greatly better than simply friend and neighbour.'

'It'll be ages before I'm free.'

'I've waited thirty-seven years – a little longer won't kill me. If only you will tell me you care enough to be my wife. Dearest Verity, what is it?' A tear escaped and ran down her cheek before she could wipe it away.

'I do try not to let it make any difference, but Michael, I don't know how I'd get on if I had to adjust to surroundings I didn't know.'

Very tenderly he drew her into his arms. 'Of course you can't leave Crocker's End. I'd rather anticipated – no, anticipated

isn't the right word – I'd dreamed of being there with you. I'd
sell the farm with cattle and machinery – with farming in the
doldrums it would sell better than most. I have a really good
herd, and a dairy farm at least brings a steady income. It would
raise enough money to be a help at Crocker's End. I suppose
I have no right to want to knuckle in on your family when I
haven't one of my own.'

'Don't say that. You are part of the family.'

'Well, think about it, Verity. Would it be such a bad thing,
being there for each other? You don't have to give me an answer
straightaway. I've thought about it for years . . .' Then, in a lighter
tone, 'So it's hardly fair of me to expect you only to want five
minutes.'

Finally the new bushes were all planted, and with regret the hired
workers took their last day's pay and went home, one or two
women to catch up on neglected housework, but the men to
sign on again at the Labour Exchange in town.

Every day Jackie was to be seen with her hoe, defying weeds
to choke the new plants, often with Michael helping, and at the
weekends Richard too, working with the same efficiency he
brought to everything he tackled. Jackie and Michael scratched
up the weeds, but the ground they covered never managed to
look as 'cared for' as that in the rows Richard cleared.

In the spring Verity and Ernest's divorce was heard. The solicitor had evidence that Ernest was living with Hilda Schofield,
and he also had confirmation from Verity that since Crocker's
End had always belonged to her, she expected no future support
from Ernest. So it was an open and shut case; by autumn of that
year, 1932, the Decree Absolute would be through and the final
line drawn under more than thirty-six years of marriage.

The young bushes thrived, and as spring came, Jackie, despite
her sickness in the first few weeks, had never felt more healthy
and vigorous. It seemed to her that she and the fruit farm were
progressing in unison. While her arms and legs were still as thin
as they ever had been, and her face probably thinner, by
midsummer she looked like a child with a pillow up her shirt.
But there was no stopping her working. Michael spent as many
hours as he could at Crocker's End, but he told no one that he

had put the farm in the hands of Scotchbrook & Downing, the auctioneers. He was approaching seventy and it was time he retired; he tried to believe that was the reason behind his half-formed plan. But in moments of truth, he knew exactly what he hoped for once that Decree Absolute was in Verity's hand.

When the manager from Findlay's came to see the crop, Jackie escorted him round the fields.

'Good fruit,' he approved, 'as good as I've seen. Another week and you'll be picking. I suggest you get the pickers in next week. We'll send the lorry with its containers on Thursday afternoon – late in the afternoon. The fresher the fruit, the better. Yes, you're going to have a good return here. Very healthy. Just the lush, ripe currants to be harvested at the first picking, mind. Then I'll arrange for the next collection on Tuesday and Friday of the following week. And we'll go on from there.'

Despite her disappointment that it hadn't been Charles Findlay himself who had come instead of this abrupt and unsmiling man, the end result was the same. Their first year was a success! Watching her visitor walk back to his car, Jackie's face broke into a smile without her even realizing it. She held her hands under her smock on her fast increasing bump, and felt herself to be one with the plump, lush fruit.

The call went out to the Labour Exchange, and by eight o'clock on the Thursday morning picking started. The casual workers were paid by the hour, and rather than go home at midday they were glad to keep working. Jackie had brought plenty of cider to help their sandwiches down.

'I've never seen such a hive of activity,' she said to Verity, who sat in the shade of a tall elm 'watching with her ears'. Michael was helping too, but although he wasn't prepared to admit it, he found it a very tiring job. How Jackie kept going he didn't know, but she looked an absolute picture, browned by her hours in the open air, taking pregnancy in her stride in the way nature intended.

The lorry arrived at about six o'clock and the baskets of blackcurrants were emptied into the large metal containers brought for the purpose, then weighed on scales in the lorry. And so ended the first day of the blackcurrant harvest. The workers were paid and went off promising to be back by seven thirty the following Tuesday.

'What a day!' There was satisfaction in Michael's voice. 'Are you going to invite me to supper?'

'I reckon we will, don't you, Mum? And probably invite you to stay and help with the washing up too, if you're a good boy,' Jackie teased. Then, more seriously, 'Wasn't it exciting, though? Seeing the lorry come, knowing how well we've done. I wish Richard could have been here for our first collection. It's only ham salad for supper, nothing very much to feed a man on.'

'It sounds just the thing,' he said. 'Now let me set the table and earn my keep.'

'OK, you know where everything is – and if you don't, Mum can soon tell you. I just want to make sure the baskets are all put away. You're the farmer, you ought to know about weather, but I can sort of smell a storm in the air. We don't want the fruit baskets getting wet. I won't be many minutes.'

But half an hour later she still wasn't back. They heard the first long rumble of thunder.

'Whatever can she be doing?' Verity said anxiously. 'Michael, be a dear and go and fetch her in. She'll go on till she drops; she just won't admit to getting tired.'

'I'll tell her we're starving, that'll bring her in.'

But although he walked all the way around the fruit fields, there was no sign of her. He must have just missed her somehow, and when he got back to the house he'd find her already there. Heavy spots of rain accompanied the lightning as he retraced his steps in the failing light. What instinct made him open the door of the shed he didn't know; if she'd found some job to do in there she would have switched the light on. Opening the door he saw the baskets were strewn across the floor instead of being in a stack. And then he saw her.

Eight

It took all Michael's strength to lift Jackie's unconscious body. No use wondering what had happened; what concerned him was whether she had damaged herself in her fall. Staggering under the weight and puffing like a traction engine, he made his way towards the yard and the back door.

'What's happened?' He heard the slur in her whispered question, but all he was aware of was a rush of thankfulness. She was conscious.

'You must have had a fall,' he gasped, fighting for breath under the strain of carrying her. 'You've cut your head. Hold on tight to me.' Talking was proving too much for him as he struggled to breathe and thankfully leant against the barn where her car was parked.

'. . . be all right . . .' She tried to force her voice to sound normal. 'My head hurts, but I can walk now.'

By that time there was steady rain. Of the two of them she looked more capable now than he did as he gently stood her on her feet, keeping a firm hold on her. He mustn't let her guess what an effort it was for him to take each gasp as the pain in his chest tightened. They moved on towards the house, and whether he was supporting her or she him they didn't question. Without warning she felt the return of the pain that had taken her by surprise in the hut as she had reached to add the last basket to the stack. That's when she had lost her balance and fallen, knocking her head on the stone sill of the window . . . Now it was happening again and she let out an involuntary cry, but Michael was using every scrap of concentration to walk the last steps to the house so he didn't notice.

'What's happened? You were such a long time,' Verity greeted them as she heard them come from the yard into the kitchen. 'Has the rain started?'

'I'd fallen in the shed.' Jackie was proud of herself. Now that the pain was loosening its grip, no actress could have done better.

'Knocked myself out. He carried me all the way till we got back
to the barn.'

Now Verity's concern was all for Michael, who hadn't spoken.
Her perception told her that something was wrong, even though
she couldn't see his expression as he leant against the door with
his eyes closed.

'Michael, Michael, whereabouts are you?' With her arms out
she moved uncertainly in the direction of the sound of his painful
breathing, but with his eyes closed he didn't see her. Following
the sound, her outstretched hand came into contact with his
heaving chest, and gently, shaken by tenderness, with the flat of
her hand she started to massage him. Jackie was forgotten. 'Darling
Michael, you shouldn't have carried her. She was too heavy.' He
covered her hand with his, pressing it tight against him. Darling
Michael, she had said. He wanted to take her in his arms . . . if
only the pain in his chest would lose its grip, but instead the
vice-like tightness spread to his shoulders and jaw. 'Have to sit
down . . . a minute . . . be all right.'

'Jackie, help him to my comfy chair. Please God, don't let him
be ill.' She hardly knew she said it. But Jackie didn't move. It was
Michael who realized something was wrong, not just with him
but with Jackie, too. She was gripping the back of one of the
kitchen chairs, her knuckles white, her face shining with sweat.

'Jackie?' He didn't put the question into words.

'Can't be . . . too soon . . .' She was speaking with an effort.
'Going off . . . all right in a minute.' It took every ounce of her
willpower to speak or even to think coherently.

All right in a minute . . . silently Michael repeated her words.
So too would he be; he must be. It didn't hurt quite as much to
breathe, but he was afraid to move in case the pain came back,
like a vice tightening in his chest, in his shoulders and jaw.

'Must get Edna Trout,' he whispered. 'Must phone.' But to reach
the phone he would have to cross the room and the hall. This
sort of fear was an unknown to him. He and Jackie looked at
each other, both helpless in a situation they couldn't control.

With that uncanny instinct she had gained with the loss of
her sight, Verity knew she had to be the one to phone the farm.
But first she must get Michael into the easy chair where she
spent so much of her life. She'd think about Jackie in a minute,

poor Jackie, but until Michael was cared for everything else must wait.

'Lean on me, Michael. It's only a few steps. You'll feel better in the armchair.' Walking on her own she knew how many steps from door to chair, but with one arm around Michael and he putting more weight on her than he realized, she held her other arm in front of her, moving it to make sure they didn't walk into anything. When her hand came into contact with the back of the chair, she sent up a silent 'thank you'.

'There you are. Now you just sit quietly for a few minutes and you'll feel better. I'm going to phone and ask Mrs Trout to come over. That's what you wanted?'

In a house she knew so well, Verity managed to find the telephone on the wall of the hall, picked up the receiver and waited for Annie Butcher to answer. Annie and her husband Derek kept the village store at the back of which, behind a grill, was the counter of the post office and a switchboard.

'Number please,' came Annie's 'telephone' voice.

'Will you give me Dinkley 457, Annie? This is Dinkley 149.'

'Hold the line, Mrs Bennett. It's ringing for you.' Annie enjoyed this part of her job; it gave her a real feeling of importance.

'Hello,' Edna Trout answered, expecting it would be Michael.

'Mrs Trout, this is Verity Bennett. Can you get on your bike and come over? I don't want to fuss unnecessarily, but it's not like Michael to admit anything is wrong with him. And Jackie, she's had a fall and they say she's hurt her head. I'm no use to either of them. And just in case – in case of what I don't know – but to be on the safe side could you bring your night things, and Michael's too?'

'Now don't you worry, Mrs Bennett. I'll get my bike and be with you before you know it.'

Relief almost took Verity's fears away. Once Mrs Trout arrived she would see just what had to be done.

Richard left London early, wanting to be home in time for Findlay's first collection. And so he might have been but for the fact that when he was no more than halfway he felt a change in the steering: the car was pulling to the left. He stopped and got out, hoping he was wrong, but sure he was right. Yes, the front nearside tyre was almost flat. Changing a wheel ought not to have delayed him too much, but on that occasion everything seemed set against him, or so he believed. The truth was that in all the years he had driven he had never changed a wheel. How Ernest would have mocked to see 'Einstein' struggling to jack the car up, not being able to get a start on unscrewing the nuts. Then, when finally he managed to get the spare wheel firmly on and let the jack down, he could see at a glance it had less air in it than the other three. So he drove on carefully until he reached a garage and had it inflated. All in all, instead of arriving earlier than usual, he arrived later.

Drawing up in his usual parking place at Crocker's End, he saw that Michael's car was still there, also two bicycles propped against the wall. Usually as soon as they heard his car someone would come out into the yard to meet him, but not this evening. The collection must be over; the workers had gone home. The rain had stopped and silence and stillness lay across the fields. How peaceful it was; already the agitation he'd felt at his inadequacy in doing a simple job like changing a wheel was calmed. Taking his briefcase off the passenger seat, he slammed the car door, subconsciously expecting the sound would bring out the reception committee. Instead, in the kitchen he found his mother kneeling in front of Michael, a scene so unexpected that he felt a second's resentment. Then he realized something was wrong.

'Mother, is everything all right?'

'Oh, Richard, thank goodness you're home. The baby's being born. No, dear, you can't go up . . .' Her sharp hearing and uncanny instinct had told her he was across the kitchen and on his way to Jackie. 'Mrs Hilliard, the laying-in-nurse, is up there with her, and Mrs Trout has come. She's with them, fetching anything Mrs Hilliard needs. I'm no use at all.'

'You've been wonderful.' Michael spoke for the first time, his voice lacking its usual vigour. 'She made the phone calls and got Jackie upstairs.'

'Of course I can go up!' By contrast, Richard spoke loudly, defying argument. But his mother heard the underlying fear.

'No, it'll worry Jackie. Mrs Hilliard knows what she's doing. It's all happened so quickly. She was all right when the workers went home, then she went to the shed . . .' And so Verity told him the whole story, ending with, 'The pains were coming so quickly I knew we must get Mrs Hilliard. Six weeks early, and in such a hurry to get into the world. By the time Mrs Hilliard got her on to the bed the baby's head was coming – Mrs Trout told us when she came down for hot water.'

'How long ago was that?'

'No time at all. But when it gets to that stage it can't be long. Don't disturb her, dear, she needs all her strength without having a husband to consider. But Richard, I want Michael to have a drop of brandy. He's had a sleep, and he's much better. But a brandy will do him good.'

'And you too, my boy, you look as if you could use one.' Michael sounded better by the minute. As long as he sat still and didn't breathe too deeply, the pain had gone, and yet he was frightened that one wrong move and it would be back. When Richard passed him his brandy he savoured even the smell of it, taking in its comforting warmth.

'Where's yours? Aren't you having one? It'd do you good.'

Richard shook his head. Perhaps Michael was right, for he had never in his life felt as he did: hollow, frightened, trembling, and even a bit sick. But that was nothing to what his beloved Jackie was enduring.

'I'm not going up to her,' he said as he made for the door, but he must get nearer to her, somewhere he could hear. And that somewhere was the landing outside the closed door of their bedroom.

'Keep pushing, and again, another big push,' said a voice he didn't recognize. That must be the laying-in nurse.

'If only you had something you could give the poor wee girl. Another pain?' And as if in answer he heard Jackie's sharp intake of breath and her soft, pathetic moan that tore at his heart.

'Push, harder, harder, head's right through, again, again, big push for the shoulders.' Mrs Hilliard's encouraging words, and from Jackie a scream that might have come from the depths of hell. 'That's it, good girl. The shoulders are through. Just one more huge, huge push. Here we are, that's my lovely girl.'

'A bonny wee boy,' Edna Trout said. 'What a brave girl she's been.' But her last words were almost lost in the baby's first cry.

'It's always a relief when they give a cry. My word, but if she'd gone full term he would have been a whopper. Now then, Mrs Bennett, my dear, this is no time for tears.'

And perhaps it wasn't, but relief expresses itself in many ways. Richard's body was shaken with silent sobs as he walked blindly along the corridor to the 'small spare', closing the door firmly behind him. There was no logic in the emotion – surely he had never had more cause for joy – yet he could no more control his sobs than he could stop the way his whole body shook. Then, following instinct rather than any coherent thought, he dropped to his knees by the side of the single bed. Gradually he became calmer and fear gave way to thankfulness.

Back in the corridor he could hear the activity in the bedroom: the splashing of water and clanking of china against a metal pail. Whatever mysteries were being performed, Mrs Hilliard had a willing helper in Edna Trout, so Richard locked himself in the bathroom where, from the mirror, the face of a stranger looked back at him. Only now did he remember how dirty he'd got as he'd battled to change the wheel: oil on his face, on his shirt, filthy hands, and add to all that bloodshot eyes and hair that looked as if he didn't possess a comb. Stripped to the waist, he washed. There was no hope of a clean shirt, for all his clothes were in the bedroom, but once his jacket was on, the oil wouldn't show. Indeed he looked and felt like himself again.

Coming out into the corridor he bumped into Edna Trout.

'Oh, you're home, Mr Bennett. You've got a fine son. I was just coming down to say when you came home you could come up, just for a quick peep. The nurse is in there still, but she'll give you a few seconds with Jackie – Mrs Bennett, I mean. Such a brave girl she was, but now she's tired right out, and no wonder.'

Richard didn't wait to answer, nor yet to hear the last of what she told him. Going into the bedroom he saw only Jackie, washed now and in a clean nightgown. Only half awake, she didn't hear him come in. Without a glance at Mrs Hilliard he went to the side of the bed and dropped to his knees, just as he had in the 'small spare'. Jackie didn't seem aware of him as she lay with her eyes closed. Her face was parchment white, her hair still wet with perspiration. Gently he took her hand, holding it to his cheek; his precious Jackie. In those seconds as he gazed at her, every previous emotion seemed to shrink into insignificance.

She opened her eyes, muttered, 'We've . . . son . . .' Then, as if her eyelids were too heavy, she closed them again.

'She needs her sleep. What about this boy of yours? Don't you want to say how-do-you-do to him? A fine young man he is, perfect in wind and limb, as you might say. Six weeks early, but like I was saying to Mrs Trout, what a blessing he didn't make her go full term. Having their young can be tough on small-built girls, but he was an obliging little poppet and no mistake. Here he is then, do you want to have a hold of him?'

And so Richard, with his aloof and unemotional manner, took his newborn six-pound son in his arms. Thrown off balance by his recent tears, weakened by something akin to worship as he'd knelt by Jackie's bed, now holding the tiny form he ached with tenderness.

'I want to take him down to show my mother,' he said to Mrs Hilliard. 'Better to take him down than to ask her to climb the stairs.'

'Poor soul, her first grandchild and she won't be able to see how perfect he is.'

'She'll be able to hold him.'

'Jacqueline's asleep,' he announced as he carried the little bundle into the kitchen. 'But I've brought your grandson down so that you can get acquainted. Are you all right perched where you are, or do you want to move to a chair?'

From where she was, on the arm of Michael's chair, she held out her arms. 'I'll have him here.' Then, the baby safely in her arms, she held him with her left arm and moved her right hand from the top of his head to the end of the bundle. He was wrapped securely in a soft shawl, his arms anchored so that he couldn't free them. Richard watched his mother, his Adam's apple seeming to block his throat. What was the matter with him? He should be celebrating, opening champagne, yet it took all his willpower to stop him sitting on one of those wooden chairs at the kitchen table and crying from sheer emotional exhaustion.

'What a day this has been,' Verity said, as if she had read his thoughts. 'The fifteenth of July 1932: the newest member of the family born on the day that Crocker's End has its own rebirth; the day Michael gave me – and himself, although he won't admit it now that he feels better – a fright that opened my eyes. So,

Richard darling, you're not the only one to be congratulated. Michael and I may be what he calls 'going at the seams', but it's never too late to look for happiness. We are going to be married. What do you think about that?'

'You really want to know?' He bent over and kissed her lined forehead. 'For as long as I can remember, when I've seen you two together, I've been conscious of what, with a child's limited vocabulary, I secretly called a ring of magic. Now I might describe it differently, but with you two it's still the same. I'm absolutely delighted.' He held his hand towards Michael who made a move to stand. 'No, don't get up.'

'I shall go home a happy man tonight, I can tell you,' Michael said, holding Richard's hand in a firm grasp. 'Your mother says I gave us both a fright, and by God, Richard, I've never been so scared in my life. Never been less than a hundred per cent, I suppose I took good health for granted. But listen, I've been waiting for Verity's answer for – I suppose I have to say for months, but in truth for as long as I've known her. I'd already decided that if she agreed to let us share the rest of our time together I would put the farm up for sale. I would never expect her to move, she knows that. It won't fetch a fortune, farming is at rock bottom. But then, these days, so is so much more. Today made me realize that, whatever her answer, it was time I sold up. I worry about my two chaps; they've been with me a long time. Perhaps when I find someone to take the place, their jobs might be safe. Both of them married and with children, you can't just throw families on the street. God knows there is unemployment enough.'

'Um,' Richard nodded, turning over the situation of the two loyal herdsmen. 'Don't worry about it tonight,; tonight we owe ourselves a few hours of – of thankfulness for where the day has brought us.' But even as he spoke the embryo of an idea was forming in his mind.

'Amen to that,' Michael agreed. 'Now, my son, how about relieving your mother of this new young man and letting me get acquainted with him.'

Richard took the bundle from Verity and put it into Michael's outstretched arms, while Verity moved from the arm of the chair to feel her way to kneel between Michael's parted knees.

* * *

That July saw the start of a new order at Crocker's End. There was no reason for Verity and Michael to wait, and so they were married in the Register Office at the Town Hall almost a year to the day after Richard and Jackie had taken their vows in the village church.

When Michael had first suggested marriage, Verity had shied away from living intimately with any man except Ernest. Marriage was for the young, she had believed. She recalled the heady excitement of letting Ernest undress her, of seeing the reaction of his own body, of feeling the touch of his hand on her. She had felt like a queen, knowing that she had the power to arouse such passion in him; she had had pride in her young and supple body. But what now? She may well have many years ahead of her, but youth was far behind. She didn't even know what she looked like any longer. Then there was something else there was no running away from: when Ernest had come home at night wanting to find sexual satisfaction, she had found no pleasure in his energetic pounding. It hadn't been like that when they'd been young: then she had felt exalted; occasionally she had reached a climax surely as powerful as his own. But that was all long ago. Michael had told her that even though he wanted the complete union of marriage, if she wasn't prepared for it, just as long as they could be together he would ask for nothing more. But on those terms she couldn't accept him.

On leaving the Register Office, the bride and groom, with Richard, Jackie, ten-week-old Toby and Mrs Trout had gone to lunch in the Chetwyn Hotel on the far side of town. Then Mrs Trout had gone back to the farm, Michael and Verity to Crocker's End, and Richard, Jackie and Toby, with a large bundle of baby requirements and a weekend case for themselves, had gone to a hotel in Shrewsbury for the night.

At Crocker's End, Michael grilled two prime steaks and cooked jacket potatoes before cutting Verity's into bite-size pieces.

'Here's a first,' he said, holding her chair ready for her to sit to the table, 'the first meal for my wife.' Then, as he pushed her close enough to the table he leant over her and tenderly kissed her forehead. 'The first of many, my darling, beautiful wife.'

'Silly,' she mumbled, embarrassed. 'The trouble is, Michael, I've no idea what I even look like any longer. Perhaps it's just as well.'

'Strange, that,' he said thoughtfully, 'it's something I've never considered. So let me give you a word picture, an accurate word picture, I promise. Not just of you but of me, too. You are as straight backed as ever you were, just as slim, too. Your hair isn't grey, it's a beautiful snowy white. Your face still has that elfin look I first fell in love with, but it's not the face of a baby elf any longer. Yes, it is lined. But who would have it any different? To live to be our sort of ages and not have lines to show for it would simply mean life hadn't touched us. Your eyes may not see, but they are as bright as ever they were.' Then, taking her hands in his, 'My blessed Verity, at last life has brought us to where we should be. Damned old fool I am.' And with her sharp hearing she was aware of what might have been missed by folk with normal sight. 'Never been so happy, so why the devil do I feel like this?' He raised her hand to his wet cheek.

'No time for weeping,' she told him gently. Then, with a new briskness in her voice, 'Now, I've heard about me – probably with more flattery than accuracy – so what about you?'

'Me? I'm an old fool knocking seventy, can't read without my glasses – or a magnifying glass if I want a telephone number – my teeth aren't my own, but I promise you I don't take them out at night, I still feel capable of doing everything I could do forty years ago, it's only when I try that nature knocks me down and usually only with aching joints. What hair I've still got is grey – not a beautiful white like yours. I've lost my waist. But, hey, my darling, as a couple we are fine.' She heard the pop of a champagne cork and then he guided her hand to hold her glass, 'So let's drink to *us*. May we live to be a hundred. God bless you my sweet Verity.'

It was surprisingly natural for her to let him help her undress. She found herself looking back at the hurt and sense of desolation she had felt when Ernest had cast her aside and realized just how far life had brought her. She thought of her wedding night with him, remembered the thrill of excitement. How different it was this time; life had indeed moved on and had brought her a new peace.

'God's in His heaven and all's right with the world,' she murmured as she pulled the bedcovers over her.

'Amen to that.'

Another minute or two and he climbed in to lay by her side, gently taking her hand. From there what was more natural than for her to snuggle close to him, to feel his arms holding her. Now, though, excitement did stir within her just as she knew it did within him. Again her mind carried her back to Ernest, coming in late, frustrated, tense, hungry for sex (probably because that woman hadn't been able to give him what he wanted, Verity thought. Yet even as the thought came to her, she knew the bitterness and hatred she had originally felt were fading). Her hand moved to caress Michael, a silent message to him that her doubts were gone.

And so, after loving her for more than half his life, at last Michael's dreams became reality. With Ernest any satisfaction for her had been in knowing she could give him what he wanted. With Michael there was that, but so much more. He awoke desires in her she had forgotten and she travelled with him until together they found fulfilment. Later, lying awake, she smiled. It wasn't the bright, ever-ready smile that defied pity; she wasn't even aware of it as she lay there, utterly content. Michael was already asleep, but how comforting it was to put out her hand and feel the warmth of him by her side.

When Toby was sixteen months old, Jackie had her second child, a daughter. Even that, Richard seemed to organize in the right order, first a son and then a daughter. She had sailed through her first pregnancy, never letting it keep her away from the work she loved, but the second time was less straightforward. She expected to be confined at home with Mrs Hilliard in attendance, but when the time came the laying-in nurse had to send for the doctor, the doctor had to send for the ambulance, and Jackie was taken to hospital. It was in the middle of a Saturday night, and while they waited for the ambulance the doctor talked to Richard about the inadvisability of her going through another pregnancy. Babies should be born head first, but this one was a breach and would have to come into the world by Caesarean section.

'I managed to turn it,' he told Richard, 'but as soon as she strained, it somersaulted back. The first confinement did her no good. You remember the child rushed into the world with almost no warning and she was badly torn internally? Now this one is difficult, she has fought for hours. Would two children not satisfy you both?' He was a kindly man who had known the Bennetts for years. 'I advise you both to consider her having a more permanent birth control devise fitted – a coil? It allows nature to reject fertilization of the egg. Should you both have a change of heart at some later time, it can be removed, but I really do advise you against it. Certainly there are other precautionary measures, but there's many a slip. Ah, I hear the ambulance.'

'She must never go through this again.' In his present state of panic, Richard sounded aggressive.

Crocker's End was having a wakeful night. No one had attempted to go to bed; even Mrs Trout, who had moved in as soon as the farm was sold and had taken over the role of housekeeper at Michael's expense, was still up. The only one asleep was Toby, and Mrs Trout was keeping an ear open in case the commotion disturbed him.

When the stretcher bearers brought Jackie down the stairs she was only semi-conscious. She knew she was being carried but had no interest, she was drowning in pain, pain which had been dulled by sedatives. Less than two hours later it was all over: the emergency operation had brought a beautiful baby girl into the world. In their relief they all looked to a cloudless future.

On the surface there was little change to the pattern of life at Crocker's End; after all, one small child or two make little difference. Of course there were the bad moments, just as there must be in any household made up of three generations – days when the children were fractious, which, in turn, made Jackie on edge and aware that their home wasn't their own. And from Michael and Verity's angle, there were days when they would have liked to have mealtimes without one or other of the children spilling food or hammering the wooden tray of the high chair with whoops of delight. But under it all there was affection and, usually, tolerance. So why was Jackie increasingly aware of a shadow of depression that had never been part of her character?

She worked outside for hours of every day, usually taking with her the pram or pushchair, depending on the age of the occupant. But by the summer of 1936, four-year-old Toby liked nothing better than to have his seaside spade and dig the earth between the bushes, copying the hoeing he watched going on. And as with whatever he did, his little sister Dulcie wanted to do the same as she stumbled along in his wake. Jackie loved her children dearly, just as she loved the hours she spent working, and yet increasingly she felt there was something lacking in her life.

The acreage of Crocker's End had increased, something that had come out of an idea of Richard's. Knowing Michael's concern for the future of his two faithful herdsmen, and in particular of their families, he had suggested that instead of applying to the Labour Exchange for workers at Crocker's End, the opportunity should be offered for them to come to the fruit farm. He had imagined that when Michael's farm was sold, if the two herdsmen agreed to his idea and were keen to learn about growing fruit, they would find accommodation to rent locally so that their children could still attend the village school. It wasn't so much the disruption to the children he had in mind, rather it was that with so much unemployment in the country, at least they would be kept in work. But one thought had led to another, and because the farm cottages were on the extreme edge of the slope adjoining Dilly Hill, Michael had made an offer: if he had the boundaries of the farm redrawn, the neighbouring hill and the cottages could become part of Crocker's End, the men and their families could stay in their homes, and what had been a grazing field could be planted out with more bushes. That way he would feel he had made an input at Crocker's End.

'But you may find it hard to sell without workers' accommodation,' Richard had warned.

'When it sells it'll be to a working farmer – just as I was when I was younger. And these days no working farmer is going to want to pay out good money for work he can do himself. I tell you, Richard, today there's no living to be made on the land. We fed the nation through four years of war, and since then we've been let down by each successive government.' Michael hadn't been prepared to look for difficulties.

So it was that by the time the toddlers were big enough to follow Jackie as she worked, Crocker's End was a major producer for Findlay's and its future seemed assured. So surely everything in Jackie's life was perfect. She had a loyal husband, two healthy and adorable children, her mother-in-law was also her friend, she was fond of her father-in-law and, an added bonus, Edna Trout had taken over much of the running of the house, even looking after the children if Jackie had to go out. So why was it that she felt flat – yes, *flat*, there was no better way of describing what for many people would have become depression. One thing Jackie relished in life was a challenge: the challenge of a completely new life when she'd come to Crocker's End; the challenge of changing the face of the fruit farm and giving it a new future; the challenge of building a full and happy marriage based on friendship and respect. When she'd put what she had inherited from her uncle into the future she foresaw for the fruit farm, she had felt it really was partly hers. But now Michael had come into the equation. She ought not to resent it, she told herself over and over, and yet because his share – especially married to Verity – was greater than hers, she felt pushed out. What was she but the wife of the son who, until he married her, had taken almost no interest in Crocker's End?

She tried to persuade herself that that was the reason for the cloud that would descend on her so often and without warning or logic. But honesty always got the better of her and her mind went to that other challenge: the challenge to build a joyous and complete union out of her marriage. Being the person she was, she made herself look squarely at where life had brought them all, and to face the truth that anything lacking must lie within herself. Richard was steadfast and unchanging. Dear, devoted Richard – and if the word 'dull' automatically wanted to follow she pushed it aside without giving it a chance – with his orderly life and his love for her and their children. She was lucky, she told herself so a dozen times a day, and there were moments when she knew it to be true. So why had she this longing for something unknown, something that would satisfy every starved and only half-understood emotion?

The children had outgrown cots and had their single beds in the room that used to be Richard's. They were brought up to a strict routine, partly out of fairness to Verity and Michael, and partly because the idea of Richard's children having anything less than order in their days would have been unthinkable. Of course on fine summer evenings Jackie could have broken the rules and let them play out of doors after their supper, but she knew that would be storing up trouble. So, as the hall clock struck the half hour at half past seven, they were both in bed. Having opened the top window, she pulled down the blind to keep out the long and tempting rays of evening sunshine.

'Not fair, Mum,' Toby objected. 'Why can't we wait up to see Dad when he gets home?' And in her heart she agreed with him, for Richard's return was the excitement of Fridays.

'Goodness knows what time that will be, Toby. He's been so busy lately, he's often very late. You get to sleep quickly, then you can both come in our bed and wake him up in the morning.'

Toby was no fool, he recognized bribery when he saw it. Not so Dulcie. Her little face positively beamed at the thought of morning and, as if to hurry it along, she shut her eyes tight. Jackie dropped a kiss on each head then left them, shutting the door firmly behind her. Instead of going downstairs she crossed the passage and went into her own room where she sat idly on the edge of the bed, gazing out of the open window at the familiar scene. Next week would see another season coming full circle; the outside helpers were booked to start picking the first of the ripened fruit on Monday morning. From the far side of the slope that used to belong to the farm she heard the children from the cottages playing; from somewhere even more distant a dog barked. Friday evening and, despite the white lie she had told the children, she knew that by now Richard would be on his way home, perhaps even within minutes she would see his car turn into the drive. Fridays were the highlight of her week, but was it because she had missed his company or was it because she knew that tonight every nerve in her body would be alive, her senses would race, and just for a few moments she would clutch at the belief that her life was full and she loved him utterly. She would tell herself that this was love – and in those moments she would believe it.

From between two rows of blackcurrant bushes she saw Michael and Verity appear. How could she, a woman twenty-six years old, envy the elderly couple? And yet, watching them, that's just what she did. They stopped walking and turned to each other, talking, laughing, his arm still round her shoulder. But of course he kept his hand on her, it gave her assurance. A woman with no sight and you envy her? Thinking it, Jackie was ashamed. But look at the way Verity bumped her head against him, like an over-affectionate animal, and the way he drew her towards him just for a second. All of it so natural, so much part of their lives. Jackie raised her face towards the evening sun, feeling its warmth. But it brought her no comfort, only a longing for something and she knew not what. Her small, suntanned hands cupped her breasts, and having no power – nor yet any will – to stop herself, she moved her thumbs on her hardened nipples. If only she could put the clock forward; if only now, this very moment, Richard could give her what she craved. What was the matter with her that she couldn't be content to live without sex from Sundays until Fridays? Her memory carried her back, as it so often did, to the times before she had known Richard, times when she had followed every instinct to find that elusive miracle. And after-wards all she had known had been shame. But that had been because of Wilhelm, because he had cast her aside. Now her life was different, now she was utterly sure of Richard's love, just as sure as she was that tonight for both of them the miracle would be there. If she were a normal, happily married woman – and she was happily married, time and again she told herself so – she would be content, and would lovemaking become part of a comfortable routine? No, it must never do that, or it would be as – she pulled her thoughts up sharply as the word 'dull' formed in her mind.

Yet, half an hour or so later, with Richard home and the four of them chatting about the week's happenings, no one could possible guess at where her thoughts had carried her in the soli-tude of the bedroom. There was an air of excitement about her. But of course there would be: Monday was to see the beginning of harvesting the currants, the culmination of a year's work.

When she had been at the newspaper shop she had read the news avidly. Now she was often ashamed at how many days went by and she hardly read the headlines. And on that Friday she only half listened as Richard and Michael talked about the rise of mili-tarism in Nazi Germany. It wasn't anything new and seemed to her as distant from the peace of Crocker's End as the man in the moon.

So the months went by, season following season. They had a

large glasshouse built and early each year Jackie took cuttings and grew them on to form new bushes. She who had come to Crocker's End knowing nothing of country ways was becoming an authority on the propagation of their stock. As Michael said to Verity, 'You'd think she was a descendant of your people. No natural daughter could have more flair than Jackie.'

Verity laughed. 'That's more than we could ever say of darling Richard, Ernest's Einstein.'

That was in the early summer of 1939. Like ostriches with their heads buried in the sand, people were clinging to the hope that, as Neville Chamberlain had assured them when he'd returned from meeting Adolf Hitler the previous year, there would be 'peace in our time'. If they took their heads out of the sand they were faced with the glaring fact that Germany had amassed a large and well-trained army, that planes were being brought off the production line as no country anticipating stable peace would do.

It was in the middle of a Wednesday afternoon that Richard arrived home unexpectedly. He parked in his usual place, and before he had even turned off the engine Jackie appeared.

'Is something wrong?' she asked him, opening the car door.

'On the contrary.' He got out, kissed her cheek then slammed the car door, in that order. 'I'm moving out from the London department. There's a new place starting in Buckinghamshire and I'm being transferred there.'

'Is that good?'

'It should be most interesting – and challenging. Yes, Jacqueline, it's good from my point of view. I've been there this morning and fixed up somewhere to stay. I take up my post on Monday, so you have me home until Sunday evening.' He sounded so matter-of-fact. She wanted to be pleased, excited even, that they had these extra days together so unexpectedly, but his manner disappointed her. Then, with a sudden change of expression, his eyes were bright as he took her hand in his. 'Can you stand having a husband underfoot for a few days?'

She laughed, raising his hand to rub her face against it. 'Toby and Dulcie will feel really badly treated, having to go to school. Tell me about the new job, you say from your point of view it's better?'

'It's a completely new set-up and, I fear, I can say no more than that. This morning I had to swear an oath of secrecy.'

'How stupid.' She felt rebuffed.

'I wish I could agree with you. It's no use running from the truth, Jacqueline. We have to be prepared. War was averted last year, but at some stage it will happen. And don't you think we have a lot to be grateful for that Chamberlain managed to get us breathing space?'

She was puzzled by his answer.

'I don't see what that has to do with your being moved out of London and it being so hush-hush that you can't tell even *me*. Are you being moved to some munitions place?'

He laughed. 'Now, can you see me being any use there? It's as much as I can manage to change a light bulb. No, darling, basically nothing changes with the work I do. As my father used to say, all I'm fit for is doing sums.' It was an attempt to change the subject, but sensing that she was hurt at being excluded, he added, 'I wish I could tell you, Jacqueline. I know anything I said would be safe with you. But I have given my word.'

Dear Richard, she thought. Anyway, she decided, even if he told her she wouldn't understand.

'I was just going to get ready to meet the children from school. Hurry up and get that dreary suit off and we'll go together. Go and give Mum a nice surprise. She's all on her own, Michael has gone to have something looked at on his car.'

Afterwards, she was to look back on that day as the end of an era, even though it wasn't strictly true.

They had been gone no longer than five minutes when another car came down the slope from the lane. The driver got out and walked through the yard to the back door, then let himself in. Finding no one in the kitchen he crossed the hall and went into the drawing room.

'Verity?' Why he put a query into his tone he didn't know.

She turned in her chair, her face moving towards the sound of his voice.

'Ernest? Are you on your own?' But what difference could it make to her whether he'd come by himself or brought Hilda with him?

'You knew my voice the moment I spoke. Dear Verity. You look just the same, not a day older.'

'Hardly true after eight years. But it's of no importance. What brings you back from your northern retreat?'

'Perhaps it's the climate of war looming. It makes us all see things clearly, sift the dross from the gold.' Then, walking soundlessly on the carpeted floor, he bent to kiss her.

'You didn't answer me. Is Mrs – Schofield? Bennett? – is she with you?'

'I am alone. Verity, my eyes have been opened. For nearly four decades you and I were together, we can't turn our backs on that as if it counted for nothing. I hurt you when I left you, I know I did. And I am truly, honestly, desperately sorry. I suppose I was chasing my youth.'

'You'd left it a bit late for that,' she answered, 'it must have been quite a chase.'

'I can't blame you if you're bitter, darling Verity. I did you a dreadful wrong, but love, real genuine love like you had – and still have – for me, is full of understanding.'

'Oh yes, I have understanding. And it's love that has given it to me—'

'So we'll start again. I see you've made great changes outside. Is the place doing well? How have you managed without a man at the helm?'

'I said love has given me understanding, and that's true. But for us it's over, Ernest. Can you not see that I wear a wedding ring?'

'But of course you do. I remember the day I put it on your finger.'

'And I remember the day I took it off again – the day you left. I'm sorry if you've been imagining me sitting at home pining for you. If you'd stayed here and things had gone on as they were, I would probably never have found the happiness that is mine now. So I should be grateful to you. Certainly I wish you no harm. Michael and I are married and I have realized just how empty our life together was. So go back to your lady friend – wife, or whatever she is.'

'You married Michael Southwell? But what the devil are you doing living here? Why aren't you at the farm?'

In a quiet, gentle voice she told him about the sale of the farm and about Jackie being married to Richard and living there with the two children. There was no rancour in her tone. But she wished he hadn't come; she wished he would leave. The past might have lost its ability to hurt her, but resurrecting it cast a shadow.

'So what have you done with your lady friend?'

'There's going to be war, we've seen it coming for some time. She has taken the boys back to their homeland.'

'Ah.' Just a simple sound, not even a proper word, but it told him that she had a clear picture of why he had come back. 'Then I am sorry you find yourself on your own. But Ernest, don't despair, who knows what is around the next corner? If you had stayed here and we had gone on as we were, I should never have found the whole and complete relationship I have with Michael. And for you, there may be some purpose in her leaving you.'

'You've grown hard, Verity. Well, I don't look for sympathy from you or anyone else. I have a good life up north, a good house, a position of respect . . .' She only half listened. She wanted him gone, not because he had any power to upset her, but because his coming back had brought home to her just where the years had brought her. She had a sense of peace.

Richard's posting made little difference to life at Crocker's End; it varied only in that instead of driving back to London on Sunday evenings, he drove to Buckinghamshire. The fruit ripened just as it did every year, the local people and one or two gypsy folk came to do the picking, and the children broke up for the long summer holiday. But there was a feeling of uncertainty. Some buried their heads even deeper and went away for their annual week or fortnight by the sea, while others cancelled their plans. Jackie and Richard came under the latter category, but they were luckier than so many that August as the clouds of war gathered. Richard wouldn't be called to serve in the forces; he was more use to his country where he was.

Gas masks were issued, and Toby and Dulcie, like their friends at school, delighted in looking like Mickey Mouse, even while their pleasure was overshadowed by a funny, unfamiliar feeling of fear as they saw the grown-ups wearing funny black rubber things with a sort of snout that made a strange noise when they breathed. When term started in September there were a lot of new children at the village school, strangers to all of them. Some of them cried a lot, one or two wet their knickers, and others didn't seem to know what to do with a knife and fork. But the teachers were kind to them and made sure no one teased them. And with the resilience of the young, the local children soon accepted them and the newcomers became part of the country community.

In towns the residents were far more conscious of the blackout than in the country where there had never been any street lights. Mrs Trout made heavy black curtains for all the windows, Jackie took their ration books to the village shop to register for groceries, and to the butcher in town for meat.

And then, secretly ashamed that they could remain so untouched, the inhabitants of Crocker's End settled down for the first winter of war. Richard came home when he could, but he worked long hours and sometimes two or even three weekends went by between his visits. Like so many people, he had had to lay up his car and his journey now entailed bus, train and taxi.

After the first year of war everyone realized it would be a long haul. The Germans were in France, England within their sights. Every news broadcast told of skirmishes in the air as young men, some no more than months out of school, protected the skies. Then, when the fear of invasion receded, came the blitz. Somewhere, surely, at the end of the tunnel there must be light and hope. If there wasn't, no one was prepared to admit it. Dogged determination had become the order of the day.

War affected nearly every aspect of people's lives, and it brought them together as nothing else could. Shortages and hardships had no power to dent the new – and some might say un-English – camaraderie between strangers: women queuing with their children's ration books to get the allocation of two oranges, or men disappointed on arriving at their favourite local to find a handwritten notice pinned to the locked door: 'Sorry, closed until brewery's next delivery. Hope to open Friday evening'. Through it all there were days of sunshine, days of rain, days when the ground was hard with frost; the fundamental things of life were unchanged. And when coal was running low, with weeks to wait before any more could be delivered, even though some might mumble exactly what they'd like to do to 'bloody Hitler', at the same time pulling their chairs closer to the kitchen range (or at Crocker's End, the Aga), there was an almost tangible feeling of unity. But the worst of winters will always pass and, like a rainbow after a storm, the snowdrops brought promise that spring would soon come round again. The blackcurrant bushes cropped well, but one difference as the country settled into a wartime routine was that it was hard to recruit locals for casual labour; they all had full-time work. The gypsy people came, but only the older ones. From first light until dusk, Jackie worked. Dick Cload and Harry Higgs had both been called up and had been replaced by two men in their sixties and one lad who had had polio and wore a steel support on his leg. Michael joined the pickers, but it was a Michael ten years older and suffering angina attacks. Yet somehow they got through.

It was in the early months of 1942 when Richard, home for a weekend, told them that he'd heard the Ministry of War had taken over land between the village and town and had built huts, put up high wire fences and made it a prisoner-of-war camp.

'Leave it with me and I'll see if it's possible to get some of the prisoners to help here. You'll never manage the pruning without more help. And Michael, you know how the cold air affects you.'

'I bet they won't allow them the freedom to come and work out of doors,' was Jackie's opinion.

But she was wrong. He didn't come home the following weekend, and it was on Tuesday of the next week that he phoned to tell her that it was all arranged and a work party would be arriving at nine o'clock the next morning.

'They won't know a thing about pruning bushes,' he warned, 'and they won't speak English either – although the chap I spoke to said that one of them did, so let's hope he's bright enough to pick it up quickly and teach the others. Anyway, it's better than nothing. Don't let Michael overdo it, will you? I know how Mother worries about him. Are you all right, Jacqueline darling? Promise me you won't try and do too much. Damn this war.'

'How much is too much?' She laughed. 'You would be proud of your son, he's a real help.' Perhaps that was a slight exaggeration, for with the short winter days, and in term time, Toby had less opportunity than enthusiasm.

The next morning, just as the hall clock struck the half hour at half past eight, a lorry turned in from the lane and came slowly down the slope. Leaving Mrs Trout to see the children had their hats – or cap, in Toby's case – and coats on and their satchels packed, Jackie kissed them goodbye and went out to greet the prison guard who had brought the new workforce.

About twenty men jumped down from the back of the lorry. But nineteen of them might not have been there; Jackie saw only one.

Nine

How could she be so sure? There was nothing unusual about a German having blond hair, nor yet about the tall, well-built frame she remembered so clearly. It was fifteen and a half years since the day which she now acknowledged had coloured her thinking ever since. He had changed, of course he had changed: an eighteen-year-old youth had become a thirty-four-year-old man. So too must she have changed. Within weeks of her thirty-second birthday, married, with two children just being seen off to school and living miles from the area that held his memories of England, probably he wouldn't even recognize her.

The men were all out of the lorry and the driver, an Englishman of course, was coming towards her.

'You are a welcome sight,' she greeted him, holding her hand out to him. 'My husband phoned yesterday to say you were coming and you would help until the winter pruning is all done. You don't know how glad I am.'

Sergeant Mitchell had never enjoyed his work so thoroughly as he had since he'd been posted to the camp.

'I'll see to it the men are brought in. I doubt if they know much about pruning, but they're not a bad bunch, even if they're not here by choice. I'll keep an eye that they work hard.'

'I'm sure they will.' She held the smile in her voice, not letting him guess her resentment that he should have authority over Wilhelm. 'And my husband was told that one of them does speak English. If I explain to him what has to be done, then perhaps he can tell the others.'

'That's a bit tricky, ma'am. No fraternizing, that's the rule.'

'I'd hardly call giving him instructions "fraternizing".'

'Yes and no.' Sergeant Mitchell wasn't convinced. 'Give an inch and they might take a foot. Blimey! But wouldn't we all do the same? No, I tell you what: you show me the way you want the bushes cut back and I'll see it's done properly. Back home, before my call-up came, I worked in the Parks Department, so me and pruning are old buddies. I'd like you to show me how much you want cut back, though; I've not cut fruit bushes before. I wouldn't mind betting most of the chaps have never so much as held a pair of secateurs. I'll just bring them right in and get them to wait down by the barn where I can see no one tries to go walkabouts.' Then, turning back towards the gang of waiting men, he blew a whistle to alert them.

As they filed past on their way to the gravel patch in front of the barn, Jackie made a pretence of concentrating on fastening the buckle on her shoe. But as Wilhelm approached she looked directly at him, willing him to meet her gaze. The first thing she was aware of as he came closer was his lack of expression; he obeyed orders, but she knew his pride was unbroken. Into her memory sprang the image of the proud youth he had been, his love for his country and his sublime confidence that even after its defeat in the Great War, nothing would hold it back. It would once again become the great nation it had been, and he would help build that greatness. Even as those thoughts came, so they were pushed away by something else: yes, he had recognized her. His expression (or, rather, his lack of it) might not have changed, but she felt rather than saw his shock. She had no hint of whether there was pleasure in the shock or resentment that she should see him in these circumstances. He had already passed on down the path.

'Now then, ma'am – Mrs . . . who is it?' Sergeant Mitchell came back, ready to be instructed.

'I'm sorry, Sergeant, I should have introduced myself. I'm Mrs Bennett, Jackie Bennett. And you?' In her natural friendly manner she held her hand out to him as names were exchanged. Sergeant Mitchell found it all more to his liking than picking up the jobs no one more senior wanted in the Parks Department. And one thing Jackie recognized in his favour was that he was quick to grasp her instructions and able to pass them confidently to his band of labourers.

She left them to their own devices. Taking her own secateurs she made her way to the lower slopes. Her mind was racing: memories from so many years ago crowded into images of what the next days could bring. No fraternization . . . but surely she could talk to an old friend, a childhood friend? Then thoughts

of childhood were pushed aside. Where was his mind as he absorbed
his instructions? Like her, was he swimming in the cool waters
of the river? Was he reliving the moments when he'd feasted his
gaze on her naked body? Standing with the secateurs idle in her
hand she shivered in the cold February air. How different it had
been on that hot August afternoon that had been the crowning
climax of their time together; their whole world was different
now, pulling them apart, separating them with mistrust. She
stooped down to start work again just as she became aware of
footsteps approaching. How could she have been so sure it was
him? No fraternization! Instinct made her squat so that she wasn't
visible above the unpruned bushes.

'This is where she wants someone to start, at this path. You
should be OK on your own; you seemed to understand. Do a
row at a time, and work your way down the slope. Tidy your
clippings and put them in a pile at the end of each row. Sure
you know what to do?'

'Absolutely sure, Sergeant.' *His* voice! The voice that had haunted
her for half her lifetime! Then heavy footsteps growing fainter as
the sergeant made his way to the upper slope.

For a while Jackie remained where she was. It was ridiculous
to feel like this. For over ten years she had been married – happily
married – and, very likely, so too had he. Just because he had
recognized her, it didn't mean that the past meant anything to
him. She even tried to tell herself that for years she'd not thought
about him. So where was the logic in feeling like this? 'I swear
I will come back,' came the echo of his voice, 'we will always be
there for each other.' But neither of them had envisaged that
when he came back he would be a prisoner of war, or that their
countries would be hell bent on destroying each other.

Standing up she looked over the dividing eight or nine rows
of bushes to where he was working. No one else was visible. No
one else existed for her as she started up the slope.

'Wilhelm,' she breathed as she turned into the row where he
worked.

He turned towards her, and standing very straight bowed his
head in acknowledgement.

'I recognized you the moment you jumped down from the
lorry. I thought you might have forgotten me.'

'My memory is clear. This is a very different meeting from anything we might have imagined. I see you are no longer Jackie Hunt; you wear a marriage ring.'

She nodded. 'I have been married ten years and have two children.'

'I too have a wife. Gizella and I have been married for only six years, and for half of that time I have been serving my country. My son, Heinrich, is four years old, but when I left our home he was not even one year old. Your husband? He is serving his country too, I have no doubt?'

'Yes. But he isn't in the forces if that's what you mean.'

'Ah, he works in the manufacture of weaponry, I expect.'

'No.'

Wilhelm looked puzzled. 'So in what way does he serve his country? In the growing of fruit?'

She laughed. 'No. He's never worked with the fruit. He is a mathematician.'

'And that keeps him from going in what you call the forces. No doubt he is engaged in work for your government? Is he able to live with you at your beautiful farm for the growing of fruit? Perhaps he is in London or at some outpost of government?'

'He's—' As if she heard Richard's voice telling her he was sworn to secrecy, she stopped short. Even in the village she had seen the placard 'Careless talk costs lives', and on the railway station in town another warning of 'The enemy within'. Wilhelm was the enemy. But how could he be? He was her friend. And yet as she cut her sentence short and they looked at each other, they were both aware of how far apart the years had forced them. 'He gets home as often as he can,' she ended lamely.

'And what husband would not? I would give so much – more than I can even tell you – to be able to do the same. And yet here I am, caged like an animal until we win this unnecessary war.'

'Unnecessary? More likely inevitable. You must have known why your country was building such an arsenal of weaponry. Certainly not so that it could rust for lack of use.'

Wilhelm smiled at her sudden anger.

'Dear Jackie. You like to believe all that you are told. My people

are a proud Arian race. Do you not see the great things Adolf
Hitler has done since coming to power? He has given us back
our rightful place in Europe, indeed in the world. If after the last
and terrible war fairness had been shown and all nations had sat
around a table together to make the peace, then none of this
need have happened. Lands would not have been stolen from us
and we should have been free to purify our stock, dismiss those
who had no rightful place amongst us.'

'Wilhelm, don't let's quarrel. War is so dreadful. People from
both our countries with their lives shattered, oh, it's too beastly.'

'Indeed, yes. We did no harm to Britain. Yet because the polit-
icians sign treaties, their countries have to defend each other.'

'So you would walk by on the other side of the road?'

'I would not. I would fight for what I see to be right. And so
I fight for my country. Or I did, until I was captured and brought
here to work like an unpaid slave or to – as you say – kick my
heels behind a high wire fence. And all the while, Jackie my
friend, what is happening to Gizella and to my son?'

'Do you get letters from her?'

'We had better cut your bushes while we talk or your English
sergeant will think I have been wasting my time and I will not be
allowed even this amount of freedom tomorrow.' He started to clip
as he spoke and, moving to the next bush, she did the same. By
the end of the day Sergeant Mitchell would be more than impressed
with Wilhelm's efforts. 'You ask whether I have letters. I hear from
my wife, short letters that tell me nothing except Heinrich's progress
– which to me is the most important thing for which I fight. I
also have had a more disturbing letter from my father. He tells me
that Gizella has not kept herself loyal to her vows of fidelity; there
are many men away from home, men hungry for love, just as she
must be. Ask your own husband how well he keeps faith to you,
and if he is truthful he will say sometimes he weakens. Just as any
man – and I expect any woman too – would do, living as one has
to in this unnatural way of separation. There are days when the
future is without hope, the tunnel is dark and seems without end.
Do you not feel it yourself, Jackie – Jackie, my first love?'

'Don't be silly, Wilhelm. We were hardly more than children.'

'Ah yes, hardly more than children. And we loved with a purity
of the spirit that one loses with the years.'

'Keep pruning,' Jackie said, pushing her own secateurs into the pocket of her duffel coat. 'Sergeant Mitchell is coming our way.' Then, speaking more loudly, 'Well done! I hope the others are making such a good job. Hello, Sergeant, I'm doing my round, making sure they are all doing it right. If this one is anything to go by, there won't be any problem.'

'I showed them clearly what was wanted, ma'am.' Then, to Wilhelm, 'You seem a bit quicker than the rest of them. But no need to stop, get on with your job.' Like so many more used to taking instruction rather than handing it out, a little authority looked like it was going to his head.

'Well done!' Jackie said again to Wilhelm, before starting up the slope. 'I don't doubt your word, Sergeant, but I want to see for myself.'

As she did her round of inspection, occasionally taking her secateurs to cut to a lower lateral, her mind was on her conversation with Wilhelm. How could he feel as he did about Hitler's invasion of Germany's neighbours? She remembered his boyish patriotism and how she had admired him for it. But, my country right or wrong? Would she have felt the same in his position? Then there was what he had told her about his wife; surely he must care if she was filling the void in her life with other men? Imagine if Richard was away for months, perhaps years, would it be the same for him? Even as she asked herself the question, she knew the answer. Richard came home at least once a month, but what if, like so many servicemen, he was overseas for years without leave? Despite the front he presented to the world, he wasn't a cold man. Without her realizing it, a smile pulled at the corners of her mouth as memory and fantasy came between her and the working prisoners.

For the rest of that day she kept busy in another area; she mustn't risk the sergeant suspecting that she and Wilhelm knew each other.

On Friday of that week, Richard phoned.

'I expected to get home this weekend, but, Jacqueline, I have to go away for a while.'

'Away? Away where?'

'I'm sorry, darling, I can't tell you more than that. And even I don't know how long before I can get back. I shall phone you, of course, at the first opportunity. How are Mother and Michael? You're making sure he doesn't try to work out of doors while this cold spell lasts, aren't you?'

'They're fine. They keep each other company by the fire. The coal is running very short, but I've managed to get some logs, so that should help until the coalman can let us have more.'

'What about the Aga? Are you able to keep that going?'

'No. We cook on the gas stove and use the geyser for hot water.'

'I hate it, Jacqueline. They keep the place fairly well warmed here, day and night. And I think of you being cold. You're sure you're all right?'

'Perfectly sure. And the prisoners are making a splendid job, the pruning will be finished by the end of next week. Sergeant Mitchell tells me they are going to work at a logging place after that.'

'I wish I could help you. Jacqueline . . . just that I miss you. And you?'

'Of course I do, Richard. Perhaps it'll only be for a week. But why should we expect to be luckier than other people – those poor prisoners, for instance?'

'Those and the thousands who will never see their homes again. But this won't do, my Jacqueline. I count myself lucky above all men – and I thank God for it. Explain to Mother why I won't be home, and take care of yourself and the others.'

As the days went by Jackie became ever more aware of Wilhelm, even though they spent very little time on their own. There was one occasion when she found him building a bonfire of cuttings at the top of Dilly Hill when she pushed her barrow load for burning.

'For once we can speak to each other,' she greeted him as she started to take her twigs and add them to his pile, never more than two at a time so that the task would last longer. 'You've almost come to the end of your time here and we've had so little chance to talk.'

'I've been carrying a picture to show you. Here,' he reached into the bottom of the pocket on his overalls, 'this is Gizella. I took it just before I left home. And look, this is my boy, my son Heinrich. Mind no one sees me showing you.'

of course, at the first opportunity. How are Mother and Michael? You're making sure he doesn't try to work out of doors while this cold spell lasts, aren't you?'

'They're fine. They keep each other company by the fire. The coal is running very short, but I've managed to get some logs, so that should help until the coalman can let us have more.'

'What about the Aga? Are you able to keep that going?'

'No. We cook on the gas stove and use the geyser for hot water.'

'I hate it, Jacqueline. They keep the place fairly well warmed here, day and night. And I think of you being cold. You're sure you're all right?'

'Perfectly sure. And the prisoners are making a splendid job, the pruning will be finished by the end of next week. Sergeant Mitchell tells me they are going to work at a logging place after that.'

'I wish I could help you. Jacqueline . . . just that I miss you. And you?'

'Of course I do, Richard. Perhaps it'll only be for a week. But why should we expect to be luckier than other people – those poor prisoners, for instance?'

'Those and the thousands who will never see their homes again. But this won't do, my Jacqueline. I count myself lucky above all men – and I thank God for it. Explain to Mother why I won't be home, and take care of yourself and the others.'

As the days went by Jackie became ever more aware of Wilhelm, even though they spent very little time on their own. There was one occasion when she found him building a bonfire of cuttings at the top of Dilly Hill when she pushed her barrow load for burning.

'For once we can speak to each other,' she greeted him as she started to take her twigs and add them to his pile, never more than two at a time so that the task would last longer. 'You've almost come to the end of your time here and we've had so little chance to talk.'

'I've been carrying a picture to show you. Here,' he reached into the bottom of the pocket on his overalls, 'this is Gizella. I took it just before I left home. And look, this is my boy, my son Heinrich. Mind no one sees me showing you.'

'My memory is clear. This is a very different meeting from anything we might have imagined. I see you are no longer Jackie Hunt; you wear a marriage ring.'

She nodded. 'I have been married ten years and have two children.'

'I too have a wife. Gizella and I have been married for only six years, and for half of that time I have been serving my country. My son, Heinrich, is four years old, but when I left our home he was not even one year old. Your husband? He is serving his country too, I have no doubt?'

'Yes. But he isn't in the forces if that's what you mean.'

'Ah, he works in the manufacture of weaponry, I expect.'

'No.'

Wilhelm looked puzzled. 'So in what way does he serve his country? In the growing of fruit?'

She laughed. 'No. He's never worked with the fruit. He is a mathematician.'

'And that keeps him from going in what you call the forces. No doubt he is engaged in work for your government? Is he able to live with you at your beautiful farm for the growing of fruit? Perhaps he is in London or at some outpost of government?'

'He's—' As if she heard Richard's voice telling her he was sworn to secrecy, she stopped short. Even in the village she had seen the placard 'Careless talk costs lives', and on the railway station in town another warning of 'The enemy within'. Wilhelm was the enemy. But how could he be? He was her friend. And yet as she cut her sentence short and they looked at each other, they were both aware of how far apart the years had forced them. 'He gets home as often as he can,' she ended lamely.

'And what husband would not? I would give so much – more than I can even tell you – to be able to do the same. And yet here I am, caged like an animal until we win this unnecessary war.'

'Unnecessary? More likely inevitable. You must have known why your country was building such an arsenal of weaponry. Certainly not so that it could rust for lack of use.'

Wilhelm smiled at her sudden anger.

'Dear Jackie. You like to believe all that you are told. My people

are a proud Arian race. Do you not see the great things Adolf
Hitler has done since coming to power? He has given us back
our rightful place in Europe, indeed in the world. If after the last
and terrible war fairness had been shown and all nations had sat
around a table together to make the peace, then none of this
need have happened. Lands would not have been stolen from us
and we should have been free to purify our stock, dismiss those
who had no rightful place amongst us.'

'Wilhelm, don't let's quarrel. War is so dreadful. People from
both our countries with their lives shattered, oh, it's too beastly.'

'Indeed, yes. We did no harm to Britain. Yet because the polit-
icians sign treaties, their countries have to defend each other.'

'So you would walk by on the other side of the road?'

'I would not. I would fight for what I see to be right. And so
I fight for my country. Or I did, until I was captured and brought
here to work like an unpaid slave or to – as you say – kick my
heels behind a high wire fence. And all the while, Jackie my
friend, what is happening to Gizella and to my son?'

'Do you get letters from her?'

'We had better cut your bushes while we talk or your English
sergeant will think I have been wasting my time and I will not be
allowed even this amount of freedom tomorrow.' He started to clip
as he spoke and, moving to the next bush, she did the same. By
the end of the day Sergeant Mitchell would be more than impressed
with Wilhelm's efforts. 'You ask whether I have letters. I hear from
my wife, short letters that tell me nothing except Heinrich's progress
– which to me is the most important thing for which I fight. I
also have had a more disturbing letter from my father. He tells me
that Gizella has not kept herself loyal to her vows of fidelity; there
are many men away from home, men hungry for love, just as she
must be. Ask your own husband how well he keeps faith to you,
and if he is truthful he will say sometimes he weakens. Just as any
man – and I expect any woman too – would do, living as one has
to in this unnatural way of separation. There are days when the
future is without hope, the tunnel is dark and seems without end.
Do you not feel it yourself, Jackie – Jackie, my first love?'

'Don't be silly, Wilhelm. We were hardly more than children.'

'Ah yes, hardly more than children. And we loved with a purity
of the spirit that one loses with the years.'

'Keep pruning,' Jackie said, pushing her own secateurs into the
pocket of her duffel coat. 'Sergeant Mitchell is coming our way.'
Then, speaking more loudly, 'Well done! I hope the others are
making such a good job. Hello, Sergeant, I'm doing my round,
making sure they are all doing it right. If this one is anything to
go by, there won't be any problem.'

'I showed them clearly what was wanted, ma'am.' Then, to
Wilhelm, 'You seem a bit quicker than the rest of them. But
no need to stop, get on with your job.' Like so many more used
to taking instruction rather than handing it out, a little authority
looked like it was going to his head.

'Well done!' Jackie said again to Wilhelm, before starting up
the slope. 'I don't doubt your word, Sergeant, but I want to see
for myself.'

As she did her round of inspection, occasionally taking her
secateurs to cut to a lower lateral, her mind was on her conversation with Wilhelm. How could he feel as he did about Hitler's
invasion of Germany's neighbours? She remembered his boyish
patriotism and how she had admired him for it. But, my country
right or wrong? Would she have felt the same in his position?
Then there was what he had told her about his wife; surely he
must care if she was filling the void in her life with other men?
Imagine if Richard was away for months, perhaps years, would
it be the same for him? Even as she asked herself the question,
she knew the answer. Richard came home at least once a month,
but what if, like so many servicemen, he was overseas for years
without leave? Despite the front he presented to the world, he
wasn't a cold man. Without her realizing it, a smile pulled at the
corners of her mouth as memory and fantasy came between her
and the working prisoners.

For the rest of that day she kept busy in another area; she
mustn't risk the sergeant suspecting that she and Wilhelm knew
each other.

On Friday of that week, Richard phoned.

'I expected to get home this weekend, but, Jacqueline, I have
to go away for a while.'

'Away? Away where?'

'I'm sorry, darling, I can't tell you more than that. And even I
don't know how long before I can get back. I shall phone you,

She took them and felt a moment's jealousy, feeling herself to be plain and colourless by comparison with the glamorous blonde he had married.

'Your wife is beautiful – like a film star.'

'She was a beauty queen. She is a true Aryan, eyes startlingly blue, hair like ripe corn – and her figure – well, see for yourself. No wonder men desire her.'

Jackie nodded, feeling small and inadequate.

'And see, look at my son. This picture she sent to me only just before I lost my freedom. A fine boy.'

'Yes, he looks a good lad.'

Wilhelm frowned. 'Good lad? That makes him sound like every other boy on the street. But he is splendid.'

Jackie laughed. 'If Toby – my son – is called a good lad, I think that's the finest of compliments. But splendid, you say. I suppose that might have been what folk said of you when I first met you.'

'I like to think so. Splendid, to my mind, has little to do with handsomeness of features, but more of a fine, strong body, of determination and – and – how I wish I had a better command of your language – of truth, honesty. That is how I think of my son.'

His words seemed to her to bring alive all that he had been when she had thrown herself headlong into love with him. Yet was that the normal affection of a father for his child? Is that how Richard would think of Toby? She knew it wasn't.

'And would you love him less if he were different?' she asked.

'Love has many guises. If he were weak of body, then of course I would love him, but differently. Instead of pride I would feel defensive. But he is sound in mind and body, have no fear of that.'

He put the pictures carefully in his pocket and she went on, bit by bit, adding her contribution to the bonfire.

'Tomorrow we finish our work here at your Crocker's End. Before twelve months have passed we shall have won this war and an armistice will have been agreed. Tomorrow may be the last time we shall see each other.' He took her grubby hand in his. 'I have so often thought of your small hands. Such pretty hands.' The way he held her gaze told her that his memories were as clear as her own. 'They were cleaner, softer too. We were so young and untouched. I can close my eyes and see us both so clearly. That afternoon stands out in my mind like a clear beacon – innocent, glorious. And you? Have you not thought of it over the long years between?' She nodded, frightened to trust her voice. 'Now you have a husband and I have a wife. Life has moved on and brought us to our own separate worlds.' He still held her hand, his thumb caressing her fingers. 'But what we shared that afternoon was surely the most important – most important . . .' and again he hunted for the right words, '. . . making of love we could ever know. Neither of us knew what to expect, neither of us knew anything of the art of loving – and yet what we found was – was – like a gift from God above.' She had seen him working in the fields for nearly two weeks, yet nothing had prepared her for the emotion his words evoked. Again she only nodded. 'Perhaps we shall never have a moment like this again, time to speak honestly to each other. Tomorrow I shall be gone from here.'

'I thought you must have forgotten,' she heard herself say.

'I shall never forget. You were mine before you were your husband's. And I, I was yours. Wherever our lives bring us, nothing can take that from us.' From the far side of the next field came the sound of Sergeant Mitchell's whistle, telling the prisoners it was time they took barrows to the bonfire. In seconds the first would trundle into view. Tilting her chin, Wilhelm raised Jackie's face and laid his lips gently on hers. 'What we had is ours for ever,' he whispered. 'Leave your barrow, I will empty it.'

Without a word she left him and went down the slope to wait in the shed for the tools and barrows to be returned. Then, just as she had each day as dusk fell, without looking at Wilhelm, she thanked them all with a smile and told them she'd see them tomorrow.

That night, sleep eluded her. Time and again she plumped up her pillows and closed her eyes, but always Wilhelm was there waiting for her. She remembered each word he'd spoken there in the smoke-filled air by the bonfire. Those other memories, which for years she had forced to the back of her mind, refused to be pushed aside. Was he lying in his miserable bed in one of those huts, thinking of her, fantasizing just as she was? Eagerly she let her mind reach out to him, excitement driving her, and when every nerve in her body came alive willingly, she let herself imagine it was he who shared it with her just as he had long, long ago.

Only afterwards did guilt cast a shadow. Many, many times lying alone she had done just what she had tonight, but this had been different. Tonight she had been mentally unfaithful. Married for ten years, with a husband whose loyalty was as certain as the dawn of each new day, mother of two loved children – and yet in those moments her fantasy had been for another man. Yet, mixed with guilt and shame was excitement. 'You were mine before you were your husband's' came the echo of his voice. By the end of tomorrow he would be gone, perhaps she would never see him again. He had said with such confidence that by this time next year his country would be victorious. But she brushed that aside as impossible; however long it took, defeat was unimaginable. Even so, where would Wilhelm be by the time the next working party came from the prison camp? Did prisoners remain in the same place? One more day . . . just one more day . . . she would let herself look no further.

'Are you asleep, Michael?' Verity whispered into the darkness.

'Um?' At her first movement he always woke, just like a young mother with her first child. 'What is it, darling? Of course I'm awake.' He was already sitting up, expecting she needed his guiding hand. Although she had striven to maintain her independence as her sight had failed, since Michael had been with her it had become important to both of them that he helped her.

'I'm worried, and yet I can't tell you just why.'

'Aren't you well? Why couldn't you tell me?'

She laughed softly, snuggling closer to him. 'Not worried about me – well, only indirectly. You see things that I can't – but sometimes I sense things that *you* can't. It's Jackie.'

'Then, my dear, you really are imagining things. I have never seen Jackie work with more energy. From daybreak to dusk she is out there – and does she ever come in and doze by the fire at the end of the day?'

'Chance would be a fine thing,' she answered, the smile in her voice telling him that shortages and hardships had no power to

mar her own contentment. 'There's not a lot of comfort with
that horrid, hissing gas fire. Perhaps Grants will deliver the coal
soon. No, it's nothing to do with her health – not bodily health.
She is restless, I can *feel* it.'

'This bloody war is enough to unsettle any young couple –
young or old, for that matter. It's not just the young who suffer
separation from the ones they love. And she says Richard doesn't
know when he'll get back from wherever it is he's been sent. Of
course she worries and of course she's lonelier than she would
ever let herself admit. Us and the children, no one of her own
age to – to – share the void all these young women must feel
in their lives. But under all that, Jackie is happy. Perhaps she looks
on all the hours she spends out there scratching away at the soil
in the cold as her war work.'

'Perhaps I'm just being silly. If only Richard could get home
like he used to. She seemed content working all the week knowing
on Friday he would be here.'

'Thank God he's not serving somewhere overseas with no
hope that in a few weeks he'll be home.'

'You see! You've put your finger on it. If that were the case,
then we would expect her to be fidgety; that's what makes me
so sure there is something else bothering her.'

'If there is, I'm sure it's nothing that a few hours of normality
with Richard home won't put right.' He drew her closer, nuzzling
his face against her short, grey hair. 'It's when something is lacking
in your life that you learn to appreciate the things that matter
most; I know that's true. A day never goes by, nor ever could as
long as we have each other, when I'm not conscious of where
life has brought me.'

'And me, it's like that for me too.' She felt the sting of tears
in her sightless eyes, tears of thankfulness and love which, even
after all these years, still encompassed the 'Ernie darling' who had
been her guiding star for so much of her adult life. There was
something of Verity that would always belong to that Ernest of
long ago. But tonight as she moved her head so that Michael's
mouth found hers, Ernest was forgotten, and Jackie too. Michael
was eighty years old, Verity seventy-six; for them, love was a gentle
thing . . . even on the rare occasions when he was still able to
love her physically in the way he longed to, there was no wild

passion, but simply a tender expression of their need for each other.

The lorry turned in at the open gateway and parked, as it always did, near the house. As Sergeant Mitchell let down the back so that the men could jump out, Jackie was coming up the slope with Toby and Dulcie.

'Good morning, Sergeant,' she greeted him, making sure she ignored the workforce in the way he expected. 'I'm just going to walk to the village shop, but when I come back I wonder if you would stretch a point for me. In the weighing-in shed there are two high shelves where the annual account books have been kept for years. I know it sounds silly when they relate to so long ago, but I want to go through them. They aren't even in order and they must go back to the year dot. I got the ladder out the other day and tried to get them down, but I'm ashamed to tell you that when a spider fell out I nearly tumbled off the ladder. To be truthful I have no head for heights, even without spiders.'

'You want me to get them down for you, ma'am?'

This was something she hadn't considered. 'No, I wouldn't dream of suggesting it. It would mean your leaving your charges without supervision.'

'Ah yes, well that was what was bothering me. I need eyes in the back of my head with some of this lot.'

'The favour I was going to ask is this: you say you have one prisoner who speaks English. May I borrow him? I'll leave it to you to explain the job to him if you prefer, but would you allow him to get all the books down from the two high shelves and sort them into chronological order and then put them back. They'll need the dust and cobwebs knocked off them. And Sergeant, could you make sure he bolts the door from the inside or, if anyone tries to open it, they could knock him off the ladder.'

'I'll see to it with pleasure, ma'am. Just as soon as I get the others given their tools and set to work, I'll explain the task to Furtmueller – Furtmueller, what a name! I ask you!'

'Thanks so much. Now we must hurry – or better still, you two go on without me or the bell will ring before you get there.'

'Yep, we'll have to run. Come on, Dulce, skates on. 'Bye, Mum.'

Toby tugged at his sister's hand, but she insisted on kissing Jackie goodbye before they ran up the slope with all the energy of youth, and disappeared.

For Jackie there was a brisk walk to the village shop where she bought a bag of broken biscuits – a treasure indeed as they were being sold without using points from the ration book – and six postage stamps. Then she turned towards home. But on that morning she didn't come into Crocker's End from the main gate; instead she opened a seldom-used one on the perimeter that led down an overgrown path to the back of the barn. The only weak part of her scheme had been her excuse for borrowing the English-speaking man in Sergeant Mitchell's charge, but that having been accepted without query, surely there could be no hitch. Before making the children's breakfast porridge she had been out to the weighing-in shed and made sure that the back door was unlocked. As no one ever used it, there were rolls of netting in front of it, but by moving them a few inches she made sure the door could be opened just far enough for her to squeeze through.

That cocktail of emotions she had experienced the previous night gripped her: guilt, excitement, anticipation of the unknown – unknown? No, be honest, she told herself, you know, you *know* what must surely happen – and of all those emotions it was excitement that gained control as she quietly lifted the latch and pushed the door open.

'I lay awake thinking of you last night,' Wilhelm greeted her as he came down the ladder, 'trying to devise a way of letting us be together. And you, my dear friend Jackie, you must have been lying awake too, but with thoughts more productive than mine.'

She nodded, feeling he must be able to read her mind and know just where her thoughts had carried her.

'These books – do you really want them down?'

'I couldn't think of anything better, anything that would mean the door had to be locked and your sergeant couldn't walk in on us. We'll have the last two down – just in case he comes banging on the door.'

'He won't. He'll be too busy showing his authority to the others.' He laid two thin ledgers on the table.

'There's nowhere comfortable to sit,' she offered tentatively, hearing her words as inappropriate to the moment, surely the moment that had been like a beacon for so long.

'Last time we found our heaven in a coarse field, so we will not complain about a wooden floor. Take off your coat. We have so little time. Last time we had hours – remember the sunshine, remember the cows who had no interest in us.'

'I remember every moment, every touch, every word.' And for her, now, it was as if there had been nothing between that summer afternoon and this moment when they were together again.

'You were mine then – that wild, passionate girl who knew nothing of the joy of love until we found it together.' He held her coat as she slipped her arms out of it, then standing behind her he unbuttoned her cardigan and pulled her against him as his hands caressed her. She seemed to be living in a dream; the future had no meaning, there was nothing but *this*.

He laid her coat on the floor then gently pushed her to lie on it. Some of the glory dimmed as he pulled her knickers down to hang over one ankle then, breathing heavily, tore open the buttons of his prison overalls, pushed them off his shoulders and down to below his knees. It had never been like this on that glorious summer day under a clear blue sky. But she wouldn't let herself harbour such thoughts. This was Wilhelm, this was the romance she had dreamed of. Lying on the ground she stared up at the wooden roof of the weighing-in shed, so familiar and yet at that moment, so alien. She closed her eyes as she felt his weight on her.

For him, it was over almost before it began. Starved of sex for so long, he lost all control. It seemed no more than seconds later when they heard the sergeant hammering on the door.

'Open the door, Furtmueller. Haven't you finished sorting those books yet? I won't have skiving.'

Wilhelm made a supreme effort. Pulling up the trousers of his overalls and grabbing the ledgers from the desk, he took two strides to the ladder and started to climb up so that his voice would come from the right direction. He replied in a surprisingly calm voice, 'Just coming, Sergeant. I have these last two to put in their place and I will move the ladder and unbolt the door.' Pride allowed him to show neither servile obedience nor resentment; if he took pleasure in keeping the sergeant waiting, he gave no sign of it.

Jackie dragged her coat as she crawled behind the kneehole

desk, then wriggled to hide in the gap between the two sets of drawers, thankful for the 'modesty screen' front that shielded her from view. She wanted to rejoice but her mind was numb. Not once did she think of Richard and their years of marriage, and yet it was as if that beacon lit so long ago had been extinguished. She felt bereft.

Wilhelm was making heavy and noisy work of moving the ladder out of the way of the door in order to give her time to hide. After that day, the lorry would come no more to Crocker's End until the summer when the fruit was ready to be harvested. If the sergeant suspected how the last minutes had been spent there would be no chance of Wilhelm being in the work party next time. Yet there was no shape to the image of summer and the next working party.

Verity's intuition seldom failed, and during the next weeks while Richard was still away, she continued to be concerned about Jackie. There were moments when she found it hard to conjure up that ever-ready smile.

It was another three weeks before Richard returned to his base in Buckinghamshire and came home for the weekend. Crocker's End had a petrol ration, but it had to be used sparingly, so when they knew Richard was coming, the hairdresser gave Verity the last appointment of the day so that one trip to town would cover both that and meeting his train. Jackie saw her into the hairdresser's where the blinds were pulled down and covered with curtains to make sure no finger of light showed, and then she drove on to the station.

It was one of those days that hadn't bothered to get light, the heavy cloud hanging low and the air chill with damp mist. Richard's train was due at six thirty, but it had got dark extra early and when Jackie put her penny in the machine for a platform ticket it might have been midnight. Her mind was darting first in one direction, then in another. Will he guess that I've been unfaithful? But how could it be called unfaithful when it had nothing to do with me and Richard. I belonged to Wilhelm first, nothing could ever take that away. I don't know everything Richard does – oh, not with other women, I know it would never even enter his head, but where he's been, what his work is all about, those are the things that make up his life and I'm outside it all. But is that fair? He would tell me if he were a different sort of man, but to Richard his word is his bond. Dear Richard. Yes, keep thinking that. Dear Richard. Toby and Dulcie are excited that he's to be home for the weekend. And I'm excited, too. Of course I am. I wish the train would come, they will be waiting to close up at the hairdresser's. She shivered, looking along the platform where in the shielded blue light she could just make out one or two other people waiting, stamping their feet to keep warm.

Then she heard the clatter as the signal fell; it was coming. Another minute and he would be here.

Doors opened and travellers climbed down to the platform: a soldier carrying a kitbag, a young Air Force officer, an elderly woman with a shopping basket – and Richard, just as immaculate as the first day she had met him. She should be thankful, she *was* thankful, that his life was so unchanged. Yet just for a moment as she watched him walk the length of the platform towards her, she imagined the thrill if he'd come home on leave like the soldier who had dumped his kitbag on the ground and was crushing his girlfriend – or wife – to him.

'You must be frozen. The train was held up further down the line.' He kissed her forehead. Then, as if the contact had relaxed him: 'Five weeks. God, my Jacqueline, I've missed you.'

She linked her hand in his. Forget everything else, just remember this is dear Richard – and be grateful, be thankful. Forget all about Wilhelm and his horrid life in that camp, there's nothing you can do about it. *This* is your life. Be grateful Richard loves you like he does.

Her resolve lasted – indeed sometimes she had no need to remind herself of it. And yet as the weeks of spring went by, Verity still felt uneasy: could she be the only one to sense the forced cheerfulness in Jackie's manner? The days lengthened, the hour changed, and with double British Summer Time came long evenings when the children learned to be useful helpers. Then came the weekend when Richard told them he had arranged for the prisoners to come back again, now that it was time to pick the first of what looked like being a heavy crop.

★　　★　　★

The lorry arrived at exactly half past eight, and from where Jackie stood outside the barn, she watched the men jump to the ground. Yes, he was there, he'd come back. And for the first time she let her imagination look towards a future that could never be the same as those two weeks of last winter, which could no more be repeated than the summer of their adolescence. Between then and the future had come the last day together, something that couldn't be pushed aside as if it hadn't happened, and yet couldn't be repeated. What had been between Wilhelm and her must never be turned into some sordid 'affair'. With the lorry parked in its accustomed spot, the men were marched down to the sheds where she was waiting to hand out the baskets.

One look at Wilhelm told her that something was very wrong. Was he ill? He looked older. 'Downtrodden' was the word that sprang to mind. And yet she knew him too well to believe that could be possible. There was no chance to speak to him, and so she stood aside as Sergeant Mitchell took control, ordering each man to his allotted patch.

'And you, Furtmueller,' he said finally when Wilhelm was the last to be given instructions, 'I'll have you right down at the bottom of the farm, start from the furthest row and work back.' Jackie was puzzled as to why his tone held a taunt, as did his expression as his eyes met Wilhelm's.

'Sergeant,' Wilhelm acknowledged the instruction with a dignified nod of his head, but there was no doubting the insolence held in the single word.

'Bloody Hun,' Sergeant Mitchell mumbled as his charge picked up his basket and moved off. 'Beg pardon, ma'am, but I tell you that one is a real pain in the arse.'

'It will be more than an hour before any of them will have a full basket, but if I'm not in the shed when they bring them will you see they just line the baskets up. The lorry will come this evening to transfer the fruit to their own container. Now I must try and scratch up something to make a picnic for the children. School holidays and they're off to the woods for the day.'

'Don't know how lucky they are, the youngsters, do they? Let's hope, ma'am, that when they grow up they won't let the world get in the bloody mess we seem to have made of it. My missus works on the buses, you know. Maybe I told you last time we were here. Not the sort of job I like to think of her doing, perhaps having a lot of louts on there of a night. No, it's not right, it isn't. Didn't like her doing it before, but now – well, I had a ten-day leave back a couple of months ago, and left her pregnant with our first.'

'Congratulations, Sergeant.'

'Yeah, for myself of course I'm chuffed as a monkey. But Mavis – that's the missus – she's feeling really rough. We live with her people so her mum keeps an eye on her, but Mavis says she doesn't know how to face that ruddy bus each morning. Her mum says it'll soon pass. I don't know nothing about these lady things. Were you rough all the time you were in the family way?'

Seeing his worried expression, Jackie forgave him his previous pompous manner with the men.

'With my second one I wasn't too frisky. But cheer up, Sergeant, like her mother says, it'll pass, and think of the end result.'

'Ah, and that's what she says. All right for us blokes, we just get the easy bit to do. Here, just look at me, won't you, standing here nattering as if I hadn't got a job of work to do. Right you are then, ma'am, I'll see the baskets get lined up ready. Now I must get on my round making sure they pick just the ripe ones. I guess we'll be here for a while until all this lot gets ripened off. Not that I mind. It suits me very well and they're better kept occupied.'

'So you sent – what did you call him – Furtmueller, was it? – you sent him to the far end of our land, right away from the others?' A statement, yet it seemed to ask him what made Wilhelm 'a pain in the arse' needing to be segregated from his comrades.

'No chance of the blighter making a getaway from right down there. A week or so ago he made a bolt for it. Of course he didn't get far; he must be up the creek to think he could mingle with the crowd dressed in his prison get-up. Anyway, we picked him up about halfway between here and the camp. I wonder word hadn't got around.'

'No, I hadn't heard. I must fly or the other children will be gone without Toby and Dulcie.'

'Nice names . . .' Sergeant Mitchell's thoughts had moved back home.

* * *

With a packet of meat paste sandwiches and two bottles of lemonade in the rucksack on Toby's back, he and Dulcie raced up the slope to the lane where the children from Michael's erstwhile farm cottages were waiting. One of the lads carried a length of rope to tie to a branch in the wood, already imagining himself something of a Tarzan. Their six weeks with no school were full of days of freedom and adventure.

Once Jackie had seen them off, she went out to the weighing-in shed and, just as she had on that previous occasion, she moved the rolls of netting to allow her to open the door and let herself out to the lower part of the land. Taking a basket with her, she squeezed out of the narrow opening then closed the door behind her. Her heart was beating fast, whether from excitement or anxiety, for there was no question in her mind that something was wrong with Wilhelm. She walked to the Crocker's End boundary and could see that he was working hard to fill his basket. Instead of going directly to join him, she went into the line between his row and the one higher.

'Wilhelm,' she hissed through the thick bushes that separated them, 'he can't see us, he's gone up Dilly Hill. But I'll keep low.' When he didn't answer, she knelt down and with her hands made a gap in the foliage so that she could see him. 'Wilhelm, something's wrong, I know it is. Can't you tell me? Don't you trust me?'

'You know I do.' On his side of the plants he too dropped to his knees, reaching to take her hands in his. 'I told you something about my Gizella. She's so lovely, of course men are attracted to her. This damn war . . . if I were there with her none of it would have happened. She's not – how you say? – an immoral woman. But she is lonely. Oh God, aren't we all lonely; lonely in our bodies and lonely in our spirits. She has gone to live in a village which I do not know, but I have a cousin there who suggested that it would be safer than the city for Heinrich. So Gizella and the boy are living with Marte, my cousin, whose husband is away serving his country.'

'Is that not a wise thing for her to do? Is it that your parents are missing them?' For it seemed to Jackie that there was nothing in what he'd said to cause his obvious distress.

'If only I could be with her everything would be well for us,

I know it would. I know that in her heart she cares just for me. But Marte has written to me with tales that drive me insane with worry and jealousy. There is an Army base on the edge of the village and each night there is dancing, drinking, lusting and lechery – how else can I say it? My son is put to bed and left, night after night.'

'In the house alone?'

'No, no, Marte is in the house. But she is out of her mind with worry. She says Gizella is so changed and – and – oh God, it mustn't be true – she suspects she is pregnant. Her letter was written weeks ago, the mail takes so long, and I do not know what state my Gizella must be in. If she is pregnant perhaps she will run away, leave our son, or take him even . . . take my Hein—' His voice broke and he left the word unfinished, holding his trembling lips tightly together in an effort to regain control.

'The sergeant says you tried to escape.'

'I had to. I wanted to get here. You are my friend, my only hope. But I was picked up.'

'We will always be there for each other' came the echo of their solemn, youthful vow.

'But even if you could get away from the district, how could you cross the Channel? Can't the Red Cross be asked to find out what is happening?' A stupid suggestion, she knew that as soon as she'd made it, but she had to say something.

'I have an address, a contact. If I can get there I will find help. I've got to find her, I've got to know.'

'And what if you find she is pregnant? Oh, Wilhelm, could you bear it?'

'I love her, Jackie. Poor Gizella, if that is what has happened to her it is cruel. She is a good, loving woman, warm and fun-loving. She needs jollity, she needs love. Some people can stand alone, some can't. I beg you, Jackie, help me.'

Her mind was racing. 'Get up and make sure that sergeant isn't coming while I think.'

He did as she said. 'No, there is no one.'

'Now listen, I have a plan. I will tell you what I mean to do and then I will take my basket and start picking from the other end of this plot. This will be the last time we will speak, so remember what I tell you.'

★ ★ ★

The children came home in time for tea, partly because they loved watching the lorry with its huge containers taking the fruit, partly because they earned threepence for every punnet they filled (for they were never given the large baskets used by the pickers), and partly because the meat paste sandwiches had been eaten by half past eleven and they were hungry. They heard Sergeant Mitchell blow his shrill whistle.

'May we get down, Mum, so we can watch the men go?' they both spoke at the same time.

'As long as you've finished. But if you get down it's no use thinking you can come back in and expect to have more.'

It was quite a decision to make, for they knew their mother was a woman of her word. But they decided that watching the men get counted into the lorry was more appealing than bread and jam – particularly on a day like today when, as Mrs Trout had said, the butter knife had only just been shown the bread and there was no cake.

'Shall I pour you another cup of tea, Mum?' Jackie asked brightly, giving no hint that she had a racing heart and a mouth that felt dry as sawdust. 'And you, Michael?'

In the winter they never sat down to tea with the children; instead, when the evenings were dark they usually had their supper early. Light evenings meant eating later, so afternoon tea – which sounded much more palatable than it proved to be in days of rationing – was an extra. Was it her imagination, Jackie wondered as she passed Michael his second cup, or could she hear excitement outside? It certainly wasn't imagination when a moment later Toby rushed in, his eyes wide.

'Sergeant Mitchell is in a real pother! He's lost one of the prisoners. The others are all in the lorry and he's charging about out there, can't you hear him yelling the man's name?'

'I'll come out,' Jackie said in a voice that was supposed to sound helpful. 'Has the sergeant checked in the shed – and what about the outside lavatory?'

But it seemed he had checked everywhere.

'That bloody man,' he greeted Jackie, 'the bugger's gone and done it again. Well he won't get away with it any more than he did last time. What sort of a fool must he be to think he won't get caught; one look at him and it's clear even to a halfwit that

he's out of a POW camp. I'll drive around the roads on the way
back and I bet I'll pick him up – hope to God I do, or I'm in
for it!'

'When did you last see him?'

'They were all here at dinner time. But he's been working
down the lower end like I told you. Damned if I know how he
gave me the slip. I'll get cracking and see you in the morning.
But I shan't give Furtmueller the chance to come out again, he's
cooked his goose proper this time.'

As the Army lorry drove off, the one from the cordial factory
arrived and Jackie saw the day's crop collected. Toby, Dulcie and
the two children from the cottages were busy picking to fill a
punnet each so there would be blackcurrants for pudding the
next day, and so, safe in the certainty that she was unobserved,
Jackie went into the weighing-in shed and looked in the bottom
drawer of the kneehole desk. Yes, it was as she'd arranged:
Wilhelm's overalls were there and – not previously arranged – on
top of them on a scrap of paper was written: 'You have kept our
promise, and for that I will keep mine and love you always. W.'

Later she would think of somewhere to dispose of the overalls, but in the meantime she pushed them to the back of the
drawer, put some cleaning rags to the front and shut the drawer.
The note she read again, then pushed it into her pocket just as
Toby rushed in.

'Mum! Mum, are you in here?'

'What's the panic? I'm just going to lock up and chase you
two off to bed. We've got late this evening with all Sergeant
Mitchell's excitement.'

'Give me the key, I'll do it. Grandpa says for you to come
quickly, there's someone on the phone for you – a man – and
he won't talk to anyone else, says he wants you.'

Ten

Pushing the key of the shed into Toby's hand, Jackie started towards the house, alarm speeding her steps. Something must have gone wrong! Perhaps Wilhelm had arrived at the address of his 'contact' and found it was a trap, but in that case how was he able to telephone? To help an enemy prisoner escape was a crime. But Wilhelm could never be her enemy. Please don't let him be in trouble, please help him to get home and to make things right between himself and his Gizella, she begged. Perhaps he was safely at the address he had been making for and wanted to tell her that all was well. In her imagination she saw him on the bicycle that she had left for him against the back of the shed, wearing an old suit of Richard's, money and sandwiches in the pocket of the jacket. She imagined the bicycle abandoned outside the station, and his relief as he bought his rail ticket. He would have been gone hours before the alarm was raised, but even if he was safely with his contact he had a long way to go before he could get to his own people. *Please* help him, watch over him. It's all so cruel, like everything in war is cruel; everywhere people inflict misery on each other. Yet even as those thoughts crowded her mind – hardly formed thoughts, rather more a silent outpouring of emotion – she was aware of something else: in keeping that solemn promise made so long ago she had come full circle, they had both come full circle. Whether or not they would ever meet again was unknown and unimportant; nothing could take from them what they had shared, but it was over. And realizing it, she felt no sadness, only a desperate wish for him to be safe and to find again the happiness he had known with Gizella.

Once indoors she rushed through the kitchen to the hall where the telephone was attached to the wall, and there, to her surprise, she found Verity and Michael, he with his arm around her as if to protect her.

'It's all right. I'm here now,' she said unnecessarily, wanting to dismiss them. But still they stayed. And as if Dulcie knew the moment had a special meaning, she too waited nearby, watching anxiously.

'Hello. This is Jackie.' She closed her eyes, preparing herself for whatever had to be faced. *Please, please* let it just be to tell me everything has gone well. I'll make up some lie to tell the others, although her mind was empty of suggestions.

'Jacqueline Bennett? I'm so sorry to have to phone you like this.'

Only Richard had ever called her by her full name. That one word stripped her of all coherent thought.

'Yes?' she murmured.

'This is Malcolm Rogers. Richard and I are in the same lodgings, he may have spoken of me. Oh God, this is difficult.'

'What's happened? Where is he? Has he been sent away again?' But that was ridiculous; if he had he would have phoned to tell her himself.

'About an hour ago it happened. I was a bit later than Richard walking back to the house and the siren went while I was on my way. I saw the plane, then as I went up the garden path I heard the screech of the bomb. A stray bomb from a single plane shedding its load as it got away. The house had a direct hit.'

'And Richard? Is Richard hurt?' She heard herself ask it. She had faced the trauma of her aunt's illness and death, of her uncle's suicide, she had felt grief touched by guilt, but never had she experienced the emotion that gripped her as she pressed the receiver to her ear. All the years she had known him, from the day he had arrived at the shop in answer to her childlike letter, to the recent months when she had felt herself to be removed from him, the certainty of his unchanging love, the joy of their shared passion, the emotion she knew to be hidden beneath the cool façade he presented, his love for his mother, his love and pride in their children, in a few brief seconds they washed over her like a great and powerful tide. 'Answer me, tell me, can't you?' she shouted into the mouthpiece.

'The rescue team are moving rubble. The back of the house is gone. His room was on the first floor at the back. Mrs Bennett – Jacqueline – I ought to have waited before I phoned you. It's not fair to have told you before there is any real news.'

'Of course you shouldn't have waited. I'll come straight away.

They'll get him out, of course they will. He'll be all right. He will. *He will.* I'm coming straight away.'

'Are there trains? Leave me to ring you again as soon as I know something more.'

'I have petrol in the car. I shall drive.'

He heard the hysteria in her voice and was frightened. It would be dark long before she arrived, and with unlit roads and so many road signs removed, she'd probably get lost. Anything might happen to her.

'Is there anyone who can come with you?'

'Don't want anyone. Tell him – when they bring him out – tell him I'm on my way. Tell him . . . tell him . . .' Michael took the receiver out of her hand. She heard him talking to Malcolm Rogers, the voice that until a few minutes ago had been no more than a name to her.

'Mum,' she said, shocked to see the tears rolling unchecked down Verity's face, 'he'd hate you to cry. We mustn't. I'll get my things. I'll have to leave the children.' She spoke in short, unconnected sentences, rushing from one thing to the next, anywhere rather than the image at the front of her mind. Richard, covered with rubble, smothered by dust, plaster, bricks . . . smothered . . . no, no, not that. Toby had come back without her noticing and both children followed her when she ran up to the bedroom and started to throw things into a suitcase; they needed to stay close to her, and yet she wasn't even aware of them.

'Let me come with you,' Michael said when, followed by her two shadows, she came back down with her case. 'I've spoken to Mrs Trout. She will see Verity and the children are looked after. Perhaps by tomorrow we'll be able to drive him home. He'll be given leave after an experience like this.' Did he really believe what he was saying? Jackie didn't know and neither did she care.

'No. I don't want anyone with me. I want to be on my own. It's important.' And so it was, but she didn't ask herself why.

As she started to drive away, Michael's voice called after her, 'Jackie! Jackie! You've not got your Identity Card with you. If the police stop you – and they are sure to somewhere on the road – you must be able to show it.' He thrust it into her outstretched hand. And then, without a backward glance, she was away. The sun was already low in the sky, casting long shadows.

How many hours would it take her? Richard knew the way so well, he would have thought nothing of the journey. But although she'd driven for more than ten years she had never made a long journey, least of all one on strange ground and by herself. As darkness fell, the shielded lights on the car made no more than a short, narrow beam to guide her. In ordinary circumstances she might have found the journey an ordeal, but she seemed to be apart from it. Twice she was stopped by the police: where was she going? Why was she driving alone so late? She showed her Identity Card and her driving licence, impatient to get away.

As she drove, her thoughts leapfrogged in a disconnected way. She was with Richard on the first day he brought her to Crocker's End, seeing him as starchy and stiff-necked; she was walking with him on the cliffs at Deremouth on their honeymoon; she was in his arms, hearing him beg her to marry him; she was reliving their joyous love making, and her guilt that while she knew he loved her with his body and soul, yet her fondness for him was based on lust – her body loved him and craved for him while her soul remained free. The thought brought another memory: years ago when she had told him about the guilt she felt because for so long she had longed to get away from the newspaper shop and not be tied to her uncle and aunt, that had been the day he had told her about loving with your soul; he had said that if two souls were united in love, nothing either in life or death could separate them.

She was blinded by tears, the empty road ahead of her had no shape. Frightened, she pulled to the kerb and stopped, hearing the harsh sobs she couldn't hold back. With her head cradled against her arms on the steering wheel, she cried. Then another thought came from nowhere, one conjured up by the echo of words she had heard long ago: 'scales fell from his eyes'. She was a child again, sitting in church between her aunt and uncle, Aunt Alice's hand on her knee to stop her swinging her leg, and the rector had been talking about someone who had been blind but the scales had fallen from his eyes.

Richard, Richard, if two souls can be united, do you know about me? I've been blind, I've been so wrapped up in every-thing else – Crocker's End and the blackcurrants, the children, yes, and these last months, Wilhelm too. Did you know, could you feel that I wasn't caring about you? Oh dear God, forgive me, don't let it be too late. What's the matter with me that it takes something like this to make me see what deep in my heart must always have been there. I used to say I wanted to fall in love with him, yet I was too pig headed to know that falling in love is nothing, *nothing* compared with real, complete love. Help me stop crying and behave properly, not like some silly kid. If Malcolm What's-his-Name has told him that I'm driving, he'll be worried until I get there. He'll want me.

She started forward again, and this time with a new feeling of calm. He would be bruised and shaken, he might even have a bone broken, but in her new awareness she saw their future as secure. Her panic had gone.

The rescue team was working on the house as she came through the village. She could see the dark shapes of their vehicles, and despite the late hour people were clustered as near as they were allowed. She parked further back and walked towards the scene. An ambulance was just pulling away and a second one still waiting.

'Move away, missus, can't come along here,' a warden ushered her out of the way.

'My husband . . .' she started.

'Mrs Bennett, Jacqueline? I'm Malcolm Rogers. You're just too late.' He must have sensed the effect his words had on her, for immediately he held her elbow as if to steady her. 'They've just taken him off to the hospital. You probably saw the ambulance.'

'I'll follow it. Where is the hospital?'

'I'll come with you and direct you. It's about four miles away.'

Without talking they got back into her car and set off in the direction she had seen the ambulance go.

'Did you see if he's badly hurt? Was he able to walk?' Please say he's only gone to be checked!

'He was unconscious when they carried him out. They wouldn't let me get near. We'll soon be there. Perhaps he'll have come round.' And perhaps Malcolm was just trying to keep their spirits up, for what he had seen in the dim light of the ambulance men's lamp from the nearest point they would let him get, hadn't been reassuring. 'We can't be far behind the ambulance, perhaps they won't even have taken him in for examination when we arrive.'

He was wrong. The large hospital building looked as black as every other building, not a hint of light anywhere as they groped their way to the entrance. There were two ambulances outside, one of which still had the back doors open. Hope was given a boost; if he'd only just been carried in they would be in time to see the doctors with him, or so they expected.

'My husband has just been brought here by ambulance,' Jackie told a nurse. 'He was in a house that was bombed.'

'He's been taken straight through. If you'd like to take a seat. I think he may be some time, so can I get you a cup of tea? It might be a good idea, you know.'

'Why will he be a long time? Has he been badly hurt? Is something broken?'

'I'll see what I can find out for you when they've had longer to check him.'

Like obedient children, Jackie and Malcolm drank the weak and sugary tea. The minutes passed slowly, an hour seemed like half a day. Then the kindly nurse came to tell them that Mr Russell, the surgeon, would like to speak to the patient's wife. Without asking, Malcolm went with her.

Jackie was ashamed. The unfamiliar sweet drink had made her feel sick – at least, she told herself that was the reason – but sitting in front of the desk, her gaze fixed on Mr Russell's moving mouth, she couldn't take in what he was saying. The room was swaying, it was getting dark. She didn't even hear him shout 'Hold on to her' to Malcolm as consciousness was lost.

She came round to find herself lying on an examination couch, Malcolm by her side and Mr Russell nowhere to be seen.

'What happened?' She tried to speak in a normal voice, but it was difficult to make any sound at all.

'You fainted. You've had quite an evening with that drive; it's a strain with such poor lights.'

She sat up and seemed to give herself a shake. 'He was telling us about Richard. I didn't hear. Malcolm, what's happening?'

'He's badly hurt, Jacqueline. Seriously badly.'

'Tell me. Please. Don't try and keep it from me. I'm better.'

'There are two seats of injury,' Malcolm began, watching her closely, 'his arm – and that includes bones in his shoulder – and his head. There is a consent form here for you to sign in case they need to operate.'

She swallowed. She closed her eyes, and for a moment he was frightened she was going to drift away again, but then he couldn't know the silent plea she was making. I've been so blind. I beg you, don't punish me by hurting Richard. It's not fair. Hurt *me* if you like, but not him.

'Jacqueline, if you can put your signature on it I'll take it to the nurse. They may not need it,' he added with forced cheerfulness. 'Then, if you're all right here, I'll go and telephone your home. They will be waiting to know that you've got here, and they'll want to know about Richard. You rest here while I do it.'

'Malcolm, be gentle with them.'

'I promise,' he answered.

And so began the longest night of Jackie's life. It was seven o'clock in the morning when a weary Mr Russell reappeared in the room where she and Malcolm waited.

They had no need to ask if an operation had been necessary; he wouldn't have been so many hours for any other reason.

'You have had a long wait. I am sorry.'

'Sorry?' she breathed. What was he telling them?

'The operation went well, I have every hope that he will make a good recovery. But there was no alternative but to amputate his right arm.'

'Amputate?' Her mouth felt so dry she could hardly form the word.

'The damage was too extensive. Broken bones can be reset, but his entire arm was crushed, shattered. Amputation was his only chance. The broken shoulder will recover, given time and rest, but I fear there is no way of eliminating the pain until it heals. The X-rays from his head are with Mr Turnball; he will speak to you himself when he has examined them.'

Some hours later, alone now that Malcolm had left her, Jackie listened as she was told the result of the X-rays. She heard the words and yet seemed to be incapable of taking in their meaning. It was too soon to be certain, but they hoped there would be no permanent brain damage. However, his skull had been fractured and a further operation was to be carried out in which he would be given a thin metal plate in his head. The news had to be told to them at home, and she found it was surprisingly easy to play her part and keep a cheerful note in her voice.

'He's strong, Mum, his heart is good, he has bags of fight in him. He'll have a few difficult weeks, but he has all of us to help him once they let him come home.'

'His right arm,' Verity croaked. 'His whole life will be changed. He loved his work' – this was something that had haunted Jackie, for with no right arm and with the damage to his head perhaps even more serious, how could he hope to carry on with the sort of work he had done? – 'he won't be able to drive, what will be left for him?' It was plain that she was crying, and in the background Jackie could hear faithful, elderly Monty whimpering as he tried to cheer her.

'To start with he'll feel like that too, Mum. But he still has all of us. We work as a team, don't we. I expect it sounds selfish, but all I want is to have him alive and home. And if he is there all the time instead of two days a week if he's lucky, then – and I know I ought not to let myself think it, but I'd be lying if I pretended it's not true – for me, and for all of us at home, it'll be a new start, a wonderful start, to have him with us all the time.'

'Jackie, forgive me, I ought not to say it, but I must. I've been so worried about you for months, about you and him.'

Jackie knew it had always been impossible to hide things from Verity; a forced and bright smile might fool those with normal sight, but Verity's intuition was hard to deceive.

'Mum,' she said, quietly and carefully, 'we none of us know how difficult things are going to be, but nothing is going to beat us. If Richard had been killed I wouldn't have wanted to go on living. We all travel along our narrow ruts; it takes something like this to jog us out of them and make us see clearly. Mum, dear Mum, don't cry. He will be well – and even having to adjust as he will, Richard will still be "whole".' Then, in an attempt to get back to normality before she used her last shilling in the telephone, 'Is everything all right at home? Are the children behaving? Are the prisoners still working – and did the one who escaped get picked up?' She asked it in the same tone as she had each of the other questions, realizing that this was the first time in forty-eight hours that she had thought of Wilhelm.

'Everything's good. Michael sees to things outside – not actually helping with the picking, I made him promise he wouldn't do that, but he sees to it that things go smoothly. But Jackie, I forgot to tell you, that rascal who got away must have gone on your bicycle. Toby noticed it was gone and they hunted high and low for it yesterday. And I tell you what else Michael discovered: that old gate down at the bottom end, the one we haven't used for years, there was quite a track made to it where someone had walked. He must have seen the gate and the bike and decided to make a run for it. Oh well, poor soul, he must be someone's son, someone's husband. When trouble comes home to you, you see things more clearly. There go the pips again. Ring again tomorrow if you—' Jackie was left with the dialling tone buzzing in her ear.

She found accommodation in a boarding house near the hospital. She knew she couldn't leave the children for long, but was determined to be with Richard when he came round after the second operation, for until that time he had hardly been aware of anything. He'd seemed to know she was there, sitting on the left-hand side of his narrow hospital bed, for if she moved her hand in his, either gripped him harder or caressed his fingers with hers, she felt his answering pressure.

'What's happened?' His voice sounded weak and distant, and then she realized she had fallen asleep with her head on his pillow.

'Richard . . . thank God . . . Richard, you're awake . . . you've come back . . .'

'Where . . . what . . .?'

'There was a bomb on your lodgings.' She kept her tone even, speaking quietly. 'Malcolm Rogers phoned. I came. You were brought to the hospital.'

'My arm hurts – can't move it.'

He was awake and that's what she had longed and prayed for; now, though, she had to find a way to tell him. How do you say to a man that a limb has been amputated? How do you tell him his head has been so seriously hurt that it is too early to be sure it hasn't damaged part of his brain. She seemed to hear the mockery in his father's voice as he called him Einstein. She willed Richard to meet her gaze, then holding his left hand firmly, she told him the truth.

He must have heard her, he must have taken in what she told him, yet she saw in his face neither fear nor anguish. Instead he looked at her with his heart in his eyes, loving her as he always had and yet with an expression she couldn't quite fathom. Could it be hope?

Her natural instinct was to say what was in her heart, which was to share with him the shock of Malcolm's telephone call, her fear as she drove to be with him, and the sudden understanding that it was he who gave her life meaning and purpose. If he'd been fit and well she could have poured out her true feelings: she could have told him about those moments when it had been as if she had suddenly been given a new vision; she could have told him that if he had died she wouldn't have wanted to go on living. But he was still too ill to face a scene so charged with emotion.

Dropping to her knees by his bed, she held his hand to her cheek.

'Darling, Richard, you gave me such a fright I think it made me grow up. And not before time.' She raised her chin a fraction, as if in the slight movement she was inspiring in him confidence to match her own. 'We can't pretend things will go on just as they were. But we're not going to be beaten. Oh, I know, it's easy for me to talk, I'm not the one to have to adjust. But Richard, you and me together, there's nothing we can't do.'

She didn't know what she expected his reaction to be, but it certainly wasn't his sudden loss of control. His mouth was working despite his effort to hold it steady, and with a choking sound in his throat, the tears came.

'Jacqueline, don't say it out of pity . . . couldn't bear . . .'

She felt shocked; how could he think that of her?

'Pity? Sorrow, but not pity. I want to hold you but I can't get at you.'

'Sorry . . . behaving badly . . . don't know what happened . . .'

She wiped his face with the palms of her hands. 'You blew your cork, just like I did. It was before I knew you were badly hurt, I was driving.' And so she told him. 'I've never prayed so hard in all my life,' she said finally, 'prayed that I wouldn't lose you and that we would share everything for long, long lives. And Richard, my prayer was answered. You are going to be well again – well, but having to learn to be left-handed. But we will share everything, everything, darling, always and for ever and ever.'

Afterwards, looking back to those moments, she always felt they were the turning point in their lives. She believed he drew strength from her confidence.

She couldn't stay away from Crocker's End too long, so two days after that she went home. Her car was practically out of petrol, but the landlady where she had lodged agreed that she could leave it in her side path until she came to collect Richard, by which time she would have received her next petrol coupons.

Perhaps of them all it was Verity who found it easiest to accept him as unchanged. Of course she knew the extent of his injuries, but because she couldn't see him there was no barrier between her and the real Richard she'd known and loved all his life. Vision gave the others a constant reminder: his head had been shaved and although his hair was growing, the long and angry scar was still clearly visible; add to that the difficulty of using just his left hand, and from Michael to Dulcie, all of them were conscious that his days took courage, determination and hard-fought-for optimism.

By the time the prisoners came again early in 1943, his broken shoulder was mended, his hair had grown and been well cut, and he was winning the battle to adjust. He had taught himself to shave using his left hand (having had plenty of cuts in the process), but tying shoelaces and ties would always be beyond him, and even shirt buttons took twice the time they had in the past.

It was always during love making that Jackie had felt they were closest, times when the rest of the world counted for nothing. Recently, though, even that was different. Now tenderness deepened passion. For him, turning over while laying in bed was well nigh impossible, and he could no longer raise himself above her. But for both of them the act of love was precious and as necessary as food and air; it always had been and it always would be.

It was in the spring that Jackie suggested they ought to have another child. Even Dulcie had finished at the local school and, like Toby, cycled to the village where they had been given permission to leave their bicycles at the vicarage and catch the bus into town where he attended the Grammar School and she Kingsley House, a private school for girls.

When Jackie made her suggestion she and Richard were in

the weighing-in shed where she was tidying the shelves while he prepared a rough draft of the figures for their tax return, ready for her to make a fair copy. He had made up his mind that by the following year his left-handed writing would flow easily. Now, at her suggestion he looked up with a frown.

'Last time was dreadful. It was the doctor who said you shouldn't go through it again.'

'That was *then*, this is *now*. There's nothing the matter with me – and anyway, the doctor said then that when we were ready I could have the coil removed. I bet if I did I could get pregnant easy as a wink. We're not too old to have a young baby, Richard – forty-six and thirty-three. That's nothing.'

It took a few weeks to persuade him, for the night Dulcie had been born still haunted him. But Jackie was sure she was perfectly healthy and they both liked the idea of a new life belonging to the future they were building.

As she had predicted, she conceived 'as easy as wink', and in March 1944 Emily came into the world as effortlessly as is possible. Even Michael and Verity, their own youth long gone, were delighted with the new addition to the family. As the Allied Invasion Force fought its way through France, and then the following year to Germany and Berlin, if Richard's mind sometimes slipped away to that place in Buckinghamshire where he had worked, and if he felt the loss of a career he had loved, he reminded himself of all that was good in his life.

And so, as the final months of the war played out, all was well at Crocker's End.

1945

When the letter arrived they were coming to the end of the fruit-picking season. That day would see the final collection by Findlay's, and anything they gathered after that would be bottled to help see them through the winter.

'Post lady, Mum. I'll go and get the letters,' Toby called, and was off, racing up the slope to the gate where Joan Hobbs, who'd delivered their mail since the early months of the war, was sorting through the envelopes.

'Only one today,' she told him, 'just the one addressed to your mother.' That in itself was a rare thing, but what was even rarer was that it bore a German stamp.

'For you, Mum – with a German stamp. Can I have it for my album?'

Obligingly she ripped open the envelope and gave it to him, then unfolded the single sheet of paper.

'Who's it from, Mum? Who do we know in Germany?'

'Just someone who lived near me ages ago, long before I came to Crocker's End.'

'Gosh, how rotten to have a friend there when they were our enemy.' He was quite impressed by 'our enemy', it seemed to him it bracketed him with the grown-ups. And, in appearance at any rate, he was ahead of his thirteen years.

'Rotten for them, too, if they had English friends. How are you and the boys getting on with the picking?' She changed the subject, diverting his thoughts on to more familiar ground.

'Wizard! Jack's going to buy a tent with his earnings. I reckon I'll hang on to mine and put it in my boat fund. I suppose now the war's over, by next year you'll have men again. Pity really, Mum. It's a great job.'

She laughed, resisting the temptation to rumple his fair hair. Crocker's End had cast its spell on him just as surely as it always had on her. Dulcie was less interested, and although she was happy enough to 'help' occasionally if the rest of the family were working, before half an hour was up she would be restless and wander off to find amusement somewhere else. On that morning, even with the opportunity to earn extra pocket money, she had preferred that she and a school friend should proudly push Emily's pram to the village.

'I'd better get on,' Toby said. 'Good job you've heard from your friend, let's hope she's all right.'

Jackie saw no reason to correct him. She watched him run back up the hill to where he'd been working, the letter still folded as it had come out of the envelope. She had recognized Wilhelm's writing on the envelope and had a feeling of thankfulness. From the past came the memory of his letters when he had gone home to Germany in 1926, how she used to watch for the postman, how she used to read and reread what he wrote. Now, purposely, she closed her eyes, the better to absorb the sounds around her;

she breathed deeply, taking in the clear country air overtoned by the smell of the blackcurrant bushes. Her mind took a sideways leap and she thought of Richard who, since the injury to his head, had no sense of smell. How dreadful that must be. Opening her eyes, she looked around her from where she stood between two rows of bushes: on Dilly Hill three older boys from the Grammar School were working, while two from Toby's form were on the slope towards the gate. As Toby had said, by next year the world would be normal again and the women who had found war work would be glad to escape their homes and earn some pocket money.

She unfolded Wilhelm's letter and started to read.

'My most dear friend, Jackie, Until now I have not written to you. But at last peace has come to our sad world and the fear is gone that to make contact might cause you trouble. I think of what you did for me, and to say that you have my gratitude is nothing compared with the debt I shall forever owe you. Gizella and I are happy, Heinrich is a fine boy in whom I have great pride, and soon there is to be a second child. I do not have to tell you of my sadness for the outcome of the hostilities, sadness too for the wrecked lives of people on both sides, and for the displaced persons. Six years in our lifetime have brought havoc. I have made a solemn vow that I will do all in my power to see my country is once again a great nation. Even today, while our land is occupied by foreign soldiers, I wish you could see the dignity of my people. They do not beg favours; they hold their heads high. So that is my vow – as solemn as the one we made so long ago – and I will keep it just as you, my dear Jackie, kept yours. I will remember you always with affection and gratitude. Wilhelm.'

'My basket is full.' Richard's voice surprised her. 'A letter?'

She nodded. 'From Wilhelm Furtmueller, he was a prisoner of war here.'

Richard looked surprised. 'Fancy one of those chaps writing.' It wasn't a question, yet she knew he was waiting to hear more, and now she knew she could tell him.

'I knew him years ago, in Brackleford. He was the one who escaped – the day you were hurt. That old tweed suit of yours I told you I had given to a beggar . . .' And so she told him of how she had taken his suit and put money and sandwiches in the pocket then left her bicycle by the seldom-used gate. 'Whatever you did, you did because you felt it was right. Just tell me one thing: were you in love with him?'

'Oh yes,' she answered, each word spoken quietly, 'many long years ago. Love or infatuation, at that age I didn't know the difference. We were still at school.' She passed him the letter.

'Poor devil,' he said as he folded it up and passed it back, looking at her very directly and willing her to meet his gaze. What he read in her eyes was all he asked. For both of them they knew the incident was closed; whatever hold Wilhelm Furtmueller might have had on her belonged to yesterday. 'I came to ask you to lend me a hand with the basket.'

She nodded, slipping her hand into his and, taking them both by surprise, just for a second nuzzling her head against his shoulder. And so they walked together to where he had filled his basket with blackcurrants, passing the greenhouse where elderly Michael pottered and Verity had her deckchair just inside the door.

'They're fine berries this year,' Richard said.

She nodded, 'Yes, it's a good year'. They each took a handle of the basket and carried it to the shed.